THE BELLWETHER REVIVALS

Bright, bookish Oscar Lowe has escaped the urban estate where he was raised and made a new life for himself amid the colleges and spires of Cambridge. Contented with his life as a care assistant at a local nursing home, he's forged a close friendship with one of the home's residents, Dr Paulsen. But when he meets and falls in love with Iris Bellwether, a student at King's College, Oscar is drawn into her world of scholarship and privilege, and soon becomes embroiled in the strange machinations of her brilliant but troubled brother, Eden. Eden's self-belief is boundless, and as he draws his sister and closed circle of friends into a series of disturbing experiments, Oscar realises the extent of the danger facing them all.

Benjamin Wood was born in 1981 and grew up in north-west England. In 2004, he was awarded a Commonwealth Scholarship to attend the MFA Creative Writing Programme at the University of British Columbia, Canada, where he was also fiction editor of the Canadian literary journal *PRISM International*. Benjamin is now a lecturer in Creative Writing at Birkbeck, University of London. *The Bellwether Revivals* is his first novel.

BENJAMIN WOOD

THE BELLWETHER REVIVALS

Complete and Unabridged

CHARNWOOD
Leicester

First published in Great Britain in 2012 by
Simon & Schuster UK Ltd., London

First Charnwood Edition
published 2012
by arrangement with
Simon & Schuster UK Ltd., London

The moral right of the author has been asserted

British Library CIP Data

Wood, Benjamin, *1981 –*
   The Bellwether revivals.
   1. Cambridge (England)- -Fiction.
   2. Large type books.
   I. Title
   823.9'2–dc23

   ISBN 978–1–4448–1271–8

Printed and bound in Great Britain by
T. J. International Ltd., Padstow, Cornwall

This book is printed on acid-free paper

FOR MY MOTHER

Prelude

June 2003

They heard the caterwaul of sirens, and saw the dust rising underneath the ambulance wheels at the far end of the driveway, and soon the darkening garden was a wash of flashing blue lights. It only seemed real when they told the paramedics where to find the bodies. There was one upstairs on the top floor, they said, another in the organ house, and one more at the foot of the garden — the last one was still breathing, but faintly. They had left him on the riverbank in a nest of flattened rushes, with the cold water lapping against his feet. When the paramedics asked for his name, they said it was Eden. Eden Bellwether.

It had taken too long for the ambulance to arrive. For a while, they'd assembled on the back porch of the rectory, thinking, panicking, staring out at the same old elms and cherry trees they'd stared at a hundred times before, hearing the wind disturb the branches. They all felt responsible for what had happened. They all blamed themselves. And so they argued — about who was *most* to blame, who should feel the guiltiest. The only one who didn't talk was Oscar. He leaned against the wall, smoking, listening to the rest of them bicker. When he finally spoke, his voice was so calm it silenced them.

1

'It's over now,' he said, extinguishing his cigarette on the porch-rail. 'We can't go back and change it.'

Just a few months ago, they'd been sitting out on the same sap-spotted decking behind the rectory, chatting about nothing too important — the rules of badminton, some Alain Resnais film they'd all seen and hated, the saddening obsolescence of the cassette tape — all six of them just winding down, a bruise of clouds spreading darkly across the Grantchester sky. They'd gathered round the same wooden patio table, picking at the citronella candle drippings on the wine bottles, throwing dry wax at the midges. Everything had been different back then — so weightless and loose and easy.

Now they watched the first paramedic working on the riverbank, feeling for Eden's pulse, strapping an oxygen mask over his nose and mouth, feeding in a drip. They heard the murmur of the other medic's voice coming over the dispatcher: 'VSA. Purple plus. Over.'

They didn't go with Eden in the ambulance. They weren't prepared to follow in their cars. Instead, they went into the organ house to see the other medic wrenching off her latex gloves. She'd placed a green sheet over the body and it was quivering on the breeze. 'Don't be going anywhere,' she warned them. 'The police are on their way.'

It had been the hottest June day but a cold breeze had been gathering strength all evening, and now it was sweeping across the garden, through the open doors of the buildings. It was blowing into the broken pipes of the old church organ — a weak and tuneless drone that sounded on and off, on and off, with the steadiest of rhythms, like some machine that had found a way to breathe.

FIRST DAYS

If a man will begin with certainties, he shall end in doubts; but if he will be content to begin with doubts, he shall end in certainties.

— *Sir Francis Bacon*

1

Incidental Music

Oscar Lowe would later tell police that he couldn't remember the exact date he first laid eyes on the Bellwethers, though he knew for sure it had been a Wednesday. It was one of those late October evenings in Cambridge when the gun-grey light of the afternoon had faded well before six, and the cobbled avenues of the old town were dark and silent. He had just finished an eight-to-five shift at Cedarbrook, the nursing home on Queen's Road where he was a care assistant, and his mind was slow and heavy, laden with the details of his workday: the vacant faces of the older residents, the pallor of their tongues as they took their pills, the give of their skin as he lifted them into the bath. All he wanted was to get home, to fall upon his bed and sleep right through until tomorrow, when he would have to wake up and do the same things over again.

By cutting through the grounds of King's College, he knew he could shave some time off the walk. In the old city, everybody cycled: the students skittered along the narrow lanes with loaded backpacks, the tourists pinballed from college to college on rented wheels. At any time of day, on any given pavement in Cambridge, someone could be found unlocking a bike from a lamppost and riding off towards the next one. But Oscar preferred the solace of walking.

He crossed Clare Bridge and took the shortcut through the grounds of King's, hearing the flat echo of his footsteps on the path, still glassy from the afternoon rain. Everywhere was quiet. The clipped lawns seemed unusually blue with the indolent glow of floodlamps, and, somewhere close by, woodsmoke was rising from a cottage chimney, giving the impression of fog. As he went by the face of the college chapel, he tried his best not to look up, knowing exactly how it would make him feel: tiny, irrelevant, godless. But he couldn't help staring at it — that formidable gothic building with its tall spindles needling the sky and its giant blackened windows. It was the picture postcard on every carousel stand along King's Parade. He'd always hated it. Up close, in the near darkness, the place only haunted him more. It was not the architecture that troubled him, but the age of the building, the scale of its history; the royalty who'd once communed there, all the serious people whose faces now thickened encyclopaedias.

A service was underway inside. He could already hear the muted thrum of organ music behind the chapel walls, and when he turned into the Front Court, the sound grew louder and sweeter, until he was close enough to make out the fullness of the instrument — a low, hoarse purr. He could almost feel it against his ribs. It was nothing like the overpowering dirges he remembered from school Christmas services, or the blundering renditions of 'Abide with me' he'd strained to sing over at his grandparents' funerals. There was a fragility to this music, as if the organist wasn't pressing down on the keys but hovering his fingers above them like a puppeteer. Oscar stopped in the entrance just to listen, and saw the sandwich board near the open doorway: 'Evensong 5:30, Public Welcome.' Before he knew it, his feet had carried him all the way inside.

Stained-glass windows surrounded him, barely showing their colours. The vaulted arches of the ceiling seemed to roll out into the distance. At the heart of the building, a wingspan of organ pipes bellowed from a wooden partition, and he could see the sombre congregation waiting in the candlelight on the other side. He found an empty seat and watched the choir filing in. The younger boys stood on the front row in their white gowns, cheerful and distracted; the older boys stood sheepishly behind them, aware of themselves in that teenaged way, fidgeting with their sleeves. When the organ stopped there was a momentary silence, and then the choir began to sing.

Their voices were so synchronised and balanced that Oscar could hardly tell them apart. They surged and retracted with the ease of an ocean, and he felt a rush in his heart as he listened. He was sorry when their hymn ended and the reverend stood to recite the Holy Creed. Across the aisle, people were gamely muttering the prayer, but Oscar stayed quiet, still thinking of the music. By the time he noticed the blonde

9

girl a few spaces along his pew, the congregation had reached ' . . . And sitteth on the right hand of God . . . ' She was mouthing the words grudgingly, the way a bored child recites times tables, and, when she saw that he wasn't joining in the prayer, gave a slow roll of her eyes, as if to say: 'Get me out of here.' The simple profile of her face excited him. He smiled at her but wasn't sure that she noticed.

Now the reverend was reading from Jeremiah (' . . . if thou take forth the precious from the vile, thou shalt be as my mouth . . . ') and Oscar watched the girl and her encumbered, self-conscious movements. Like him, she didn't seem to appreciate the strange etiquette of the church. She kneed the hymn book to the floor midway through the sermon, causing the reverend to pause, and while his dreary lesson continued she toyed with the bezel of her watch, until two pale-faced choristers began a new hymn and the organ started up again.

The only time the blonde girl sat still was when the choir was singing. Her chest rose, inflated; her lip quivered. She seemed awed by the tapestry of their voices, the clarity of their sound, the swelling harmonies that flooded the yawning space above them. Oscar could see her fingers counting out the rhythm on her knee until the final 'Amen'. The choir sat down and silence — like a deployed parachute — descended in the chapel.

At the end of the service, people filtered out by order of importance: first, the choir and the clergy in a procession of white, then the congregation.

10

Oscar hoped he could follow the girl to the door, get close enough to spark a conversation, but he ended up between a group of men debating the merits of the sermon and a softly spoken French couple consulting their guidebooks for the route home. He lost the sound of her small, scuffing steps behind him as she disappeared into the crowd. Weary tourists moved slowly along the aisles, putting on their jackets and packing away their cameras; young children slept in their fathers' arms while their mothers baby-wiped their fingers. Oscar couldn't see the girl anywhere. He put some change on the collection plate as he went out, and the reverend said, 'Thank you, good evening.'

In the vestibule, the air seemed colder, sharper. Darkness had settled fully over the city and Oscar could feel that familiar, constricting tiredness returning to his shoulders. He turned his collar to the night. It was then, as the crowd dispersed in front of him, that he saw her in the shadows, leaning against the grey stones of the chapel.

She was reading an old paperback, tilting the pages into the second-hand light of the vestibule with one hand, and cradling a clove cigarette between the fingers of the other. Her reading glasses were too big for her face — square with rounded corners, like large projector slides. After a moment, she glanced up from her book and smiled.

'One thing I know about church,' she said, 'is to learn where the exits are. It's like being on a plane. Have to get out in an emergency.' Her

11

accent was genteel, proper, the stuff of elocution lessons; but there was also something uncertain about the way she spoke, as if she was trying hard to rough up the edges of her sentences (she had dropped the 'g' of 'being' and it sounded strange).

'I'll try to remember that for next time,' Oscar said.

'Oh, I don't think you'll be coming back in a hurry. Too much Jeremiah, not enough choir. Am I right?'

He shrugged. 'Something like that.'

'Well, I can hardly blame you. They were almost perfect tonight, weren't they? The choir, I mean.' She offered him her cigarette pack and he shook his head. 'Sometimes the beaters aren't concentrating and their timing suffers, but tonight they were really with it.'

'Yeah, I thought so too.'

As Oscar stepped closer, she studied him with a quick motion of her eyes. He wondered if she would see the same things in his face that he saw in the bathroom mirror every morning — those straight, innocuous features that might just pass for handsome, the beginner-slope nose that water streamed down when it rained, that narrow jaw he'd inherited from his mother. He hoped that she could see past his workclothes: the faded leather jacket he wore over his nursing uniform, and the trainers he'd put through the washing machine so many times they were clean but somehow grey.

'Are you sure you don't want a cigarette? I hate smoking on my own, it's so depressing.' She lifted the paperback and examined its cover. 'What about Descartes? We could smoke *him*. There's enough material here to roll a good cheroot.' She snapped the book shut before he could answer. 'Yes, you're probably right. Descartes would be a bit dry, wouldn't he? Much too heavy on the stomach . . . ' There was a moment of silence. She drew on her clove again. 'So do you have a name?'

'Oscar,' he said.

'Os-car. That's nice.' She spoke his name out into the night, pondering it, as if she could see it scrolling across the sky, on a banner pulled by an aeroplane. 'Well, Oscar, don't take this the wrong way or anything, but church doesn't really seem like your scene. I was watching you in there — you didn't know a bloody word of any of the hymns.'

'Was it that obvious?'

'Oh, it's not a bad thing. I'm not exactly St Francis of Assisi myself.'

'To be honest, I just sort of stumbled in. Something about the music, the sound of the organ. I can't quite explain it.'

'That's my excuse, too.' She breathed out another whorl from the side of her mouth. 'My brother's the organ scholar. That was him playing tonight. I'm just a tag-along.'

'Really?'

'*Really*. It's not the kind of thing I'd bother to lie about.'

'Well, he plays that thing better than anyone I've ever heard. You can tell him from me.'

'Oh, he doesn't need any more positive

13

reinforcement,' she said, laughing at the thought. 'His head's going to swell up like a bloody zeppelin when I tell him you only came inside for the music. He'll take all the credit for that. I love my brother dearly, but I'm afraid the humility gene passed him by.'

Oscar smiled. He could see the Gatehouse beyond her shoulder, yellowed by the desklamps in the porters' lodge, and she was almost outlined by the glow. 'I suppose you're a postgrad,' she said, flitting her eyes towards him again. 'I can tell postgrads from fifty paces. You're all baggy leather and comfortable shoes.'

'Sorry to disappoint you.'

'Alright, okay then — a post-doc. My radar's off.'

'I'm not any kind of student,' he said.

'You mean, you don't go here *at all*?' It was as if she'd never met anyone from beyond the hallowed grounds. 'But you look so — '

'So what?'

'*Serious.*'

He didn't know if this was a compliment or an accusation.

'I mean, you're practically a fully fledged member of society already,' she went on. 'I bet you pay taxes and everything. How old are you?' She raised her cigarette to her mouth, left it waiting at her lips. 'I'm sorry. I know it's rude to ask that question, but you can't be much older than I am. Sometimes I can't imagine what else there is to *do* here besides study.'

'I'm twenty,' he said.

'See, I knew you weren't much older.'

14

She was not the sort of girl Oscar had grown up around: the mouthy teens who talked inanely on the back rows of buses and blocked the smoggy corridors of nightclubs on weekends, whose drunken kisses he'd experienced with cold disappointment on dark, windless recs. She had pedigree — that much was clear from her voice — and he liked the way she looked at him, curious not judgemental. There was depth to her, he could tell. A kind of unashamed intelligence.

'I work at a place called Cedarbrook. It's a nursing home,' he told her. 'But you don't have to pity me — I know how to read and write and everything.'

'*Pity* you? Christ, I envy you,' she said. 'Cedarbrook. That's the lovely old building on Queen's Road, isn't it? They have all that beautiful wisteria growing on the walls.'

'Yeah. That's the place.'

'Well, anyone who can make wisteria bloom like that every spring deserves a trophy. I walk past that house quite often, just to look at the gardens.'

'I can't take any credit for the wisteria. Not my department. But I'll pass it along.'

She looked down at the scuffed black toecaps of her shoes, rocking on the edges of her feet. 'This is my little corner of the world. I'm a King's girl. Medicine, second year, if you can believe it.'

'Must be hard work.'

'It's not too bad really. Not *all* of the time, anyway.'

Oscar could only try to imagine the way she lived. He'd been in Cambridge long enough to know the hours the students worked, to see them on the other side of library windows late at night, red-eyed, ruffle-haired. But he knew as little about the everyday lives of Cambridge students as they knew about the daily machinations of Cedarbrook. What went on inside the closed-off doorways of the colleges was an enduring mystery to him. He only knew that it was better to be near to these places, to walk by them and imagine what high-minded discussions were unfolding inside, than to be somewhere like home, where every conversation was audible on the high street and the only landmarks were shopping centres.

When he asked for her name, she replied: 'It's Iris. Like the genus.' And he laughed — just a short vent of air from his nose, but enough for her to step back and say, 'What's so funny?'

'Most people would say *like the flower*, that's all.'

'Well, I'm not most people. I'm not going to say it's like the flower when I know perfectly well that it's a genus. And I'll tell you something else.' She broke for a gulp of breath. 'I know exactly which variety I am. *Iris milifolia*. The hardest one to look after.'

'But worth the effort, I'm sure.'

She gazed back at him proudly, the lights of the college buildings reflecting in her lenses. Though Oscar could feel the tiredness more than ever now, weighing down his eyelids, he didn't want to leave. This was where he was meant to be, talking to this strange pretty girl, with her clove and bergamot scent and her copy of Descartes. He wanted to stretch the moment out as far as it would go, tauten it until it broke apart.

'Listen, this might sound a little, y'know,' Iris said, letting the sentence drop away. She scratched the side of her arm and glanced at him. 'It's just, my chamber group has a recital later this week, out at West Road. If you're not doing anything on Sunday night, would you like to come? We could really use all the support we can get.'

He didn't need a second to think about it. 'Yeah, okay. I'll be there.'

'Won't be hard to get a ticket at the door, believe me,' she said. Then, for reasons that weren't clear to him, she laughed out loud.

'What?' he said.

'It's nothing. It's just — you're really going to go, aren't you?'

'Yeah.'

'Just like that?'

'Yeah.'

'But you don't even know if we're any good. I haven't even told you what instrument I play. I could be the world's lousiest trombonist, for all you know.'

'I'm not doing anything else that night. And if your brother's an organ scholar, you can't be all that bad.'

'How inductive of you,' she said. 'Do you even know what an organ scholar is?'

'No, but it sounds important.'

'In the college, *yes*. In the real world, *no*.' She

told him that two scholarships were awarded every couple of years at King's. There was great competition for places amongst undergraduates, and usually a first-year and a third-year were appointed. Her brother was one of the only students in the history of the college to be awarded a scholarship twice. 'A normal person wouldn't want all the extra hassle in his final year, but that's my brother for you. He's irregular.' It was the organ scholars' job to play at the chapel services; they worked on a shift rotation: one week on, one week off. They also assisted the Director of Music in his duties. 'If the Director can't make it for some reason, the organ scholar has to conduct the choir. It hardly ever happens, though. Maybe once a year. My brother's always hoping something horrible will befall the Director, but he's healthy as an ox.' She stubbed out her clove on the drainpipe. 'Anyway, I'll be very glad to see you on Sunday, if you still want to come.'

'Are you an organist too?' he asked.

'Me? No. *God*, no. I play the cello.' She gave a little sigh, as if she'd been saddled with an instrument she had no interest in. As if one day in a school music lesson all the triangles and tambourines had been doled out, and her teacher had handed her a hunk of wood and said, *Here, play this until I find you something better*. 'I haven't been practising much recently. Not the recital pieces, anyway.'

'Why not?'

'Because studying medicine is quite demanding of my time.'

'Right.'

'And in my free time I read stuff like this.' She raised the book. 'Things my brother tells me I should be reading. I suppose I'm a glutton for punishment that way. *The Passions of the Soul*. Tell me honestly: am I wasting my youth? Should I just be out there getting drunk with the rest of them?'

'That would be a bigger waste, I think.'

Her face slackened. 'My problem is, I'm too easily steered off course. Have to be doing several things at once.'

'You're a butterfly catcher,' he said.

'What?'

'That's what my father would call you.'

'Well, I suppose that's a kinder phrase than *hyperactive*. He must be more patient than my parents.'

Oscar just nodded, peering at the ground. It was strange to hear someone speaking well of his father, because he rarely thought of him that way. He could only recall the rain-soaked building sites where he spent most of his school holidays, helping to heave plasterboards up narrow flights of stairs, and all the weekends he lost stuffing insulation into wall cavities, filling skips with office debris. He could remember the bitterness of his father's voice when they used to argue on the job: 'Go then. Leave me. I'll do it myself. You've always got somewhere better to be, don't you? A butterfly catcher, that's what you are.' This was not patience, Oscar knew, but a resentful kind of endurance.

By the time he turned back to Iris, her

attention was elsewhere. She'd noticed something over his shoulder and was gathering herself
to leave, fixing her scarf, patting down her coat.
The remains of her cigarette lay trodden at her
feet. 'My brother's here,' she said. 'I better go.'

Oscar heard the gentle tinkling of bike spokes,
and spun around to see a man in a pinstripe
blazer wheeling a shiny Peugeot racer, dynamo
lights strobing on the path. His corduroy
trousers were turned up at the ankles, and a
mass of wavy hair was spilling from the edges of
his bike helmet. There was something ungainly
about the way his blazer hung on his body
— shoulders and elbows still prominent beneath
the fabric, like a sheet thrown over an upturned
table.

'Just a sec,' Iris called to him. She took off her
glasses and pushed them into the top pocket of
her coat. Without them, her face was more
evenly proportioned. 'Here,' she said, tossing the
Descartes to her brother. 'Say what you like
about French philosophy, but it's no good when
you read it in the dark.'

Her brother caught the book and stuffed it
into the back of his trousers. 'I'm not letting you
off the hook that easily. You're getting it back
first thing tomorrow.' He squinted at Oscar as if
appraising an antique. 'Who's your friend?'

'This is Oscar,' she told him. 'We've been
shooting the breeze, as Yin would say.'

'Oh, yeah? About what?'

'Religion, flowers — all the big issues.'

'I see.'

'Did *you* know the iris is a genus?' she said.

Her brother lifted an eyebrow. 'I think I knew that *in utero*.' Propping the bike-frame against one knee, he leaned to offer his slender hand to Oscar. 'If we wait for her to introduce us, we'll be here all night. The name's Eden.' His grip was solid and unforgiving. 'Thanks for keeping her company.'

'My pleasure,' Oscar said. He couldn't quite see Eden's face — it was partly drawn over by the shadows of the chapel spires — but he could tell that his skin had the texture of a seashell, smooth yet flawed. 'Was that really you playing in there? I've never heard an organ sound so good.'

Eden glanced up at the sky. 'Oh. Well. Thank you. I try my best.'

'You couldn't save his soul, though,' Iris said. 'He's a non-believer.' She perched side-saddle on the crossbar of the bike, placing an arm around her brother and kissing him softly on the cheek. 'Shall we go?'

Eden received the kiss, barely reacting. 'Yes, let's,' he said, 'before the porters catch me on this thing. I've already been warned about riding through.'

'I don't know why you insist on cycling. Just take a cab.'

'It's become something of a battle of wills. First man to blink loses. Can't let that happen.' Eden lowered his voice to say something into her ear and she laughed, hitting his arm playfully. 'Shut *up*,' she said. 'Don't say that.' Then, with a stiff movement of his legs, Eden started to pedal away. 'Good to meet you, Oscar,' Iris said.

'Yeah. Same.'

'See you Sunday.'

'Yeah. Sunday.'

They were quite a sight, the two of them: Eden pumping hard at the pedals just to keep the bike upright, and Iris with her long legs stretched out a few inches above the ground. As they approached the Gatehouse, where the lawn turned at a right angle, she called out into the hazy lamplight, but Oscar couldn't quite tell what she was saying.

★   ★   ★

Dr Paulsen was sleeping in the leather armchair by the window. His head was limp against his shoulder, heavy as a lettuce, and the sun was edging across his face. 'How are we this morning?' Oscar said. He gathered a pillow from the bed and waited for the old man to stir. It was after nine a.m. and he knew that Dr Paulsen would want to be woken; unlike the other residents, he was not a man who was happy to sleep the day away. He didn't like to waste time on television the way the others did, or spend a whole week assembling a jigsaw that only revealed a picture of a sunny foreign vista he was too old to visit. ('I've never understood the concept of the jigsaw,' he once said. 'I mean, the picture's already on the box — where's the mystery?') His room was very different from the others: bright with natural light, dense with furniture and books, and the scent of urine was fainter here than anywhere else in the building.

22

Oscar put this down to the extra care the nurses took in emptying Paulsen's bottle — the old man was so cold to most of them that they were terrified of spilling a drop.

Dr Paulsen lifted his head, a web of drool caught against his chin. 'Oh, it's you,' he said, looking at Oscar, dew-eyed. 'Is it that time already? I was having a wonderful dream about . . . well, about something. I think Rupert Brooke was in it. Somebody was swimming naked in the Cam, anyway. If I were thirty years younger, I would've found it all quite arousing.'

Oscar placed the pillow behind the old man's neck. 'Are you coming down for breakfast today? Or are we still keeping ourselves to ourselves?'

'I haven't decided.' Paulsen sat upright in the chair. 'The more I look at these same four walls, the more I feel like Edmond Dantès. A heroic bearer of injustice.' He narrowed his eyes at Oscar. 'You're very chirpy this morning. What's got into you?'

'Nothing.'

'Rubbish. Did you get a pay rise?'

'No.'

'Good. The rates here are already extortion-ate.'

Oscar smiled. With a groan, he lifted Paulsen up by the elbows, and when the old man was steady on his feet, he said: 'Actually, I sort of met somebody last night. A girl.'

'Hand me my dressing gown, would you?' Paulsen said. 'I have to process this information.' Oscar retrieved the old man's silk robe from the hook and held out the sleeves for him. Slowly,

Paulsen reached his arms through and, with knotted, arthritic fingers, made very hard work of tying the cord. 'Okay, let's pretend this imaginary girl you're talking about is real. Tell me about her. I'll humour you for a moment.'

'Oh, she's definitely real.'

'Convince me,' Paulsen said.

Oscar tried to describe Iris in every last detail — the glossy whites of her eyes, her cigarette smell, the gentle drape of her hair against her neck. When he told him about the book she'd been reading and where she was studying, the old man interrupted: 'Warning lights are flashing now. But go on. Tell me you got her phone number.'

'I didn't quite get that far.'

'You're hopeless,' Paulsen said. 'It's a good job she's imaginary.'

Dr Paulsen was the only resident at Cedarbrook whom Oscar could talk to. He was born in Oxford but had been an English professor at Cambridge and a Fellow at King's College for over thirty years. He kept a library in his room, hardbacks stacked alphabetically by author on dark wood shelves. There were more books in his room than anything else, in fact; more novels and poetry collections and anthologies than stripes on the wallpaper. He wouldn't let the other nurses touch them, but he allowed Oscar to read them in his company, and, for a year now, he'd been letting him take home a book at a time.

They had an understanding between them. Oscar was the only nurse who recognised

Paulsen's need for privacy. The others tried to force him to be sociable; they'd set a place for him at the dinner table and wonder why he wouldn't come downstairs, meal after meal after meal. The old man could be gloomy, abrasive, downright rude. But in the few years Oscar had been working at Cedarbrook, he'd found a way to overlook Paulsen's fits of temper, because he knew he was capable of genuine kindness. And he was learning so much from the old man, simply by reading the books he recommended. In the last six months, he'd read novels by Graham Greene, Herman Hesse, the collected stories of Gianni Celati, Katherine Mansfield, Frank O'Connor, Alexander Solzhenitsyn, and essays by George Orwell. He had almost forgotten how much he loved to read; the private cadence of the words as his eyes passed over them. His parents were the kind of people who owned bookshelves but no books. They didn't understand the pleasure of reading and never thought it was something they needed to encourage. In their lives, books were optional, things foisted on children at school by dishevelled English teachers. Oscar was raised to believe that if he stayed in his room reading about made-up worlds it meant he didn't appreciate the life he had, the possessions his parents had worked hard for, like the TV and the video and the newly turfed back garden. If he read books, his father would ask him if he was okay, if he was feeling unwell, and whatever happened to that friend of his who came over once for tea. Back on his parents' estate in

Watford, life was easier if he didn't read. So he trained himself not to want to.

But ever since Dr Paulsen invited him to borrow from his library last year — 'Choose something. Anything. I don't do recommendations' — Oscar had begun to recall the joy of reading. Sometimes he could get through three or four books a month if things were slow at Cedarbrook, more if he worked nights. There were evenings when all the residents had been put to bed and the nurse-call buttons were no longer chiming, and he could spend long hours in the empty parlour, reading in the lamplight, his fingers dry against the pages, smelling of antibacterial soap. These were the times when he was happiest.

'Alright, let's go and see what they're passing off as breakfast,' Paulsen said. 'Might as well start making an effort.' He held out his arm, like a gentleman asking a lady to dance. Oscar retrieved the old man's walking stick from the foot of the bed and placed it into his hand. 'Should I expect a red carpet or what?'

'They'll be sounding the trumpets for you.'

'Good, good.'

Oscar led him down the dim corridor. After a few steps, the old man spoke into his ear: 'Listen, you want to be careful.'

'About what?'

'About fraternising with Cambridge girls. Their daddies don't like them being with boys like you for too long. They consider it a waste of school fees.'

'Well, I'll keep my wits about me.'

'Make sure you do. Besides — ' Another resident, Mrs Brady, stepped out into the hallway and Dr Paulsen went quiet. He stopped walking. She peered at them both and creased up her face, confused. There was a silent standoff between them, like two old cowboys meeting in the thoroughfare of a pioneer town. Then Mrs Brady turned, disappearing back into her room, and Dr Paulsen started walking again. 'What was I saying?'

'Besides.'

'Right. Yes. Besides, Cambridge students are very strange people, in my experience. They know so much about science and literature it makes them have peculiar habits when it comes to other things. Like dancing, and decorating their homes. You're best away from people like that. Stick with the salt-of-the-earth types like me.'

'I would,' Oscar said, 'except you're the strangest person I know.'

They reached the top of the stairs. He took the old man's cane and heaved him safely into the stair lift. Paulsen said: 'I should have a copy of the Descartes somewhere. It's yours if you can find it.'

'Thanks.'

'Just don't go scribbling love hearts in the margins.'

Oscar smiled. He placed the cane across the armrests, as if it were a drop-bar on a roller coaster, and when he was sure that Paulsen was secure, he pressed the green button and watched him descend, gradually, noisily, to the floor below.

2

Empires of the Passions

Oscar sat near the back of the concert hall. He could hear every small sound in the tight acoustics of the room — the drumming of people's fingers on the armrests, coats being folded up, the stowing of wet umbrellas. Onstage, a grand piano was set up with its lid propped open, and rows of vacant chairs and music stands stood around it in a perfect arc. A single cello was laid out sideways on the maple floor.

He browsed the concert programme and found Iris's name amongst the list of players. It looked strange in print, asymmetrical, a short word followed by a longer one, like a lorry hauling its load across the motorway: Iris Bellwether. He liked the breathy sound of it, the way it left his tongue. Further down the schedule, it was printed again: 'Iris Bellwether — Cello — *Elégie* (G. Fauré)'.

People were slowly gathering in the hall, but there were plenty of empty seats around him. Reserved conversations pervaded the room, and spikes of laughter kept rising in the foyer. Suddenly, he felt an invasion of his space, a looming presence over his shoulder. The floor creaked behind him. Oscar turned to find a tall man removing his sodden overcoat, spreading it out to dry over the arms of two seats. He could

28

only see the man's back, but he knew right away that it was Eden. There was something familiar about the rangy, languid movements of his body, and the wreath of curls that gave his head an accidental roundness.

When Oscar called out, Eden turned and dipped his head like a customer addressing a shoeshine. 'Oh, hello there,' he said. 'I'm afraid I've forgotten your name.'

'Oscar.'

'That's right. I knew it began with an O, but I was thinking: Oliver? Owen? I knew it wasn't Orville, at least — I deserve some credit for that. Anyway, it's very good of you to come.' He was dressed oddly, in the kind of outfit that seemed to have been assembled at short notice: a bright yellow turtleneck that was far too tight on the shoulders; pebbly black trousers, soaked at the ankles. He had a silver ear-stud that glimmered in the soft light. Sitting down, straight-backed, assured, he pinched at the crease in his slacks and surveyed the concert hall. 'Not a bad turn-out for a rainy Sunday. She'll be pleased. Have you seen her?'

'No, but I've been keeping an eye out.'

'I'm sure you have,' Eden grinned.

There was a small silence between them. A group of rain-spotted women headed up the aisle and took their seats. Eden flitted his eyes towards the ceiling and sniffed, as if noticing a bad smell. 'Actually, I'm glad I've bumped into you. Will you be coming to the party later? Just a little after-show thing, at our place. All very low key.' There was barely a chance to give an answer.

'Iris was going to ask you but — well, I saw you first. Will you come?'

'Alright.'

'We'll share a cab. It's still torrential out there.' Eden leaned back and stretched, revealing two large sweat patches below his armpits. He looked at his watch. 'They're starting a bit late, aren't they? Preening themselves, no doubt. Somebody needs to tell them hairspray won't make them sound any better.'

Somehow, Oscar couldn't imagine Iris fussing over her hair backstage. She seemed to be the kind of girl who paid little attention to her appearance. Maybe she spent a few minutes perfecting her make-up in the mornings, just to present the illusion of effort, but she wasn't the sort to keep an audience waiting for her nail varnish to dry.

'You left quite an impression on her, you know,' Eden said. 'She likes you.'

'Really?'

'Yes. Really.'

'How can you tell?'

'She's not difficult to read. For the past few days it's been Oscar this, Oscar that. That's the thing about Iris — she doesn't just get a bee in her bonnet, she gets an entire swarm. You could probably find honey in there if you cracked her open. I don't see what all the fuss is about, personally.'

Oscar smiled. 'What's she been saying about me?'

'Oh, come on now,' Eden said. 'Let's not be schoolgirls.'

It was the first time that Oscar had been able to get a good look at him. He wasn't at all like his sister. He had the narrow features of a field spaniel: a long, freckled nose; thin, almost invisible lips. And his eyes — there was something particularly striking about them. They had a noticeable glaze, like buffed apple-skin.

Without warning, the house lights dimmed and Oscar's heart began to rabbit in his chest. One by one, the chamber group took to the stage, Iris at the back, head lowered coyly into the hot light bearing down from the gantry. They positioned themselves accordingly — string section, woodwind section — settling into their chairs, giving momentary plucks and blows to check their tuning.

Oscar felt the pressure of a hand on his shoulder. 'Is it true you work at Cedarbrook?' Eden said, leaning in close. His tone was friendly but probing; his breath smelled vaguely of alcohol.

Oscar nodded.

'You've no idea how wonderful that is,' Eden said. 'It's such a treat to be able to speak to a regular person.' The hall doors closed behind them. A murmur of expectation bulged in the auditorium. 'Let's sit down at the party later. Just you and me. I bet you could tell me all kinds of things.'

Oscar wondered what he could possibly teach someone like Eden. He could tell him how to make sure an old man took his pills, or how to change a colostomy bag, or how to lift an old lady from a chair without straining his back. But he doubted if Eden had the stomach for this kind of education.

Onstage, Iris was poised behind her cello, ready with her bow. 'God, just look at her,' Eden said, pointing. 'She's a lost little lamb up there. The way she sits behind that thing, it's no wonder she can't get an even vibrato. I mean, *sit up straight, girl*.' His outstretched arm was a blur in the corner of Oscar's eye. 'But I suppose you've got to hand it to her; she's the prettiest thing in the room. Almost makes you feel bad for the others.'

The first notes of the clarinet were throaty and faltering. Eden heaved out a long breath, leaning back into the darkness.

★   ★   ★

Rain was thrashing outside, ricocheting against the roof of the taxi. Eden squeezed into the space beside Oscar and closed the door. He was prolonging the speech he'd started as the cab pulled up, though Iris didn't seem to be listening: 'And I know I said this last time, but your *Elégie* is definitely improving. You're getting it right in the middle section now. You really *were* like a young Eva Janzer tonight. Not that I'm old enough to have seen Eva Janzer alive but, you know, I'm extrapolating . . . ' The cab moved slowly away from the concert hall, heading towards Silver Street. 'When are you going to ditch the rest of them? That group makes you look so amateurish.'

'I don't know,' she said. 'Soon maybe. I haven't decided.'

She leaned her head against the misty

windowpane. Oscar could feel the press of her hip against his thigh. She seemed tired, bothered. Her skin was mottled pink and her hair slightly frizzed by the rain. She looked at him. 'What do *you* think, Oscar? How did I sound tonight? Be honest.'

Oscar was still thinking about her fingers, how they slid so effortlessly across the strings, how every note she played — whether it was deep down in the bassiest reaches of the instrument, or right at the very limits of the fingerboard — was crisp and true. He was remembering the shy, hesitant way she held herself on the stage, how she sat crooked over the neck of her instrument. But he found it very hard to come up with an answer to her question — how *had* she sounded tonight? — because, as he'd sat there listening, he'd been unable to concentrate on anything but Eden, sniffing and exhaling behind him. He'd focused on Eden's presence so much that the group's music had become a thick cloud of notes, an incessant blur. During her solo, he'd watched her right arm sweeping the bow, but for a good few moments he couldn't make out the melody. It was as if he was seeing her on 8mm film, with no sound but the steady clicking of the cinema projector, a noise so constant and inscrutable that it may as well have been silence.

There was no way he could explain all of this to her. 'Your brother's right,' he said instead. 'You were incredible. I can't believe you'd even think about giving it up.'

'Not the cello *full stop*,' she replied. 'I could

never give *that* up. Just the chamber group.'

'I don't know. I thought you sounded good together.'

'Well, my father says it's getting in the way of my studies. Something has to go and the chamber group's top of the pile.' She sighed. 'Nearly a year I've been playing with these people, and we're still not getting any better. It's hard to see the point any more.' Her expression turned thoughtful. 'Maybe there's no use in it anyway. Performing in public, I mean.'

'How come?'

The cab slowed, and she checked the position of her cello case in the passenger seat. 'It's like Eden keeps telling me: why bother getting up there and playing if you can't really make them feel anything?'

'I felt it,' Oscar said. 'Don't be so hard on yourself.'

'You're just being kind.'

'It's basic musica theorica,' Eden interrupted. He twisted round as much as his seat belt would allow. 'She's explaining it badly, that's all.'

'How am I *supposed* to explain it?'

'Well, I usually start with Pythagoras.'

'The triangle chap,' Iris said brightly, though Oscar didn't need telling. 'Except triangles weren't his whole shtick. He had this theory about the planets, too — the Music of the Spheres.'

'Yeah,' Oscar said, 'I've read about that.' He'd come across it in one of Dr Paulsen's history books, when he'd been reading about Alexander the Great. This had led him to Aristotle, then to

34

Plato, and then to Pythagoras. He remembered the premise, but it was a little blurry in his mind — a mathematical theory about the configuration of the planets, how they're supposed to sound distinctive notes as they move around the sun, creating one giant harmony. He'd found the whole idea appealing, if a little contrived.

Eden seemed impressed that he'd heard of the theory. 'I'm not sure what it says about our college when a humble nurse knows more about the ancient Greeks than you do, Iris.'

'Eden!' she snapped back at him.

'What?'

'That's an awful thing to say.' She turned to Oscar, shaking her head. 'I'm so sorry. I can't take him anywhere.'

Oscar half-smiled. 'It's okay.'

'What are you apologising for?' Eden rolled his eyes, thinking, as if he were hearing the minutes of their conversation being read back to him by a courtroom stenographer. 'Oh, right, yes, *okay*. Perhaps a little condescending.' He peered at Oscar vaguely. 'Sorry. I can't stop myself sometimes. No hard feelings, eh?'

'No hard feelings.' Oscar caught the sympathetic eyes of the taxi driver in the rear-view mirror. 'I don't know why you're so hung up about me being a nurse,' he said, to nobody in particular. 'It's not all that interesting.'

'Well, that's because you don't see the kinds of advantages it gives you,' Eden said. 'It's natural. A rocket scientist would tell you the same thing — nothing very interesting, nothing to make a fuss about. But that's not how it really is. I bet there are all kinds of things about Cedarbrook that would fascinate someone on the outside.' He turned to face the road. The taxi's wipers were frantically disseminating the rain, brake-lights fuzzing in the windscreen. 'Let's hope Jane's got a good fire going or it'll be freezing when we get there. Nothing spoils the mood of a party like a bitter cold.'

'Didn't you leave a note?' Iris said.

'Yes, but you know Jane. She's so dozy sometimes it's a wonder she can turn the lights on.'

Iris laughed, touching Oscar gently on the arm. 'That's his girlfriend,' she said. 'He's not being cruel. She really is away with the fairies most of the time.'

'In any case,' Eden said, 'we're celebrating tonight. Farewell to the chamber group, and good riddance.'

'I told you, I still haven't decided about that. You can throw as many goodbye parties as you want, it's not going to influence my decision.'

Eden bent forward, grinning. 'Oh, come on, Iggy. Wise up. When I think of all the effort you put into these things, it makes me so — I was going to say *angry*, but that's not the right word. I'm not angry; I'm embarrassed. There are so many better uses for a talent like yours.'

'Right,' Oscar said. 'She should perform solo.'

'No, it's more fundamental than that. Her whole philosophy on music is completely misguided. It's just — *wrong*,' Eden said, his voice growing louder.

Oscar was a little stunned. 'I'm not sure I get

what you're saying.'

'We're not having this discussion again,' Iris said. She glared at her brother. 'I'm warning you.'

It didn't stop Eden from continuing his point. 'I'll try and put it more simply,' he said, smirking. 'My sister is what we music scholars like to call a Cognitivist. Broadly speaking, that means she has some very cold-hearted ideas about how music works. She's an intelligent girl, but wrong about *so* many things on *so* many levels.'

'We disagree, okay? Let's just leave it at that.'

But Eden ignored her. 'She thinks that the sadness we feel when we listen to a sad piece of music — let's say Mahler's Ninth — isn't real sadness at all. To her, it's some nameless sensation, a general feeling of having been moved by the beauty of the music. She doesn't think composers know how to arouse our emotions, or manipulate our feelings through the placement of the notes. According to her, when Mahler brings us out of that fourth movement — *poof!* — we all cry tears of generality. Are you following this?'

Oscar nodded, though he was still perhaps a page or two behind.

Eden began to laugh. 'At least, that's how she used to think, before I started to show her the light. She may have changed her mind in the last couple of hours.'

'I don't know *what* I think,' Iris said, folding her arms.

'Now there's a cop-out for you.'

'Shut up, Eden.'

'She'll figure it out for herself one of these days. It's just a matter of time.'

Oscar watched the two of them like a spectator at a tennis match, his eyes moving from Iris to Eden and back again. He was beginning to understand that this kind of dispute was somehow unexceptional to them, just another quarrel in a lifetime of disagreements.

The taxi stopped at a red light on Hills Road. Iris gazed out of the window, irritated. 'Did you ever stop to think that I could be right about this?' she said. 'That maybe I'm the one who's got it figured out and it's you and all your Emotivist friends who've been stumbling in the dark?' Her voice was dry and pleading. 'You're not always right about *everything*, you know. Why can't you let me have an opinion without trying to convert me to *your* way of thinking? And — ' she breathed, calming herself down, ' — and how did we get back onto this stupid bloody subject anyway?'

Nobody answered. The cab moved away from the junction.

It was then that she placed her palm on Oscar's knee. Her hand was warm, so light he could barely feel it. She left it there for a long moment, not even looking at him. Then she pulled it back again, absently, and tucked it underneath her leg. 'It's not like any of this pontificating makes a difference to me. If I leave the chamber group, it won't be for any deep philosophical reason. It'll be because I'm tired of it. Same reason I dropped all the other groups I was in. Same reason I dropped my first boyfriend and the lacrosse team at boarding school.'

Oscar was still learning how to be around the two of them, but he felt so at ease in their company — more alive somehow. They were the kind of sophisticated people his father never let him be friends with when he was younger — 'the high and mighty crowd,' his father called them, the ones who lived in the detached houses out in Cassiobury. Oscar would see them in the wing mirror of his father's van, wandering home from the grammar school in their smart black blazers; the kids whose parents his father built extensions for, but with whom he was too proud to share a cup of tea after a day's work, fearing their good crockery and their vast, expensive kitchens. Now here Oscar was, holding his own amongst the same type of people. He felt a similar contentment in the presence of Iris and Eden as he did with Dr Paulsen, as if they had reset the clocks so he could live an hour ahead of the person he used to be.

It was nearly ten thirty when their taxi pulled up outside a three-storey tenement on Harvey Road. A light was on in the front window, venting through the collar of the drawn curtains. The rain had stopped and the taxi motor hummed in the soundless night. Eden paid the driver with a twenty and told him to keep the change. There was something about the thoughtless, distracted way he handed over the money that made the gesture seem patronising, like he was unaware of the note in his hand, uninterested in its value

— just a boy buying rides with fairground currency.

They got out and Eden took his bike from the boot, locking it by the wall. Oscar helped Iris carry her cello case up the steps to the front of the house. There was a round blue plaque beside the entrance that said:

Sir Charles Staunton
1852–1924
Composer — Organist — Conductor
Professor of Music
Cambridge University
Lived here 1884–1893

'This used to be our great uncle's house,' Eden said. 'My parents seem to think we got our musical genes from him, but I prefer to think I'm less predictable than all that. I play his stuff sometimes at the chapel, though. You ever hear the King's choir sing *Night Motets*?'

'No.'

'Well, you should. The man had a gift for choral music.'

In the hallway, Oscar took off his shoes and stacked them on the pile with the others. There was a giant mahogany coat-stand behind the door, laden with damp umbrellas and waxed jackets that smelled of upturned soil. The party was already underway, beating in the room beside them. He could hear the steady thump of the stereo behind the wall.

'Everything you see here — the skirting boards, the dado rails — they're all the original fixtures,' Eden said, lifting his voice slightly over the din. 'J. M. Keynes lived in the house over the road. It's not as fancy a neighbourhood as Iris likes to tell people, but I suppose it's better than being in some dingy little room in the college.' He waved an arm at his sister. 'Better if she gives you the tour. She cares more about the history than I do.'

'There's not much to tell,' Iris said. She got to the foot of the stairs, leaned her cello case on the balustrade, and threw her coat on top of it. 'Our mother used to live here, when she was at Emmanuel. She used to rent the top floor to some postgrad who was seeing my father at the time — that's how they ended up meeting each other. Now they own the building and the ones on either side. Funny how life works.'

'Don't worry about the noise levels,' Eden added, pointing to the air. 'The neighbours wouldn't dare complain.'

As soon as he said it, the sounds of the party became more present in the hallway. Oscar could hear splinters of deep male voices, girlish laughter, the clink of glasses. A ska record came on the stereo: an eager, bouncing rhythm. 'Sounds like Yin's got his LPs out for the occasion,' Eden said. 'God save us all.' He gestured towards the living room with an open palm, urging his sister forwards. 'Lead on, maestra, lead on. Everybody's waiting.'

There were twenty or so people maundering in the living room: girls perched on the arms of chesterfields, boys slumped in leather wingbacks by the gleaming fireplace, couples dancing half-heartedly, others standing by the stereo speakers, browsing through records. What looked like an antique harpsichord was pushed against the far wall, a lace tablecloth and a vase of roses set upon the shiny teak lid. The room had its own bouquet, a mix of drying denim, firewood, and the musky odour of bodies. Oscar had never seen a party quite like it.

When they came through the door, everybody turned. Three girls rushed over to greet Iris in a pincer movement, wrapping their arms around her, screeching: 'Oh my God, Iggy, you were am-a-zing!' 'I nearly cried at the end!' 'I just *love* your dress, by the way!' The rest of the crowd hung back, waiting for their moment. Then a stocky, acne-scarred man in a cream linen jacket came over and took her by the palm. 'I hear you nailed the Fauré,' he said. 'Good for you.' He was a short, pear-shaped thing, about twenty, with razored sideburns and teeth like a dry-stone wall. His words were pronounced in a measured way, as if to conceal his slight German accent.

'Thanks, Marcus,' Iris said, hitting him on the stomach skittishly.

'If you play some Bach next time, I promise I'll come and listen.'

'All you ever want to hear is Bach,' Eden said. 'You're so obvious.'

Marcus tilted his hands in the air, spilling wine from his glass. He trampled it into the rug. 'Why bother yourself with hobbyists like Fauré when you can perform the music of a master? That's all I'm saying.' He glanced at Oscar, raising his eyebrows. 'And who do we have here?'

Iris made the introductions. She explained how she'd met Oscar at the chapel and Marcus stood there, nodding courteously as she talked. He hardly seemed interested in what she was telling him until she mentioned Cedarbrook, then his grey face brightened. 'The place with the wisteria?' Marcus asked. 'Oh, how lovely. Did you know about this, Eden?'

Eden blinked a few times. 'Of course.'

The four of them small-talked for a while. Marcus was in the final year of a music degree and writing a dissertation on the death of J. S. Bach. He was quick to make sure Oscar knew how little shame he felt for being at Downing College: 'It isn't one of the glamour colleges, but so what? Back in Germany, in my parents' little mountain town where people still churn their own milk, they treat me like royalty. I should really go home more often, come to think of it.' Marcus took a large swig of wine, so big he had to pool it in his cheeks before gulping it down.

'It's still not a real college like King's, though, is it?' Eden said.

'You keep out of it. I'm chatting with your friend here.'

Eden laughed. 'Did you say *vitt*? Chatting *vitt*?'

'Oh, stop it.' Marcus turned to Oscar. 'They're always making fun of my accent. If they had the balls to go to Germany and talk German they'd get a rude awakening.'

'Excuse me,' Eden said, 'you're only half German. And I didn't hear anyone laughing at my accent when I was in Heidelberg with you.'

43

'That's because we don't laugh in people's faces. It's funnier to do it behind their backs.' Marcus smiled. 'Do you know what they call Oxbridge students in Germany?' He moved a step closer to Oscar, lowering his voice. 'Pretzels.' He let the word hang a moment. 'All that dough leaves a bad taste in the mouth.' He giggled wildly at his own joke. 'Actually, I heard somebody say that at a formal dinner. Or it might have been Alistair Cooke on the radio. But it's true, don't you think?' He raised his glass and dredged the last trickle of wine from it.

Somebody took the opportunity to change the music. The first bar of 'Can't Stand Losing You' blared from the speakers, and Iris looked over to the stereo. 'Oh, I just *adore* this song,' she said, and held out her hand, willing Oscar to take it. 'Will you dance with me?'

Oscar looked at her expectant face, dewy with sweat. There was no way he could refuse her.

'I warn you,' Eden said. 'She doesn't dance very often. It might put you off her for good.' He leaned an arm on Marcus's shoulder and whispered into his ear. Marcus responded with a squint of his eyes, as if measuring something on Oscar's face. 'Yeah,' Marcus said, giggling. 'That's what I assumed.'

Oscar felt Iris take his hand, her soft fingers closing around his wrist. She led him into the small crowd of dancers in the middle of the room. When she let go, he felt her absence on his skin like a draught. She closed her eyes, dropping her shoulders to the beat of The Police, dipping her hips, shifting her pale bare feet and lifting the long hair away from the back of her neck, her fingers steepled at the base of her skull. Her lips moved silently around every lyric — she knew them by heart.

The longer they danced, the less conscious Oscar felt of himself and his surroundings. He lost sight of Eden and Marcus, and stopped wondering what they were thinking about him, what they were saying to each other. The beat of the music seemed to lock itself to the beat of his heart. He hoped that he could stay there with Iris on the makeshift dancefloor, a couple forever heel-stepping to a perpetual rhythm. When the first song died out, another one kicked in, then another. They danced closer to each other, Iris turning her back, rolling her hips, sinking. He tried to follow her movements, placing his fingers gently around her waist — she didn't tell him to stop. The skin on her shoulders was moist with sweat, and he was almost out of breath. He wanted to kiss her, there at the base of her neck.

After four or five tracks, Iris was finally tired. 'Oh, I haven't danced in ages,' she said. 'I need a clove like you wouldn't believe. Wait there.' She smiled and walked off, scouting for a cigarette. He watched her move into the hall, out of sight, and the breadth of the room began to widen. His chest heaved and settled, and he was suddenly remembering himself — *early shift tomorrow, can't stay too late*. The night was beginning to creep over him like tidewater.

'You guys seem to be getting along okay,' came a deep voice from behind him. An American accent, or possibly Canadian; it was difficult to tell. 'I don't think I've ever seen Iggy dance with a guy before. Wish I knew your secret.' A broad-bodied Chinese man was standing there, beer in hand, one thumb hooked in his belt-loop. 'You want a drink?'

'No thanks, I'm fine.'

'Suit yourself.' The man sniffed. His face was wide as a dinner plate. 'I'm Yin,' he said. 'I take it you're Oscar.'

'Yeah. How did you know?'

'I was just talking with Marcus and Eden.'

'Oh.'

'They say you work at some nursing home.'

'Why does everyone keep mentioning that?'

'Hey, I was just making conversation.'

Oscar went to sit down on the chesterfield, feeling a sudden ache in his feet. Yin followed, taking a seat right up beside him. His aftershave was the same as Mr Antrim's in Room 15, a foreign, citrus fragrance that smelled too sharp in the flatness of autumn. 'Okay look,' Yin said, 'I admit we were talking about you, but not in a gossipy way. I guess we're all so institutionalised that it's kind of a thrill when we get to meet someone normal. If we could get by without leaving our colleges every day, we would.'

'You're not in your colleges now.'

'Not technically.'

'Not *actually*.'

'No, man, believe me, it's not as black and white as all that. It's like — ' Yin cleared his throat gently. 'It's like Eden and Iggy — they're allowed to live outside college grounds. They're the only undergrads I know who *are*. Apparently,

46

it distracts us all from studying if we live off campus, like we'd never read so much as a cereal box if we lived among the bright lights. But the only people Eden knows are college people anyway. So coming here isn't really any different. This place is like Bellwether Hall or something.'

'How come they get to live off campus and nobody else does?'

Yin flexed his eyebrows at the thought. 'Let's just say their family has plenty of sway around here.' He rubbed his fingers together. 'Buildings have been paid for. Donations have been made. You know what I mean. My parents do fine by anyone's standards, but I'm still sharing a bathroom over at St John's. That's how it goes.' He let out a weary laugh, clutching his forehead as if the zing of his aftershave had given him a headache. 'I'm sorry. I don't usually talk this much. I guess I'm a little drunk.'

Oscar shifted right. The closeness of Yin's wide body had started to bother him. He searched the room for Iris but couldn't find her. Eden was nowhere to be seen. The party was now just a gathering of backs turned towards him, strange faces making polite conversation. Marcus was talking to a brunette by the drinks table; a studious couple were standing timidly near the doorway, making eyes at each other. Nobody was dancing any more but the music was still fizzing in the speakers.

Yin leaned forward, elbows on knees, and said: 'I don't even know most of the people here tonight. They must be Iggy's classmates or something. We don't throw parties that often

— you can probably tell.'

'Do you know where she went?'

'She'll be back, man. Relax. Have a beer with me.'

Oscar looked at his watch. It was getting on for midnight already. There was nothing to do but wait around. He didn't want to seem too eager, to go about the house looking for her, room after room. She would only be smoking a clove out by the back door, or chatting in the kitchen with her college pals. They would only glare at him if he interrupted their discussion, and she wouldn't be able to give him her full attention. So what harm was there in having a drink with Yin?

'Cool,' Yin said. 'I'll see what I can rustle up.'

Oscar flicked through the stack of records over by the window. They were mostly 45s from the eighties, pristinely kept in polythene sleeves, and each one had a white label on the reverse that said: PROPERTY OF YIN TANG. He set them down on the windowsill. Through the seam of the curtains, he could see out onto the tenement steps. And there she was, outside with Eden, smoking, talking, gazing across the quiet floodlit street. She seemed red-faced, upset.

'Drink up.' Yin appeared beside him with a bottle of Tuborg. For a second, he glanced down at Iris through the window, too, and then pulled his eyes away, nudging the bottle into Oscar's arm. 'I think you should stick around awhile. This whole thing's gonna wind down soon, I guarantee it. Then we'll get back to normal.'

'What's normal around here?'

48

'I mean it'll just be the five of us. Me, Marcus, Jane, and *them*.' He nodded at the window, at the shapes of Iris and Eden on the steps. 'We're a pretty closed circle most of the time. Our parties tend to fizzle out fast.'

Oscar stayed in the living room, talking with Yin on the chesterfield, until they'd drunk a few more beers between them. Yin was from California, and that made him very different from the others. He was chatty, laid-back, but he spoke frankly at times, never worried about offending Oscar's sensibilities. He was studying for a degree in history. Though he lacked Eden's intellectual bluster, it didn't make him any less sophisticated. He spoke about important, complex affairs like weapons of mass destruction and the Bush administration in a brisk, uncomplicated way, as if they were categories on a game show, and talked freely about his life and family in San Francisco. Sometimes, he let out a deep guffaw to emphasise his jokes.

Yin seemed to hold such a deep affection for the Bellwethers that it spilled out each time he spoke. He would always move the conversation back to them: 'Yeah, I mean, my mom's side of the family is weird that way. They don't let anyone get close to them. It's a Chinese thing, I guess. But then, maybe *not*. It's kind of the same deal with Eden and Iggy, too. We've always had our own little clique going' — he pronounced it 'click' — 'and I guess we all like it that way, otherwise we'd let a few more people into the circle.'

'So why don't you?'

Yin grinned at him drunkenly. 'I don't know. I guess we don't meet too many people we like that much. It's hard for people to come in from the outside. We've known each other a long time.'

'Oh.'

'Don't worry about it. You're doing fine. You've already got Iris on your side — that's pretty clear — and Eden won't let just anybody hang out with him. He must have a good feeling about you or you wouldn't even be here . . . I, on the other hand, am still to be convinced.' Oscar couldn't tell if he was joking until his face cracked into a smile and he began laughing through his teeth. 'No, I'm kidding. You're okay by me.'

Yin was right about the party winding down. Around midnight, the last few guests were putting their coats on in the hallway and others were mounting their bikes outside. The final seven-inch was spooling on the record player. There were only four of them in the room: Oscar, Yin, Marcus, and Jane, who'd taken a seat on the other chesterfield, her thin legs crossed and stretched out.

Oscar knew very little about her. She was a reedy girl with tangerine hair and a star-map of freckles on her face. There was nothing especially attractive about her if you studied her features one by one, but somehow when they were put together in a jumble like they were — small eyes, pale skin, short ears, thin nose — she was quite pleasing to look at.

Soon, Oscar heard the front door close and

Eden came striding into the living room. 'Mind if I turn down the din?' he said, and flicked off the stereo without waiting for an answer. The silence made everything seem louder somehow: the strain of the leather upholstery against Marcus's back, and the scuff of Iris's feet upon the hardwood as she came in from the hall after her brother, looking solemn, tired-eyed.

Eden collected a few wine bottles and took a seat beside Jane. There was something so cordial and Victorian about their behaviour towards each other — a smile here, a kind look there, but not a single touch between them — and Oscar found it strange that they could be so close together on the couch and yet so distant at the same time. They listened while Marcus and Yin discussed the art of punting: whether a traditional wooden pole was the best choice on a cold day, or if a metal pole and some sturdy gloves were more appropriate. It was the cause for some debate.

Oscar watched the orange flames whip steadily against the hearth. His head was foggy with beer, and the voices in the room felt heavier now. Only Iris seemed to be completely sober. She went to turn off a couple of lamps and it gave the lounge a sedate, womb-like feeling — warm, safe, certain. Then she began clearing the mess, sweeping things into a cardboard box.

'For God's sake, Iggy, will you stop tidying up,' Marcus said. 'You're making us all feel guilty. I'm getting itchy just watching you.'

'Leave it, sis,' Eden agreed. 'Petra will do it tomorrow.'

'Petra?' Yin said. 'Tell me that's not your cleaner.'

Eden blushed, his cheeks turning as ruddy as the open fire. 'She's more than just a cleaner; she's a bloody godsend.'

'When did you get her?'

'A few weeks ago. From one of those agencies. She whistles when she hoovers, like one of the seven dwarfs.' Eden snapped his fingers. 'For heaven's sake, Iggy, come and sit down.' He patted the empty space to his left. Iris set the cardboard box down on the floor, dusted off her hands, and went to join him.

'I can't believe you have a cleaner,' Yin said. 'That's so bourgeois.'

'There's nothing wrong with having a cleaner,' Marcus said. 'My parents had two when I was growing up. They were the only people who ever played with me. I loved them like sisters.'

'Well, *that* explains a lot,' said Jane.

Eden stared across the room. 'What do you think, Oscar? You're the only one here who's done an honest day's work in his life. Is there anything wrong with having a cleaner?'

Oscar gave the question less thought than it probably required, and his words came out a little harder than he intended. 'As long as you treat her well, and pay her what she's worth, I don't see the harm. We've all got to make a living. If there weren't rich Cambridge students like you lot, too lazy to pick up your own socks, there'd be more people out on the streets.'

The room went quiet, and their eyes all seemed to turn in his direction. 'Nicely put,' Iris said, a wide smile on her face.

Yin smiled too. 'I guess we deserved that.'

'Do you remember that time at prep when the House Parents made us clean the boarding house, so we sellotaped ham under Ian Ashbee's bed?' Eden said to Marcus, laughing. 'For weeks, nobody could figure out where the smell was coming from. Ha! The look on his face!'

'Why did they make you clean the boarding house?' Jane said.

'Marcus stole a box of KitKats from the tuck shop.'

'For you. I stole it *for you*.'

'Yes, and we *both* got punished.'

'Hey, what about the time you Tipp-Exed the whole of 'Kubla Khan' on the common room wall?' Yin said. 'That was classic.'

'You could've got expelled for that,' Iris said. 'Dad didn't think it was so funny.'

'He has no sense of humour. They were never going to kick *me* out.' Eden leaned back, satisfied with himself. 'I was practically running the Oratorio Choir for them, I seem to recall.'

'And anyway, what kind of idiot thinks Coleridge is graffiti?' said Marcus. 'They should have thanked you for elevating the décor.'

'My point exactly.'

One school story was regaled after another, and for the first time all night, Oscar began to feel genuinely excluded. He was drawn to the urbaneness of their lives, their refinement and culture, but he just couldn't find a way into their discussion, no matter how hard he tried to interject. They were pulling memories from a private source, from some reservoir of experiences they'd all shared. All he could do was sit there and listen, and watch Iris as she laughed along, telling her own anecdotes about 'midnight bridge club' and swimming regattas. For a while, she barely even looked at him. If she asked him a question directly, it was only to confirm something she already knew: 'Isn't that the most hilarious thing you've ever heard? Oscar, isn't that just brilliant?' The more they talked, the more disconnected he felt.

They were like a family. They called each other pet names: 'Edie', 'Iggy', 'Yinny', 'Janey' (only Marcus seemed left out in this regard, though Yin once called him 'Em'). They teased each other, correcting Marcus when he mispronounced a word, and goading Yin by asking which country was most doomed: one with a flagging NHS, or one with a thriving NRA? Oscar knew he couldn't compete with this kind of friendship. He had never been as close to anyone as they were with each other. It gave him a despairing feeling in his stomach, like stumbling on a crowded pavement. His attention began to wander.

Iris must have noticed. She turned to him and said: 'Oh, this is probably so boring for you. I'm sorry.' Her smile seemed to lighten the space between them all at once. 'We always do this — end up talking about the old days. And then we wonder why nobody wants to spend any time with us.'

'I'm a bit lost, that's all,' he said. 'I mean, it sounds like some of you were at school together and some of you weren't. How do you all know each other?'

It was Jane who spoke up. Her voice was prim, gravelled. 'Marcus and Eden met at prep — the King's school. They were both in the chorister programme until they were, what, twelve, thirteen? It's *such* a demanding programme they have there; every boy has to learn about five instruments and rehearse with the choir eight hours a day. Can you imagine? I'd go spare.'

'It wasn't so bad really,' Eden said.

Jane continued: 'They met Yin later, at Charterhouse. The three of them were Gown-boys.' Yin raised his glass and nodded proudly. 'And I boarded with Iris at St Mary's. I'm sure we didn't mean to end up at Cambridge together, but here we all are. The Bellwethers and the flock.' Jane smiled, revealing a small gap between her front teeth.

'I think you just called us all sheep again,' Marcus said. 'I hate it when you do that.'

Eden reached for one of the wine bottles that were standing at his feet and went about uncorking it. 'Alright, I've got a better story for you, and not about the old days,' he said. 'This one's about Oscar.' He began filling up every-one's glasses, and when he reached Oscar, he tilted his head and winked. 'You should tell them how *we* came to meet.'

Oscar shifted in his seat, head still woozy. 'God, I don't think I can remember.'

'I heard it already,' Marcus said. 'You were flirting with Iris outside the chapel.'

'He wasn't *flirting*,' Iris said.

'Alright then, he was talking to you perfectly innocently outside the chapel, with no lurid thoughts in his mind whatsoever. Along comes Eden, blah blah blah.'

'That's not the whole story,' Eden said. He looked at Oscar. 'Do you mind if *I* tell them?'

'Go ahead. I don't even know what you're on about.'

Oscar listened as Eden relayed the events of Wednesday evening in detail. ' . . . and I was sitting up in the organ loft, and noticed him straight away. Picked him out as a heathen like *that*. He looked so bloody awkward, so unsettled. He was just staring at the choir like he could see the words coming out of their mouths. Afterwards, Iris tells me the only reason he went into the chapel was because he'd heard the organ. Ask him, he'll tell you. He hasn't been to church in years.'

'Well, he's hardly the only non-believer in the world,' Jane said.

'Yeah, big deal,' Yin said. 'My uncle Sun Fat is practically a Satanist. Who cares?'

Oscar got the feeling he was being examined. His mouth was going dry.

Eden sat back and folded his arms. 'You're missing the point. I wasn't supposed to be playing on Wednesday. The other organ scholar, Barnaby — it was supposed to be his night. But he'd sprained his wrist, so, like a trooper, I covered for him. And I thought, sod it, I'm not going to stick to Barnaby's boring old programme — Krebs, Gibbons, Bruna — we've heard it all before. The Director won't care if I change the voluntary. So I played something different, something by Mattheson.'

'You *didn't*,' Marcus said.

'Too bloody right I did. And look — ' Eden grinned, gesturing towards Oscar with outstretched arms. 'It worked. Living proof.'

Oscar was having difficulty following their discussion; his mind was clouded with drink, bleary with tiredness. But his head was just clear enough to know that he resented being talked about this way, as if he were something Eden had found flattened on the street and brought inside for the others to prod with a stick.

'I don't get it,' Jane said.

'He played the Mattheson piece, Jane. Keep up,' said Marcus. 'It's really quite extraordinary.'

'I still don't get it,' she said.

Oscar finally spoke up: 'Who the hell is Mattheson?' It came out rather bluntly.

Silence fell in the room.

'Johann Mattheson,' Eden said. 'He's my fixation *du jour*. I could talk about him all day, every day, for the rest of my life, and I still wouldn't tire of talking about him.'

'Oh God, please tell me you're not going to do your big Mattheson spiel,' Iris said.

'He wants to know,' Eden replied. 'Who am I to deny him?'

'Oscar, listen to me, there's still time.' Iris looked at him with a pitying sort of expression — mouth pursed, brow lifted. 'You should get out of here before he bores you into a slow death.' Oscar didn't respond. He needed to know what point Eden was trying to make.

'Fine,' she said, 'don't say I didn't warn you.' She rose from the chesterfield and picked up a few stray glasses. 'I'm going upstairs to lie down. There's only so many times a girl can hear the same story.' She carried the empties into the kitchen and didn't return.

When Eden started to talk, a certain glee stretched over his face. Johann Mattheson, he told them, was a German composer and theorist. He'd once been a musical prodigy, playing the organ at churches in Hamburg from the age of nine, and singing in the chorus of the Hamburg opera. Handel was one of his contemporaries, and they were close friends for most of their lives, until rivalry eventually got the better of them, ending in a duel. 'It was a proper sword fight outside a theatre — the real McCoy,' Eden beamed, 'and Mattheson nearly killed him, so they say, but a button on Handel's coat stopped the blade and saved him.' He was a prolific composer, writing mostly church music — 'What they like to call *sacred* music. He was a master at it' — and several operas — 'Okay, his operas are tedious, I'll admit it, but there are some incredible ideas in there, some really profound musical things happening.' Most of his compositions, Eden said, were lost during the Second World War. But it was Mattheson's theories about music that he was most interested in — in particular, a book called *Der Vollkommene Capellmeister*.

Oscar kept hearing Iris's footsteps through the ceiling. He wondered what she was doing up there, if she'd be coming back down.

'Mattheson and Descartes go together like cheese and wine,' Eden went on. 'I've really become quite enraptured with the man's ideas. I've read everything he's written, everything there is to read about him — diary extracts, letters, postcards — anything I could get my hands on. I've even started to collect things — anything he might've touched.'

'A man needs a hobby,' Marcus said.

'Yes, true, but it's more than that. He was really onto something in *Capellmeister* but he never quite followed through with his ideas. I think he got rather scared by what he could achieve. Oh dear, I'm not explaining this very well . . . ' Eden paused, looking up, as if the answers were somewhere in the gilded swirls of the light fixtures. Then he landed his gaze on Oscar. 'Remember what I was telling you in the cab, about Emotivism?'

'Some of it,' Oscar said. He mostly recalled the warmth of Iris's hand on his knee, how well she'd endured her brother's sermon on the failings of her chamber group.

'Well, let's extend that line of enquiry . . . ' Eden sipped his wine. 'If I told you there is music that makes you happy, and some that makes you sad, you wouldn't disagree with me, right?'

Oscar shrugged. 'I suppose not.'

'Well, Mattheson believed — and *I* believe — that composers have the power to affect and manipulate your emotions, your passions, as Descartes put it. When they're writing music, they have the potential to make you feel

59

whatever they want you to feel. Sort of like a chemistry experiment: if certain elements are put together in a certain formula you get a certain reaction. Would you say that's a big leap to make?'

'I don't know,' Oscar said. 'Maybe.'

'Well, Descartes didn't think so. He said even those with the weakest souls can acquire an absolute command of their emotions, if — and I quote — *if art and industry are used to manage them*. And Mattheson believed the same thing. He said that, in some structural way, music and emotions resemble each other. The man was a genius, and I don't use that word lightly.' Eden waited. There was a glimmer of something in his expression that made Oscar feel uneasy, a slightly manic thrill in commanding the whole group's attention. 'Mattheson took Descartes's ideas and applied them to music. In *Capellmeister*, he basically lays down a set of instructions for composers, to show them how to induce certain emotions through their work — to achieve that empire over the passions Descartes was talking about.'

There was a long moment of quiet. Everyone looked at each other.

'Don't mean to be dim,' Jane said, 'but what does any of this have to do with Wednesday night?'

Eden put his hands together and set them on his lap. He recrossed his legs. 'It's simple. The piece I played for the voluntary, which Oscar heard, was by Mattheson. It was a piece he composed for a Lutheran church in Hamburg

— I'm talking centuries ago. Marcus and I found the notation in a little antique shop in Heidelberg. We only paid fifty euros for it. They didn't even realise what they had, but we've had it verified. It's the real thing.'

'So?' Jane said.

'So this piece, as far as I can tell, is something he wrote towards the end of his life. Back then, he wanted to see if he could prove his theories in his compositions — to write music that could make people feel a love for God. Sort of like revival music.'

'That's exactly what Oscar felt,' Marcus said. 'Amazing.'

'Come on,' Jane said. 'That's a pile of nonsense and you know it.'

Eden shook his head. 'He said so himself — the only thing that took him inside was the sound of the music. He was lured in. Mattheson lured him in.'

'I don't know,' Oscar said. 'I just liked the sound of the organ, that's all. It didn't make me find God or anything. Not even close.'

'You liked the sound of the organ because Mattheson designed it that way. He gave you those emotions — curiosity, hope, safety, love. It's all in there. You heard it and you couldn't help but go inside.'

'Maybe,' Oscar said. 'But, trust me, I'm still an atheist.'

Eden laughed — a short exhalation of breath. 'Alright, fine. I admit it didn't make you *believe* in God. I'm not sure such a thing is possible, and I don't think Mattheson thought so either. But it brought you into his house. You came into church and sat down, which is precisely what that piece of music was intended to do.' Eden leaned forward. 'I'm just saying you didn't have an arbitrary compulsion to attend evensong on Wednesday. You were guided there.'

'If that were true,' Jane said, 'the whole chapel should've been full of people like Oscar.'

'What do you mean?' Yin said.

'You know. Heathens. Heretics. Non-believers.'

They all laughed.

'Maybe he was the only heathen who happened to be walking by,' Marcus said.

Jane stood up, straightening her skirt. 'When did you both go to Heidelberg anyway? I don't remember that.'

'In August,' Eden said. 'It was just for a weekend. You were in Italy.'

'Did Iris go with you?'

'No. She stayed behind. What does it matter?'

'It doesn't.' Jane shrugged. She seemed to let the subject drop, but then picked it back up again. 'I don't remember you saying anything about going to Heidelberg, that's all. I might have wanted to go to Heidelberg myself.'

'You were in Italy. With your parents,' Eden said. He stressed each word like he was punishing a dog.

'Yes. And if I'd known you two were going antiquing in Heidelberg, there's no way I'd have gone anywhere with my bloody parents.' She went to the far end of the room and returned with a crystal decanter. 'Would anyone care for some port? It's just about late enough.'

'Not for me, thanks,' Oscar said.

'It's the good stuff,' Jane said. 'That's one of the best things about Eden — he can drivel on and on, but he's always got a decent port in the house. Come on, have a glass.'

'Thanks, but I really should be going. I've got work in the morning.'

'Oh. Right you are,' Jane said. 'More for the rest of us then.'

The sound of Iris's footsteps above them had stopped now, and Oscar was already regretting his decision not to follow her. It felt like they'd hardly had a chance to speak since they'd finished dancing. He got up and made for the hallway.

As he neared the door, Eden called out: 'I could prove it, you know.' His voice sounded like dry, distant thunder in the quiet of the room. 'We could have a demonstration, right here in the parlour.'

Oscar turned. 'Prove what exactly?'

'That Mattheson knew what he was talking about. That he was really onto something.'

'It makes no difference to me.'

Eden shrugged. He seemed a little hurt. 'I'm just saying, I could prove it. If you came back tomorrow night, we could have a demonstration, and then you'd believe me.'

Oscar lingered by the doorjamb. 'Why does it matter if I believe you or not?'

'Because,' Eden said, his tone softening, 'because my sister likes you. And it would do her good to know we agree on something.' He looked away, as if the mention of Iris bore no

63

significance, but Oscar heard it for what it was: a tentative endorsement, an invitation to spend more time with her. And Oscar could see no better reason to come back tomorrow than the prospect of getting close to her again, even if it meant indulging Eden for a while. 'Okay. I'll come,' he said. 'If it means that much to you.'

Eden gave a faint smirk. 'I was thinking eight o'clock?'

'My shift might run over.'

'That's alright, we'll wait for you.' Eden accepted a glass of port from Jane and gestured towards the ceiling. 'Tell Iggy to come back and drink with us.'

Oscar said goodnight and headed into the hall. He went up the cold wooden staircase to look for her, expecting the old boards to creak under his feet, but every step was close to soundless. The bathroom door was open at the top of the stairs and a shaving light was on above the washbasin. He nearly walked straight past, but then he noticed a pale arm drooping over the side of the bath, an ashy cigarette between two of its fingers. Iris was laid out in the empty tub, asleep. She was still wearing her recital gown and looked impossibly comfortable, her neck lolling towards the tiles, a peaceful look upon her face. He didn't want to wake her. Down in the hallway, he wrote his number on the pad by the telephone, tore it off. The others were still talking in the next room, and he imagined the cheery rumble of their voices lasting until dawn. He found her brown coat hanging by the door, slipped the note into the pocket, and went out into the night.

3

A Reversible Lack of Awareness

The next day, things were quiet at Cedarbrook. Oscar spent his breaktime in the conservatory with *The Passions of the Soul*. It was an awkward translation and he made slow progress to begin with. The language was dense, arrhythmic, old-fashioned (relying heavily on words such as 'thither' and 'oft'), and a significant percentage of Part One seemed to focus on the digestion of meat in the human body. He put the book away and vowed to try again during his next break.

He wanted to speak to Dr Paulsen about it, but the old man was not in a talkative mood. His first attempt at communal dining had gone smoothly, in that he'd managed to eat breakfast with the other residents without catapulting poached eggs at them, but his second attempt, an evening dinner of boiled ham and potatoes, had not been a great success. Oscar had reported for his shift at eight, only to be informed by Jean, the staff nurse, that there had been a ruckus in the dining room the night before: 'Your friend Paulsen tried to pull off the whole tablecloth.' Jean was a big woman; when she got upset, her jowls shook and her ID badge flapped against her breast. 'He was spitting at everyone, throwing mustard, potatoes. It was ugly.' Oscar had gone up to Paulsen's room to see if he could

65

find out what the problem was, but the old man wouldn't speak.

At quarter to five, Jean came to the nurses' station and told Oscar he could leave early, so he walked straight back to his flat to shower and change out of his uniform. He ate dinner, left the dishes soaking in the sink, then sat under the pale kitchen light and tried again with Descartes. The prose was no easier to consume. It was just the kind of book that somebody like Eden would admire, he thought: leaden with concepts, light on entertainment. Still, he liked the way Descartes treated the soul and the body as separate things. It read to him like an owner's manual — a step-by-step guide to the mechanics of emotions.

By the time Oscar got to Harvey Road, it was very dark, and the flickering security light on the house across from Eden's gave the whole street a haunting neon shine. Marcus answered the door and showed him inside. 'What's it like out there?' he asked. 'The radio said it might hail tonight. Any sign of it?'

'Not that I could tell.'

'Hard to know when hail is coming, I suppose. I wonder how they predict these things, these weathermen. No more reliable than palm readers, if you ask me.'

The others were waiting for him in the living room. All the furniture had been rearranged: Eden's antique harpsichord was set up, dead centre, and a leather wingback was positioned in the shallow curve of its body. The fireplace was glowing. Both of the chesterfields had been pushed back along the far wall, and Iris, Yin, and Jane were sitting there in an oddly straight alignment, like passengers expecting a train. A soft, auburn light bathed the room — twenty or so candles were wavering in jam jars beside the golden castors of the harpsichord. Iris waved at Oscar sedately, a simple lifting of her fingertips. He smiled back at her.

'Glad you could make it,' Eden said. He was perched on the window ledge with the curtains drawn behind him, sipping from a china teacup. A stack of papers rested at his feet, bound in a manila file and tied with red ribbon. The room seemed bigger, barer, with the rugs scrolled and propped up in the corner, reminding Oscar of church halls and children's parties and pass-the-parcel.

The rest of them said hello. They all looked slightly fretful, reluctant to move. Oscar sat down next to Iris, on the arm of the couch. 'I'm not sure I like the look of this.'

'Me neither,' Iris said. 'Did you bring your Ouija board? I think we're having a séance.'

'Very funny,' Eden said. 'Nothing wrong with a little atmosphere. It all adds to the effect.'

Yin leaned forwards. 'This is gonna be something to write home about, I can tell.'

'Well it better not take long,' Iris said. 'I've got a supervision paper due tomorrow and I could do with making a start sometime this decade.'

'Alright, alright. Thank you, my dear sister, for your cynicism. It's been duly noted,' Eden said. 'Now the guest of honour is here, we can get things started.' He looked at Oscar, then

67

gestured towards the wingback with his eyes. 'Would you mind taking a seat?'

'Me? Why me?'

'Because you're the one I said I'd convince.'

Oscar didn't move. 'You don't need to prove anything to me. I told you before, I don't really care one way or the other.'

Eden rucked up his face. 'Oh, come on. If you didn't care, you wouldn't be here. You'd still be lazing on the couch watching *Taggart*.'

'He's got you there,' Jane said.

'I didn't know *Taggart* was on,' said Yin. 'I should've stayed home too.'

'Come on now.' Eden pointed to the wingback again, palm upturned, willing Oscar to sit.

'Go on,' Iris said. 'I really need to finish that paper.'

Feeling the weight of expectation upon him, Oscar walked over to the wingback and sat down in its worn, supple leather. 'Just promise me this isn't going to hurt.'

'I guarantee it,' Eden replied. At once, he clicked his fingers, pointing to the far corner of the room. 'Yin, Iris, Jane, take one of these and go and stand by the clavichord, please.' He untied the ribbon on his file and doled out a booklet of sheet music to each of them. They didn't get up from the chesterfield, just sat there, amused, peering at their booklets. 'Come on, humour me, will you?' Eden said, and they got up. 'Marcus, you know what to do.'

Marcus nodded and left the room. He came back in carrying Iris's cello case and proceeded to set it on the floor and open it, slowly

68

unlatching the clasps. 'Hey, be careful with that,' Iris said. 'The bridge is a tiny bit loose.' Marcus removed the cello and the bow, dragged one of the dining chairs close to Oscar in the wingback and sat down. In a deliberate, focused motion, he began rosining the bow.

'Okay then. Good.' Eden exhaled a long breath. He walked over to the keyboard end of the clavichord and stood there momentarily, drumming his fingers on the teak. Then he took a bundle of keys from his trouser pocket, searched for the right one — a delicate, tarnished little iron thing — and unlocked the lid. With a flurry of his fingers, he played a brisk run of notes. Marcus droned a deep, scratchy burr on the cello. Eden hit the corresponding notes on the clavichord, until he was satisfied they were both in tune. 'Alright, let's get started, shall we?'

'What are we supposed to do?' Iris said.

'You're my choristers.'

'Oh God, I was afraid you'd say that.'

Eden ignored her. 'Yin, you can be the beater. The rest of you just read along with the notation.'

'You might've given us some warning,' Jane said. 'I haven't warmed up.'

'You'll do fine. You've done this a hundred times before.'

'Not *this* we haven't,' Yin said.

'You all were in choir at school, weren't you? Have a quick read through and note my alterations in red. It's just a madrigal — Baroque — a three-part harmony. It'll barely challenge you.' Eden lifted his eyebrows at Oscar. 'Just sit back, okay. Close your eyes, and try to empty your mind of thoughts. Can you do that?'

Oscar wasn't completely sure he could, but he nodded.

'Take your time. Just let yourself relax.'

There was a long silence. Oscar fidgeted in the chair, hearing people moving around him.

'Okay, I'm going to ask you a few questions,' Eden said. 'And I want you to respond with the first thing that comes into your head. The *very first thing*. There are no right or wrong answers, only honest ones.'

'What?'

'Just run with it.'

'This is mad,' Oscar said. 'I'm opening my eyes.'

Eden's voice came back at him sharply: 'Stop being such a bloody girl and answer my questions.'

Oscar went quiet.

'What is your full name?'

He let a few seconds go by, then relented. 'Oscar James Lowe.'

'And how old are you?'

'Twenty.'

Eden struck a high note on the clavichord. 'What are you most afraid of?'

Oscar thought about it. He was afraid of a lot of things, but there was one fear that stood out above the rest. 'Old buildings,' he said. The high note continued to sound.

'Next question. Which bones have you broken in your body?'

He remembered the only serious injury he'd

ever had, playing cricket for the school team, and the uncomfortable Fiat Panda ride to the hospital with Mr Hamilton, his old PE teacher — he could almost feel the agony of it again. 'The middle finger on my left hand,' he answered.

'Okay.'

Eden waited. 'If a house were on fire, and you were stuck inside, would you want someone to risk his own life to save you?'

He responded quickly: 'No.'

The high note stopped.

He opened his eyes. 'Is that it?'

'Keep them shut,' Eden said. 'Empty your head again.'

Oscar seemed to be sitting there for a long time, eyes closed tight. Nothing appeared to be happening. He could hear nothing, sense nothing around him, and he began to feel embarrassed; he was sure they were all playing a trick on him, that they would all erupt with laughter at any moment. Just as he was about to open his eyes again, the melody of the clavichord bit through the silence. It was an arresting kind of sound — brittle but sweet, light but pure — and the music seemed to cascade around him like falling snow.

The tune was slow and mournful to begin with, and it relaxed him. With each note, he felt his body loosening. The air flowed smoothly through his lungs and his heartbeat seemed to regulate itself. *Dah-dah-dah-dah-dah*. His arms tingled, and the tension in his shoulders eased away, like creases smoothed out with an iron. He was getting so comfortable, so calm, that he

71

found himself smiling. But suddenly the tempo shifted, and the music became frenzied, discordant. Jarring notes speared the air, sharp and strange to his ears. At once, the cello joined in. The instrument was right up close to him, and its deep, languorous music seemed to shake the slackened muscles of his arms and legs.

That's when he felt it: an urgent warmth at the base of his neck.

The voices came next. Yin's deep baritone drawing outwards, then Jane and Iris in unison, their sweet, songbird tones off-setting it, forming a volley of words that Oscar couldn't quite understand. The singing and the fluid cello countered the spikes of the clavichord, anchoring the music, giving it gravity. He wasn't sure if it was just his mind playing games with him, but he swore he was falling out of consciousness. The music pushed and retreated in his head, steady as the tide. He was falling away. He could still hear the voices of the others, but they were muted now, just words passing through a long, dark tunnel. His eyelids felt heavy. There was a metallic taste in his mouth. A dry ache on his tongue. A sedating heat against his neck. And the next thing he knew, he was wide awake and blinking.

Iris was on her haunches, looking up at him, one hand on his thigh, the other touching his face. 'Oscar, can you hear me? Oscar?' She seemed slightly panicked.

'Woah,' he replied, adjusting to the light. 'I think I fell asleep.'

Everyone laughed, and the sound seemed to

pull him further into consciousness.

'Can you feel anything?' Iris asked. 'Are you alright?'

'Yeah. I'm okay, I'm just a bit groggy. What happened?'

She replied in a wary kind of way: 'Look down.'

He peered at his feet. Nothing. He checked his right side. Nothing. Then, as he looked towards his left, he saw it — a thick roof-nail, about four inches long, skewering the loose skin on the back of his left hand, just below the knuckle of his middle finger. He flinched, feeling like he might throw up, and tore his eyes away. 'Jesus! What the hell have you done? You said it wasn't going to hurt.'

'I think if it hurt you'd be screaming by now,' Eden said.

Oscar waited a few seconds for the pain to register, but it didn't. He gave it another moment, allowing his brain the chance to catch up. But he felt nothing. 'You hypnotised me?'

'In a manner of speaking,' Eden said.

There was still no pain in his hand at all. Everything else felt fine — he could wiggle his fingers and feel the leather against his skin.

'I told you I could prove it,' Eden said.

'By sticking a nail through my hand? Thanks a lot. If I get some kind of infection, I swear, I'll — '

'Oh, relax,' Marcus said. 'It's been sterilised. Perfectly clean.'

'You might be a little sore in the morning, though,' Iris said.

'Take it out. Take this thing out of me *right now.*'

Eden shook his head, folded his arms. 'If I take it out, it'll hurt. Trust me, you'll want me to put you under again. It'd be like a dentist pushing a rotten tooth back into your jaw. Not very nice.'

'Just get this thing out of my hand, okay? Or I'm going to — '

'Going to *what?*' Marcus laughed. 'Calm down.'

Yin spoke up then. 'Okay, come on, guys, fun's over. Take it out, Edie. Give the guy a break.'

'Fine, not a problem. It'll just take a sec.' Eden looked at Oscar. 'Lean back. Close your eyes.'

Again, the silence. Again, the brooding melody of the clavichord, followed by the cello, followed by the heat and the voices, followed by drifting, drifting, drifting. Something like an ether consumed him, gradually. When he woke up, the furniture was back in its right place. A dressing was taped to his hand. And the five of them — Eden, Iris, Marcus, Yin, and Jane — were all sitting around him, in an arc of chairs, leaning on their elbows, talking.

'I didn't understand the questions at the start,' Jane was saying.

'Oh, I was just having some fun with him,' Eden said. He was not paying attention to Oscar as he woke. 'Smoke and mirrors, that's all. I could've kept him under a lot longer if I'd wanted to.'

Oscar felt a pain in his left hand, like a searing burn, and he grabbed for it with his right, as if

74

holding it might lessen the agony. He didn't understand why he was hurting. The last thing he remembered was sitting down in the chair and Eden telling him to empty his mind.

'Hello. We've got movement,' Eden said. He tilted his head and waved. 'Morning, sunbeam.'

Oscar looked at them with wet eyes. 'Fuck. Did I pass out or something?'

'Yep,' Eden said. 'You were out for the count.'

'What happened?'

'I'm not sure. I think it might have been Yin's aftershave.'

Everyone laughed, and Yin gave a sarcastic titter.

'Don't you remember anything?' Iris asked. There was a softness to her voice that felt to him like genuine concern.

'I remember sitting in the chair and you all starting to play, and then — ' He broke off. 'My hand is killing me.' Oscar stood, flexing the fingers of his sore hand. A sort of panic came over him. It was not the pain itself that made him fearful, but the strangeness of it, the fact that he didn't know where it had come from. 'What the hell happened to me?'

Iris was about to speak, but Eden placed his fingers upon her shoulder. 'You had an accident,' he said. 'We were halfway through the demonstration and you fainted. You fell onto one of the candle jars and cut your hand. Are you alright?'

'I did?' Oscar looked at the others. Their faces were blank, static, and he didn't know how to read them. Another surge of pain gripped his hand. 'It hurts like mad.'

'I dressed the wound. It'll heal up fine,' Iris said.

Eden held out his palm. 'Let me see.'

'What?'

'Let me take a look at your hand.'

'Why?'

'Because I say so.' Eden's voice was dry and hollow.

'You better let him look,' Iris said. She smiled at Oscar in that way that he couldn't resist. Her pupils were steady, reassuringly set. Reluctantly, he put his hand into her brother's palm.

Eden removed the dressing. Two small lesions were seeping, an inch apart. The wound looked like a snake bite. A yellowy bruise was starting to spread across the swollen skin. The sight of it made Oscar light-headed. He turned away.

'Oh, it's not that bad,' Eden said. 'I've seen worse. On horses.'

'Are you sure I don't still have some glass in there?'

'You'll be fine.'

He winced as Eden placed his other hand over the wound. 'Hey! What are you doing? That kills. Stop it!' But Eden only gripped harder. His fingers viced. There was an urgent heat in his hands. 'For fuck's sake, stop it!' Oscar shouted. But Eden wouldn't release his grip. He only extended it over Oscar's wrist and stared into his face. His eyes had that weird sheen about them, that purity of focus. The pain was still there in Oscar's hand, but more overwhelming was that deep, distracting heat coming from Eden's fingers.

76

'Let go of me!'

Eden squeezed harder and harder. His face was concentrated, sneering.

'I said, let go!'

Iris took a timid step backwards.

'Edie, can't you just leave him alone now?' Jane said.

'Yeah, man, don't hurt the guy,' said Yin.

But Eden's skinny thumbs kept pressing and twisting, pressing and twisting. Then he quickly released his grip, and Oscar reeled backwards. 'What the fuck is wrong with you?' he shouted. 'Are you trying to torture me or something? Jesus!' He was shaking with anger and could feel the blood rising through his body. A queasiness came over him. He wanted to get away from this dark room, these people. He was too frantic to speak. Hauling on his coat, he ran out into the hallway. The leather caught underneath his heels as he stepped hurriedly into his shoes, but he didn't stop to adjust them.

He was still struggling with the latch on the front door when Iris rushed out to the hall. 'Hey, come on, don't go,' she said. 'It's Eden being Eden, that's all. Will you let me explain?' She stared at him with a look of regret — not as if she were sorry, but as if she were somehow disappointed in him. 'He went too far, I know. We all got a bit carried away in there. But *please*. Please don't leave. He was just trying to — oh, I don't know what he's trying to do.'

Oscar said nothing. He couldn't find the words to express how angry he was, how much he objected to being made a fool of,

77

experimented on, *used*. He stood there in the dim hallway, breathless, shaking his head. Iris turned her eyes to the floor. It was as if she had seen something in his face — a sight that could explain his feelings much better than words. 'Look, perhaps it's better for everyone if you go home and cool off,' she said. 'I'll call you, okay?'

'Don't bother,' he said. The words sounded so definite, so final. He pulled back the door with his good hand, walking out into the fading remnants of the night, where the glow of TVs burned blue in upstairs windows along the street, oblivious and unreachable. All he wanted was to go home and get up for work again in the morning and never see Eden Bellwether again.

* * *

Nobody at Cedarbrook noticed the wound on Oscar's hand — none of the residents, none of the other nurses — because the next day it had almost disappeared. He'd gone back to his flat, swallowed a codeine with a gulp of vodka, and fallen asleep with the wound still aching. The medicine had kicked in overnight, or so he assumed, because he'd woken up feeling no pain at all. The cotton dressing was spotted with blood, dried to a blackish burgundy. But, lifting it back to check the skin underneath, he'd found only two faint scabs below his knuckles, no bigger than freckles. It didn't seem possible. He had the vaguest memory of the night before: the initial panic of seeing the wound, the mention of broken glass, and the sheer persistence of Eden's grip on his hand. Maybe, in the anger of the moment, the injury had seemed worse than it was. Maybe he'd overreacted. But if he'd really fallen, like Eden said, shouldn't there have been some indication of it: a lingering soreness in his body; a bruise, a mark — *something*?

Still, he was glad that he didn't have to explain his injury to anyone at work that week. It was better that way. No fuss, no questions, no time to dwell on what a fool he'd been. From Tuesday to Sunday, he harboured the shame inside him like a pilot light. He stayed behind an extra few hours at the end of every shift, helping Jean and the other nurses. He signed himself up for nights the week after, five in a row — and weekends — every available slot until the end of November.

Dr Paulsen was easy to evade. He'd withdrawn into his room again, still raw from the incident at Sunday dinner, and too stubborn to press the nurse-call when he needed attention. So Oscar arranged for Deeraj to take the old man his meals, and empty his urine bottles, and change his bedding, and bathe him. In exchange, he agreed to take on all of Deeraj's least favourite duties. 'You can start with Mrs Radnor's corn plasters,' Deeraj said, 'and then you can shave Mr Clarke, and I'll see what else after that.'

For two weeks, Oscar found no time to read — or rather, no will. The thought of it overwhelmed him now; seemed futile and humiliating. A whole fortnight had passed by the time he noticed *The Passions of the Soul* was still lying on his night table, untouched. On

79

Monday morning, he gave it to Deeraj.

'What am I supposed to do with this?'

'I need you to return it to Paulsen for me.'

'No chance,' Deeraj said. 'If he thinks I've been anywhere near his precious books, he'll start with the spitting again.'

'But I can't give it back to him myself.'

'Why not? I thought you two were friends.'

'I just can't, okay.'

Deeraj chewed on his lip. He gathered a fresh set of towels from the store cupboard. 'Sorry, pal. Better handle this one yourself.'

Tuesday was a pleasant, sunny day — a break from the flat grey weather that had pervaded the previous week — and Oscar worked so hard through the morning that he had completed most of his duties by early afternoon. He walked down to the foot of the garden and stared at the vines of wisteria. They would bloom an intense purple in the spring, covering the front of the building, but for now, they only gave the building a feeling of unmet potential.

He was gazing around the newly turned flowerbeds in the Cedarbrook grounds when he heard a high, scratching knock from above him. He looked up towards the building. Dr Paulsen was standing at the window of his room, rattling the handle of his cane against the glass. *Tack-tack, tack-tack*. He was wearing a tweed blazer, and a panama hat, white as a picket fence. Motioning his arm slowly, he gestured for Oscar to come inside.

The Passions of the Soul was in the staff room, and Oscar went to retrieve it from his

80

locker before going upstairs. There was a bar of light under the old man's door. Oscar called hello as he went inside but heard no reply. Paulsen was waiting at the foot of the bed, one hand gripping the crook of his cane. The floor was a chaos of clothes. 'I can't seem to work the telephone. All this dialling nine and zero first,' he said. 'Would you be so kind as to order me a taxi?'

'Where are you going?'

'The Orchard.'

Oscar moved deeper into the room and began picking up clothing: musty Argyle jumpers, scratchy tweed trousers, dress shirts. 'You can't just take yourself off to The Orchard. Don't be silly. You know the rules. Things like that have to be arranged.'

'I can go wherever I want, son. Don't you tell me what I can and can't do. People used to open doors for me, you know. They'd stand up when I entered the room.' Dr Paulsen got up to emphasise his point. Then he gave a long, forlorn sigh. He removed his panama and held it to his chest. 'I'm sorry, I didn't mean to snap at you. I'm a bit impatient today.'

'Don't worry.'

'It's just that I got this letter from a dear friend of mine last week, saying he wished to meet me at The Orchard. I told him, quite categorically, that I would be there.'

'And who's going to look after you?'

'I've never missed an appointment in my life.'

'That's not the point.'

'This man is a very, *very* dear friend of mine. I

81

haven't seen him in such a long time, and last time I checked, this place was not a prison.'

Oscar folded up more of Paulsen's clothes and set them in a careful stack on the bed. He wondered where the old man had found the strength to dress himself, and with such neatness and co-ordination. 'Okay, look,' he said. 'I'll call you a taxi, but I'll have to go with you.'

'Thank you.' Paulsen sniffed. 'But I don't need a chaperone.'

'They're not going to let you out otherwise.'

'And who's going to stop me?'

'About twenty nurses.'

'Pah! Let them try!'

Dr Paulsen nodded towards the shirt Oscar was folding. 'What did you do to your hand?'

He was amazed that Paulsen had noticed — he could've sworn the wound was no longer visible. 'You can see that?'

'With my eyes? I can hardly see a thing. It's just strange that you've been folding everything with one hand.'

'Oh.' Oscar breathed. He pushed both hands into his pockets.

'I hope you haven't hurt yourself.'

'No. I'm fine.'

'Good.' Paulsen reached into his blazer. 'Would you like to see the letter from my friend?' The old man handed over a piece of lavender paper. It bore a scent like cigar smoke. Oscar unfolded it and read it quietly to himself. At the end, the letter was signed: 'Deepest Love, Herbert Crest'. He folded it back up and returned it to Paulsen. 'This says he wants to meet on Tuesday the nineteenth.'

'Yes. I can read.'

'Today is Tuesday the twelfth.'

'Oh, no, are you sure?' A disconsolate look came over the old man's face. 'And I've got my glad rags on and everything,' he said, lowering himself onto the bed. 'Well, consider this a week's notice. Next Tuesday, I'm going to The Orchard and nobody's going to stop me. Are we clear?'

'I'll let the Staff Nurse know.' Oscar smiled. He stayed for a moment, putting the old man's clothes into drawers, rehanging them. He felt the bulk of *The Passions of the Soul* in the apron pocket of his uniform, but he knew it wasn't the right time to return it. Dr Paulsen was lost in thought, rocking back and forth at the foot of the bed.

He was on his way out when Paulsen called to him: 'Have you ever been up in a balloon?'

He turned in the doorway. 'Excuse me?'

'A hot-air balloon. Have you?'

'No.'

'Well, you should. It's the most incredible experience.' Paulsen exhaled emphatically. 'I don't think a man can say he's truly lived until he's seen the world from up in a balloon. You can see for miles. You can breathe the air. Everything's so tranquil up there, and the only noise comes from the birds flapping through the clouds, and the whooshing of the gas every now and then. I swear, you don't even realise how vast the world is until you get higher. When you can look down and see your own house, the old

turf you've trodden your entire life, all of this — '
He gestured with his arms towards the window;
beyond the glass, the well-tended grounds of
Cedarbrook were doused in sunlight. ' — you
realise just how insignificant it all is. From up
there, the fancy old colleges are like rabbit-
droppings. You really must go up in a balloon
one day.'

'Yeah. Maybe I will.'

'Go this weekend. Take that girl of yours
— what's her name? The student?'

'Iris,' he said. The word rang in his head.

'Take her. There's nothing more romantic.
Herbert and I used to take balloon rides every
few months. We couldn't get enough.'

'I don't think I'll be seeing her anytime soon.'

The old man didn't seem surprised by the
news. He gave a long, protracted blink but his
expression didn't change at all. 'Herbert was a
King's boy, y'know. A strange young thing, he
was, when I met him. Only owned three outfits,
wore them in rotation, whatever the weather. He
used to have this smell about him — musky, a bit
sweaty. It wasn't completely unpleasant. There
was so much to love about him. I don't know
what he saw in me, I really don't . . . Can't
remember why I'm even telling you all this now.'
Paulsen took a long moment to recapture his
train of thought. A sprig of hair had sprung up
on the back of his head and he smoothed it
down with his fingers. 'I suppose what I'm saying
is, it'd be nice to take him up in a balloon one
more time. I think he would like that. It's been
ages since we saw each other. Sometimes, you

can hold a grudge for so long you forget why you were holding onto it. And before you know it, half a lifetime has gone by and all you've got is an empty fist and a lot of regret.' He gave a small cough, clearing his throat dryly, and hung his panama from one finger, as if spinning a plate. 'I suppose I should put this back in the wardrobe until next week.'

'I'll see what I can do about The Orchard,' Oscar said. 'Maybe I can take you there myself.'

Paulsen nodded. 'Now you're talking.'

Later, when Oscar was filling out his time sheet in the staff room, he found himself distracted by the thought of hot-air balloons. He tried to imagine standing in the basket, peering down at the tiny world, but it only made him feel lonely and directionless. And so he pictured himself sharing the flight with Iris, her lithe hand operating the gasflame, her long hair stirred by the wind, and he realised the picture looked so much better this way. He'd missed the comfort of thinking about her, day by day, the company of her image in his mind.

He didn't quite feel ready to go back to Harvey Road. Instead, he went home and looked for the name Bellwether in the phone book. He tried the number before work the next morning, hoping she would answer. It rang four times and then her frail, friendly voice came through the receiver. All she said was 'Hello,' but it made his heart quicken.

'It's Oscar,' he said.

'Oh, Oscar, thank goodness.' She exhaled loudly. 'I'm so glad to hear from you. I wanted to call so many times and explain, but I couldn't think of how to . . . it doesn't matter. We're talking now. That's what counts.' They navigated around the subject of her brother with awkward small talk about the recent hail showers. She began to tell him about an ice storm she'd once seen in Montreal, but he interrupted her. 'I was thinking we should get a cup of tea or something. Like normal people,' he said. 'Are you free later?'

'Yes. That would be nice.' He could almost hear her smiling. Then she asked, 'Where?', and his mind wiped itself blank. All he could think of was a funny-looking place by Magdalene Bridge, an Italian chain bistro with phoney terracotta walls.

She arrived nearly ten minutes late, sporting a grey bobble hat that barely covered her ears, and a pair of mittens made from the same thick, whiskery wool. The sight of her coming down Magdalene Street brought a tremor to the backs of his knees. A soft ache built inside him. He was still angry with her, but it didn't seem to matter any more. She was carrying her cello case, strapped over two shoulders like an unwieldy backpack, the weight of it bending her body forwards. A cyclist steered quickly to avoid her as she crossed the road without looking.

Stopping before Oscar, she set the cello down by his feet. They shook hands, daintily, like they were perfect strangers. 'Sorry I'm late. I got out as soon as I could,' she said. 'Our director was going on and on about our bowing. I told him, *Mike, if we were any more in sync we'd be*

86

Siamese twins, but he didn't really see the funny side. Have you been waiting long?'

'I just got here.' She didn't need to know that he'd been standing nervously in the doorway for a quarter of an hour. 'I thought you were giving up the chamber group.'

'No. I decided against it. My father will just have to lump it. And besides, it annoys the heck out of my brother.' She looked away. 'We should get a table.'

They found a place beside the biggest window in the café. The austere grey buildings of Magdalene College stood proudly on the riverbank. Everywhere Oscar turned, the college and its pristine lawns were in his peripheral vision, lurking, pressing. It was getting on for four o'clock, but the sun was still slanting down, casting silhouettes upon the river. Punts were idling along the water, and for a moment he sat there quietly with Iris, watching them collide with tame little bumps. A Japanese family steered into the embankment while an old man in a straw boater went by serenely, a parade of mute swans following in his wake. There was a tension in the silence. For the first time, he felt uneasy being alone with her.

Iris poured her Darjeeling. 'So look,' she said, 'sooner or later, one of us is going to have to talk about what happened the other week.'

'I know.'

'I want you to know how sorry I am. Things got out of control.'

'Well, I think I might have overreacted a little bit.'

'That's understandable. You were injured, after all, and Eden only made things worse.'

'I should've let you explain.' He tried to look into her eyes, but her face was pointed down towards the spoon she was whirling in her tea. 'I mean, I haven't known Eden that long, and I don't know what he thought he was trying to prove with that stunt of his exactly. I don't even know how I ended up hurting myself. But that's not what upset me. It was when he wouldn't let go of my hand, and I looked at *you* — it seemed like you didn't want him to let go. It felt — ' He stopped to make sure the words came out right. 'It felt like maybe you were enjoying seeing me like that, under his control. It was like you were laughing at me.'

There was a balanced sort of hush in the bistro. Iris looked out of the window towards the river, now empty of punts, the water hardly disturbed. 'I wasn't laughing at you, Oscar — I'd never do that — and I certainly wasn't enjoying it. But there are things about Eden I knew you wouldn't understand, unless you saw them for yourself.'

'What things? What are you talking about?'

'Honestly, I think he's going funny in the head. I mean *ill*.' She tapped her temple with her fingertip. 'That whole performance the other night was so demeaning. I've been dying to call you and apologise but — oh, I suppose I was afraid you wouldn't speak to me. I just don't have anyone I can talk to about this. Not really. I find myself worrying about him *constantly* these days. It's making me feel so desperate.'

'You can talk to me,' he said. 'I mean it.'

She smiled. 'You've got a kind heart, Oscar. I could tell that about you the moment I saw you.'

'What is it that you're so worried about?'

'*Him*. My brother. His delusions of grandeur.' She paused, sipping her tea thoughtfully. 'I really want him to see a psychiatrist. But you've seen what he's like. Can you imagine him listening to a word I say?'

'Not really.'

'I've tried to bring it up with my parents but, well, they listen less than Eden does. My father's dead-set against psychiatry in general — he can't sit still long enough to talk properly about anything, let alone his emotions — and my mother's always at church, or too busy with her meetings to care about anything that's important to *me*. But this feeling I have about Eden's been building for a long time, and I'm really at the end of my tether. I didn't mean for you to get caught up in it all.'

Oscar fidgeted with his coffee cup, lacking the appetite to drink it. 'So why didn't you warn me not to come the other night? If you were worried about what he might do . . . '

'Because.' She shrugged. 'I was being selfish. I wanted to observe him in action. I wanted to see what he was going to do to you. And I know it was wrong of me, to use you like that, but you've got to appreciate: I was trying to gather evidence.'

'What do you mean?'

'You know, something I could talk to a psychiatrist about, ask for advice on.'

'It sounds like you're trying to get him committed or something.'

'I just want a professional opinion, that's all.'

Oscar leaned back in his chair. 'What exactly do you think is wrong with him?'

'I'm not sure yet. I've been reading all these textbooks about behavioural problems, but his symptoms — if you can even call them symptoms — change all the time. The psychiatrist I spoke to seemed to think there was nothing too concerning about it.'

'You spoke to someone?'

'Yeah, last week. I made an appointment with this woman I found online — Dr Heller. She has this private practice near King's Lynn. Middle of nowhere. Took me forever to drive there.'

'And?'

'And nothing. She doesn't psychoanalyse people based on second-hand information, apparently. But if my brother would like to make an appointment himself . . . Ha! I told her there was more chance of it raining cantaloupes.'

Oscar felt the strangest hint of sympathy now for Eden. It didn't seem right for her to be talking this way, as if her brother were some rabid animal she was trying to snare. This feeling must have shown on his face, too, because she started to backtrack. 'I don't know, maybe I'm just being too sensitive about it, over-analysing things. Maybe there's nothing wrong with him at all.' She leaned away. 'Truth is, if you know my brother's history, this sort of behaviour is quite normal. You get used to it after a while. He has very odd ways of showing his affection. When he took your hand like that? He wouldn't do that to just *anyone*, you know. He thought he was helping you. I bet there's hardly anything there now, right? Can I look?' She reached across the table and put her hands on his, settling them. Her skin was soft but cold. She turned his left hand over and looked for a wound, grazing the space gently with her thumb. She didn't seem the least bit surprised to see it had healed. 'God, I wonder how he does it.'

'I've been wondering the same thing.'

'If I could just know *how*, I might understand *why*.'

'You don't seem very shocked.'

She shrugged. 'It's a magic trick, that's all. I'm used to them by now.'

'He's done this kind of thing before?'

'When we were younger. All the time.' Their eyes fixed together for a second, and he could see the tiny bistro lights in her pupils. She said: 'Oscar, I need your help with this. You're the only one I can ask.'

'With what?'

'With my evidence gathering. I need to have proof of his behaviour. People need to start seeing how he really is.'

'I don't know, Iris.'

She carried on, as if she hadn't heard: 'If I could just get him to put something down in writing. Give him your email address maybe . . .'

'I don't think that's a good idea.'

'Why not? We'd only be doing it to help him.'

'Yeah, but I'm not going to spy on him.'

'No, no. It wouldn't be as clandestine as all

91

that. I'd just be giving him your email, that's all.' She made small circles on the tabletop with her finger. 'He never writes to me, so all I have are my observations, and apparently they don't count for much. But if I could just get some clear proof of the way his mind works, how he communicates with people. Then I could take it to a proper psychiatrist and get an opinion on it. *Please*. I can't tell you how much of a help that would be.'

She had never seemed so vulnerable before. She was asking him earnestly for his help — how could he refuse her? He told her his email address and she wrote it on her wrist with a biro.

'I need you to print off copies of anything he writes to you,' she said excitedly. There was a hopeful look on her face now, and a relief that was apparent in the loosening of her posture. 'Don't look so guilty about it. We're only doing it to help him.'

'I know, it's just — I suppose it feels dishonest. What makes you think he'll even write to me?'

'Because I've told him he needs to apologise.'

'Oh.'

'And once I tell him how your hand is, he won't be able to resist. He'll want to gloat about it.' She shook her head. 'That sounded cruel. I didn't mean it that way. I only want to help him, that's all. You've got to believe me when I say that.'

'It's okay. I believe you.'

A splinter of sunlight broke through the window and focused in a narrow beam on the floor of the café; then, just as easily, the sun moved behind a cloud and the shaft of light disappeared. 'You know, I thought about something the other night, after you left. I was thinking about the King's choir. I go there to listen to them all the time, not just when Eden's playing.' She made a plinth with her fists and rested her chin on them, glancing up at him. From this angle, she was at her most beautiful, her face tapering into an elegant V. 'Do you know what I think about when I hear that choir? Absolutely nothing. I don't have a single thought in my head the whole time they're singing. They just relax me so much, I feel as if I'm free. I stop thinking about all the bloody tests I've got to take, and all the things my father says I *simply must* achieve while I'm here. When that choir sings, I'm just a girl in a room, listening. And I don't care what it is they're singing about, it's just nice to feel free for a while. Now — ' She sighed. 'How much of that has to do with Johann Mattheson or Descartes or anything Eden says, who knows? Who cares? Mattheson's just his latest obsession, that's all. It used to be Plato, and Nietzsche, and Walter Benjamin. Before that, it was somebody else. I'm bored of hearing about my brother's fixations. But I know something for certain. That feeling I get when I listen to the King's choir? I feel the same way whenever I'm with you, Oscar.' She twisted the ends of her hair. 'Somehow I feel like I could tell you anything.'

★   ★   ★

93

His flat was cold, the bed unmade. She pulled a gold cigarette case from her coat pocket. 'I'm going to smoke a little — you don't mind, do you? It calms me down.' She wandered around his room, ran her hands over the surfaces, picking up any possessions that caught her interest — a plastic snow-globe from Edinburgh, a squash ball, a postcard from Kew Gardens — considering them for a moment before replacing them exactly as she found them. As she lit a clove and took a long drag, she examined the books that were stacked up on his floor, studying their spines with a tightened expression. The more of them she saw, the wider the smile spread across her face. 'How come you have so many copies of *The Colossus*?' she asked. 'It worries me, you liking Plath.'

'You don't like her?'

'Are you kidding me? I adore her. But I'm a Cambridge girl with overbearing parents. What's your excuse?'

'I just like her point of view. The first time I read that collection, I had a borrowed copy. Then I saw it at a market stall and bought it. Then I saw it again and bought it. I couldn't stop myself. I'm over it now.'

'Are you sure you're straight?' she said. 'Don't give me that look — I'm just teasing.' She tapped ash blithely on the carpet. 'So what's your favourite Plath poem?'

'I don't know.'

'Of course you know. Tell me.'

'Probably 'Full Fathom Five'.'

'Huh,' she replied, turning down the corners

of her mouth. 'Interesting.' The smell of clove was strong now, sweet as molasses. 'Do you write any poetry yourself?'

'Sometimes.'

'I don't suppose you'd care to share any.'

'You'd suppose right.'

'One day,' she said.

Quick-stepping to his bedside drawers, she levered them open with her free hand, and when she found nothing worth mentioning, went to browse his CD collection, standing beside him at the cheap pine cabinet that housed his stereo. She was so close he could smell bergamot through the haze of cigarettes. 'I don't know why you were so downbeat about your flat. It's perfectly lovely. A bit dusty, but nothing compared to my house. Those old tenements are impossible to keep clean.'

'I thought you had a cleaner,' he replied.

She ignored him.

He pushed Play on the stereo and the sound of the King's College choir rose up in the room. Iris had brought along a copy of their latest CD. It was a good recording, but the choristers weren't the same, and their voices weren't as rich or resounding as they'd seemed that Wednesday night in the chapel when they'd first met. 'People always look at the speakers,' Iris said, musingly. 'When the music's on, we always look at the stereo or the speakers, like we're trying to see the music coming out of it. What d'you think that means?'

'It means we're all stupid.'

'Yes, but it's rather sweet, too. Don't you

think? There's something innocent about it, something childlike.' She moved closer to him, twisting up the volume dial with one hand, placing the other against the small of his back ever so lightly. 'Oh, wow, just listen to that.' She turned her body a fraction, swaying towards him, blowing cigarette smoke behind her, eyes closed. The cheap cabinet rocked on its feet. He looked at the olive-green shadow on her eyelids: a forgiving colour, safe but indefinite. He was quivering, reluctant to make a wrong move. She opened her eyes, staring back at him. Then, without looking away, she reached into the back pocket of her jeans, drew out her cigarette case, and stubbed out her clove against it. She snapped the case shut and set it down on the cabinet. Grabbing at the collar of his shirt, she pulled him towards her.

'Are you sure about this?' he said, almost whispering.

She nodded. Her hair collapsed across her face and he tucked it back behind her ear with his thumb. Their foreheads touched together, and they waited, as if listening to some silent countdown. They kissed — that first quick touching of lips, that toe-in-the-water kiss before the high dive. He smiled at her, and asked her one more time, 'Are you sure?' The voices of the choir cleaved through the dusty air of his flat, swarming around them like seagulls above a shipwreck. She pressed her body against him, and they fell back upon the bed.

'If I wasn't sure,' she said, 'I wouldn't be here.'

* ★ ★

In the Watford estate where Oscar grew up, the houses all looked the same. Square, innocuous brick-piles, clad in cheap grey stucco, with rectangular concrete driveways. If a new family moved into his estate and decided to update their property — to paint their front door a vivid orange, say — the effects would ripple through the community. Soon, every door in the estate would be daubed a vibrant colour, until the rows of nondescript houses had the palette of a child's drawing. The only house that ever stayed the same was his own.

This is what he was thinking about as he lay in bed next to Iris. They were naked below the duvet and she was sleeping on her side, facing away from him. He kissed her bare shoulder and put his hand across her stomach; she stirred, gripping his forearm, drawing him closer to her. She asked what was on his mind.

'Nothing,' he replied. 'Just thinking.'

'Don't feel guilty. I knew what I was getting myself into.'

He didn't feel guilty, just unpractised. Only a few girls had stayed the night with him before, and they'd put their clothes back on right after and watched TV, gone into the bathroom to shower, or just fallen straight to sleep with their mascara streaking his linen. And he'd been left alone each time to listen to the night traffic halting at the junction outside his window. But Iris had not fallen asleep so quickly; it had taken her some time to gather her thoughts, lying breathless on her back, flattening the cover down over her breasts. The only thing she wanted, afterwards, was to talk.

She'd told him about the country farmhouse in Grantchester, where her parents lived. It had once belonged to some rich South African who'd made his fortune from diamond mining in the 1850s. The man was a devout Christian, and he'd installed his own private chapel at the foot of the garden. It was only a small building — in her words, 'about the size of a modest village hall' — but it had an adjoining rectory for the resident minister. When her parents bought the place, they converted the chapel and the rectory into guesthouses, restoring the old pipe organ so that Eden could practise on it whenever he was at home.

Iris had explained all this to Oscar, slowly abrading the skin of his collarbone with her fingertips. He had listened with a sinking feeling as she'd talked about family barbecues by the river at sunset, marquee parties in the back garden, cherry blossoms and playrooms and moonlit punt rides, family holidays in Martha's Vineyard and the Florida Keys, as if these were the obligatory details of an ordinary childhood. When he'd asked her what her parents did to afford all of this, she'd been only too happy to tell him. Her father was a paediatric surgeon who'd made 'all kinds of sensible investments' over the years. ('He became a partner in a telesurgery company about ten years ago when nobody could even conceive of it catching on — I mean, who'd want a robot operating on their only child, right? — but now the technology's booming and he's got a share of all these patents everybody wants.') Her mother's family were wealthy, too — 'a line of investment bankers on my grandmother's side' — and aside from being executrix of the Charles Staunton estate, her mother had a portfolio of companies for which she was either a board member or a silent partner. ('I think most of them trade in precious metals. Silver. Platinum. Not so much gold these days. Palladium is the new gold, apparently — massively sought after in China.')

The more that Iris had talked about her home and family, the more uncomfortable Oscar had felt beside her. His voice had softened with every interjection — 'Oh, that's really . . . that's great, that must've been nice' — and he'd gone very quiet, so quiet that she'd fallen asleep. While he'd listened to her gentle snoring, his mind had drifted to his own family, his own childhood back in Watford. And he'd woken her before these thoughts made him too melancholy.

'So what now?' she asked, turning to face him, kissing him.

'I don't know. It's been a while since I've done this.'

'Me too.'

'I suppose we just play it by ear.'

'It feels strange. Sort of like we're cheating.'

'Cheating on who?'

'Nobody. I'm just saying it feels that way.' She sat up. 'My father cheated on my mother a long time ago, before Eden and I were born. She told me about it once. I suppose that's made me inclined to feel guilty about sex.' Her leg slid

99

over him. 'What about your parents — are they still together?'

He adjusted his head on the pillow. 'Yeah, just about.'

'You don't talk about your family much, do you?'

He stayed quiet.

'How often do you see them?'

'Every now and again.'

'Well, when was the last time?'

'I don't know.'

'God, I can't imagine not knowing the last time I saw my parents.'

He moved his arm away from her.

She let a moment go by then said, inquiringly: 'Are you ashamed of them or something?'

'No. Of course I'm not.'

'Well, I don't understand . . . '

He couldn't bring himself to tell her what she wanted to know. His parents were uncomplicated people, but they were difficult to explain to somebody like Iris. She wouldn't understand the smallness of their expectations, how all they'd ever wanted for him was to reach an age where he could look after himself — find a job, move out, work hard, get by, just like *they* did when *they* were seventeen — and maybe one day give them a grandchild they could boast about to the locals at the George and Dragon. How could he explain to her the helpless feeling of being told to skip an exam to finish off a plastering job with his father, or the ache of seeing his school reports used as scrap paper for takeaway orders? He was not ashamed of his parents, but he didn't

100

want to be like them. He was not ashamed of where he was from, but he didn't want to go back there. These were the poles of his heart. He could no more explain them to Iris than he could resolve them.

She got dressed in front of his mirrored wardrobe, fixing her bra nimbly, raking her fingers through her hair to straighten it. He stayed in bed, watching her. A grimy light pooled in the room and, outside, the moon was already a pale blur in the sky. He could make out the scrawl of his email address, still on her wrist. She put on her coat and retrieved her CD from the stereo. Looking down at him from the edge of the bed, she asked: 'Will you let me know as soon as you hear from Eden? I can't tell you how much better I feel, knowing there's a plan in action.' Her voice was heavy, serious. She squeezed his fingers and kissed him on the forehead. At the door, she heaved the straps of her cello case over both shoulders. 'Be safe,' she said, and walked out.

He slept for a good few hours, and, when he woke, he found himself wanting to call his parents. It had been a long time, over six months, since he'd last spoken to them, and though he didn't have much news to tell them, he felt an urge to hear their voices again.

His mother answered, adopting her best telephone manner. 'How are you, son? Haven't heard from you in ages.' He filled her in on events at work, and she told him all about the goings-on in the estate, gossiping about people he used to know. His cousin Terry, she said, had

101

been in a fight with a bouncer in town; he'd had seven stitches across his eyebrow. 'I hope you're staying out of trouble. I suppose there aren't many fights to get into in your neck of the woods, eh? Not unless you're scrapping with the toffs. I'll put your father on.'

There was a noise of someone jostling with the receiver, before he heard the gruff voice of his father: 'Yeah.'

'Hi, Dad.'

'Oh. It's you. Hi.'

'How's everything?'

'Same as ever. You?'

'Fine.'

'Uh-huh.'

He was long used to awkward gaps in conversation with his father. 'Just thought I'd see how you were doing.'

'Mm-hm.' His father paused. 'It's always quiet this time of year. Not much doing.'

'Things'll pick up.'

'Yeah. Anyway. I think your mother wants another word.' Oscar could hear the muted sound of his parents bickering, and the signature theme of the ITN news. His mother came back on to remind him to call more often, and to check in with his cousin Terry. 'Better go, son,' she said, 'your father's calling.' And then the line went dead.

There was no more sleep left in him, so he got up and turned on his computer. It was an old machine and took a while to grind through its gears. An email was waiting in his inbox. The subject line read: 'Apology'.

Dear Oscar,

I'm terrible with computers, so I hope this message gets to you. I would genuinely like to thank you for giving me this chance to apologise for my behaviour the other night, and to explain myself — not many people would be so accommodating. Here is what I know my sister would like me to say:

I'm very sorry, Oscar, for putting you through that silly ordeal the other night. For making you feel embarrassed. For hurting you. I'm deeply sorry for it all. I'm afraid I rather lost control of myself. I hope you'll find it in your heart to forgive me. Oh please please please.

But that isn't what I'll say. I won't insult your intelligence or your integrity with that kind of tripe. Because I know you don't need an apology from me. What you need is my approval.

Iris tells me that your hand has more or less completely healed. *I am* tremendously glad about that, though I'm not in the least bit surprised. I had no doubt that it would be better by morning. The other night was probably an unusual experience for you, Oscar, but for me it was quite ordinary. You wouldn't believe the extent of my capabilities, though perhaps you might permit me to show you one day.

I know what Iris thinks about me, and I'm really very glad that you've taken it upon yourself to help her. She has her reasons for trying to make it seem like I'm ill (most of them are quite worthy reasons, too). But, Oscar, I'm not ill (and even if I were, I certainly wouldn't be stupid enough to write to you admitting it). So I'd appreciate it if you wouldn't pronounce me a lunatic just yet, because, contrary to what you thought were my cruel intentions the other night, I do actually like you. I find you interesting — much more than any of my sister's former *objets d'affection*. There's a depth to you that isn't clear from the surface. I always find that an intriguing quality in a person.

In any case, I'd prefer it if you didn't reply to this message. I'm not interested in having a pen pal. But what's become very clear to me these last few weeks is how much my sister seems to like you. Really, she's never talked about anyone as much as she talks about you. Just between us, I think she might be in danger of falling in love, and that's certainly never happened before, not with any of the awful rugby types she tends to go for.

So, instead of an apology, I'd like to invite you for dinner with my parents on Thursday night. Iris will be there, naturally, and I'll invite the others, too. It'll probably be an enormous bother for you to come all the way out to Grantchester, but I'd be very happy if you did. The food is always good (my parents hire caterers). Dress smartly but don't try too hard.

Yours madly (*cough cough*),

Eden B

4

The Harmony of What Exists

Oscar watched the dark, distant meadows of Grantchester become a colourless blur in the passenger window. The dim headlights of Iris's Saab shone down on the gravel, presenting only a narrow band of the road ahead, and it seemed as if the night was being projected on the windscreen — a corner of the world, right there, for them only. As he finished reading Eden's email aloud to her, keeping his voice steady, Iris barely looked beyond the steering column to see what was approaching; she just turned the wheel left and right, and the road seemed to follow her. 'And that's *everything* he wrote? There wasn't some PS you didn't read?'

He folded up the printout. 'See for yourself.' He reached into the footwell behind Iris's seat and slipped the email into her bag. 'He's on to you.'

'On to *us*.'

'Right.'

'I can't believe he said you needed his approval. Who does he think he is?'

'I know.'

'He's so unbelievably arrogant. And what he said about me *falling in love* and *rugby types* — I don't go for rugby types! I mean, really, that's just plain devious. To presume that just because we've been — ' She broke off. Her mouth closed abruptly. The car slowed and she steered into a clearing, flanked by tall evergreens. 'I should never have let you agree to this. Eden is one thing, I can handle him — but my parents? God, you'll never want to see me again after this.'

'It'll be fine.'

'It's too soon for you to be meeting my parents. They're the kind of people who scar you if you don't know them very well. I hadn't planned for this.'

'Well, if I don't make an effort with Eden, I won't get him to open up to me. And isn't that what you want? He might be less guarded tonight.' He put his hand on her knee and she looked at him, soothed. 'Compared to mine, your parents will seem like John and Yoko.'

She laughed, as if a bug had caught in the back of her throat. Then her face turned solemn. The light of the road flickered on her taut skin. 'You don't have to put yourself through this — not for me. Not if you don't want to.'

He didn't answer, and she seemed to accept this as a resignation. But his silence was for something else. There was another reason that he'd agreed to go to the dinner — something in that email, one simple line that rattled him every time he read it: *There's a depth to you that isn't clear from the surface.* He'd imagined that Dr Paulsen might offer a compliment like this one day, perhaps when they were discussing a book of poetry or going through the Review section of the newspaper together. But the words had come from Eden, and part of Oscar wanted to find out

106

if they were genuine.

'I should warn you about a few things,' Iris said. 'Shoes off at the door. If they offer you wine, don't ask for white — they'll think you're a philistine. If my father offers you brandy after dinner, that's a good sign, but you should politely say no, because it's oh-so-expensive and he secretly hates wasting it on people.' She paused. 'Call my mother Mrs Bellwether — my parents don't shirk pleasantries. Shake my dad's hand firmly but not too firmly and make sure your palm isn't sweaty. He thinks you can tell everything about a man by his handshake. What else . . . ? Yes, right, this is very important. I don't smoke. Never have, never will. Got it?' He nodded back at her. Loose gravel snapped against the body of the Saab. She peered at him from the corner of her eye. 'You look very handsome in that suit, by the way, or did I tell you that already?'

'Actually, you didn't. But I'm glad you like it.' It was the only suit he owned, plain navy, single-breasted. He'd worn it to his interview at Cedarbrook three years ago, and to his grandfather's funeral last February; it was a fraction tight across the chest now, but he could leave it unbuttoned. 'And you look stunning, as always.'

She was wearing a long leather overcoat the colour of buttercream, with saucerlike buttons done up to the top. Her hair was raked back and she had on tiny earrings, two little beads of gold. She was driving in stocking feet because she couldn't work the pedals with her heels on. 'I

107

haven't even shown you my dress yet.'

'I don't need to see it. I know how you'll look.'

'Don't. You're getting me all flushed.'

Ahead of them, the Bellwether house came into view. Oscar had to take a breath. It stood, wide and tall and flawlessly white, nestled in an acreage of countryside so verdant that it could almost be seen in the dark — not in clear detail, but simply as a presence, as a sway of grass beyond his sight, a motion of branches, a shimmer of water far away. Fallow farmland lay behind the canopy of the firs and pines that edged the driveway, and as the car surged forwards, the trees flashed by him like some flipbook animation.

He had never seen a house so well designed before. It was grand but not imposing, expensive but not tasteless, homely yet palatial. It was hinged at the middle by a large glass atrium, and the upstairs windows were set with cast-iron balconies, overlooking the immaculate lawns of the front garden and the straight line of the driveway. There was a circular fountain in the approach, babbling gently, and Iris brought the car around it in a slow turn, tyres crunching on the shingle. She stopped at the face of a double garage. The doors lifted automatically and she parked up beside two other cars: a Land Rover and a silver Alfa Romeo. He guessed that the Bellwethers' garage had about the same square-footage as his parents' terrace. It was as neat and organised as a show-home, all polished concrete and halogen bulbs. He could only imagine the amount of material his father could hoard in a place like this: enough timber cut-offs, aluminium joists, and salvaged kitchen cabinets to last a lifetime.

'We'll go in the front way,' Iris said, 'otherwise I'd have to take you through the kitchen and, God knows, my mother wouldn't want you to see the caterers at work — spoils the illusion.' Iris had a key, but she didn't use it. Instead, she rang the bell and stood waiting with Oscar, holding his hand lightly. After a moment, the door was pulled back by a woman in a black uniform. She nodded and smiled, but said nothing, extending her palm to the atrium.

They went inside and the woman took their coats. Iris had on a filmy dress with a floral pattern that hung loosely from the ridges of her shoulders, and the fine bones of her clavicle stood out in the serene light. She was beautiful, Oscar thought, but not quite herself. He noticed the chandelier above them — an arrangement of icicle crystals, hanging together to form an abstract shape, like an elaborate baby mobile. A magnificent wooden staircase peeled downwards from the second storey, ending at the great woven tapestry under their feet.

'Iggy, is that you out there?' came a voice from an adjoining room.

'Yes, Dad,' Iris called back, 'we're *both* here.'

Her father emerged into the atrium, clutching a tiny glass of sherry. He was a lot shorter than Oscar had imagined. A horseshoe of grey hair was set around his bald crown and a few straggly wisps were jutting out where a fringe should be. His beard was ghost-white and neatly trimmed. He went straight to his daughter and gave her a gentle kiss on the forehead. Then he stood back, awaiting an introduction. Oscar dried his hand against the lining of his pocket.

'Oh, right. Oscar Lowe, Theo Bellwether. And vice versa.' Iris grinned, and gestured towards Oscar like he was the newest Bentley on the forecourt.

Her father held out his broad palm. 'Hello there. So glad you could come.' They shook hands thoroughly. 'Can I get you both an aperitif?' Theo lifted his glass and studied it under the light. 'I must say, the sherry's somewhat *overtly* dry tonight. I prefer something with a lighter touch, but still — can I?'

'No, Dad, I'm driving.'

Theo flicked his eyes to Oscar expectantly.

'No thank you, Mr Bellwether.'

'I suppose I'm a bad salesman. Come inside, the pair of you. Everyone's here already. We've been having an impossible discussion with Eden. You can both weigh in.'

Iris raised her eyes. 'Oh, that'll make a nice change.'

'I'm afraid my son is quite unstoppable when he gets the wind in his sails,' Theo said, walking across the atrium, his back towards the pair of them. 'I keep telling him he should join the Debating Society but with all the other things he's got going on, he just doesn't have the time. Still, he's inherited his father's flair for the dialectical.' He led them into an expensively arranged sitting room. It was decorated with matching cream settees and footstools, bespoke wall cabinets that held crystalware and ornamental plates, towering shelves that housed a vast collection of

hardbacks, thick textbooks, innumerable encyclopaedias. The Bellwethers' collection made Dr
Paulsen's seem like a book-stand at a jumble
sale. Oscar wondered how many of them had
actually been read.

The room was edged with a moody light, and
angled lamps were glimmering softly above the
paintings on the walls. 'My wife would want me
to point out the pictures,' Theo said, stopping to
check his watch, which he wore with the face on
the underside of his wrist. 'They're new. She's
been collecting this young artist lately. Candice
Feldman — have you heard of her?'

'No,' Iris said.

'Me neither,' said Oscar, studying them from
afar. They were abstracts: splotches of iridescent
oils on newsprint, hung in clean white frames.

'Oh, well, I'm sure you will have in a year or
two. Come, sit.' He motioned towards the
settees.

Eden was leading a discussion from one side
of a chaise longue, with Jane sitting blank-faced
beside him. Marcus and Yin had an armchair
each, and both were wearing tweed, as if they'd
arrived from a clay-pigeon shoot. A blonde
woman in a plain red dress was perching on the
lip of the settee — Mrs Bellwether. She bore no
obvious resemblance to her daughter, other than
her shade of blonde and a general air of
calmness and contemplation. She was wearing a
silver necklace with a locket, which seemed
slightly faded, perhaps antique. They were all
holding their sherry glasses the same way, with
one hand pinching at the neck of the crystal, the

111

other cupped underneath the base. It reminded Oscar of the way his father used his free hand as an ashtray when he smoked indoors.

'Yes, sweetheart, except you're failing to grasp the most important part,' Eden was saying to Jane, who now looked perplexed. 'The only way that man can truly have free will is if the soul is a separate entity. Otherwise, we're all just products of our neurons, of chemical processes that we're not in control of. Let me explain it simply.' He paused. 'If I want to move my glass to my mouth to drink, I can do so, but I haven't *chosen* to do so — the thought is just a chemical function. It's an event that my brain has conspired to create, because it likes the taste of sherry. Whereas, if a man has a mind, a soul that's distinct from the body, *he* is the engine of his own actions; he determines when his hand moves towards the sherry glass. You see?' Jane creased up her face. 'Okay. Imagine a man in a coma. He wants to move, but his body just won't respond — yes? Well, there are people who have such a conception of their own free will that they can recover from those kinds of accidents; they can make use of what bodily functions they have left. They blink, they sniff, they twitch their noses to communicate their will. The soul awakens the body.'

'Son, I'm not sure you've quite reasoned this one out,' Theo said, placing a hand on his wife's shoulder. 'To say that thought is solely a chemical function shows an ignorance of basic human neurology.'

Iris kissed her mother. 'Hello, Mum.'

112

'Hello, darling. You look pretty.'

'Thank you.'

'And this must be Oscar.' She didn't stand to greet him, just shook his hand limply, bowing her head. 'What an interesting suit.'

'Thank you,' Oscar said.

Eden paused his discussion to acknowledge their arrival, gently raising his chin — no word of hello. Oscar couldn't help but feel nervous seeing him again, hearing that haughty, persuasive voice. He sat down with Iris on the settee, a good few feet away from Eden. Jane waved at them and smiled.

'Look, I'm not saying the Cartesian view is without its flaws,' Eden said, narrowing his eyes at his father. 'But perhaps if you hadn't had the notion of dualism completely quarried out of you at medical school — '

'Tss! It has nothing to do with medical school. It's about seeing more logic in another viewpoint.'

'Like what, Mr B?' Jane asked, and Eden gave an audible huff.

Theo canted his head. 'Well, you don't have to be a dualist to believe in the human soul. A soul is an holistic entity, the way I see it — the mind and the body together. Let's take that man in the coma: he's unable to function, not because his body is broken, but because part of his brain is broken. Neurologically, he's lost certain capacities, and therefore his wholeness as a person has been compromised. His free will has been corrupted. Temporarily, he's an empty vessel, because his brain is no longer working in

113

combination with his other facets.'

'So the man may as well be dead — right?' Yin asked.

'No, he's just . . . out of alignment. Compromised. Temporarily, perhaps terminally.'

'I really don't get it,' Jane said. 'I can't ever keep up with these discussions.'

'I'm saying that the brain has the ability to right itself, given time, like an upturned canoe. And as long as the man's other facets remain uncompromised — namely, that he is still breathing on his own — his soul can be fully restored.'

'But what happens to his soul in the time that his brain isn't working and he's compromised, as you put it?' Marcus asked. 'Does it just cease to exist?'

Theo thought about this for a second. 'No, no, his soul still exists, just not cohesively. The same way the picture on a jigsaw is still a complete picture, even when the pieces are lying in the box unassembled.'

'I can't stand jigsaws,' Jane said. 'The final picture is never worth the effort.' Oscar thought of Dr Paulsen turning his nose up at the puzzles in the store cupboard.

'You can always rely on Jane to get to the meat of the issue,' Mrs Bellwether said. She gave a girlish chuckle.

Marcus crossed his arms. 'Do you want to know the annoying thing about this argument? There's no way to prove who's right. It sort of makes me want to slip into a coma myself.'

Theo laughed. 'Right!'

114

'I mean, all of this posturing over what we are, why we exist, it's so frustratingly unknowable. Sometimes I wonder why people bother. The answers will come when we die.'

'But what if they don't?' Oscar said. Everybody looked at him. He felt he'd spoken out of turn. It was the first time he'd experienced a gathering like this: people who weren't afraid to think, express, debate. He'd grown up believing that to reveal your intelligence was to show your weakness to others. It was better to do your homework the night before school, because if it was done on the schoolbus in front of other boys they'd goad and tease and shout — 'Swot! Suck!' — and the girls would think you were soft. It was right not to talk about the complex affairs of the world over the dinner table with your family, but to talk instead of sport and weather and television programmes, because nobody liked to think of heavy things as they were eating. This is what he'd been raised to think.

'Well, go on,' Theo said. 'Don't be shy.'

Oscar began tentatively: 'I just mean to say that it's only religious people who believe they're going to be given answers when they die, that there's some sort of place, like Heaven's Gate, where you queue up for a final verdict from St Peter. But really — ' He cleared his throat. 'What if it's like the Buddhists say, and we're reincarnated into another form? Or what if we just die and that's it — nothing else? Then we'll just go from one state to another without ever knowing why we existed. That would be the biggest joke of all.'

When he finished speaking, there was silence in the room. He felt Iris's hand sliding over his, and the squeeze of her fingers. Marcus and Yin looked away. Theo was thoughtful, dazed. Mrs Bellwether sipped at her sherry.

Then Eden said: 'I forgot to mention that Oscar is an atheist. It completely slipped my mind.'

'Are you really, Oscar?' Mrs Bellwether said, apparently shocked.

'Yes.'

'You don't believe in *any* kind of higher being whatsoever?'

'No.'

'No grand scheme for our lives?'

'No.'

'*Well*,' she said. 'I feel sorry for you, Oscar, if that's the case.'

'It's alright, Ruth,' Theo said. He stared at Oscar with an unswerving focus. 'Everyone is entitled to a belief system. We respect the views of others in this house, don't we?'

'Of course.'

'Well, then.'

'Does it concern you that Oscar is an atheist, Mother?' Iris asked.

Mrs Bellwether gave a tight little shake of her head.

'We should remember our Thomas Aquinas,' Eden said.

'What's that supposed to mean?'

Eden stared back at Iris, blankly. 'For those with faith, no explanation is necessary. For those without, no explanation is possible.'

'Yes, God has a plan for all of us, I'm sure,' Mrs Bellwether added.

'Mum, that's *so* condescending.'

'What your mother means,' Theo said, 'is that she doesn't think of Oscar any differently just because he doesn't believe in God. Because she knows the Lord believes in *him*, and that's all that really matters.'

'Oh, please.' Iris gave a scornful laugh. 'I don't know how you can sit there decrying Eden's ideas about the soul one minute, and then come over all pious on Oscar. It's total hypocrisy.' She moved her body closer to Oscar on the couch — stiff, resolute.

Theo set his sherry glass down on the side table. 'It's nothing of the sort. Just because I don't believe in Descartes's idea of the soul, it doesn't mean I can't believe in the soul itself, or in God, for that matter. How many doctors do you think go to church every Sunday morning?'

'They're all hypocrites too.'

'Iris!' Mrs Bellwether said. 'Where is this coming from?'

Theo waved his hand at his wife to quiet her. 'There was a recent study in America. Seventy-odd per cent of doctors said they believed in God. Ninety-odd per cent said they regularly went to church.'

'Don't go quoting random statistics at me,' Iris said. She leaned back against the cushions. 'Statistics prove nothing in this case.'

'Look,' Theo knuckled his beard, widening his stance, 'a man can belong to science *and* to God, darling. They don't make such awkward bedfellows. Ask Francis Bacon, ask Isaac Newton, Faraday, Boyle. Even Einstein believed in God.'

'Rubbish!'

'Oh, I think you'll find he did.'

Eden spoke up: 'Actually, he's right. Einstein agreed with Spinoza's idea of God. He said God reveals himself in the harmony of what exists. That the universe without a creator is an impossible premise.'

'There you go, son, I knew I'd taught you *something* sensible.'

Marcus leaned forward, pleased with himself: 'Science without religion is lame, but religion without science is blind. I believe that's what Einstein said. Or maybe it's the other way round . . . '

'Oh, listen to you all, quoting famous men,' Mrs Bellwether said. 'And here I was wondering where those school fees were going.'

'I'll memorise some quotes for next time, too — make myself look more intelligent,' Jane said, and let out a high laugh that nobody else participated in.

'Iris, my darling, you're going to find this out for yourself one day. Medicine is not a godless pursuit.' Theo's voice was softer now, more fatherly, but it reminded Oscar of the tone in which Eden sometimes spoke — lofty, self-congratulatory. 'When you do your first residency and come to deal with life and death on a regular basis, you'll find yourself reaching out for God. I'm certain you will. Why? Because it's in your nature, much as you rail against it. You should be more like your

118

brother. He might have misguided ideas about life, but at least he's smart enough to appreciate the fundamentals. He knows better than to question the values of his parents.'

'*What?*'

A bell sounded at the far end of the room. Another woman in a black uniform retracted two sliding doors, revealing a large mahogany table set with white linen and silverware. 'Ladies and gentlemen, the first course is ready to be served.'

'Oh, thank heavens for that,' Eden said. 'I could eat a pony.' He jumped up from the chaise, Jane following at his heels. Everyone filed into the dining room. When Oscar passed by on the way to his seat, Eden touched his shoulder, whispering: 'Thanks for coming. Isn't this a blast?'

Oscar was relieved that Iris's place setting was next to his. They sat across from Eden and Jane, while the Bellwethers took either end of the table. Marcus and Yin filled the space that was left. They were wearing different shades of tweed but with the same broad pattern; when they sat down, Theo referred to them as 'Holmes and Watson', and the two of them remained unusually subdued for the rest of the evening. (Oscar noticed that Marcus and Yin weren't quite themselves around Theo. They seemed scared to say anything he might disagree with. And they were always so eager to impress Mrs Bellwether by complimenting her home, her furniture, her crystal. All evening, they were an awkward double act: Marcus would say something toadying, like, 'You've got such an eye for these things, Mrs B,' and Yin would follow up with the same few words of agreement: 'Oh, yeah, *totally*.')

The caterers served up a starter of goat's cheese with a rocket salad. Oscar understood about the cutlery — the working from the outside in. He knew about holding a wine glass by the stem. But what he didn't understand were the other etiquettes of formal dining — when it was appropriate to speak, and to whom, and of what. He was so worried that he might embarrass himself that he said almost nothing until the main course was served: a loin of beef with organic vegetables and tiny horseradish potatoes, with a wine that Theo took great pleasure in announcing as 'a deft little Barbaresco'. It had been a long time since Oscar had eaten so well. He was used to the meals at Cedarbrook, where the flavour of everything was boiled out and there was a taste of communality to it, of food left waiting in great metal vats.

'So, Oscar,' Mrs Bellwether said, 'why don't you tell us something about yourself. We know you're an atheist, but that can't be the sum total of you.'

'Well, what would you like to know, Mrs Bellwether?'

She smiled. 'Iris has said you're not at Cambridge. I presume you have a profession of some kind.'

'I work at a nursing home — Cedarbrook.'

'That place with the wisteria,' Eden added.

'Ah, yes.' Mrs Bellwether chewed her beef for a moment. 'So you're a nurse?'

120

'Sort of.'

'Surely one's either a nurse or not a nurse.'

'I'm a kind of nurse. A care assistant. I'm unqualified.'

'I hope you don't mean you're unqualified for the position itself,' Theo said.

Oscar just smiled.

'Well, I think it's very selfless of you to do a job like that. Very noble. You might even say *Christian*.' Mrs Bellwether paused. 'You're helping people every day. Like my husband. Did you know he was a surgeon?'

'Yes. Iris told me.'

'I don't practise any more,' Theo said. 'I retired young. These days I'm more involved with the training side of things.'

'He teaches surgeons to become better surgeons,' Mrs Bellwether said.

'Getting into the robotic surgery game before anyone was taking it seriously — that was my biggest achievement. People laughed at me at the time, but they're not laughing now.'

'So, not meaning to be crude about it,' Jane said, 'but do you have to, you know, *clean up* all the old people?'

'She means do you have to wipe their dirty bottoms,' Eden added.

Oscar expected an outcry from Mrs Bellwether, but it never came. She simply looked down at her plate. Theo said: 'Eden, come on now. *Dinner table*.'

There was a pause. The room's eyes fell on Oscar. He set his knife and fork down across his plate. 'Yes, actually, that's exactly what it means.

121

That's what caring is — helping people when they're helpless.'

'But doesn't that make you feel — ' Jane checked herself. 'I don't know — undignified? To have to do that. To wipe up after them.'

'Actually, no. Just the opposite. It's the patients who feel undignified.'

'Yes, but, *really* . . . I don't know how you can do it. Just on a practical level.' Jane shivered at the thought. 'I wouldn't even do that for my own mother.' She picked up her bread roll and began to butter it fiercely. There was a quiet in the room; eyes flitted across the table. It was as if everybody was looking at each other, wondering: Would *I* do that for *you*?

'You know, I don't even think about it any more,' Oscar went on. 'It's just something that needs to be done, so I do it. It's a perfunctory thing. Like it is when we all go.'

'Stop. You're ruining my gravy,' Marcus joked, pushing his plate away. Everyone laughed.

Oscar thought back to his shift that morning. He'd gone in to see Mrs Kernaghan in Room 3. As he'd helped her out of bed, he'd noticed the smell, and then seen the way her nightdress was clinging to the backs of her legs, the liquidy stain on the bedsheets. Mrs Kernaghan had never had trouble with incontinence before. She'd given him a look of terror when she realised what had happened. She'd said: 'I knew it, I could smell it, but I hoped it was a dream.' He'd drawn a bath for her immediately, and sent for one of the female nurses to wash her and clothe her for breakfast. Later, he'd spoken to Dr Paulsen about it, to warn him that he should be especially considerate of Mrs Kernaghan's feelings today. 'The old dam finally burst, huh?' Paulsen had said. 'I knew she wouldn't be able to last out. It comes to us all in the end.' Oscar had lost count of the times he'd bathed Dr Paulsen, sponged off the backs of his frail old legs. The first time, Paulsen had been silent, resigned to the indignity of it. The second time he'd said: 'Now you've seen the worst of me.' The last time, he'd said: 'I shit more sense than I speak these days,' and giggled.

'Let's change the subject, shall we?' Theo said.

For the rest of the meal, Oscar evaded further interrogation from the Bellwethers. They talked mostly of things that affected the family: the upkeep of the house at Harvey Road, the débâcle (as Iris put it) of her last recital, her continuing progress with her studies. 'She really set the benchmark with her transcript last year,' Theo said, 'but, Oscar, I keep telling her there's still room for improvement.' It was noticeable that when Theo pressed Iris about her grades, Mrs Bellwether held back from the discussion, and Oscar couldn't tell if this was out of discretion or indifference. She was quick to ask Eden about the new Dean of his chapel — 'Which seminary did he come from again?' — but seemed less interested in the scheduled repairs to the Harrison organ. Eden made no mention of Johann Mattheson or his theories in explaining how everyone had come to know Oscar. 'It was one of those happy accidents,' he said. 'Iggy got talking with him outside the chapel after

123

evensong, and I suppose we all just hit it off.'

Mrs Bellwether sat up, looking at Oscar with a new enthusiasm. 'What were you doing at evensong? I thought you weren't religious.'

'The choir,' Iris said. 'He went to hear the choir.'

'Oh, yes. The choir *is* magnificent.'

'They're a national treasure.' Theo topped up his glass. 'Jane, I meant to ask, how are your parents faring in Tuscany?'

'They love it out there. Slowly getting used to the language.'

'I should think so. Will you be going out to see them?'

'After the exam term, maybe.'

'School first, eh? That's what I like to hear.'

While Theo quizzed the rest of them about their post-graduation plans, Oscar stayed around edges of the conversation, politely responding with smiles. Jane said she would likely take a job in publishing after her degree, though she really wanted to be a war correspondent like Kate Adie — 'Anyway, I've still got a whole year to decide on things.' Yin was considering a return to California next year; he'd had some interesting offers from acquaintances in Palo Alto. 'I know exactly zero about IT, but somehow they don't see that as a drawback.'

Mrs Bellwether seemed to take for granted that Marcus would be going on to a Master's programme: 'There's marvellous security in academia, if you're smart enough,' she said. 'Just think, you and Eden, *postgraduates* — and Iris not far behind.' Then, as if it were an afterthought, she turned to her daughter and said: 'You haven't said anything about my new paintings, by the way.'

'They're good, Mum. Accomplished.'

'I think they're fabulous, Mrs B,' said Marcus.

'Oh, yeah, totally,' said Yin.

Mrs Bellwether clasped her hands together. 'I'm so thrilled with them, I can't tell you how much. And the artist is really quite lovely. So humble, for someone so talented.'

'You make her sound like Rembrandt,' Eden said.

'Well, even Rembrandt was an unknown painter at one time in his life. I saw the sketches for her new exhibition — so wonderful.'

Eden's face tensed a little. His eyes fell towards the tabletop and he began meddling with the salt cellar. 'I'm sure they'll make you a decent profit.'

'That's what your father said. I might auction one off for the church.'

'Yes,' Eden said, dourly, 'that'll go down well.'

They all retired to the drawing room after dessert. It had the conscious extravagance of a hotel lobby: leather sofas, candelabras, a grand piano, and a marble fireplace. Theo stood behind a rosewood cabinet, stacked with cut-glass decanters, and began removing the stoppers and sniffing the contents of each bottle, as if about to commence some explosive chemistry experiment. Eventually, he chose one and lifted it. 'Alright. Who'll share some Delamain with me? Oscar, I know you're game.' Theo raised one eyebrow.

'Thanks, Mr Bellwether,' he said, ignoring Iris's suggestive cough.

'Some of the best cognac you'll ever drink, this,' Theo went on. 'Three grand for seventy piddling centilitres.'

'Let's all have some!' Eden said.

'Yes, I'm always up for Delamain,' said Marcus.

'Oh, terrific.' Theo stared downwards, glue-eyed. He took eight glasses from the cabinet and poured a conservative measure of brandy into each of them. When he finished pouring, he looked at the decanter, as if trying to aggregate how many precious centilitres he had wasted on his guests. He dished the glasses out, one at a time.

They all sat drinking for several minutes, talking very little, until Eden jolted forwards in his armchair and said: 'Would anyone like to hear something interesting?'

'Depends what it is,' Theo said.

'Just a little article I found. I meant to tell you about it at dinner.' He set his brandy down and stood up, digging his left hand into his trouser pocket. Oscar had never seen Eden dressed so smartly. The suit he was wearing was not ill-fitting, but it looked unusual on him, the way a military uniform looks on a child. He had on a pair of brown Oxfords that clashed with the whiteness of his pinstripes, and the loop of his tie was visible underneath his collar. After a moment, Eden removed a folded square of paper and sat down again, opening it. 'Really is an amazing story. I discovered it online, in the *New*

126

York Times archives. Shall I read it to you?'

'What's it about, dear?' Mrs Bellwether asked.

'Hypnotism.'

'I'm not sure I like the sound of that.'

'Trust me. It's fascinating.'

Iris drew herself forward on the sofa, but said nothing. She flashed a glance at Oscar.

'*Hypnosis by Handel in Downtown Manhattan,*' Eden began, reading in a slow, steady tone. '*Dr. Marcelo Fernandez escorts his final patient of the day into his office and asks her to lie down on the couch. 'Close your eyes. Try to relax,' he tells the woman. 'Let me know if — '*'

'Where exactly is this leading?' Theo interrupted.

'If you listen, you might find out.' Eden opened his mouth to continue reading, but Theo stopped him, thrusting one arm forward as if to halt a train. 'But it's so interesting,' Eden said. 'There's this man in New York who can hypnotise people in lieu of anaesthesia.'

'Oh, *I* see.' Theo gave a pitying laugh. 'What is he, some kind of shaman?'

'No, he's actually a qualified doctor like you. Listen — '

'Alright, son, put it away now. Let's get back to our evening.'

'Dad, he only wants to read it. You're being a bit extreme,' Iris said.

Oscar could tell by the calmness in her voice that she didn't so much want to hear her brother's article as to watch him expose his strangeness before their parents, but she was smart: she made it seem to Eden like she was firmly in his corner.

Theo said: 'No, I'm being perfectly rational. I've seen the results of that kind of witchdoctory in my clinic too often, and I won't hear another word about it.'

'It does sound a little profane, darling,' said Mrs Bellwether. 'Your father doesn't have to hear it if he doesn't want to.'

Marcus and Yin remained silent, making eyes at each other.

Eden smiled. 'Well, how about if I just leave it out for people? Over there on the piano. And if anyone wants to look at it, they can do so of their own free will.'

Theo inhaled his brandy and sighed. 'Alright. Fine.'

'Wait, we're back on free will again?' Jane said. 'I haven't had a chance to look over my notes from last time.' She had a knack for diffusing the tension in a room. Oscar could see what the others liked about her: she was self-deprecating, constantly downplaying her intelligence and positioning herself as the slowest member of the group, when she might well have been the brightest of them all. She had a sense of humour that seemed naïve, but he recognised it as something more than that. It was her way of forging her own identity within the group: an endearing, calculated dumbness.

They sipped their brandy as Eden walked across to the piano and set the article under a vase of orange lilies. He sat down at the keys and began to play the sober chords of the funeral march. Everybody laughed, apart from Theo, who just gave a restrained smile.

'Why don't you play something for us, dear?' Mrs Bellwether called out.

Eden seemed thrilled to be asked. 'Yes. Sure. What would you like to hear?'

'Anything you want to play is fine with me.'

'Alright.' Eden began to play a slow, melodious tune. The chords were soft and simple as a lullaby.

'What is that? Chopin?'

'It's Schumann,' Marcus said.

'Ah, yes.'

'Did you know,' Eden called out over the music, his fingers still working the keys, 'that Schumann had Manic Depression?'

'Really?'

'He was quite doolally with it near the end. Ended up throwing himself into the Rhine.'

'This is one of his later works, isn't it?' Marcus said.

Eden nodded slowly. The gentle tenor of the piano idled through the room. '*The Geister Variations*. When he wrote this, he thought he was being guided by the voices of dead composers. I'm sure Theo wouldn't have any patience for old Schumann whatsoever.'

'Sshh,' Theo said. 'It's poor manners to talk while you're playing.'

Eden closed his eyes. The soft, sparse chords seemed to roll on forever.

When he finished, there was a thin smattering of applause, led by his mother. 'Oh, Edie, I do miss that sound. I remember a time when it was all anyone could hear in this house, morning, noon, and night. It was like living at Carnegie

129

Hall. Now we come down for breakfast — don't we, Theo? — and we say to each other, *it's so quiet.*'

'What about Iris?' Oscar said.

Mrs Bellwether cornered her eyes at him. 'I'm sorry?'

'Didn't you ever hear Iris playing her cello?'

'Yes, of course we did.' The skin on her chest became radishy; she fingered her locket. 'I meant Iris too. You could always hear her out in the garden, playing something or other. She's always played very nicely.'

'Like a young Eva Janzer,' Theo added. 'I've always said that.'

'But music's never really been her passion, not like it is for Eden. Iris has more important things to focus on than the cello. She's always wanted to follow in her father's footsteps, haven't you, darling?'

Iris just nodded. When all eyes were turned away, she gave Oscar a small kiss on the temple, and squeezed his knee, as if to say, 'Thanks for trying.' He was glad to be that person for her, the voice who pleaded her case in runaway discussions.

'So why don't you come to the chapel any more?' Eden asked his parents. 'You haven't been to a service all year.'

His mother looked at Theo, then answered: 'You know we try to get out there as much as we can, dear. But it's always so busy on Sundays.'

'Weekends are tricky for us,' Theo said. 'You know that.'

'Plus, there's the parking in town midweek. Around King's especially. So many tourists.'

'Your mother prefers St Andrew's these days. Much more convenient, and the new minister is quite entertaining. He has a way with a sermon.'

'Yes, of course,' Eden said. 'It's just that you said you'd come when you could.'

'And we haven't been able to, son. That's all there is to it.'

Mrs Bellwether sat up very straight. She looked at Oscar as if he were one of her abstract paintings that she was training her eyes to appreciate. 'Will you be staying over, Oscar? There's plenty of space for you boys in the organ house. Jane can stay with Iris in the rectory.'

'No, Mum, we're driving back,' Iris told her. 'I have to go to the library first thing.'

'You can drive there in the morning, can't you?'

'Yes, but, I don't think Oscar — '

'Of course. He must have to be at work early.'

'Actually, tomorrow is my day off,' Oscar said. 'I'd be happy to stay.'

'Well, that settles it.'

'Are we calling it an evening already?' Theo said, looking at his watch. 'I suppose it *is* quite late.' He downed the last of his brandy with a murmur.

Marcus and Yin both declined the offer to stay over. There was unfinished work that couldn't wait another day. 'We've got a gruelling all-nighter planned,' Yin said. 'Too many distractions here.' They bantered playfully with Mrs Bellwether for a while, until she agreed it would be better to let them leave. In the atrium, they said their goodbyes, donned jackets and scarves, and headed for Yin's BMW.

'Will you show Oscar to the guesthouse, Eden?'

Mrs Bellwether said, stepping tiredly upstairs. 'Your father's just about ready to fall asleep. And I have early appointments tomorrow.'

The Bellwethers said goodnight. After they retired to bed, the house seemed quiet and cavernous, and Oscar was starting to feel flushed with the afterglow of brandy.

'*Suivez-moi*,' Eden said, and led the way through the empty kitchen. The caterers had left the dishwasher whirring and the leftovers foiled up on the counter. Eden flicked a switch on the wall, dousing the back garden with a gentle blue haze. The lawn stretched out, long and shapeless, disappearing into ivy-coated trees and rampant hedges. Oscar could just make out the quiet bend of the river, where tall grass and thistles swayed; a wooden punt lay upturned on the bank, sleek in the moonlight. Just before the water, set off amid a tiny patch of woodland, there was a limestone building. It was a peculiar shape: oblong but with a glass roof that rose acutely from one side. Another, simpler building was connected to it, with a sheltered porch made of polished wooden beams.

They went along a brick path, between flowerbeds and cherry trees. Iris breathed in the night air contentedly, holding Oscar's arm. Jane and Eden walked ahead of them, muttering to each other, keeping their hands by their sides.

When they reached the doorway of the first building, Eden stopped. 'Look, I think we need to get one thing straight here. I don't see any reason why Oscar and I have to bunk together, do you?'

'No,' Iris said.

'Right then. I'll stay with Jane in the organ house, and you both have the rectory.'

'Won't your parents mind?' Oscar said.

'Of course they'll mind,' Eden said. 'But there's no reason they should find out. Besides, it's about time they woke up and smelled the twenty-first century.'

'Fine by us. It's not like we haven't shared a bed before,' Iris said. She drew Oscar closer and kissed him on the lips.

Eden rolled his eyes. He unlocked the door to the smaller building — the rectory — reaching in to turn on the lights. Then he spun round and handed the key to Oscar. 'Do be gentle with her. She lost her virginity in that bed, you know.'

'*Eden,*' Jane said. 'That's no way to talk about your sister.'

'I was kidding. She knows I was kidding.'

'Lucky for him,' Iris said, giving Jane an uncomfortable smile.

'Goodnight then,' Oscar said.

'Goodnight,' Eden replied. 'Remember, the walls are thin.'

'Shut up, Edie.' Jane dragged him away. They walked around to the other side of the building, vanishing into darkness.

It was cold inside the rectory. Iris went to turn on every radiator she could find, then sat down at the foot of the queen-sized bed, pulling the woollen quilt around her shoulders. The room was open plan: a simple bedroom encroached on the lounge; a small kitchenette with breakfast stools was set against the far wall, and the French windows opened out onto the porch decking. It had the feel of a country bed and breakfast, and bore that same impersonal fragrance: potpourri, carpet cleaner, laundered towels.

'I thought you handled it very well tonight,' Iris said. 'My parents can be difficult when they want to be. I was proud of you, standing up for yourself like that.'

The truth was, Oscar wasn't sure if he liked her parents at all. They had that impossible confidence that comes from wealth, the self-righteousness that comes from piety. How many times had he spoken to Ruth Bellwether, only to have her blinking back at him silently, showing no sign that she'd even been listening? And when Theo had been lecturing Yin on American foreign policy over dessert, Oscar had noticed that his views were borrowed from the talking heads on current affairs shows: 'We've not been winning many hearts and minds lately, I can assure you,' Theo had said, spooning pannacotta. 'We're losing the propaganda battle — that's where the real war on terror lies. It's in the media, not in the caves of Kabul.' Oscar was sure he'd heard someone make the same point on *Newsnight* a while ago. But he told Iris: 'I thought they were nice. A bit different, maybe.'

'Oh, sweetheart, that was their best behaviour you saw tonight.'

'Do you think they liked me?'

'Hard to tell. My father gave you his cognac. And they invited you to sleep over. That's something. But then again, you're not the first boy they've let stay overnight.'

'Oh.'

'Don't worry, I didn't let them *all* in my room.'

'Was that true what Eden said?' he asked.

Her body straightened. 'About me losing my virginity in here?'

'Yeah.'

She shrugged. 'Does it matter?'

'I suppose not.'

'Well then. It's not true.' She smiled, then fell back on the bed. 'Oh, I'd give anything for a cigarette.'

He went to sit beside her. 'Does Eden usually take on your father like that?'

'How do you mean?'

'You know, first they were at odds about Descartes and everything. And then that thing with the article. It seemed like your father was used to it.'

'Yes, they're always jabbing at each other lately. It's been getting worse. I think my brother's finally figured out which buttons to push, and Dad keeps rising to it. Not that it makes any difference.'

'Why not?'

'He'll always be the golden boy, no matter what he does. They let him get away with anything.' The quilt dropped from her shoulders and she stood up. 'Notice they didn't ask him any questions about his lectures or exams. They just assume he's on top of it all. But I get the grand interrogation: *What did you get for that virology paper, Iris? Who's supervising you now?* It's ridiculous. And that whole fuss he made

135

about them not coming to the chapel — if *I'd* said anything like that I'd have been yelled at.' She paused, remembering something. Her expression brightened. 'Oh, yes, yes, I almost forgot.' She twisted around, retrieved her clutch bag from where it had landed by the pillows, and rummaged inside it, pulling out two pieces of paper. 'I've been evidence gathering.'

The first piece of paper he recognised immediately — it was the printout of Eden's email. 'Exhibit A,' Iris said, dropping it back in the bag. Then she held up the second piece of paper: 'Exhibit B.' She placed it between them on the bed. 'I swiped it from the piano as Marcus and Yin were leaving.'

He looked down at the article. 'You've read it already?'

'Mm-hm.' She kissed him softly on the forehead. 'I'll get myself ready for bed while you read. I'm sure you'll have plenty to say.'

Hypnosis by Handel in Downtown Manhattan

The New York Times February 4, 1992

Dr. Marcelo Fernandez escorts his final patient of the day into his office and asks her to lie down on the couch. 'Close your eyes. Try to relax,' he tells the woman. 'Let me know if it's too loud for you.' He clicks a remote control, turning on a stereo at the far end of the room. Classical music begins to stream from three round speakers embedded in the ceiling.

'Now, I want you to

136

take deep breaths in through your nose and out through your mouth,' Dr. Fernandez says, with his soothing Latino voice.

'Try to ignore the world outside. Forget about your subway ride, all those people. Just focus on the air coming into your lungs, and listen to what I'm saying. Soon, you're going to be floating off with the music, and you'll start to feel very calm and relaxed.'

I am here as an observer. Dr. Fernandez has been working with criminal investigators in the NYPD for several years and, upon hearing of the book I am researching (about non-scientific methods of forensic investigation), he has invited me to his office in Lower Manhattan. He has promised to demonstrate his advanced hypnotherapy practices, which include today's musical technique.

'They've been using music to hypnotize people since forever,' Dr. Fernandez tells me after the session with the female patient. 'Baroque music is particularly efficacious because it stays around 60 beats per minute, which is the same as the human heart rate.'

Dr. Fernandez is a 58-year-old former vacuum cleaner salesman from Chicago. Since he began working as a professional hypnotherapist twenty years ago, he claims to have hypnotized 'at least thirty people a week,' including high-profile trial witnesses and sports stars. Chronic pain sufferers and cancer patients are some of Dr. Fernandez's most regular clients, as well as those seeking to overcome minor phobias, drug addictions, or alcohol dependency. Some people want to lose weight fast. Some are curious about their past lives and ask to be regressed. 'You wouldn't believe the crazy requests I get,' Dr. Fernandez informs me. 'My job is never boring.'

The woman I observe being hypnotized is a dog-walker from Long Island City. She has acute tendonitis in her knees and has come to Dr. Fernandez to help her manage the pain. At the end of the session, she tells me: 'He has such a kind way about him. I'd trust him with my life. And he sure makes my knees feel better.'

Cynicism & Negativity

Over the years, Dr. Fernandez has spent a great deal of time and energy trying to educate the public — and fellow doctors — about hypnosis. Having earned his M.D. at the Pritzker School of Medicine at the University of Chicago, he now chairs the Professional Hypnotherapy Association of America. 'I meet with a lot of cynicism and negativity from the medical profession,' he explains. 'Some doctors still call what I do 'mesmerism' or 'animal magnetism' — these are the terms doctors used back when we thought the Earth was flat! It's incredible that even today, when the benefits of hypnosis have been proven by countless scientific studies, there are still those who want to decry it.'

Dr. Fernandez cites television shows which 'greatly trivialize' hypnosis as the major culprit. 'It's damaging, yes. Every time I see a guy hypnotized into clucking like a chicken with his pants down, I can't help but feel undermined.'

Regardless of the skepticism from the medical fraternity, Dr. Fernandez's practice is thriving. His office is located in a picturesque neighborhood close to 14th Street. The décor is not unlike a typical family doctor's office, à la Norman Rockwell: high white ceilings, oak furniture, and tasteful green wallpaper. Pinned to a noticeboard in his office, there is a letter from a former New Jersey Senator, which thanks Dr. Fernandez for 'helping [him] get past the pain of [his] amputation — both physically and mentally.'

The speaker system in Dr. Fernandez's office has been designed to meet his precise sonic specifications, accentuating certain bass frequencies. He owns a vast collection of classical music but mostly relies on the work of Baroque composers. 'Bach or Handel get the best results in my experience,' he says, 'but it depends on the patient. There are those who respond more to Vivaldi, or even Johann Mattheson.'

Positive Suggestion

My previous experiences of observing hypnotherapists in action have taught me that first-time clients are often anxious about what the process entails. Dr. Fernandez agrees that most newcomers fear that the effects of hypnosis will not wear off.

'I always reassure them that they'll remain in complete control of their faculties. They should always be able to remember everything afterwards — sometimes they may not remember it all right away, but it comes back to them after a day or so, maybe a week.'

In *Counting Down from Ten*, his most recent book, Dr. Fernandez explains that his musical approach to hypnosis has proven effective because it makes the unconscious mind even more susceptible to suggestion. Melodic refrains encoded in the Baroque music, he states, are reinforced by his vocal repetition of key phrases. These are absorbed into the unconscious mind of patients during hypnosis and remain in the conscious mind when they awake.

Many cancer sufferers approach Dr. Fernandez prior to starting chemotherapy. 'People can get pretty frightened about what lies ahead, and I try to help them with that as much as I can,' he says. Dr. Fernandez has discovered that recounting positive stories about chemotherapy while the patient is in a hypnotized state has enabled many of his clients to endure extensive treatment regimes without incurring hair loss. Furthermore, he has found that clients scheduled to go under the knife require little or no anesthesia and recover more quickly from surgery, after only a few sessions with him.

On Dr. Fernandez's desk there is a framed photograph of him standing beside Dr. Kenneth Jensen, founder of the New York Cancer Patients Forum. For several years, he has worked with the organization and many of his referrals come via Dr. Jensen himself.

Martha Velinski was one such referral. Diagnosed with lung cancer in 1986, she turned to Dr. Fernandez for help. In a recent interview printed in the Cancer Patients Forum newsletter, Mrs. Velinski reveals that three years of hypnotherapy sessions with Dr. Fernandez made her feel more confident about her recovery, enabling her to endure chemotherapy with a positive outlook. In subsequent surgeries, she needed only a quarter of the dose of anesthesia she had previously required and bled less during each operation.

'Before Oliver Wendell Holmes coined the phrase 'anesthesia,' doctors defined it as 'a reversible lack of awareness.'' Dr. Fernandez smiles proudly. 'I wouldn't say that's too far off the definition of hypnosis, would you?'

[To read this story in full, subscribe now: www.nytimes.com/subscriptions]

Editor's Note: Subsequent to the original publication date of this article, we are sad to announce that Mrs. Martha Velinski died following her protracted battle with lung cancer.

When he finished reading, Oscar had a single picture in his head. It was the image of his own left hand, a roof-nail speared through it. Every fuzzy detail of that night at Harvey Road came back to him then, in a torrent. He could feel a helpless anger building inside him.

Iris was in the bathroom, brushing her teeth, and the squeal of the water pipes was all too present in his ears. He closed his fist around the article, scrunching it into a ball. The door was ajar and he pushed right inside. She looked at him, pausing the action of her toothbrush. 'I don't know why you showed this to me,' he said, standing at the jamb. 'You must have known what it would do.'

She spat out a dash of toothpaste and rinsed her mouth. 'I knew you'd be mad at me.'

He threw the article against the wall and it rebounded into the bathtub. 'I can't believe you just stood there and let him put a nail through my hand.'

'I know. It was stupid. But — '

141

'But nothing. Stop defending him.' He caught sight of his reflection in the darkened window and stepped away, recognising the buckled, angry face of his father. 'I just want you to be honest with me, Iris. If you're using me to get at your brother, if that's all this relationship means to you, then we'd better end it now.'

She went quiet, pensive, dabbing her lips on the guest towel. 'First of all, I think you're getting a bit ahead of yourself. It's been, what, a month? We've slept together *once*. That doesn't mean we're in a relationship. Not yet, anyway.'

'Well, maybe we should call it off, before things get too serious.'

'I'm not saying I don't *want* to be in a proper relationship with you. Oh, Oscar, you're being unfair.' She bent to retrieve the article from the bathtub, and started to unfold it. 'You've no idea what it means to have a brother.'

'What's that got to do with anything?'

'A lot, actually. You don't seem to realise how hard it is for me to talk to anyone about this. Eden and I have always been so close; we've always relied on each other — for support, yes, but mostly for *company*. Can you imagine how big and scary a house like this feels to a little kid? Do you know how easy it is to be lonely around here? We needed each other when we were younger, if only to get through the summer holidays, but now we don't need each other so much. He can see it, I can see it. It feels like the older I get, the less I want to be around him. That's hard to come to terms with. But you seem to think I can just separate myself from him like *that*.'

The snap of her fingers echoed in the bathroom. She leaned her hip against the basin, studying herself in the mirror. 'It's not your fault, I know. You're an only child and that's just how it is. What's strange is that all of my friends are only children, too — even my parents are only children. I don't have anybody to talk to about this kind of thing. Not properly. How nice it'd be just to be able to compare stories. To know what's normal and what isn't.' She began to smooth out the article against her stomach; the paper rustled softly. 'But I don't have anything to judge him by. I've got all of these memories and no way of knowing if they're strange or ordinary.'

He took a breath, feeling his anger subsiding. She was a hard person to stay mad at. All it took was the sound of her sighing gently, the sight of her eyes welling with tears, and he would start to forget what had brought them to arguing.

'What kind of memories?'

'Oh, I wouldn't know where to start. They all just blur into one. It's funny — all of my memories of growing up here seem to be of the summertime. I only remember being with Eden in the school holidays, maybe the odd Christmas here and there. But it's always sunny in my memories.'

She walked towards him, and he moved aside, letting her through into the bedroom. She folded the article in half and put it down on the bedside table. At the dresser, she took off her necklace, her earrings, let down her hair and combed it with her fingers. 'If I tell you this,' she said, 'you've got to promise not to tell anyone.'

'I promise.'

'You can't say a word to the others.'

'I won't. I swear.'

She sat on the edge of the bed and removed her shoes, stowing them away neatly. 'He was always doing that kind of thing when we were little — hypnotism stuff, like he did with you. We'd be lying out on the grass in the back garden, and the sun would be burning down and the birds chirping away, and suddenly he'd touch my shoulder and say: *Want to play a game?* And I'd say okay. He'd tell me to sit up, close my eyes — and I would. I completely trusted him when we were that age. I looked up to him. He was so clever and talented, and funny . . . Anyway, he'd start to sing to me, this quiet, simple little tune, like some old-fashioned lullaby. I'd be squinting my eyes against the sunshine so all I would see was this orangey-red colour, and with the heat on my face and everything I'd start to feel light-headed. Then I'd hear Eden's voice telling me to wake up. And when I'd look down, there'd be one of my mother's big safety pins stuck through my leg — I mean, closed shut, pushed through the skin by my ankle, my shin, my calf. It varied, depending on his mood, I guess.'

'You mean this happened a lot?'

'All the time, when we were little.' She got up, turning back the bedcovers. 'Is that normal? I don't even know any more.'

'Of course it isn't.'

'You mean brothers don't hurt their sisters sometimes?'

'No. Not just for the sake of it. That's abuse.'

'Well, I think that's a rather strong word for it. There was nothing malicious about it. I never felt so, anyway. And it's not like I could go to some therapist and say *my big brother hurt me*, because he didn't hurt me. I never felt a thing. Not once. But I'd look down and see a bit of blood and start crying my eyes out all the same. I'd run off somewhere and he'd come to find me. I could be hiding under the bed, in my mother's wardrobe, in the attic. He'd always find me. And then he'd tell me it was okay, that I shouldn't worry, because he was going to heal the cut for me, no problem. He'd make me swear not to tell our parents. Then he'd place his fingers over the cut and hold onto it really tightly, staring into my eyes. And I'd feel a kind of warmth. It was nice. And somehow — don't ask me how — he'd make it disappear. The next morning, it'd be gone completely. Just like he did with your hand the other night.' She looked at him tenderly. The lamplight made her eyes seem tired, older. 'That's why I don't need you to be angry with me about all this, Oscar. Just understand that the other night was hard for me, too. It was like being a little girl all over again. For the first time, I was watching the same magic trick happen to somebody else, and I didn't know what to do.'

'What else did he do to you?'

'Oh, it doesn't matter now.'

'Yes it does. I need to know.'

'It was always just stupid, silly stuff like that. There was nothing sexual about it, if that's what you're thinking.'

'I wasn't.'

'Well, good.' She sat on the edge of the bed, staring down at the carpet. 'It was just stupid kids' stuff.'

'Like?'

'Like, I don't know. Like, he would pretend he could predict things that were going to happen, future events. Just mundane things, nothing big. Or he'd pretend that he could hear the voices of people in houses as we passed by in the car. Sometimes, we'd be driving somewhere and he'd say into my ear: *The man doesn't want to put the house on the market, but the woman is insisting.* And then, the following week, there'd be a For Sale sign on the lawn. Or sometimes, he'd just be sitting there in the drawing room and he'd say: *Mum will come home later with nine cans of lentil soup and a jar of gooseberry jam.* And she *would.* Or he'd say: *Tomorrow, the Canadian dollar will come down by point three five.* And you'd look in the newspaper the next day and it had come down against the yen by exactly that amount. I don't know how he did it — I still don't know to this day — I wish I did. He was full of tricks like that.'

'He probably just read your mother's shopping list. Or he must've seen a property ad in the paper, or, I don't know, made a lucky guess.'

'Probably,' Iris said. 'And when we were little, those things didn't bother me so much. I could bear them. But now he's started doing this stuff all over again, and I can't keep pretending it's okay.' She got up, turning her back on him. Casually, she unzipped her dress and pulled it

146

over her head, standing there before him in her underwear. He thought it was the most elegant she had looked all evening.

'Do you know what he said to me yesterday? He told me he could make you agree to this dinner. That it would be so simple. All he'd have to do was utter the magic words.'

'Did he now.'

'He said you wouldn't be able to resist.'

'He's so conceited.'

'Yes. I told him so. He just laughed.'

'So what were these magic words of his?'

'Something about your depth of character. I mean, can you believe the nerve of him?'

Oscar stayed quiet, hoping the disappointment — the shame — wouldn't show on his face. He watched Iris removing her underwear without a single thought as to his presence. She stood naked in front of him, fluffing her pillow, then slid under the duvet. She sat up against the headboard, flattening the cover across her stomach. 'Look at you, over there in your suit. You look so handsome. Come to bed. I can't spend any more time worrying about my brother tonight. You're right. I've wasted enough time caring about him for one day. That little speech he gave about Schumann — how he went mad and threw himself in the river — that was all for our benefit, you know. He was toying with us.'

'Yeah, I'm starting to see that.'

Oscar removed his suit jacket and threw it onto the floor. He went to sit on the bed, removing his shirt. As he kicked off his shoes, he felt her hands upon his back. She was kneeling behind him now, massaging him. He felt her lips on the back of his neck. 'I know we've only slept with each other once,' she said, 'but I think we can add to that tally before the night is out.' Her voice was soft. 'I want us to be together a long time, Oscar.'

He turned and took her in his arms, leaning her back against the mattress, feeling the coldness of her stomach against his, the give of her breasts against his chest, the scissors of her legs around his waist. He kissed her hard — so hard he could feel her teeth through her lips — and their tongues touched, wet and heavy, sweet with cognac and toothpaste. She stared right into his eyes as if to focus him, as if to bring their minds together as well as their bodies. She rocked with the pressure of him, and he felt taken by her, seized by the very warmth of her. And the heat of her quickening breath against his ear as he pushed himself inside her was like sunlight burning through a window, magnified and startling. He had to turn his head away. As he did, he saw the article on the nightstand, and his eyes fell on three words he had somehow missed before. They stared back at him: black, static, incontestable. She clawed at his back trying to recapture his attention. 'What, sweetheart? What is it?' He rolled away, breathless, three words resounding in his head:

' . . . by HERBERT CREST'

5

Fantasies of Unlimited Power

Dr Paulsen was sitting in his usual armchair by the window, staring out across the grounds of Cedarbrook. A magazine was spread over his lap. It was late in the morning and the sky outside was dreary as newsprint; there was a fine, almost invisible spray of rain in the air that clung to Oscar's face like a fever-sweat. His steps were heavy, purposeful, and as he made his way into the old man's room, the floorboards groaned underneath the carpet in the usual places. Paulsen heard the sound and craned his neck to say: 'I told you — smoked fish is not a breakfast item. Do I look like a sea lion? I want boiled eggs or nothing at all.' When he saw it was Oscar, he removed his glasses, polished them swiftly with his sleeve, and put them back on. 'Oh, I'm sorry, son, I thought you were Deeraj. He's been trying to force kippers on me all morning. What are you doing here on your day off?' He closed his magazine and gestured to the empty chair across from him.

Oscar sat. 'Is the library open? I need to make a return.' He lifted up *The Passions of the Soul*.

Paulsen took it and held it lightly, as if it were made of some explosive material. 'Took you long enough.'

'I've been a bit busy lately.'

'I see.' The old man smirked. 'Back on, is it?'

'What?'

'With the King's girl. You've a terrible poker face.' Paulsen leafed through the pages and studied the binding. 'No coffee stains, no muddy fingerprints, no cracks in the spine. I've taught you well.' He set the book down on his lap. 'So tell me: what did you make of Mr Descartes?'

'I didn't agree with a lot of it, but I liked it. It was original, at least.'

'Well, you're certainly right about that. Bearing in mind the context of the times he was living in. To say the soul is more or less located in the pineal gland — he could've been hanged for heresy.'

'I like how he identifies all the emotions, sort of like a periodic table.'

'Yes, that's a good way of looking at it.'

'It's clever. Not easy to read, but it definitely made me think.'

'That's all we can ask for from philosophy, wouldn't you say? If you come to it looking for definite answers, you're going to be disappointed.'

Oscar leaned back. He took a moment to stare out at the Cedarbrook grounds. In the rainy front yard, three gardeners in blue overalls were raking up leaves and turning the soil in the lawn borders. Cars zipped by on Queen's Road, one after another, and the speed of them seemed at odds with the torpor of life inside Cedarbrook: the one-step-at-a-time along the corridors, the spoon-by-spooning of mealtimes; food that took all morning to cook and to serve, only to be taken away cold, unfinished, an hour later. Inside the wisteria-coated walls of this building, time was a slow and ponderous engine. It was one of the things Oscar liked most about the place.

He looked at the old man earnestly. 'Can I ask you something, Dr Paulsen?'

'Of course. What is it?'

'You might not want to talk about it.'

'Try me.'

He edged forward. 'This old friend of yours, Herbert Crest — '

'Herbert?' Paulsen's eyes widened. 'What about him?'

'I don't suppose you know what he does for a living.'

The old man lifted his chin. 'Has that staff nurse put you up to this?'

'No, it's nothing like that. I'm just curious.'

'You can't stop me going to meet him,' Paulsen said. 'I'll break out of the window if I have to.'

'No, I know. Don't worry about that.'

'So how come I'm getting the third degree?'

'I'm just asking. I'm curious.' Oscar removed the *New York Times* article from his pocket and showed it to Paulsen, who looked down at it, glasses slipping along his nose. 'Could this be the same Herbert Crest?'

The old man glanced over it, then gave a short, dry laugh. 'That's his handiwork, alright. Where did you get it?'

'From the internet.'

'You've been checking up on him.'

'No, no, nothing like that.' Oscar put the

151

article away. 'Somebody happened to show it to me last night, and when I saw the name, I — well, I couldn't believe it. I thought it had to be a coincidence, that it was some other Herbert Crest.'

Paulsen seemed dubious. 'I've never really believed in coincidences,' he said. 'Everything happens for a reason. The older I get, the more I'm sure of it. What's the date on that piece?'

'1992.'

'He'd have been living back in Connecticut then. I think he's moved to Boston again now.'

'Has he written other articles?'

'Probably more than you could count. That's how he makes his living.'

'He's a journalist?'

'A psychologist. Writes books — great hulking things — that's how he makes his money. He does news articles by way of promoting them. Help me up: I'll show you.'

Oscar lifted him by the elbows. Dr Paulsen took a moment to regain his sense of gravity. They walked towards one of the immaculately ordered bookshelves. 'I've only got a few of them. I must admit, I stopped collecting him a few years ago. He changed his publisher, and his books are quite hard to find over here, not to mention expensive. Take whichever one you like.' He pointed to a selection of cloth-bound hardbacks of varying colours. 'I've still got the dust jackets somewhere around here. I can show you his picture. Wait there.' He went over to the drawers by his bed.

Oscar ran his fingers across the titles on the

spines: *Selfhood in the Modern World. Engines of Grief. The Predatory Instinct. Solitude and the Self-Image.* His hand stopped on *The Girl With the God Complex.* He slid the book out slowly. It felt solid and compact in his hands. As he turned back the cover, the pages fell open at a dedication: 'For Abraham'. He leafed backwards to the author's biography:

Herbert Crest was born in 1934 and grew up in Boston, Massachusetts. He was educated at the Worcester Academy and King's College, Cambridge, where he studied Philosophy and Psychology. In 1961, he completed his Ph.D. at the Psychological Laboratory, Cambridge, and in 1969, he became a Fellow of the Research Centre at King's College. He now lives in Bloomfield, Connecticut. His interests include poetry, collecting miniatures, and lawn tennis.

'Here we are now,' Paulsen said, suddenly behind him. He was holding a fold of paper; the dreary morning light glinted against it. 'Of course, he was much younger in this photo. What would he be here — forty, forty-one? Put on a little weight. Still beautiful, though. Look at those eyes.' Paulsen showed him the grey-scale author photo on the dust jacket.

Herbert Crest stared back with remarkably clear eyes, as white and opaque as fondant icing. He had an amiable sort of face, broad and fleshy, with cheekbones like kneecaps, and straight dark hair that draped across his forehead in an effortless side parting. His face was clean shaven, his tie loosened. There was something almost apologetic about his pose: a half-hearted smile, one eyebrow cocked, a dimple forming at the side of his nose. It was a salesman's face, the sort you could trust without ever knowing why. 'I think I'll just borrow this one for now.'

'Okay, son. Whatever you want. But I'm keeping the dust cover.'

'I'll bring it back soon.'

'No rush. Just know this — ' Paulsen turned away, heading back to his armchair. 'If you have to come with me on Tuesday, then so be it. But you're sitting at your own table and buying your own bloody scones. Are we clear?'

Oscar left the old man alone. He'd agreed to meet Iris that evening. She was in labs and rehearsals for most of the afternoon, and he had nothing better to do with the rest of his day off than to think about her, what she was doing, who she was talking to. The drizzle had stopped falling but the pavements were glazed with puddles and there was a closeness to the air — sometimes cold, sometimes warm. He walked to Jesus Green and sat on a damp bench under a beech tree, watching the grungy-looking kids in the skate park for a while, seeing the way they scratched up and down the halfpipe on skateboards and BMXs.

That morning, he had woken with Iris's head upon his chest. Her hair was splayed out across her face and over his shoulder, rising and fluttering with each sleepy breath. The sun had not risen yet. He had lain there for a minute or

154

so, just watching her. He knew that he loved her, but he wouldn't say it until he was sure she felt the same — and he didn't know if he'd ever be certain. She had stirred, making the faintest moan, drawing the tiny face of her wristwatch close to her eyes. 'Oh, damn,' she'd said, 'my parents will be up already. We've got to get moving.' They'd dressed quickly in the darkness of the early morning, made the bed, and slipped quietly out of the rectory, careful not to be seen leaving together. Iris had slunk along the path like a cat burglar, around the side of the building to the organ house, and he had followed her, trying to keep silent. When she'd rapped her knuckles lightly on the door, it had edged backwards.

No place had ever overwhelmed Oscar quite as much as that organ house. One long and spacious room took up the entire building. It was dark and solemn as a cathedral, though he could imagine how it would flood with daylight once the sun was up. At the far end, pressed right up against the wall, there was a large and brilliant organ. Its console was made of five separate keyboards, tiered like a wedding cake and curved like an amphitheatre; it was built out of cherry wood in a boxy, uncomplicated fashion, and inlayed with ivory buttons and gilded switches. Above this console, a narrow formation of metal pipes was gathered into a wooden frame, aligned in a perfect regiment, like so many cigarettes packed into a case. The rest of the room seemed inconsequential: there was a four-poster bed, a wardrobe, and two identical couches facing each

155

other across a sheepskin rug; there was an en-suite bathroom raised up on a platform with a standing bath, a shower, and a lavatory, all hidden discreetly by a bank of concertina screens. But there was no sign of Eden or Jane, and the main house was empty come breakfast time.

Oscar had driven back to Cambridge with Iris, wondering how he would ever be able to get used to the Bellwethers' way of living. He'd got a bad feeling from that organ house — not the same fear that came over him whenever he passed by the old colleges, but something similar — an anxiety that came from not belonging there, from intruding on a private world.

Now, the kids in the skate park were dispersing in front of him, trundling off in separate directions with their boards under their arms. He leaned back against the bench, opened *The Girl With the God Complex*, and read the preface. It engaged him more than he expected. There was something about Herbert Crest's prose: it was plain and unfussy but wonderfully descriptive. He had that gift for making real lives seem cinematic. Oscar read chapter one, then chapter two, and before he knew it, he was halfway through the book and the evening was beginning to descend around him.

The book was made up of a single case study, that of an American teenager whom Crest called 'Jennifer Doe' (her real name could not be given). She had come to Crest's attention when his psychiatrist friend in California, Dr Isaac Leibman, called to seek a second opinion on the

156

diagnosis he had made. Leibman painted a troubling picture of Jennifer Doe: she was a girl with 'severe delusions of her selfhood', a girl who refused to acknowledge the authority of her own parents, her teachers, police officers, county judges, or the correctional officers at the juvenile facility where she had been incarcerated since the age of fourteen, after drowning her five-year-old brother in a public swimming pool. Dr Leibman said that the only reason Jennifer had ever given for murdering her brother was: 'My sisters told me to.' But Jennifer had no sisters. When Leibman asked if she could name them, Jennifer told him: 'Clotho, Lachesis, and Atropos.' These were names from Greek mythology, the names of The Fates. In the book, Crest wrote:

The Fates (also referred to as Moirai, the Daughters of Zeus, or The Daughters of Necessity) were important deities in Ancient Greece, responsible for deciding the path or 'thread' of every human life. They were three sisters: Clotho, the spinner, who made every thread on her loom; Lachesis, the measurer, who determined the length of each thread with a ruler; and Atropos, the decider, who cut the thread with her scissors. Dr Leibman had diagnosed Jennifer with Compensatory Narcissistic Personality Disorder (more commonly referred to as a God Complex) with Borderline Personality traits, and on the basis of what he had told me I saw no reason to disagree with him. But I was also

157

aware that the God Complex diagnosis is far from a routine conclusion in psychiatry. It is very rare for a patient to exhibit genuine symptoms of this state of mind, and seldom are therapists brave enough to apply such a verdict to a patient in their care, even those with unfettered Narcissistic Personality tendencies. Dr Leibman, I realized, was not just a colleague asking for professional validation, he was a friend reaching out to me for help.

By the end of the book, Oscar felt he knew Herbert Crest like an old friend. He admired the kindness that was implicit in the long paragraphs of loving description, where Crest seemed to speak of Jennifer Doe affectionately, never judging her, always keeping his focus on what was rational and sensible, while allowing the fullness of Jennifer's personality to shine through, paraphrasing her lengthy speeches and detailing her slightest behaviour. She was not just a patient, or a diagnosis, or a murderer to him, but a whole person. In the pages of the book, she was flawed, complicated, deluded, even dangerous, but she was also greatly human, and Oscar imagined it took a certain kind of mind to be able to capture a person so completely and so compassionately.

The book got under his skin. There were aspects of Jennifer Doe's behaviour, certain things she said, that seemed unerringly familiar. Like the part when Crest asked her to explain how she could possibly know she was a messenger for The Fates, and she replied: 'I could tell you, but you wouldn't be able to understand it. You'll figure out the answers for yourself one day. Just a matter of time.' Eden had said something very similar to Iris once — Oscar was sure of it. There was also a moment when Jennifer Doe gave Crest a 'long, mellifluous stare', after she'd guessed the suits of five cards in a row from his pack: 'That's nothing, Dr Crest,' she had told him. 'You wouldn't believe what else I can do.' Hadn't Eden written more or less the same thing in his email a few nights ago?

In chapter four, Crest explained Narcissistic Personality Disorder, outlining the diagnostic criteria he'd helped to develop for the American Psychiatric Association. With every new point in the list, Oscar felt his heart tightening:

NPD sufferers exhibit a pervasive pattern of grandiosity (in fantasy or behavior), need for admiration, and lack of empathy, beginning by early adulthood and present in a variety of contexts, as indicated by five (or more) of the following:

1. Has a grandiose sense of self-importance (e.g., exaggerates achievements and talents, expects to be recognized as superior without commensurate achievements).

2. Is preoccupied with fantasies of unlimited power, success, brilliance, beauty, or ideal love.

3. Believes that he or she is 'special' and unique and can only be understood by, or should associate with, other special or high-status people (or institutions).

4. Requires excessive admiration.

5. Has a sense of entitlement, i.e., unreasonable expectations of especially favorable treatment or automatic compliance with his or her expectations.

6. Is interpersonally exploitative, i.e., takes advantage of others to achieve his or her own ends.

7. Lacks empathy: is unwilling to recognize or identify with the feelings and needs of others.

8. Is often envious of others or believes that others are envious of him or her.

9. Shows arrogant, haughty behaviors or attitudes.

Oscar could hardly wait to tell Iris about it at dinner. They met at an Algerian place on Mill Road, where a man sat at a flaming grill in the front window, gleefully turning kebabs. Their table was at the far end of the room, away from the smoke and the smell of burning coals. Iris took gentle sips of water as he told her about Herbert Crest's book, and Jennifer Doe, and what he'd read about Narcissistic Personality Disorder, how he thought it might be what Eden was suffering from. Her face held no expression as he talked, but occasionally she gave a quiet nod, or lifted her chin, or *mm-hmm*-ed in agreement. Finally, she said: 'Oscar, this is all very sweet of you, but don't you think I've already thought of it? I mean, I've read nearly everything there is to know about these kinds of personality disorders. But I'm not convinced that Eden has any of them in particular — not entirely convinced, anyway. He's more complex than that.'

'Yeah, I know, but once you read this, you might feel differently.' He pushed the book across the table. She didn't pick it up, just looked down at it, as if it were some fly that had landed on the tablecloth.

'What's the point?' she said. 'It'll be another dead end. Sure, my brother's losing it, but he doesn't believe he's some Greek God like this Jennifer girl you're talking about.'

'That's not all it's about, though. You should read it.'

'Look, sweetheart, thanks for trying. I just don't have time to waste on reading books I know aren't going to help.'

They ate in silence for a while. The waiters seated a large party at a long table near the window, and the burr of chatter rose up in the room. Smoke continued to billow from the grill, steaming the windows. Oscar grew tired of listening to them. He leaned forward and said: 'I don't want to go on about it, but there's a

161

chance I might get to meet the guy who wrote that book on Tuesday. And I thought I could try to talk to him about Eden, not mentioning any names, of course. But, you know, maybe I could get his advice.'

'You can't just go up to somebody at a book signing and ask him to psychoanalyse your friend.'

'Who said anything about a book signing?'

'Well, I just assumed — are you saying you *know* this Crest fellow?'

'Not exactly. He's more like a friend of a friend.'

'Why didn't you mention it before?'

'Because I needed to find out if it was the same Herbert Crest. And now I know it is — '

'Oh, for crying out loud, this is so typical.' Iris took three large gulps of water as if to cool herself down. 'Don't you see what my brother's up to? He's playing with you, Oscar. He's playing with us both. He must've found out your connection to this Crest fellow and he's having some fun with us.'

'I don't see how he could know anything about it.'

She laughed. 'That's precisely the point. It's how my brother gets his kicks. He likes to prove his intelligence, his power over people; he likes to astound you with things then pretend like they're nothing, like it was barely an effort, when really — do you see what I'm talking about?' She paused to catch her breath. 'That's why I know it's more than just a simple diagnosis with him. Everything's just one big game to my brother.

162

He revels in the meddling. As soon as I get close to someone, he finds some way to drive a wedge between us. He's done the same thing all my life.'

'Why?'

'Oh, you don't want to hear my stupid theories on it. Let's just eat.'

'Tell me.'

She set her cutlery down, folding her hands. 'Because, deep down, he's frightened of losing me — that's why. Because if I ever get married and move away, he won't be able have power over me any more. And that's what he needs, to feel power over *everyone*. It's what sustains him.' She sighed. 'It's how he does it that's so frustrating. He manages to mess with my life so subtly that there's no way of proving it, so when I tell my parents about it, it looks like I'm the one causing trouble, telling stories. But I'm not!' She stared at Oscar, reaching across the table to take his hand. 'Oh, I'm sorry, I'm sorry,' she said. 'I should never have dragged you into this.'

'Don't worry about me. I can handle myself.'

'I know you can.' She smiled. 'That's why I need you with me, every step. We can't let my brother ruin this.'

'We won't.'

She leaned back. 'You're serious about me, aren't you, Oscar? Please say that you are.'

She asked it so straightforwardly that he was numb for a moment. He had to move his eyes away. 'I'm more serious about you than I've ever been about anyone,' he said, keeping his voice steady, and when he looked up, he found her

163

eyes were glazed with tears. She began to dab at them with the side of her finger. 'I can't tell you what it means to hear that,' she said. 'In my family, nobody ever says that kind of thing out loud.'

They held hands as they walked into town. The night was oddly warm and the streets were still wet with rain. They went through Parker's Piece, straying from the footpath to take a shortcut across the grass. There was a muddy line in the turf, made by the feet of countless people who'd taken the same shortcut before them. A desire line. He'd learned the term from Dr Paulsen, who'd pointed out the worn grooves of wheelchair tracks in the Cedarbrook garden last year.

Iris seemed to like the phrase. 'Eden says English is unromantic, but I think he's wrong about that. We have so many beautiful words for ordinary things.' She took deep breaths of fresh air, peering across the open park. 'If I had to choose my favourite word in the English language — actually, my favourite thing in the world, full stop — do you know what it'd be?'

'What?'

'Petrichor. It's the word for how the earth smells after rainfall.'

He kissed her on the cheek, walking on. 'You're too smart for me, miss.'

'Don't say that. You're just as clever as I am.' He felt her tugging at the bend of his arm. 'You could be anything you wanted to be.'

'I don't know,' he said. 'Lately it feels okay being who I am.'

She smiled and pulled him closer. 'Well, that's just fine with me, too.'

When they reached the coffee house by Emmanuel College, it was closed and shuttered over, so they headed straight back to Oscar's flat. His room was dim and damp. He threw Crest's book onto the bed and cleared away the dishes from the floor. Iris smoked a clove by the window while he lit some candles and put Nina Simone on the stereo. They lay down beside each other on the bed, listening to that deep, drawling voice, that frostbitten piano sound. Iris picked up *The Girl With the God Complex* and, without saying a word, she took her glasses from her pocket and began to read. He unbuttoned her blouse with one hand as she turned the pages, smoothing his fingers across her breast. They lay there together until he fell asleep. It was very late by the time he woke up again. The music had stopped but Iris was still reading in the sallow light with her blouse undone and her glasses at the tip of her nose, still cradled in the bend of his arm. 'I like how this Crest fellow writes,' she said. 'You were right about him.'

She turned back a few chapters, locating a certain paragraph and tapping her finger on it: '*Sometimes, NPD sufferers are trapped in an endless cycle of trying to prove their abilities,*' she read aloud. '*They may set themselves extraordinary, impossible challenges to solve or overcome, only to battle with the feelings of failure and incompetence that these self-imposed challenges create* . . . I've got to admit, it's ringing a few too many bells.' Finding her place

165

again, she carried on reading, and soon she gave another hum of recognition.

'Listen to this part: *In a family like Jennifer's, where nobody talked about their pride or love for each other, the smallest compliment would seem to her like the loudest affirmation.* It's like he's been living in my house for years.'

6

The Rightful Order of Things

Oscar wheeled Dr Paulsen across the car park. The Orchard was alive with midday shadows and he could see a glimmer of footprints in the dewy grass beyond the tea pavilion. Pale autumn sunlight slanted down through the apple trees and the birds were trilling in the hedges. Women sat alone under half-bare branches, sipping tea from dainty cups. Couples shared ploughman's lunches across green patio tables. Young men lazed in deck chairs with their headphones on. 'Just park me under that big one over there,' Paulsen said, pointing to an apple tree that was taller and wider than the others. 'We're a little early. Here — ' The old man reached under the blanket on his lap, pulling out a twenty-pound note, 'get me a scone with all the trimmings and an Assam, and whatever you want for yourself. Bring the tray over, then make yourself scarce. Understand?'

'Where should I go?'

'I don't care. Just keep out of earshot. I don't like airing my linen in public.'

Oscar bought the tea and scones from the pavilion and delivered them. Then he found a free table in a patch of grass that was warm with sunshine. He sat in a deck chair, quietly drinking an Earl Grey, staring at the resilient green of the trees. It was the first time he'd ever been to The Orchard, though he'd heard so much about it from the old man. According to Paulsen, the greats of English literature had walked in the tall grass here — Virginia Woolf and Rupert Brooke; J. B. Priestley and E. M. Forster; John Betjeman and A. A. Milne. Oscar had always wanted to see it for himself, but he'd been too afraid of their shadows to visit alone. Now he was experiencing it for what it was — trees and grass, sky and mud, weeds and flowers — something beautiful and unruined. He wanted to come back here with Iris and lie with her under the same tree that Ted Hughes had once lain beneath with Sylvia Plath, dreaming up poems for each other. (Lately, he'd been trying to write something of his own. The title had come easily, and he'd sketched out a decent first line — *You are the first thing about the morning that I recognise* — but so far he hadn't been able to think of anything good enough to follow it.)

He looked over at Dr Paulsen. The old man was sitting with his hands folded on the tabletop and every so often he would tilt his head, as if he'd caught sight of Herbert Crest approaching from some hidden aspect of the tea pavilion. Then he'd turn away again, feigning a new appetite for his uneaten scone.

Around half-past the hour, Oscar saw someone approach the old man's table. For a long moment, Paulsen barely regarded the person in the baseball cap who was standing before him, but then the two men exchanged words — a few short sentences that sounded to

Oscar like the distant rumble of a boat engine — and Dr Paulsen looked up, beaming. He opened out his arms and embraced the man, who stooped down, slapping two palms against his back. The man removed his cap, revealing a scalp as smooth and shiny as a cricket ball, and sat down at Paulsen's table, gazing at him. It was Herbert Crest. He looked different from his picture on the book jacket. Now he was skinny and ghostly and frail. From a distance, it seemed like the daylight was coming through his body, the way a torchbeam shines through dust.

The two men talked for a long time. Their conversation was broken only by frequent peals of Crest's laughter, and Paulsen's enthusiastic cackling. Oscar wondered what they were discussing, trying to imagine what these two fragile old things had once meant to each other. Neither man had seen the other in twenty years, but it seemed as if they were continuing a conversation they'd only started at breakfast. Their bodies had an easy, uncomplicated language.

Soon enough, Oscar found they were both looking back at him. Paulsen motioned with his hand — one glacial movement, inviting him over. The two men kept their eyes on him as he approached. 'Herb wanted to meet you,' Paulsen said.

'He's been singing your praises all afternoon,' said Herbert Crest, getting up slowly. His voice was thin and rusty, and he spoke with the rolling, curling vowels of a Kennedy. There was a bony fragility to his handshake. 'Anyone who can

169

impress Bram Paulsen is somebody I need to meet.'

'It's a pleasure,' Oscar said.

'To meet me, or to look after this old guy?'

'Both.'

Crest grinned. Now that he was closer, Oscar could see the scar on the top of his bald head — a long, straight, fleshy seam.

'Oscar's quite a fan of yours,' Paulsen said. 'Could hardly shut up about your book in the car.'

'Which one?'

'*The Girl With the God Complex*.'

'Ah. You liked it, huh?'

'Very much.'

Crest lowered himself into the deck chair. 'I always thought it was my best. Sold worse than any of them, though. Funny how that works.' He cleared his throat. 'Not that book sales have ever bothered me.'

Oscar took a seat beside him. 'I loved the way you wrote about that girl. It was like you really felt something for her.'

'Kind of you to say.'

'I wondered what became of her.'

'The girl?' Crest wet his lips with a slither of his tongue. 'Y'know, she almost got better there for a while.' He darted his eyes towards the sky. 'She died, though, couple years after the book came out. Angela. That was her real name.'

'Oh.'

Crest rubbed at the dry stubble on his cheek. 'Cut her wrists up pretty bad, so they told me. I guess she couldn't stand living with us mortals any longer.' He tried to laugh, but it sounded weak and insincere.

'I'm sorry to hear that,' Oscar said.

'Not as sorry as I was, believe me. But, hey, what can you do? What can any of us do? Death is part of life and all that crap.' Crest gave Dr Paulsen a warm smile. 'Y'know, I tried to get the publisher to reissue that book, but they wouldn't touch it. So I told them where to go. Ha. I guess that's why the big boys won't publish me any more — I'm too much of a hot head. Bram can testify to that.'

Paulsen blinked.

'It's too late to change me.'

'Are you still writing?' Oscar asked.

'I'm working on a book right now, as it happens. It's kind of why I'm here.' Crest went quiet. 'Listen, would you mind getting me some water? I'm dry as a sandbox and I've got a long ride home.'

'Yes, some water would be nice,' Paulsen said. He gave Oscar a heavy look. It was an expression he recognised, one that said: Take the hint.

Oscar bought a bottle of Perrier from the tea pavilion. A couple of women were holding a conference about what kind of cake was best, coffee or carrot, and whose turn it was to pay. They side-stepped along with their tray, slowing the line. When he arrived back at the table, Herbert Crest was gone.

'He had to rush off,' Paulsen said. 'A call came through.'

'Oh. Damn.'

'You don't have to pretend you're sad about it.'

'No, I'm — there was something else I wanted to ask him, that's all.'

'Just be glad you got to meet him. I wasn't planning on introducing you two, but he spotted you right away. The first thing he said when he sat down was: 'I know that's your nurse over there, Bram, you can't fool me. I've got mine waiting in the car!' He always could see right through me, the bastard. God, I love him.'

Oscar wheeled the old man back through the trees, across the pebbles of the car park. The sunlight was fading but there was a pleasant smell in the air of some distant bonfire. He heaved Paulsen into the passenger seat of the minibus, then folded up the wheelchair and put it in the boot. As he started the engine, the old man thanked him. 'You made it very easy for me today, Oscar. I won't forget it. That boy Deeraj wouldn't have left me alone for a second with his fussing and hovering. But not you. You're a good lad. I almost felt alive again today.'

The old man barely said another word on the drive back to Cambridge. He just gazed out of the passenger side, at the rolling smudge of the hard shoulder, the steel girders, the combed rows of farmland. It was early evening and the sky had grown purple. The tyres droned on the carriageway tarmac.

As they neared the edge of the city, Oscar couldn't hold from speaking any longer. He knew that Dr Paulsen had no wife, no children, no remaining family. Not a single person had ever come to visit him at Cedarbrook the whole time he had known him. Herbert Crest, he

172

realised, was the only person the old man had left in the world. 'Tell me to butt out if you want, but I've got to ask — '

Paulsen removed his hat, but didn't speak.

'What happened between the two of you?'

The old man hardly moved. His eyes surveyed the road. 'I was completely and utterly in love with that boy. And he was in love with me.' He stared dead ahead, not even blinking. 'After what I did to him, it's incredible he still wants to talk to me.'

It was strange that he still referred to Crest as a boy, as if a younger version of him still existed somewhere.

'What happened?'

'It doesn't matter what happened. It was stupid and childish, and I'm not proud of it. I made a fool of myself. It was all very ugly. But there's no point dwelling on ancient history. I've made my peace with it now.'

'I've never seen you as happy as you looked today.'

'Ah, you've a good heart, son, you know that? It's funny, in some ways, you remind me of him — of how he used to be.' Paulsen looked at him warmly. 'I can't tell you how good it felt to see Herb again, face to face. I still love him, not in the same way. I think we've become very different people, him and me — but, oh, that boy was the greatest love of my life. He meant everything to me. Still does.' Paulsen gave a quiet sigh through his nose. He rolled the brim of his panama around in his fingers as if preparing a pizza dough. 'He looked so ill, didn't he? Did

173

you see his eyes? They used to be so bright and clear. They were practically dead already.'

'Is he sick?'

'Very.' He tapped at his temple. 'Brain tumour.'

'Oh no, I'm so sorry.'

'Hardly your fault. If anyone's to blame it's the pathetic excuse for a god we have up there. I'm nearly twenty years older than Herb — I've known him since he was eighteen. You'd think I'd be the one to go first, wouldn't you? But no. Sod the rightful order of things. If there's any kind of god up there, he's one cruel, miserable old bugger.'

The news that Herbert Crest was dying did not come as a surprise to Oscar. He'd suspected it the moment he saw him arriving at The Orchard, seen it in the ghostly pallor of his lips, the grey circles around his eyes, the sound of his breathing, as if each inhalation brought a wave of pain. But it unsettled him to have these suspicions confirmed. By the time the old man finished telling him about Crest's illness — the surgeries, the chemo, the joy that came with the short remissions and the despair that came with the relapses — he felt utterly deflated.

'I'll never complain about anything ever again,' the old man said. 'Not when I think of Herb struggling like that. I know he's not the only one out there with a tumour, but seeing what it's done to him, well, it just brings it all home to me. I'm a lucky man. I've never thought of myself as lucky before. I'm just so glad I got to see him again.' The doctors had given Crest no

174

more than two years to live, and that time had almost passed. He was visiting every person that he'd ever loved, Paulsen said, so that he could tell them how important they were to him — and, most of all, to say goodbye. 'I was third on his list. That's good enough for me. Even if it all ends up in this book of his, I don't care.'

'He's writing about it? About dying?'

'Sort of,' Paulsen said. 'Sounded to me like it's more about wanting to survive. What was the title he had? Oh, damn, it's gone clean out of my mind.'

'He looked too sick to be writing anything. It's a wonder they even let him on a plane.'

'He lives in London now.'

'Oh.'

'Been here the last few years. Strange to think of him being here all that time, on the same shores. I always thought he was an ocean away.'

They stopped at traffic lights on Barton Road. A parade of cyclists wheeled over the pedestrian crossing, their coat-tails billowing behind them. Oscar could hardly hear the engine, and he wondered if he had stalled it, but when he pressed the accelerator it gave out a tinny rev.

'I can't remember the title he had for the life of me. Oh, my stupid old brain.'

'It doesn't matter.'

'Yes it does. Once the short-term memory goes, that's it, I'm done for.' Paulsen thought hard; his face was one big crease of concentration. 'I can remember the publisher. Spector and Tillman. But the title. Damn, what was it?'

The lights blinked green and Oscar moved the

minibus forwards. Turning onto Queen's Road, he could see the outline of Cedarbrook in the distance, and as they drew towards it the shape swelled upwards and outwards. It was lit from the ground with floodlights, and the angles of the beams against the bricks reminded him of the Bellwether house. He steered through the open gates, driving around the side of the building, parking in the back yard, amid a fleet of other buses. It felt like he was a cruise-ship captain coming home to dock.

A lamp was on at the nurses' station, and one of the new auxiliaries was sitting there filing her nails. She brought out the day book and Oscar signed his name beside 'Paulsen, Abraham'. He put the old man in the stairlift and walked him, step by step, back to his room. He took off Paulsen's jacket and shoes and pulled the blanket over him as he lay down and closed his eyes. 'Sleep well,' he said. Hanging the old man's jacket over the armchair, he felt something in the outer pocket — a crackle of paper behind the lining, crisp under his fingers. He checked that Paulsen was asleep before taking it out.

It was the letter from Herbert Crest. There was a shakiness to the handwriting he hadn't noticed before. The ink was blotted with rainspots. On the back of the envelope, there was a printed gold label with his name and address: 'Dr Herbert Crest, 41 Cartwright Gardens, Bloomsbury, London WC1 2BQ'. Oscar pushed it back into the old man's jacket, drew the curtains, and left.

Downstairs, the auxiliary was still filing her

nails. He went around the desk and sat down beside her. The computer screen was blinking with a spam ad for online poker. She peered over his shoulder as he brought up the web browser and typed 'herbert crest spector tillman' into the search engine.

There was a direct link to Herbert Crest on the Spector & Tillman site. When the page uploaded, a small black-and-white photo appeared in the top right corner of the screen. Crest was gaunt-faced but still had a dusting of thin white hair and the sharp tendons of his neck were hidden behind a turtleneck sweater. He was leaning the weight of his head on his chin and clutching a pair of frameless spectacles in his fingers. Underneath, there was a block of text:

New and Forthcoming Non-Fiction Titles

DELUSIONS OF HOPE (Fall 2003)

by Herbert M. Crest

Dr. Herbert Crest is the critically acclaimed A.P.F. Gold Medal Award-winning author of *The Fraudulent Mind, Solitude and the Self-Image*, and *Distant Relations*. Continuing the tradition of these artfully constructed psychological case studies in his latest book, Dr. Crest finds a new focal point for his investigations — himself. *Delusions of Hope* details the author's private battle with a malignant brain tumor. With courses of radiation and chemotherapy at an end, and surgical options exhausted, Dr. Crest struggles to find an alternative remedy for his illness. The book follows his path from reiki therapists to acupuncturists to Sudanese witch doctors to spiritual healers, as Dr. Crest tries to determine the psychological foundations of hope and what it means to place one's trust in things beyond the cold, hard logic of science. In so doing, he seeks to find an answer to the question: What is survival really worth?

7

Dead Reckoning

When the call came, Oscar was dreaming of his parents' house. The ground-floor windows were swirled with white chalk and an endless spray of orange butterflies was funnelling out of the open doorway. As he made his way along the path, he could see his father sitting in the living room on a raggedy sofa, dressed in hessian pyjamas; the butterflies seemed to form a halo around him. His mother was in the kitchen, fixing the handle of a broken pan, and just when he was about to call out to her, the buzz of his phone on the nightstand pulled him awake.

A brittle, distant voice came over the line: 'Oscar, I know it's late, but you need to get to Downing as soon as you can.' There was no hint of emergency in Eden's tone. 'There's been an accident. Iris is hurt.'

Oscar found it difficult to speak. When he tried, the words refused to come out, and he could only make a short, desperate sigh that amplified in the receiver. He managed to gather himself enough to say: 'What happened?'

'It's all this fog,' Eden said. 'She was knocked over. A van, they're saying. Wait a sec — ' There was a scratch as Eden covered the mouthpiece, and Oscar could hear a muted mumbling. 'Sorry. Policewoman was telling me something. I'll meet

179

you by the porters' lodge, okay? Be quick.' The line went dead.

He threw on some clothes and hurried out into the night. While he'd been sleeping, a thick fog had descended over the town and he could hardly see what was in front of him as he ran. Tips of buildings peeped out of the whiteness. Things that he'd never even noticed before — chimney pots, TV aerials, skylights — he now relied upon to guide him, like some pilot with broken instruments, flying by dead reckoning. Pavements he'd walked along every day on his way home now seemed treacherous and unfamiliar. He followed them as well as he could, running harder than he'd ever run, unsure of his direction. The fog made the city a foreign country. He ran almost by memory, fingering shop windows along Regent Street, metal railings, bits of wall, slowing when he felt the pavement was about to end. The mist was cool against his face and the air felt dense and hard to breathe. He didn't stop running, though his lungs burned and his muscles ached.

Outside the gates of Downing College, the blue lights of a police car flashed solemnly. From a distance, the pulsing light seemed downy and mild, but when he got closer to the porters' lodge, the blueness was colder, harder, cracking the night apart with steady blinks. A uniformed policewoman was sitting inside the squad car. The engine was running and she was speaking into the radio on her collar. He could see Jane now, too, pacing near the college gates. Eden was with her, hands buried deep in the pockets of his overcoat.

'Oh, Oscar, thank God!' Jane strode towards him and hugged him tightly. 'Don't worry, don't worry, she's alright. She's alive. But she's been injured quite badly.'

He couldn't catch his breath. He felt sick. 'Where is she?'

'Addenbrooke's. Her parents are with her.'

The squad car moved away from the kerb, making a three-point turn in the road.

He looked at Eden. 'What the hell happened to her?'

'There's no need to sound so accusatory. This is hardly *my* fault.' Eden arranged the lapels of his overcoat. 'All I know is what the police told me. A van hit her, somewhere on Silver Street.'

'*When?*'

'Two, three hours ago. She was on her way to meet us,' Eden said, nodding towards the fog-cloaked grounds of the college. 'We were all playing mah-jong in Marcus's room, and the next minute this policewoman shows up.'

'Did they catch the driver?'

'It was a hit and run — in thick fog — they've got no chance.'

The urge to run was still in Oscar's feet. His head was thrumming. 'I need to get to the hospital,' he said. 'Now.'

'We *all* need to get there. Why the bloody hell do you think I called you?'

'I'll drive us,' Jane said. 'Don't worry. Everything will be okay. There's no need for any bickering.'

Oscar had to wait with Eden at the Downing gates while Jane fetched the car. He was too anxious to talk, imagining Iris on the quiet bend of Silver Street, alone and terrified. He began to kick at the kerbstone.

'You know,' Eden said, looking past him, 'she was lucky — her cello case took the brunt of it.' Eden removed a handkerchief from his pocket and blotted the tip of his nose. 'Then again, if she'd ditched that group weeks ago, like I told her to, she wouldn't have been coming home from practice in the dark.'

'All I care about is that she's okay,' Oscar said. 'That's all any of us should be thinking of right now.'

Eden kept quiet. There was no brotherly concern in his manner; he was leaning nonchalantly against the iron gate, investigating his handkerchief, as if it were a tourist map. 'My parents are with her. If she was in any danger, they would've sent for me by now.'

'Sent for you?'

'Yes,' Eden said, turning his eyes to the quadrangle. 'They'd have sent a car for me, or one of my mother's church friends would've come to get me. But they haven't, so she must be okay.'

'I wish I could say that put my mind at ease.'

'Just putting things in perspective,' Eden said.

The swirling fog showed no signs of breaking, but Oscar could see a flurry of shadows near the library. He was glad when Yin and Marcus emerged from the mist, heading for the porters' lodge. They both seemed tired and downcast, but Yin's face was particularly ruddy, his shoulders slouched in his puffer jacket. 'That's the whole point,' he was saying to Marcus, who trailed behind him, 'the last time we played mah-jong I had my bike stolen. I'm telling you it's cursed or something. We can't play it any more.'

'Accidents happen,' Marcus said. 'Don't get all Chinese about this.'

'What's *that* supposed to mean?'

'If you want to blame anything, blame the weather,' said Eden, stepping towards them. 'And the fact that my sister can't look both ways before she crosses the road.'

Yin folded his arms. 'Man, I can't believe you're making jokes about this. She's really hurt.'

'Gallows humour, Yinny, not lack of concern. You're starting to sound like Oscar.'

'She was talking to the paramedics,' Marcus said. 'That's a good sign.'

'We better hope so,' Yin said.

Oscar saw headlights approaching from the Hills Road junction. 'Is that her? Is that Jane?'

'Settle down,' Eden said, squinting into the darkness. 'Plenty of room for all of us.'

★ ★ ★

The Bellwethers were already sitting in the empty A&E waiting room when Oscar and the others arrived. Theo had an arm around his wife's shoulder and she was pressing her head into the slope of his neck, eyelids closed. They were dressed as if they'd been pulled out of some grand occasion to be there — he in a dinner suit with the bow tie slightly askew, and she in a

183

sequined gown and a diaphanous wrap that concealed the ageing skin of her shoulders. Theo was idly flipping through a magazine on his knee, one-handed. He didn't get out of his chair when the five of them entered the room, just raised his chin at them. Mrs Bellwether stirred, levelling herself.

Theo told them to sit down, and they did, hunching towards him. He told them that Iris had broken her femur. 'They've just taken her into surgery, but the signs are good. It's not too bad a break.'

'Oh, thank heavens,' Jane said.

'I spoke with the surgeon. He's more than competent. They do these procedures every day.'

'She really had us worried,' Yin added. 'We thought we'd lost her.'

'Well, she's in a lot of pain at the moment,' Theo said, 'but she's going to be fine, thank God.'

Marcus said: 'I knew she'd be alright. She's a tough old bird.'

Eden didn't talk. He stood up, walked across the waiting room to the water cooler, and began to fill up a paper cone. He drank it down, then filled another, and another.

Mrs Bellwether looked at Oscar. 'Don't worry, dear, she's going to pull through. Iris is made of sturdy stuff. She'll be back on her feet in no time.' She continued to fold and refold her cashmere gloves upon her lap. 'When she was a child, she got into all sorts of scrapes. Gashed her knees, cut her tongue, even broke her collarbone once. But she never complained, always healed up quickly. That's the thing about Iris, she's always been an incredibly fast healer. Hasn't she, Theo?'

Her husband nodded. 'What? Oh, yes, incredibly.'

Oscar couldn't take his eyes off Eden, who had finished at the water cooler and was now walking back to his seat. 'Well,' he said, 'when will you be moving her out of this rathole?'

'Soon enough,' Theo said. 'When she's had some recovery.'

'What d'you mean *move her*?' Yin asked.

Marcus leaned towards him, lowering his voice. 'He means when is she going to the private hospital.'

'Ah.'

'What's wrong with *this* hospital?' Oscar said.

'Oh, nothing,' Eden said. 'It's just, I want her to be comfortable.'

'She'll be fine here.'

'No she won't. She'll bloody well hate it. Sharing a ward with a bunch of strangers, only a little curtain for privacy? That's not my sister.'

'We'll be moving her, son, don't you worry,' said Theo. 'She might even be alright to come home. It depends on how well the procedure goes.'

Oscar didn't like the idea of unsettling Iris during her recovery. 'Sounds like you're the only one who's uncomfortable here, Eden.'

'Puh!'

'Iris won't mind sharing a room for a while.'

'Well, that just shows how little you know her, doesn't it?' Eden folded his arms. The sleeves of his jumper were so short that they rode up, revealing pale moley skin. 'We're not all capable of dossing down with the proletariat, you know. She won't even drink water if it's out of the tap.' He turned to his parents, as if sharing a private joke. 'Only been in the picture five minutes and already telling me he knows best.'

'Alright, cut it out, the pair of you,' Theo said. 'You're making a scene.'

'You have to get her out of here immediately. She'll have MRSA before you can blink.'

'Eden, that's *enough*,' Mrs Bellwether said. Her voice was as firm as it had ever sounded; it echoed against the magnolia walls. Eden looked away, cowed.

'When can we see her?' Jane asked.

Theo rubbed his eyelids. 'She'll be in surgery for a few hours yet. After that, she'll be groggy with the anaesthesia. Could take a while. You should all go home.'

'We've only just got here,' Oscar said.

'I know, but you'll be no use to anyone sitting around this place all night. You've all got work to do, I'm sure. Go home and sleep and come back tomorrow. She's going to be fine — just broken bones, nothing that can't be fixed.'

Eden pushed his hands into his pockets. 'What are you going to do?'

'We'll see how she is. If she's okay, we'll go back to the house. And if she needs us, there's a bed-and-breakfast over the road. We'll stay there for the night.'

'A bed-and-breakfast? You?'

'Needs must.'

'Well, I thought it'd take a worse disaster than this — '

186

Theo looked at his son, mouth ajar. 'Excuse me?'

'I was just saying — '

'Go home, Eden.'

'I just meant — '

'If you think there's a worse disaster than your sister being in emergency surgery, my dear boy, I'd really like to hear it.'

Eden stayed quiet, staring at the floor. 'She's not dead. That's all I meant.'

Jane gasped: 'Eden!'

With this, Theo rose to his feet. Mrs Bellwether reached out for him, trying to hold him down, but her effort was limp, halfhearted. Eden seemed shocked by his father's anger. He wilted into his chair.

'You better hope those words don't end up haunting you, son,' Theo said, stooping over him. 'All surgery, *any* surgery, is life and death. What the bloody hell is wrong with you? I've just about had it with your glibness.'

Eden gave an apologetic tilt of his head, but Oscar thought he could see him repressing a smile; his mouth seemed to draw upwards into the slightest, most imperceptible of sneers. Nothing seemed to register behind his eyes; he was not tearful, not obviously rattled nor openly remorseful. He just got up and said, 'Well, if that's all,' and walked right out of the waiting room. The automatic doors parted and closed behind him. Nobody followed. Outside, the fog was still heavy, moving like the slowest cloud that ever passed across the sky.

★　★　★

Oscar couldn't leave the hospital until he knew that Iris was okay, until he'd seen that for himself. He said goodbye to the others — to Jane, who offered her car for him to sleep in; to Marcus, who wrote down his mobile number and asked to be kept in the loop; and to Yin, who gave him the coins from his wallet so he might have some change for the coffee machine. If the truest measure of people is how they act in an emergency, then they were all good people, he thought. He could not say the same about Eden.

The Bellwethers stayed with him in the waiting room, until an RGN came through the swing doors and told them there was a more comfortable room upstairs, closer to the operating theatre. They went up silently in the lift. Theo's arm didn't move from his wife's shoulder. He kept leaning to whisper consoling words into her ear. When they got to the family room, she lay down on one of the couches and Theo covered her with his dinner jacket. He went to sit beside Oscar, staring across at his wife as she slept. 'We were at a function,' he said, gesturing at his dinner suit almost apologetically. 'Wren Library benefit. Hence the attire. My mobile rang and — well, here we are.'

'I was sleeping,' Oscar said. 'Came as quick as I could.'

'There's no need to stay, you know. I can handle this. No harm will come to her on my watch.'

'The harm's already been done.' Oscar stared down at the linoleum. 'I can't go home. I love her. I need to know she's okay.'

This seemed to get through to Theo. 'Yes, I

suppose you do.' He made a small sound with his nose — a tiny release of air. 'Want to know the irony of all this?'

'What?'

'I thought if anything was going to derail her school year, it'd be *you*. Medicine doesn't let you take any lateral steps. You can't skip a lecture or not do the reading. You certainly can't miss an entire bloody term. This is really going to set her back.' He gave Oscar's thigh a swift double-tap, getting up. 'Shall I go and see if I can find anything out?' He headed for the corridor, tucking in the loose tail of his shirt.

Oscar waited. The hands on the wall clock hardly seemed to move. In the corner of the room there was a tiny red table and a chair — a kid's desk-set. White paper, crayons, and felt pens were spread out upon it and a few messy pictures had been taped up on the notice board, beside posters for group therapy, grief counselling. He thought about writing Iris a letter, something she could read when she woke up from surgery. He knelt down at the tiny table, took a sheet of paper and a pen, and tried to write, but the words just wouldn't come. The clock crept around to three a.m. He closed his eyes and thought of her.

He imagined them together, drinking Pimm's under the apple trees at The Orchard, lying in the lush grass. And he smelled the scent of her, still on his clothes — the same smoke and bergamot that clung to everything in his flat; he could smell her on the pages of every book she'd ever pulled from his shelf. He heard the voices of the King's choir whenever he came through his front door, and the sound of Fauré whenever he crossed the Magdalene Bridge. She had made his life worth writing about. So he wrote it down the only way he could.

Around four, Theo came back. He gently nudged his wife awake with two poised fingers. 'They just brought her out,' he said, looking at Oscar. 'The surgeon's on his way.'

'Did you see her?'

'Only briefly. They were wheeling her into recovery. She looked fine. I think it went well.'

The surgeon — a towering black man with a moustache and a kindly face — came in to speak with them. His name was Mr Akingbade and he was still wearing his pale green scrubs. Oscar could see no bloodstains on him, just two large sweat patches underneath his armpits and one on his chest. A nurse in a blue uniform lingered near the doorway, her back against the dimmer switch.

'It went as well as it could have,' Mr Akingbade said. 'I am very confident.' In his slow, African voice, he told them he'd repaired the femur by drilling through the bone and driving a metal rod through the hollow, then stabilising it with a series of screws. It was an intra-articular fracture, a bad one, but not as bad as some he'd seen. 'We'll keep an eye on her, of course, but she's going to be alright. In a few days, you'll be able to take her home.'

Theo pulled Akingbade aside to discuss the finer details of the surgery; they talked in hushed, murmured sentences, all nods and gestures. The nurse stepped forward and said: 'Would you all like to see her? You can't go in, but you can look through the glass.'

They walked down the corridor and stopped outside a large room with a viewing window. Curtains were drawn across it on the inside, and the nurse went to slide them back. As the door opened, Oscar could hear the steady blips of a heart monitor.

Iris lay helpless in the bed, an oxygen mask over her mouth, both hands resting beside her. Her left leg was braced with a foam and metal contraption. The line of a drip was connected to the back of her right hand, and a series of round discs were stuck below the neckline of her hospital gown. She was still under the anaesthesia, but there was a serene expression on her face that he recognised. He knew then that she would be okay. He allowed himself to breathe out.

Mrs Bellwether had said nothing in the surgeon's presence. Now, her eyes swelled and she seemed to sniff back an emotion that was rising in her — Oscar couldn't tell if it was sadness or exhaustion. Then she turned to Theo: 'Do you think the Mulgrews found it strange, the way we ran out like that?'

'I'm sure somebody will have told them it was an emergency.'

'I don't want them to get the wrong impression. It was such a lovely benefit. I hope we didn't put a dampener on things.'

'Darling, that *really* doesn't matter right now.'

'We should go,' Mrs Bellwether said. 'It's four in the morning.'

'Are you staying, Oscar?' Theo asked.

'Just a bit longer,' he said.

They said goodnight to him, and went down in the lift. Oscar stood at the window, peering in at Iris, soothed by the regular noises of her monitor. He watched her until he could hardly keep his eyes open any longer. On his way out, he gave his letter to the nurse. She told him she'd leave it on Iris's bedside table.

Dear Iris,

I tried to find another way to tell you how I feel about you, but nothing seemed quite good enough. So I offer you this: an attempt at a poem that I've been working on for a while. I know you'll think it's far too gushing and sentimental. And okay it owes too much to good old Sylvia. It might just be the worst poem you'll ever read (or at least the worst poem you'll read tomorrow). But that's just it. That's why I wrote it. Because I can't wait for you to tease me about it the next time I see you. I can't wait to see you laugh and look at me with pity, because, after tonight, any look from you will be enough. You make me want to write my whole life down.

I love you,

Oscar xxx

PETRICHOR

*You are the first thing about the morning
    that I recognise.*

Not the way the sun crowns in the
window, spears drawn,

the dose of salts the new day throws upon
my other pillow
where old impressions of your breath still
maunder like a sigh.

Not the sound of hot brakes spraining at
the junction, buses
clearing out their throats when sweat-back
joggers hoof on by

with music cranked to cancel out those
airborne noises.
No, I smell your risen voice and know that
I have woken

into something that feels better just for
knowing. You are there
like a linen cast over an easel: a concession
to a coming afternoon.

Oscar didn't go home. He went to Cedarbrook
and slept on the futon in the staff room; because
it was only four hours until the start of his shift.
He took a shower and changed into a spare
uniform, then ate breakfast with the early-bird
residents in the day room with the sun half-risen.
Somehow he managed to mumble and stagger
through to lunchtime without anybody noticing
his tiredness, until Mr Cochrane on the second
floor asked him, with a tone of contempt,
whether he was taking any recreational drugs.

On his lunch hour, he went to talk with Dr Paulsen, who was eating his meal alone in his room, as usual. The word from Deeraj was that the old man wasn't in a fine mood — he'd barked at one of the agency nurses when she tried to change his duvet. But Oscar saw no signs of Paulsen's foul temper when he went in to say hello. The old man was standing at the bookshelf, reading *The Girl With the God Complex*. His body was leaned awkwardly — one hand gripping the book, the other gripping the shelf — and his cane was lying by his feet. 'I don't remember this book being so interesting,' he said, turning a page and peering at him. 'Thanks for bringing it back.'

'How long have you been standing there like that?'

'Oh, I don't know, half an hour maybe.'

'Come on, old man.' He took Paulsen by the elbow and walked him over to the armchair. 'It'll do you no good leaning like that. You'll be sore in the morning.'

'Yes, yes, alright, don't fuss.' Paulsen dropped into the chair and groaned. He went back to the book. 'This part right here — ' He held one finger to the page, underscoring a single sentence. 'He actually quotes Nietzsche. Anyone who knows Herb will tell you, there was a time he could hardly bring himself to say the man's name — like an actor with *Macbeth*. But it's right here, look — he actually paraphrases the man.' He read aloud: '*As Friedrich Nietzsche once wrote, the irrationality of a thing is no argument against its existence. Jennifer Doe insists my rational brain is not equipped to comprehend who or what she is. The more I listen to her, the more I can see value in Nietzsche's point . . .* Value in Nietzsche's point! Herbert Crest, wash your mouth out with soap and water!'

Oscar was listening but his eyes were closed. It was a struggle to stay upright. He needed the support of the wall.

'Late night, I take it?' Paulsen said.

He shook himself awake. 'You could say that.'

'You're welcome to sleep on my bed. I won't tell.'

'I'd love to. But I can't.'

'Why not?'

'I've still got three hours of my shift to go.'

Paulsen shrugged. 'So tell them I've made a big mess and you have to clear it up. Say I've done it in my tracksuit bottoms again. That should buy you some time. I'll lock the door.'

Oscar relented. He slept in the old man's room for over an hour, and by the time he woke up, he felt more able to face the world. Outside the window, grey clouds were slouching through the sky. Paulsen was back at the shelves, still examining Crest's book. 'I've been wondering,' he said, not looking up from the page, 'how come you left school so young?'

Oscar rolled away, straightening out the pillows. 'Oh, I really don't want to get into that. Not right now.'

'Why not?'

'Because.'

'*Because?* That's all you have?'

'Yeah.'

195

'*Because* is not a complete sentence, it's a conjunction. You'd have known that if you'd stayed in school.'

Oscar gave out a long, heavy breath. 'There were other things more important to me at the time, okay? Let's leave it there.'

'What could be more important than your education?'

'Leaving home, having my own life, money in my pocket.' He got to his feet, arranging his uniform. 'Why are you so interested all of a sudden?'

'I don't mean to pry. It's just that reading this book again has made me think about Herbert. Not Herbert now — I mean when he was younger. I feel like I've been getting to know him all over again.'

'What's that got to do with me leaving school?'

'You remind me of him, that's all. The way you see the world and think about other people — you're so alike. That effortless compassion you both have. Quite aggravating really, the pair of you.' Paulsen smiled. 'And yet, the more I think about it, the more I see the differences between you. Your lives are complete opposites. I found that comforting at first, but now I think it just saddens me.'

Oscar shifted on his feet. 'How'd you mean?'

The old man took a moment before he answered, as if proofreading the words in his head, making sure they came out as he intended. 'When I think of the life that Herbert had and compare it to your life — and then when I see how similar you both are, how your minds work

196

in the same way — it makes me sad, because I know that if you only had a scintilla of his education, you could achieve more than Herbert ever could. And Herbert's achieved plenty. So what was it, son? Did you not get the grades?'

'It doesn't matter. I'm here now, aren't I, and that's all that counts.'

'I don't think it was the grades. You're too clever for that.'

'Marks weren't the problem, okay, but I don't want to go into it. Not today.'

'A-ha! I knew it!' The old man paused, eyeing the window. 'A smart boy like you shouldn't be here wiping food off my chin. He should be at one of those colleges out there with all the other smart boys his age. So, come on, what was it?'

One day, Oscar would tell the old man everything. He'd already imagined how it would go. It would be some rainstruck afternoon when the whole of Cedarbrook was trapped indoors and there was nothing to do but sit with Dr Paulsen and talk about the past, while the other patients watched quiz shows down in the parlour and the staff all bantered quietly in the corridors. He would tell the old man about the nursing home he used to work at — the one in Watford where he'd once helped his father build an extension — and how he'd got talking with the staff nurse there about a care assistant job, how she'd made it sound so worthy and dignified. He would tell the old man that leaving school had not been a choice for him but a necessity — a chance to get away from his parents' closed-off estate and find his own place on the other side of town; just a little bedsit above a bookmaker's, nothing fancy, but somewhere he was free to see whatever kind of people he liked, have a broadsheet newspaper delivered to his own door if he wanted, spend weekends in London or walking in Cassiobury Park, feeding the ducks with his own stale bread. He would tell the old man that independence had been his biggest priority when he was seventeen, that he'd secured it by sacrificing the luxury of an education — something he felt he could always return to when he was older. He would tell him that getting the job at Cedarbrook and moving to Cambridge had been the biggest achievement of his life. And if the old man were to say, 'Yes, but don't you regret leaving school? You could've been so much more,' he would look away and smile, and explain the feeling that pricked his spine every time he wandered through town, passing by those ancient college buildings, and how he'd trained himself to ignore it. Soon, the rain would begin to soften outside. The noise of the residents downstairs would get louder, and the nurse-calls would start ringing again. And Oscar would tell the old man his only regret: that the was living the unremarkable life his parents had always expected from him.

But this discussion was for another day. The past wasn't something he felt ready to talk about with Dr Paulsen yet. He thought of it as a stinging wasp he'd trapped inside a glass: though he could still see it there, long sedated, he didn't feel secure enough to lift away the glass and release it.

'I don't need you to feel sad for me, Dr Paulsen.' He placed a hand on the old man's arm. 'Just let me keep coming up here to talk to you. That's enough for now.' He smiled, turning for the door. 'Thanks for the siesta.'

★ ★ ★

Iris said she couldn't even remember stepping out into Silver Street, or where she was supposed to be going. She didn't know the size, shape, or colour of the van that had hit her. She could hardly even recall the feeling of being hit or riding in the ambulance. All she could remember was that, before she'd seen the blazing headlights emerging from the fog, there had been a tiny moment when she'd known what was about to happen to her. She said it was like time had ruptured for a second, and the earth had stopped spinning. It had given her enough time to twist her body around. 'It was the strangest thing. It was instinct. I turned my back so the cello case would protect me. I didn't even know why I was doing it; I just knew it would save me. And it did. That little moment saved my life.'

Lying in her hospital bed against a bank of pillows, she talked in slow, uncomfortable phrases. Her caged leg creaked when she made the slightest move. She closed her eyes. 'Oh, this morphine is lovely, but it's making me so tired.' He thought that she was falling asleep, but then she looked at him, smiling. 'Thanks so much for your letter,' she said, 'and the poem.'

'There were things I needed you to hear. I

199

know I'm a terrible poet.'

'Nonsense. It was the most wonderful poem I've ever read.'

'Shut up. It was awful.'

'No it was *not*. I mean, I'm hardly an expert, of course, but who cares about a piddly thing like technique anyway? It's the intention, the emotion that counts.'

He stroked her wrist with his thumbs. 'I'd be more comfortable if you teased me about it.'

'That's what I'll never understand about you, sweetheart. When people try to pay you compliments, you tell them they're wrong, that something must be wrong with *them* for thinking nice things about you. Well, I'm not going to apologise. I love the poem, and I love you for writing it.'

He knew there was a difference between *I love you* and *I love you for writing it*. But the sound of the words still emptied the breath from his lungs. It was the first time he'd ever heard them spoken — by Iris, or any girl he'd ever been with — and they sounded much less formidable than he expected. He kissed her dry lips and she groaned with pain. 'Oh, this leg is just *agony*. I feel like a mashed potato.'

'Go easy on the morphine. You don't want to get addicted.'

'Does that really happen to people?'

'A lot.'

'Then I suppose I'll just have to get used to the pain, won't I?'

Hospital noises flooded into the room — the clack of nurses' heels in the vinyl corridors, the dulled-out conversations of soap actors on next door's television, the coughs and wheezes of patients — sounds he knew so well.

'Have you heard from Eden?' she asked. 'I thought he would've been in to see me by now. Funny, my parents seem to be in a bad mood with him. Did something happen?'

'He went off somewhere last night. Your father had words with him, in front of everyone.'

'You're kidding!'

'He was acting blasé about everything — you know how he is. Anyway, your dad really gave him what for.'

She shook her head, wondering at the idea. 'Do you know, I can't even imagine what that must've been like. What did my mother do?'

'Nothing really. Your dad was angry enough for both of them.'

'Oh, I'd give anything to have been there. No wonder they kept changing the subject when I asked about him.' She stared towards the window, thinking. Her eyes turned to thin slats. 'He'll probably keep his distance for a few days, let things cool down. But he'll visit me. I know it. He won't be able to keep away.'

In fact, a week went by before Eden came to visit. Oscar arrived at the ward at the usual time, carrying a few books he thought Iris could pass the time with. He stopped when he saw Eden through the darkened glass of her room and held back in the corridor, peering in from an angle. That tall, wiry frame of Eden's loomed like the shadow of an oak tree at the end of her bed. He was wearing a long black mackintosh and his hair was pulled back into the slightest ponytail with a bright blue elastic. His ear-stud caught the light of the corridor and glinted. Oscar didn't feel guilty about eavesdropping. He saw it as insurance against a possible disaster.

'These doctors can only help you so much, you know,' Eden was saying. 'I mean, I'm sure you'll be back on your feet by the summer, but can you really afford to take so much time away from study right now?'

'You're sounding just like Dad.'

'Yes, well, Theo knows what he's talking about. Missing out on a whole term will set you back a year, maybe two.'

'I can catch up. All I have time for now is reading.'

'It's not just about reading. What about your labs? And that placement you were going to do? You'll miss out on that. They'll give the job to somebody else. Someone who can actually stand up. Have they told you how long it'll take before you can walk again?'

'I'm not worried. Things will work themselves out.'

'I don't know how you can be so calm about this, Iggy.'

'Don't call me that. I've told you to stop calling me that.'

'Yes, yes, fine. But you know what I'm saying. This is very important.'

'There's not much I can do about it. I just have to accept it.'

'Nonsense.' Taking a step back, Eden unhooked

the clipboard from the foot of the bed and perused her medical notes. It made a thick, metallic sound when he put it back again. 'I can help you.'

'You going to attend my lectures for me? Take my exams?'

'No, no, don't be silly, of course not. You know what I mean. I mean I can *help* you.'

Oscar moved in closer to the door.

Iris lifted her chin. 'Ah. Well, why didn't you just say so?'

'I've been trying to,' Eden said. 'You haven't been listening to me.'

'I don't know. You really think you could fix me? This isn't exactly superficial damage I've got here, Edie. The doctors say I'm going to need months of physical therapy.'

'You won't need any of that, I promise.'

'Well — I don't know — I'm not sure.'

Oscar couldn't tell if she'd seen him standing there, or if she could see anything beyond her brother's broad, flat shoulders. He got the impression that she was amusing herself somehow, that she was toying with Eden for the sheer pleasure of it. And though all he could see was Eden's back and those white socks that stood out from the bottoms of his cords, he could tell that Eden was not aware that he was being strung along. There was a resoluteness to his stance, a patience in his manner.

'If I did let you try,' Iris went on, 'how exactly would it work?'

'You just leave all that to me.'

'But what would I have to do?'

'Nothing. Just lie still.'

203

She paused. 'Alright.'

Eden drew his heels together slowly. 'I promise you, you'll be back on your feet before the spring.'

'I'll believe it when I see it,' she said. 'When would we have to start? Now?'

'No, no, not here. As soon as they let you come home. When are you being discharged?'

'Friday. They need the bed. You should've seen how happy the doctors were when I asked for home care.'

'Well, what do you expect from an NHS hospital? I tried to get Theo to move you, but that boyfriend of yours made a big fuss. Sometimes I wonder what the pair of you have to talk about.' Eden drummed his fingers on the bedframe. 'I take it you'll be staying in the rectory when you come home.'

'No, the organ house. More space in there. You don't mind, do you?'

'Not at all. In fact, it couldn't be better.'

'Good, because I'm rather looking forward to being waited on.'

'I wouldn't count on Mother sitting at your bedside,' Eden said. 'Or Theo either. He's been peacocking his feathers over your surgery, but once you're home it'll be a different story.'

'If you say so.'

'I *know* so.' Eden sniffed. 'Next week then. That's when we can start. I'll get everything prepared.'

'Alright.'

'And don't bother worrying about all of this now.' Eden gestured towards his sister's legs. 'I'll have you feeling better soon.'

He walked over and offered his cheek, pointing at the exact spot he wished to receive her kiss. 'Be well, sis,' he said.

Oscar retreated quickly into the corridor. He waited until Eden came striding out of the room, heading for the lifts.

'You're a terrible snoop,' Iris called out. 'I saw you the second you arrived. You heard every bit of it.'

'So what if I did?'

'Don't get defensive — I'm glad you were there. It's the first time anyone's been around to witness my brother's ego in full swing.' She nodded at the books under his arm. 'They for me?' He set them down on the table-tray and kissed her. She shuffled the books in her hands like playing cards, studying their covers one by one. 'We're going to be ready for him this time,' she said. 'You heard how he was talking. He doesn't care about me, he doesn't care about my surgery, he just sees it all as some big opportunity for him to prove how clever he is. He's too full of his own importance to even notice what he's doing. Well, I'm going to make sure we catch him this time. He's starting to slip. Oh, you brought me *The Fountainhead*. Is this actually any good? I've heard so many bad things about it.'

Oscar didn't answer, and she satisfied her curiosity by flipping the book over to read the blurb. 'How do you mean, catch him?' he said.

'We're going to get everything on tape. I don't

really have a plan yet, but I will. It's too good a chance to miss. If he wants to use me as some sort of guinea pig, fine. But we'll be there, ready with a plan of our own. All we have to do is think of one.'

LAST DAYS

Like a man travelling in foggy weather, those at some distance before him on the road he sees wrapped up in the fog, as well as those behind him, and also the people in the fields on each side, but near him all appears clear, though in truth he is as much in the fog as any of them.

— *Benjamin Franklin*

8

The Remote Possibilities

Oscar felt bruised by the city the moment he stepped off the train. King's Cross thundered with a million tiny sounds: the heel-march of commuters, the scrape of wheels against the tracks, the rainfall on the rooftop, the clash of deployed umbrellas. He was hardened to the London rain, the way it made the whole town feel dirty, claustrophobic. Walking by St Pancras, he kept his eyes down. The giant old station with its dense red bricks and its soaring clock tower was the building that terrified him most in the world. When he was nine years old, his father had left him alone in the van one afternoon, parked facing St Pancras; and while he went off to see a man about some work at the Camden Library, Oscar had nothing to do but stare at that gothic railway station, noting every shadow under its spires and gables, imagining ghosts on every balcony.

By the time he got to Cartwright Gardens, his shoes were wet through. It was an attractive crescent of terraced houses — some were flats now, and some quaint little hotels — one sweeping curve of bricks that seemed perfectly round-edged, as if the place had been built around the lip of a saucer. At the centre of the crescent, where there might have been a park square, there was a tarmac tennis court without a net.

On the steps of number 41, he found Herbert Crest's name written on the buzzer and pushed it. 'Yes, hello?' came his muffled voice after a moment.

'It's Oscar Lowe.'

'Ah, you're right on time. It's the ground floor on your left.'

The lobby was bright and smelled like snuffed candles. It was modest and friendly, the kind of place where the residents had a committee and chatted on the stairwell, where neighbours stopped by uninvited and pushed wrongly delivered mail under each other's doors.

A young black nurse emerged from Herbert Crest's apartment, zipping up her raincoat over her uniform. Passing by, she said: 'Two hours — that's all you get. I'll be back later, yeah?' Then Crest appeared in the doorway, his face as pale as a sugared almond, and she called out to him: 'Don't forget to take your Dilantin, Herbert. Listen for the alarm clock.'

Crest waved Oscar inside. They went through the narrow hallway into the living room, where the old man gestured towards his leather couch like a practised psychiatrist. 'There's nothing the matter with Bram, is there? I know you said there wasn't on the phone, but I need you to put me at ease.'

'No. I'm here about something else, someone else.' Oscar removed his coat and sat down.

'You'll forgive me if I don't believe you. Bram Paulsen works in mysterious ways. I told him back at The Orchard — we're okay, him and me. Can't we just leave it at that? I don't want to hear any second-hand apologies.'

'This isn't about Dr Paulsen. He doesn't even know I'm here.'

'Good. Glad we understand each other.' Crest slowly levered himself into an armchair. 'Oh, damn it, I forgot to pour the coffee. Would you mind? Once I'm down it's hard to get back up again.'

The apartment had the solemnity of a doctor's office. Papers and files were piled into an organised mess on the bureau, on the dining table, on the floor. There was a serious regiment of medicine bottles lined up on the coffee table. A laptop computer was humming on the ottoman beneath the window and there was a glass display case in the corner of the room, which housed a collection of tiny ornaments arranged in a meticulous formation.

Oscar went into the nook of the kitchen. Two mugs and a cafetière were set out on the counter, ready to pour. The calendar on the fridge was sketched with reminders, the first week of February already crossed out. Crest called: 'So do you think we might cut to the chase here, kid? I have to get back to my writing before noon.' He left no gap for a response. 'My editor's a hardass, worse than my nurse. She wants my final draft done by the end of March, and I've got a pile of notes to get through. I think it's her way of telling me it has to be finished before I die. I said to her, *Listen here, Diane, I think you're taking the word deadline a little too literally.*'

211

Oscar laughed. He carried two cups of coffee back into the room and handed one to Crest.

'You're a handsome kid, aren't you? I can almost tell what Bram sees in you.'

Oscar gave an awkward smile.

'Oh, relax, I'm too old and too sick to make any moves on you. Just take it as a compliment.'

He sat down and sipped his coffee, feeling Crest's eyes upon him. There was a pause between them. Inside the apartment, the city felt gentler, like something containable. Pigeons circled the sky outside the window. The rain had stopped but there were still spots of it descending the glass.

'So, come on, kid, out with it. Don't hold back.'

'It's kind of a long story.'

'Oh, everybody always says that. If you want me to say *start at the beginning*, I'm not gonna.'

'Are you this tough with everybody?'

'I learned from the best, remember.'

Oscar explained everything he knew about Eden Bellwether. About how they'd met at King's College Chapel, and all the things he'd said about Descartes and Johann Mattheson. About how he'd been hypnotised and injured by him, and how the wound had disappeared a few days after. About Eden's email and the *New York Times* article, and the way Eden seemed to figure out their connection to Dr Paulsen, as if he wanted the two of them to be brought together somehow, as if he were playing games with them. About all of the things Iris had told him of their childhood, the stunts Eden had pulled when they were kids, the damage he'd done, the wounds he seemed to have healed. About everything he'd learned about Narcissistic Personality Disorder from Crest's own book.

Crest just sat there all the while, nodding, making noises of interest and agreement, scratching the stubble on the underside of his chin. He seemed intrigued by what Oscar was telling him, contemplating his words, stopping him sometimes, mid-flow, to ask a question or make a comment ('And you say you had no awareness afterwards that you'd been hypnotised?' 'You mention predictions — what kind of predictions?' 'Did you feel in danger? Or did it all seem like harmless fun?' 'That's the thing with these kinds of charlatans — they all think they're infallible, unshakable, but, trust me, if you stick around long enough observing them, the mistake always comes.'). By the time Oscar told him about Iris's accident and how Eden had promised to heal her before the turn of spring, it was well past noon, and the coffee had gone cold in his cup. There was tiredness in Crest's eyes; they kept drooping towards the carpet and closing over. The daylight was heavy on his sheer bald head.

'Well, alright, Oscar. I've listened to you, and I've got to admit it's mysterious. This friend of yours could be an interesting case. Bottom line, though: I can't help you. I don't have much time left, and it pains me to let a good opportunity slip by, but I've really got to concentrate on my book right now if I'm gonna get through all these edits by next month. I'm sorry you came all this way for nothing.'

'But your book is partly why I'm here,' Oscar said. It came out more desperately than he intended. 'What I mean is, I think Eden would be a perfect case study for you.'

'Maybe so. I just don't have any time to waste on discovery.'

'But what if he could actually help you?'

'Excuse me?'

'He might really be able to make you better.'

Crest laughed so loud it seemed to hurt his whole body as it came out of his throat. 'You're kidding me, right?' He looked like a teacher who'd been asked an inappropriate question by a child in his class.

Oscar chose his next words carefully. 'I don't really believe he could heal you, Dr Crest. But then again, I'm not completely sure that he couldn't — not enough to rule out the possibility, even if it's just the tiniest, tiniest possibility. And isn't that what your book is meant to be about? Those remote possibilities? Isn't it about trusting in things that seem like madness?'

'You're in the right ball park, I guess.'

'All I'm saying is, Eden's the strangest, most conceited person I've ever known. He probably has some kind of illness, maybe NPD, I'm not sure. But even if he *is* ill, it doesn't mean he's not onto something. The irrationality of a thing is no argument against its existence, right? You wrote that yourself.'

'Actually, Nietzsche wrote it, I just quoted him.'

'Well, couldn't you just take a look at it? See it

214

for yourself before you make any decisions.' Oscar picked up his coat from the arm of the couch. The wool was damp and smelled musty to him now, like those patients' wardrobes at Cedarbrook that were filled with old dinner suits, worn once and hung out for generations of moths to feed on. Stuffed into the inside pocket, the cardboard sleeve of the video tape was still dry. He took it out and showed it to Crest, whose eyes narrowed at once. 'Do you have a machine I can play this on?'

Crest studied the black cassette. 'In the bedroom,' he said.

★ ★ ★

The plan had been beautiful in its simplicity. Oscar and Iris had conceived it across the stiff linens of her hospital bed only two months ago. Every avenue of it had been considered. They'd talked it over so many times as she'd lain there in recovery, studying the dots on the suspended ceiling, her leg braced and elevated. It was a practical plan, disaster proof. And it had worked without a hitch.

In the days before Iris was discharged from the hospital, Oscar had put everything together. She'd given him her credit card and told him not to worry about how much any of it might cost — just to get whatever they needed. He'd found a website called The Spy Shop and bought the smallest video camera they had. It was a black and white pinhole camera, small enough to be concealed inside a book on Iris's dresser; digital,

215

with good resolution, and a long thin cable that could run down and hook up to a video recorder in the cupboard beneath. From the same site, he'd bought a seed microphone, which had a head no bigger than a wood louse and could be contained inside a pillow — the webpage had said it was the same model the police used undercover. The parcels had arrived at his flat the next morning, tiny and light as jewellery boxes.

Iris came home from Addenbrooke's on a brisk afternoon in early December. Everyone was there to meet her, waving in through the passenger window as her father's Alfa Romeo halted on the driveway.

Her parents stepped out of the car first. 'Okay, everyone, stand aside, give her space,' Theo said, and went around to open the door. Iris hobbled out with her father's help and the aid of crutches. Her left leg was held straight by a metal scaffold and she struggled to stand upright, keeping all of her weight on her right side, wincing with the pain.

'Welcome home, Iggy,' Jane called out, and everyone sounded their hellos.

Iris just nodded. Slowly, slowly, she moved along through the side gate and into the back garden, her crutches rattling over gravel and flagstones, everyone following patiently behind her. Reaching the organ house, she seemed surprised by the GET WELL SOON banner that was stretched out across the doorway — thick blue letters painted on a bedsheet by Jane earlier that afternoon, hung by Marcus and Yin. Inside,

216

the organ house was adorned with bouquets of flowers, helium balloons, and paper chains. There was a Christmas tree twinkling with fairy lights in the far corner, and gold and silver tinsel was strung across the room and around the posts of the bed like parcel ribbon. The door to the big oak wardrobe was open and all of Iris's clothes — moved from Harvey Road — were hanging inside dry cleaning bags, freshly laundered. 'You shouldn't have gone to all this trouble,' she said, standing in the willowy light. 'I've only broken my leg.'

'We're just glad you're back,' Yin said. 'You had us all worried.'

'Yeah. It's a celebration,' Oscar said.

'You're too important to go stepping in the way of traffic,' Marcus added. 'Don't do it again.'

'Hear, hear,' said Theo, helping Iris onto the bed, twisting her legs around and propping them on a mass of pillows. Again, Iris rocked with the pain. Oscar, seeing her pain, felt it too. The others looked at her with faces of sympathy — all except Eden, who simply loitered near her bed, expressionless, saying nothing at all. He stood with his arms folded, his right hand fingering his weedy left bicep, as if practising a piano tune.

'Come on, everybody — out.' Theo clapped his hands together, shooing them back into the garden. He turned to his daughter. 'You need to rest that leg awhile, okay? I'll come back later with your tablets.'

'You don't need to fuss over me, I'm fine.'

'Nonsense. I've taken the day off work.'

'Oh, Dad, you needn't have done that.'

'Tough luck.'

'Where did Mum go?'

'She went back up to the house. Had to make a call.'

Iris threw her head back against the pillow and looked around the room. 'It's so lovely in here. The light is so gentle.'

'As long as you're comfortable.'

'Thanks, everyone, for looking after me like this,' Iris said. 'I have such good friends. Come in and see me later? I want to hear all your news.'

Everybody started filing out, waving goodbye-for-now. Eden trailed slightly behind, hands deep in his pockets. Oscar could see him in the corner of his eye. 'Wait, hang on, sweetheart!' Iris called out.

Eden turned first. 'Yes?'

'Oh, no,' Iris said, her voice softening, 'sorry, I meant Oscar.'

There was a palpable silence in the room. Eden cleared his throat a little meekly and said: 'Of course. Of course you did.' He walked away, head lowered, and Oscar could smell the stale odour of his body as it passed by him in a gust. Jane went to catch him up, calling, 'Eden, darling, slow down!' The others followed. And soon it was just the two of them, alone in the great yawning space of the organ house.

Iris made sure the doors were closed before she took his hand and asked: 'Is everything set?'

'I did it this morning, first thing. Nobody saw me.'

'You're sure?'

'Sure as I can be.'

'So where is it?'

'Where's what?'

'The camera, dummy.' Her eyes flicked from wall to wall.

'Best you don't know. Then you won't give it away.'

'Yes, okay, makes sense.'

'I just need to show you how to work the microphone.' He took the tiny device out of his pocket and instructed her how to switch it on. 'Keep it inside your pillowcase, okay? It'll pick everything up, though, so try to keep your head still. And the wire runs right along the skirting board, so don't be too rough with it.'

She smiled wearily. 'Wow. This is almost exciting.'

'I wouldn't think of it that way, if I were you.' He kissed her lips — they were parched and briny. 'Your dad's right — you need to get some sleep.'

She closed her eyes. Cold daylight fell down through the glass ceiling. The helium balloons quivered with the gentle draught. 'Do you think this'll work?'

'Probably not,' he said, 'but anything's worth a try.'

★　★　★

The video played out now on the dusty TV screen in Herbert Crest's bedroom. It was a black and white image, a little misty around the edges, the way silent movies tend to be, but

219

the clarity of the picture was good enough: nothing out of focus, nothing too pixellated. After a minute of scratch and fuzz, the TV speakers jolted on and began to hum with the drawl of organ music. There was a surging quality to the sound — a flood of notes followed by a slow and searing drone, going back and forth, back and forth.

The camera didn't move. It zoned in on one section of the organ house, where Iris lay half-under the covers on the four-poster bed, her left side exposed, her leg braced. In the near distance, there was the blur of a familiar shape — a shadow swaying in the chalky light, like the silhouette of a candle flame against the wall. It was Eden. He was sitting at the organ console with that unmistakably straight back of his, fingers sprawling across the keys at an urgent pace, then slowing. As he played, he stared straight ahead, never down at his hands. He tapped the sole of his left foot against the pedals, emphasising the rhythm. And as the music lurched on, it gathered force, until the passive tap of his foot became a stamp. Through all of this, Iris didn't move a muscle in the bed. Her eyes were closed. 'It goes on like this for another twenty minutes,' Oscar said. 'I'll wind it forward.'

'No, hold on,' Crest replied. 'Leave it. Let it play out.' He folded his arms, eyes trained on the television. They stayed there together in the shade of the bedroom, with the outside world closed off behind the curtains, until the music stopped. Eden twisted on the organ stool, turning his pale face towards the camera at last. Even from far away, there was that familiar buffed-apple sheen in his eyes.

They watched as Eden stood up and walked out of the picture. A few seconds later, he came back into the frame, carrying a set of wooden ladders, and placed them at the side of the organ console, beneath the column of metal pipes that towered over it. Without a sound, he climbed the ladders. Only his legs remained in shot. He stayed there like that for a long moment; then finally he began to step down. Bit by bit, the top half of his body came back into the frame. He held something under his right arm: a bundle of fabric, bright white and limp.

'What's he got there?' Crest asked.

'Keep watching,' Oscar told him.

Eden jumped the last rung of the ladder. Hurriedly, he carried the bundle over to Iris, who was still lying in the bed, unmoving. She seemed to be asleep. He loosened the brace around her leg. She didn't even flinch. Then, carefully, delicately, Eden lay a white towel from the pile upon her broken bones. It looked heavy and sodden, and steam appeared to rise from it. He lay another one over her, then another, coating her whole leg in white. There were several of them lined up along her left side. Just above the knee, where Iris's fracture was at its worst, he placed another, doubling up. He stretched his arms out in front of him, the heels of his hands pointed down at Iris's leg. He lowered them until the flats of his palms were barely a centimetre above the towels and held

221

them there, trembling. Minutes went by. Nobody moved. Then Eden simply walked away, towards the camera — he was so close that his hip almost brushed the lens as he went by. Iris remained perfectly still on the bed — the only movement was the rise and fall of her ribs as she breathed. Oscar must have watched this video twenty times, but this was the first time he'd noticed the trails of tears on her cheeks, captured by the light.

With a dull flicker, the screen went blank. Crest kept staring at the TV set, though it was playing nothing but a flatline of grey. He scratched his scalp. 'How many of these tapes do you have?'

'This is only the first one. I've got twenty-odd more just like it.'

'Are they all the same?'

'Identical, more or less. Apart from the music — that's the only thing that changes. He did the same thing every day for four weeks, but he played a different piece of music every time. Until she got better.'

'In four weeks she recovered?'

'She was on her feet by the new year. You'd have to see her to believe it.'

Crest sniffed. 'Well, her leg couldn't have been too badly broken — '

'It was. I can show you the X-rays.'

'X-rays can be deceptive.'

'You're right, it doesn't make sense, I know it doesn't. But what can I say? At the start of December, her leg was basically held together by screws and nails. The surgeon told us it would be at least six months before she could put any weight on it. By Christmas, she was up on her feet. Now it's February and she's walking around the place like nothing ever happened.'

'I don't believe you,' Crest said. He snapped his head away. He rubbed his jaw. He sighed. 'How do I know you're not playing me for a fool here? No offence, but I hardly know you. Why should I trust anything you're telling me, just because you know Bram Paulsen? Hardly a ringing endorsement. No, no, this doesn't change anything, not really.'

There were noises now in the hallway: the latch on the front door snapping shut, a set of keys being dropped onto the telephone table. A deep, Caribbean voice called out: 'Herbert, I'm back. Everything okay?'

'I'm in the bedroom!'

After a moment, the nurse came to poke her head around the door. 'Oh,' she said, seeing Oscar was still there. 'Didn't mean to interrupt. Did you take your Dilantin?'

'Yes, yes, stop fussing,' Crest said.

'Alright, I surrender. Just making sure.' She closed the door.

Crest waited a second, listening to her disappearing footsteps. 'Let's not tell her I lied. One missed tablet won't kill me.' Then he turned his eyes again to the TV screen. 'The thing with the towels — what was that?'

'You really want to know?'

Crest nodded.

'He wraps them around the pipes of the organ.'

'When they're wet?'

'I think so.'

'Huh.'

'All I have to go by are the videos, and what Iris can remember.'

'She doesn't remember all of it?'

'No, just little things. The before and after.'

'Are you suggesting the towels absorb the music in some way?'

'I'm not suggesting *anything*. I'm just telling you what I've seen.'

Crest began to bend his ankles up and down, as if he wanted to stride across the room but his body wouldn't let him. 'Normally, these people pretend they're channelling some ancient spirit or other. They say their souls have been possessed by some religious character, always with a name like Jehosephat or Jeremiah, and they always happen to talk like Hannibal Lecter whenever they're channelled. I've seen so many of these idiot charlatans, and they're all the same. *This* guy, though — he's not pretending to be channelling anything, is he?'

'No, I suppose not. He talks a lot about Johann Mattheson, that's all.'

'Mattheson, huh? That's interesting.' Crest went quiet again, scratching the same dry spot on his scalp. 'Alright, so tell me this, kid — what's in it for you?'

'What do you mean?'

'Come on, don't play coy. You know what I'm talking about here. Why should I help this guy? What are you getting out of it?'

'Nothing.'

'Bull*shit* nothing. You want this guy out of the way. He's making problems between you and this girl, right? This, what's her name — Iris. That's what your agenda is here. No need to be ashamed about it. I just want you to be upfront with me.'

When Oscar looked at Crest, he couldn't help but think about what Dr Paulsen had said — about the two of them being alike, how they both thought about life the same way. He stared down at Crest's gaunt face and those dark, swollen eyes that wrinkled at the corners, wondering if he was seeing a reflection of himself in another fifty years.

'I'm here because, deep down, I know that Eden's ill. And if everyone goes on allowing him to think he's got some godly powers to heal the sick — even if he's clever enough to make other people believe it too — something terrible's going to happen. You're right, I love his sister — and I don't want to ever see her in pain again — but that's not what this is about.' He stopped, feeling the weight of Crest's attention. 'Because I'm also willing to accept that I might be wrong — that there's the tiniest, remotest chance that Eden has some kind of power or understanding that nobody else has. And, knowing that, how can I not report it? Isn't it my duty to tell somebody who might be able to figure it out one way or another, who might even stand to benefit from it himself? The way I see it, we have nothing to lose.'

'We're not the only ones to consider here,' Crest said, steepling his fingers. 'You're not thinking about what might happen to the kid when I prove he's not so special after all. A realisation like that can tear someone apart. Look what happened to Jennifer Doe.'

'Yeah, I've thought about that.' Oscar turned off the television and pushed the button to eject the video. He waited, tapping the lid of the VCR.

'It doesn't concern you?'

'Not when I remember she drowned a five-year-old.'

The video slid out of the machine with a robotic noise. Oscar already had his fingers on it, pulling it free, but Crest said: 'Leave it.' His voice was weary, sore-throated. 'No promises.'

9

Near Allied

Oscar waited for Iris to finish her second cigarette on the steps of the University Library. It was past nine, but the building was still open, and there was a warm light behind the carousel doors. She was telling him things he'd long grown tired of hearing: how she would never be able to thank her brother enough for what he'd done but, oh, what a drag it was to be back on her feet again, how sometimes she wished she could've just stayed in bed all year. 'I keep thinking back to being in the hospital,' she said. 'It was so lovely to be taken care of like that — all those doctors and nurses making sure I was okay, bringing me things. Nobody expected me to study when I was in there. My father didn't even talk about coursework. All I was expected to do was watch the telly and read *Cosmo*. And I know that life can't go on like that forever, but now we're halfway through term and I'm feeling guilty about having one measly cigarette break, I just get this horrible urge.'

'What kind of urge?'

'I don't know. To run out and break the other leg, I suppose.'

'Don't say things like that,' Oscar said.

'Alright, calm down, I was only kidding.' She tossed her cigarette to the ground and trampled it. 'I just wish I could spend the whole night with you instead of Moore and bloody Dalley.'

'Who?'

'It doesn't matter.' She looped her arm through his. 'Can't we just hide out here for a little bit? I don't want to go back in there yet.'

The change in Iris was becoming more obvious and troubling to him. Now that she was back on her feet again, there was a general impatience about her. She was easily distracted, unable to settle, and smoking more cloves than usual — at least a pack a day. They could hardly get through a meal together without her telling him she needed to rush off somewhere. Back in January, they'd been midway through dinner at their favourite Algerian place and she'd told him she was so bored of the food that she never wanted to eat there ever again. Last weekend, on a perfectly nice February afternoon, they were having coffee in Market Square and she'd emptied out her cappuccino onto the ground and told him it was 'an insult', then gone into the café to demand a refund. When she'd moved back to Harvey Road for the start of the Lent term, he thought it would make things better, bring everything back to normal. He thought it would be easier for them to find time for each other without the constant commuting to Grantchester, but it had only become more difficult. Lately, they'd relied on these fleeting moments of togetherness between her study sessions and his shifts at work. 'What can I say, sweetheart?' she would tell him. 'I'm playing catch-up with everything now. I've got to read seven chapters before my supervision tomorrow or it's game over for me on the entire Tripos.' But this wasn't what troubled Oscar most. Even when they did find time to be together, the spectre of Eden was always looming over them.

She talked about her brother differently now — so lovingly and magnanimously. Gone were all the hopeless doubts of November. She was convinced by him. Conscripted. 'He's really an extraordinary person, you know. There's a selfish side to him, of course, but that's true of anyone,' she would say. Often, Oscar would catch her examining her leg like it was a prosthesis she was trying on for the day; or he would overhear her talking on the phone to her parents, saying: 'You should really come down to King's one night and hear him play. I think he misses seeing you in the crowd. Oh, alright, if you're going to be pedantic, the *congregation*. Will you just come out one night? He wants you there, I can tell.' Sometimes it took all of Oscar's strength and resolve not to shake her by the shoulders. He wanted the old Iris back, the girl he'd known before the accident, who could finish a meal, and find time for him each night, and talk about her brother reasonably, without such blinkered sentimentality. Most of all, he wanted to remind her of the plan they'd made before Christmas.

Now they were both looking out from the steps of the library for somewhere to go. Across the street, the windows of the West Road Concert Hall were bright yellow, and beyond the surrounding trees, a private tennis court for the Fellows of Trinity College was bathed in the shimmer of lampposts.

Iris noticed the soft, inviting light hanging above the fence. 'Let's go in there,' she said.

'What for?'

'I don't know. We'll improvise.' She strode off towards it, without looking back to see if he was following.

He could hardly believe that she was the same girl whose bedside he'd been tending just a few months ago. She walked with only the slightest trace of a limp on her left side. There was a bounce in her step, more poise and purpose. The scarring on her leg was still visible, but barely. He wanted nothing more than to get near enough to touch her again. She seemed to have been keeping him at arm's length since coming back to Cambridge. If she took a shower before bed, she would dress herself in the bathroom and emerge in baggy, washed-out pyjamas, and sleep with her back towards him. If he tried to kiss her neck, she would flinch, pull the covers around her. And if he ever tried to raise the subject of the plan they'd made, or mention the idea of meeting Herbert Crest, she'd divert the course of the conversation to something else: the follow-up appointments with her surgeon, the lymphocyte slides she was studying with her lab group, her exam timetable. It worried him.

The tennis court was coated in leaf skeletons. Iris went over to tighten the sagging net with the crank-handle. Then she hunched down on the service line, awaiting some invisible top-spin serve, twirling her make-believe racket in her hands. 'Come on, Oscar,' she said. 'I'll let you be

Agassi.' She lunged to the right, to the left, swatting the air with her fist to practise her imaginary strokes, making *pock* sounds with her lips. 'When we were kids, Eden always wanted to be Ivan Lendl. We made our own grass court in the garden. He wasn't very good, but he tried very hard, took it all very seriously. He'd come out wearing his tennis whites, sweatbands and all. I don't know why anyone would want to be Ivan Lendl.'

Oscar let it go. He moved to the opposite side of the net.

'Here comes my serve.' She threw the invisible ball into the air and smashed it towards him. It bounced in, somewhere close to the tramlines, or so she claimed with a pointed finger. 'Fifteen-love. Don't be holding back on me now. I want to see your best groundstrokes.' Her exhalations steamed.

He felt a little self-conscious, swiping at the air and pretending to follow the path of the ball, though he found himself anticipating her returns and considering his footwork. They back-and-forthed like this for several points. He assumed she'd grow bored soon enough. 'Advantage Agassi,' she called out. The faint moonlight settled on her face.

'Shouldn't you be taking it easy?' he said.

She shrugged. 'Dad says I'm okay to run on it.' She swung her arm and hit another imaginary serve. He just stood there. 'That was a let.'

'Iris — you need to be careful.'

'I'm fine. You heard what the doctor said — I'm the fastest healer on the planet. And if I break it again, so what?' She hit another serve. 'I'll just get Eden to fix it for me.'

He folded his arms. 'You can't be serious.'

'Hey, I thought you were Agassi, not McEnroe.'

'You don't really believe that, do you?'

'What? About Eden?'

'Forget it,' he told her, and walked away. 'I don't want to hear it.'

'Oscar — '

She came after him. He heard the shuffle of her steps over his shoulder as he reached the fence.

'I was just kidding. God, you're no fun lately — what's the matter with you?'

He turned and looked at her sternly. '*Me?* There's nothing up with *me*. It's you, Iris. You're practically another person. It's like the last few months didn't even happen.'

'I don't know what you're talking about,' she said, flitting her eyes away.

'Do you know how often you bring him up?'

'Who?'

'Oh, for God's sake, Iris, you know who.'

'Well, he *is* my brother. And he *did* fix my leg. I'm just proud of him, that's all.'

'You really believe he healed you.'

'Of course. It's my body, I should know.' Her fingers groped for his arm. 'Sweetheart, look at me. Look.' She gestured to her legs, as if presenting a new pair of shoes, jumping on the spot, dancing around. 'Look at what he did. How can I not believe him any more?'

'It wasn't him, Iris. It just seems that way. It's a coincidence.'

'Of course it was *him*. It had to be. I know I was sceptical about it before, but — '

'Sceptical? Iris, you thought he was mentally ill. You begged me to help you prove it.'

'Well,' she said, and paused. 'That was before.'

Oscar had seen her change of heart coming. It had been a gradual thing: an occasional compliment about Eden on the phone had turned into questions about the ethics of their plan each time Oscar had come to visit, and finally a lack of interest in seeing the videos, an unwillingness to even acknowledge them. Somewhere between the first towel Eden placed on her leg and the first free steps she took across the organ house floor, she had given herself the licence to trust her brother completely, after so many years of resentment and accusation. It had brought her a new kind of happiness, and sometimes Oscar felt guilty for trying to dismantle it. But he kept reminding himself of the conversation they'd had back in November, when she'd sat with him by Magdalene College and made her first appeal for help. How distressed she had seemed then, how close to breaking.

He tucked a strand of her hair behind her ear. 'Look, there's something I need to tell you, Iris,' he said, then waited, wondering if it was the right thing. 'I know you said you didn't want me to do it, but I went to see Herbert Crest last week.'

She stared back at him, deer-eyed. The slightest noise came from her mouth — a gentle wash of air. All she said was: 'Oh.'

'Don't you want to know why?'

She shook her head.

'We had a plan, Iris.'

She stayed quiet.

'I know you feel differently now, but I'm trying to keep to that plan we made. We decided it together, didn't we? We promised we wouldn't back out. One of us has to see it through. I promised to help you with your brother, and that's what I'm going to do. No matter what.'

She looked down at her leg as if it were some toddler who'd come clinging to her side, overhearing a conversation much too adult for its ears. Her smooth, pallid kneecaps showed through the rips in her jeans. 'Fine, if you want to get Crest involved, get him involved.' He could tell from her tone that she wasn't serious. 'But he's only going to find out what I found out. And he's probably going to wish he hadn't.'

'You're not mad about it?'

'Your heart's in the right place, I suppose.' She removed the pack of cloves from her coat and shook the last one out, holding it tightly between her lips. The matchflame brightened her face. She took a long, laboured drag and blew the smoke out, slow and even. 'Do you know how hard it is to sit in a library, learning about the clinical relevance of blah-blah-blah when you've seen what I've seen? I can't care about what it says in textbooks any more — all that pointed, straight-down-the-middle science talk. It used to make complete sense to me. But now I can't even get to the end of a chapter without thinking about my leg, and what Eden did. It makes a mockery out of everything I've ever held important. Those textbooks seem so out of step now, so conventional.' She gave another limp shrug of her shoulders, peering up at him. 'So, maybe you're right. Maybe I *have* changed lately, I'll admit it. But only because my whole world just feels so bloody different now. I don't know how to go back to where I was from here.'

★   ★   ★

Oscar woke up alone at Harvey Road the next morning. Daylight was pressing on the windows and Iris had left her usual mess of clothes on her side of the bed. Downstairs, the clink of cutlery was rising from the kitchen. He got dressed and went to get himself something to eat. Eden was at the breakfast counter, slicing the top off a boiled egg with a steak knife. He must have heard Oscar's footsteps in the doorway, because he didn't look up from what he was doing, just said: 'If you want anything for breakfast, tough — there's nothing in. But I can offer you some orange juice. It might be a day or two past the sell-by.' He shook his fingers, wincing with the heat of the egg, and the severed top fell onto his plate.

'Where is everyone?'

'Gone to class. Left the wolf alone with the lamb. Tut tut.' Eden was still holding the knife, about an inch or so from his face. He twisted it around a few times, set it down beside his plate, then opened his book on the table and began reading.

Oscar went to pour himself some orange juice.

It smelled a little fermented, so he filled a glass with tap water instead and stood there drinking it.

'Don't you have work or something?' Eden said, hardly lifting his eyes from the book.

'Night shift.'

'How awful.'

'You get used to it.'

There was a sudden stirring from the washing machine. 'Well, please don't stick around for my benefit,' Eden said, chewing. He turned a page and added, nonchalantly: 'If you're going to stay over again, do me the courtesy of keeping your mouth closed. I can hear you snoring from the next room.'

This is how Eden had started to talk lately. He would utter snide remarks to Oscar when they were alone together, making no eye contact, and sometimes his voice would sound almost threatening. The disquiet between them had only worsened over the Christmas break. Though Oscar had spent most of the holidays at Cedarbrook, racking up the hours at triple pay, he'd accepted the Bellwethers' invitation to join them for lunch on Boxing Day. He'd expected it to be a grand occasion, all cravats and champagne and seafood canapes. He'd imagined a fleet of cars on the driveway, and an assembly of distant Bellwether relatives packed inside the house. But it had turned out to be a quiet affair: just him, Iris, Eden, and their parents, gathered around that too-large dining table. Oscar had taken his seat beside Iris, her crutches leaning on the chair next to her, and Eden sat across from them, supervising their behaviour.

Halfway through the meal, Theo asked Oscar if he had a favourite patient at Cedarbrook, someone to whom he might have given special attention. He qualified this by saying: 'Everybody has favourites. It's inevitable. When I was doing my first rotation at St Albans, there was an old dame called Mrs Garrett in the Renal Ward. She was always telling me how handsome I was and trying to get me to go out with her daughter. Anyway, I scrubbed in to observe her surgery and the poor woman died on the table — it was all very heartbreaking. For the rest of my rotation, I thought I was some sort of surgical Jonah. I was afraid to get close to patients after that. I got over it, of course, but I'll always remember Mrs Garrett's face.'

Oscar could have told Theo about Dr Paulsen, but he chose not to. His relationship with the old man was not something he wanted to discuss across the dinner table; it was not some inane topic that could be passed around like cranberry sauce for everyone to dip into. So he just said: 'No, I don't really have any favourites. I try to treat everyone the same.'

'That's admirable,' Mrs Bellwether said.

'Yes, very,' Theo agreed.

At this point, Eden had pushed his plate away. 'Oh, please. Of course you have a favourite.' He eyeballed his parents. 'His favourite is someone named Paulsen. Dr Abraham Paulsen, if I recall it correctly. Room 12, second floor. Isn't that what you told me?'

That had left Oscar almost speechless. He removed his napkin from his knee and politely

237

dabbed his lips. 'I don't remember telling you that.'

'Oh, well, ignore me. Perhaps I got it wrong. Or perhaps you were a little, you know — ' Eden made a tipping motion with his hand, as if drinking from some miniature champagne flute. '*In vino veritas* and all that. There's no need to lie about it.'

Iris weighed in: 'Alright, Eden, I think you've made your point.' She placed a hand on Oscar's knee, beneath the frill of the tablecloth. Her voice had an engaged sort of tone. If she was trying to take someone's side by entering the conversation, Oscar wasn't sure whose. She turned to look at her mother. 'He wasn't trying to lie. I'm sure he just didn't want to discuss it, did you, Oscar?'

He didn't know what to say. He'd expected her to defend him, not give some half-hearted apology for his presence. 'I — '

'A lie of omission is still a lie.' Eden tilted back in his chair.

'Stop badgering the boy and finish your lunch,' Theo said, standing to retrieve the carafe of burgundy from the centre of the table. 'I wish I'd never brought it up.'

Oscar had excused himself from the table and gone into the bathroom just to have some time alone. He had a seasick feeling in his bones, and it stayed with him long after Boxing Day. It was still there now, as he stood in the kitchen at Harvey Road, watching Eden spoon the whites of his eggs into a cereal bowl. There was a stale air coming in from the hallway and the washing

238

machine was turning slowly. He drained his water and set the glass down on the counter. 'Can you tell Iris I'll call her later?'

Eden gathered his book and went back to reading. 'I'll be sure to pass it on.' His pupils rolled upwards. 'Will that be all? Or would you like to stay and help me fold my delicates?'

'Just make sure you tell her.'

Oscar went into the hallway to look for his shoes. They were lodged between the wall and a pair of Jane's wellingtons. He was tying his laces when Eden appeared by the doorjamb, picking his teeth. 'I've been thinking,' Eden said. 'You really shouldn't worry about my sister's — you know — her patterns of behaviour.'

'Her what?'

'Don't tell me you haven't noticed. She always goes for the rough diamond types. First there was that ghastly labourer she slept with, and then the rugby players, and those other handsome but ordinary types — ' Eden stopped, inspecting the floor. 'And now there's you. There's a pattern. If you ask me, I think she likes a project. Someone she can put a shine on.'

'Is that right?'

'Just an observation.'

'I don't remember asking for your observations.'

'Shame.'

'And I really don't care what you think.'

If Eden was startled by the sudden failure of their courtesy, it didn't register on his face. 'That's what I'm telling you,' he said, stepping forward. 'Why should it matter what anyone thinks? My sister knows who she wants. She can be incredibly stubborn about things.' Eden was staring at him with that usual self-congratulatory smirk. 'We don't need to discuss it if you don't want to. I just thought it might be concerning you. Like this thing with the old man.'

'What old man?'

Eden placed a hand on his shoulder. 'Come on. You know who I mean.'

Oscar could see his own tiny reflections in Eden's eyes, bearing down on him. 'I don't know what you're talking about,' he said.

Eden gave a short snicker. 'Listen, you don't have to play dumb with me. My sister tells me everything. I mean *everything*. All I'm saying is, people have a habit of letting other people down, breaking promises they made to each other. And I really hope you're not going to be another one of those people.'

'You're not making any sense, Eden.'

'I want you to say it.'

'Say what?'

'I want you to say you'll keep your promises.'

Oscar felt the pinch of Eden's fingernails upon his shoulder. 'Fine. Okay. I'll keep my promises.'

Eden removed his hand and smiled. 'Very glad to hear it.' He straightened out the front of Oscar's coat, backing away along the hall. His stocking feet made no sound. 'There's a quiet little place I know, not too far from here. Plenty of greenery, not many people. If there's a certain somebody who wants my help, I'd like to meet him there.' He got as far as the kitchen door, then turned. 'Thursday week is good for me, but stay by your phone in case I change my mind.'

10

Wives of the Above

'Isn't that him, in the corner?' Iris pointed to the far end of the hotel restaurant, where Herbert Crest sat alone at a large circular table. It was nine a.m. on a Thursday morning, and the Crowne Plaza was half empty, just a few businessmen loading plates with croissants at the buffet, a mother feeding her baby out in the lobby. 'You might've warned me. He looks so fragile.'

'What did you expect?' Oscar said.

'I thought he'd seem more — I don't know — '

'Alive?'

She gave a rueful nod. 'Yes, I suppose I did.'

They walked across the monogrammed carpet to Crest's table. 'You'll forgive me if I don't get up,' the old man said. His skin was oily, shellacked with colourless pimples. 'The mind's still there, but a decent wind could blow me over.' He waved a hand at the empty chairs in front of him. 'Sit, sit. I woke up with an appetite. Let's eat before it abandons me.'

'Are you feeling okay?' Oscar asked, sitting down.

'So-so. Thanks for checking.'

'Your nurse isn't with you?'

'She's up in the room. I'll page if I need her.'

Crest pulled at the peak of his baseball cap, gazing at Iris across the table. 'Well, I've got to say, you're quite a picture, honey. Something told me you'd be prettier in person — I was right.'

Iris smiled. 'Nice to meet you too, Dr Crest.'

'Now *there's* a sentence I don't hear very often.' Crest gave a croaky laugh, leaning forward. He nodded at the envelope in Iris's hand. 'I see you brought what I asked for.'

Iris slid it towards him. He removed two X-ray films and studied them under the light of the mock chandeliers. 'Well, I'm not a bones man,' he said, 'but I know enough to see this was a pretty bad break. Would you mind walking around a little so I can take a look at your gait?'

Iris did as he asked, striding between the tables, where businessmen looked up from their laptops, admiring her. Oscar watched Crest watching her.

'Can I sit down now?' she said, returning to the table.

'Of course you can. Thank you, sweetheart.'

'So you believe me?'

'Oh, I never doubted you. I just needed to check something out.'

'What?'

'It's not important right now. Let's order, shall we?'

They talked about nothing but Eden over breakfast. The whole meal passed by like a preparatory meeting between lawyers. Crest wanted to know so many things. He began by questioning Iris about what he called Eden's 'methodology', and she told him what little she could recall. 'I passed out every time, so I can hardly remember anything. You've seen the videos — you know as much as I do. But I do remember feeling this lovely warmth surging through my leg when I woke up. And I remember my brother telling me not to try too hard to listen to the music beforehand, but just to let it fall over me — like the rain, that's what he said. I should let it fall over me like the rain. And it did sort of feel like that. It put me to sleep.'

'Do you remember anything about the music?' Crest asked.

'If you mean, could I hum the tune for you now — no. If you mean, do I remember it being there, all around me, and what it felt like — yes, I do. It felt wonderful. Soothing. I really mean that.'

'I wasn't questioning your honesty.'

'Well, good, because I don't have any reason to lie.'

Crest rested his elbows on the table. 'What about those towels he put on the organ pipes — can you tell me anything about that?'

'No. I don't remember any of that. It surprised me when I saw the videos.'

'You don't recall *anything*?'

'No.'

'And what about Eden himself, while it was all going on — did he say anything to you, or mention anything else out of the ordinary?'

'No. Nothing I can remember.'

Crest was being polite about it, but Oscar

knew he was frustrated with Iris's answers. The up-and-down motion of his eyes gave him away. He went on to ask about Eden's relationship with his parents.

'Well, he's always been the golden boy,' Iris answered, 'but he's been arguing more with my father lately. They both sort of look up to each other, I think. That sounds strange, but it's true. They talk to each other like they're work colleagues sometimes. Eden calls my father by his first name. It can be quite peculiar, I suppose, to people on the outside, but they've been that way all my life. It's not strange to me.'

Crest looked at Oscar. 'Did you find it peculiar?'

'The first time,' he replied. 'But I'm sure if you met my parents you'd find *them* twice as peculiar. People have their own habits.'

'I guess so.' Crest paused. 'Did they put any kind of pressure on him?'

'How'd you mean, pressure?' Iris said.

'You know, academically, socially.'

'Hardly at all. But then again, the academic life always came naturally to Eden. *I'm* the one they lean on most about grades. Really, my brother always seemed to have some sort of immunity from their expectations. I'm the one who they pushed towards a medical career. And socially? Well, we've always sort of existed in our own little bubble. Boarding school can do that to you. We don't live the same way as your average Cambridge students. I suppose we're kind of on the fringes of things, but deliberately so. We like to be on the outside looking in. That's how we've always been. But we still have a close-knit group of friends, don't we, Oscar?'

He nodded and smiled. The waitress arrived with their plates.

'Oh, at last,' Crest said. He stared at the well-presented breakfast on his plate: lean bacon, lightly poached eggs, granary toast, a ramekin of beans. 'I was hoping for something a little less healthy.' Crest cackled, throwing his napkin over his lap and flattening it out with his palms. 'So, tell me, honey, what should I expect when I meet this brother of yours today? Suspicion? Humility? What?'

'Oh, you won't find a humble bone in my brother's body,' she said. 'But he has every right to feel superior, given what he's capable of. He's a remarkable person, really.'

'Remarkable how?'

'Well, you know . . . ' She paused, chewing. 'You've seen the videos. There isn't enough room in his head for all of the things he knows about.'

'Is that so?'

'You'll find out for yourself, soon enough.'

Oscar looked at her, thinking this was the kind of sentence Eden might well have spoken himself. But if Iris recognised this fact, she didn't allow it to show. She set about refastening her earrings, absently.

'Tell me about what he was like as a child,' Crest said.

'Oh God, *really*. Do we have to go into all of that?'

'You don't think it's important.'

'It probably has some bearing on things, I

suppose, but I don't buy all of that Freudian Oedipal nonsense, if that's where this is heading.'

'No, I prefer to steer clear of Freud. I've always been more of a Jungian, anyway. But I'd still like to know about your life together as children. I do think it's important. If you don't want to talk about it, I won't push you.'

Iris blurted out: 'It was mostly idyllic.' She said it proudly, resolutely.

'What's your idea of idyllic?'

She told him about the cherry blossom trees, and the marquee birthday parties, and the tyre-swings by the riverbank, and the backyard tennis court; about the history of her parents' house, the rectory, the organ house — all of the things she used to tell Oscar about when they lay together in bed at night, holding each other in the darkness. How he missed those nights. It had been months since they'd held each other like that.

'We were given just about everything we ever asked for,' she went on, citing the grand piano that Eden had been given for passing his Grade 8 music exam when he was nine, and the family holidays to Tuscany and Egypt and Long Island and Barcelona. 'When my brother was sixteen, he asked for a diamond tie-pin from this famous antique jewellers in London, and my parents got it for him. It cost a fortune.'

'Is money important to him?'

'No. He treats it like — like, I don't know, talcum powder or something. He's got so much of it, he throws it around everywhere without thinking.'

'And what about you?' Crest said, his voice turning sympathetic. 'Did *you* ever get anything?'

'I got plenty. We were never competitive like that — he got things, I got things. I was never jealous of him.'

'Wasn't suggesting you were.'

'I know, but still.' Iris took a gulp of Darjeeling.

'Was he ever jealous of you? Of anything you were given?'

She gave this a small amount of thought, looking sideways at Oscar. 'Nope.'

Crest struggled to cut through his bacon, then gave up. He picked up his coffee and slurped it. 'Can you think back to the very first time your brother healed you? And I'm using that word advisedly, for want of a better one.'

'Oh, I don't know, it was a long time ago.'

'How old were you?'

'Hard to say exactly. Seven or eight.'

'See, I'm trying to pinpoint what I like to call a trigger moment. An event that seems innocuous and ordinary but is actually the opposite. Oscar's already told me a few things, but I guess I'm looking for something more. Can you remember anything that might've happened around that time — something that might've happened earlier that day, or vaguely around that timeframe?'

She folded her hands on the table. 'I really can't remember that far back. We were just little children.'

Crest looked at her, heavy-lidded. 'Okay.' He turned a little in his chair, facing Oscar. 'May I speak candidly here?'

'Of course,' Oscar replied. 'It's difficult for her to remember, that's all.'

'Yeah, but I think it's important that we're all on the same page.' Crest twisted back to Iris. He wiped his hands on his napkin, finger by finger. 'This is a delicate situation with your brother, and I've got to say before we go any further, my stance going into this thing is that he isn't blessed with any kind of special powers, however much you might believe in him. In fact, I think the whole idea of healing — spiritual, alternative, whatever you want to call it — is totally preposterous.' Casually, he scooped up some beans with his fork and left it hanging over his plate. His words were frank, but his expression was kindly. 'That being said, I've seen a lot of dimestore healers over these past few months, believe me, and what intrigues me about your brother is that he doesn't fit the typical mould. He doesn't seem to be in it for the money, at least. Maybe for him it's about the adulation of his family, the prestige, or maybe he likes to be able to prove how smart he is to his friends. I don't know. But as a psychologist, I find him a very compelling subject, and that's the only reason I'm here today. I'd like to get to know him further. Don't get me wrong, I have a GPM tumour in my skull — I'd be very happy if he could rid me of my problems — but I think we all know that's beyond him. Right?'

Iris just tilted her head. She was about to say something, but Crest wasn't done.

'I don't know how much Oscar's told you

about my new book. I've been writing a lot about hope. My theory is that hope is a form of madness. A benevolent one, sure, but madness all the same. Like an irrational superstition — broken mirrors and so forth — hope's not based on any kind of logic, it's just unfettered optimism, grounded in nothing but faith in things beyond our control.'

She smiled politely.

'I know you think your brother healed you. The way you were striding around the place just now, I could tell. Hell, you're probably even a little proud of the guy, right? That's to be expected. But you're gonna have to get this into your head from the beginning, honey — I'm not here to prove anybody right or wrong; I'm just here to see what I can learn about your brother, and hopefully I can help him. Okay?'

It surprised Oscar to see how relaxed she was about the situation. She leaned forward, placing her fists beneath her chin. 'That's perfectly alright, Dr Crest. I can understand why you'd think that,' she said. 'I used to think exactly the same way. You have a very modern mindset.'

'Please, call me Herbert.'

'Okay. Herbert then.' She grinned at him. 'It is — it's a very modern mindset. Instead of a blind faith in God or spirituality, like we had back in ancient times, now we have this devotion to the logic of science. In facts, in what's provable. And that's fair enough, I suppose. But our modern faith in science has become just as blind as our old-fashioned faith in God.'

'No, honey, I think you'll find it's called

evolution. We've come a long way since the olden days.' Crest looked for support from Oscar, but he kept quiet, not wanting to be disloyal to either of them. 'Science deals only in facts. And facts, as you point out, are provable. They're tangible things we can quantify and assess. So, for that very reason alone, they're worthy of our faith. Religious faith, on the other hand, relies on storytelling — and that's not a trustworthy foundation for anything.'

'Right. I believe in science,' Iris said. 'I'm not saying we shouldn't trust science more, I'm just saying we shouldn't close the door on everything else entirely because of it.'

'Okay, I can sort of see your point there, but — '

'Look, Herbert, it's a matter of open-mindedness, that's all.' She cut him off, and Crest looked rather taken aback. He laughed, reaching for his coffee cup. 'We have to keep the door open — just a crack — to ideas we think are preposterous. We can't completely decry faith in God just because we can't prove God exists. That's illogical in itself. There are things we can prove with science today that we couldn't prove a hundred years ago — quantum physics, let's say. Einstein could've pioneered advances in quantum theory but he didn't because his faith in God limited him. He couldn't extend his line of thought that little bit further because he was blinded by what he believed in — the harmony of what exists, or whatever. But the same is true of people now, of people who believe so rigidly in science that it stops them following up

250

on ideas, different modes of thought that could lead to breakthroughs. It works both ways. People need a faith in science *and* a faith that science doesn't have the answers to everything. Even scientists need to be open to miracles.'

Crest wagged his finger. There was a little more colour in his face now, and Oscar wondered whether all this debating was doing him good. 'Ah, but quantum theory was always potentially provable. God can't ever be proven to exist. He can't ever be proven *not* to exist either.'

'I think you're wrong about that. I read your book about Jennifer Doe. You weren't *completely* convinced she was deluded.'

'Oh, I'd say I was ninety-nine point nine per cent.'

'Right. That's our margin of probability. Point one of a measly per cent. It's a tiny little margin, but it's there all the same, and we shouldn't ignore it. That's all I'm trying to say.'

Crest downed his coffee. It was clear that he wasn't used to being interrupted by anybody, and he was trying not to let it affect him. He signalled to the waitress. The skin on his cheeks was blotched red now, and his neck seemed bloated, too big for his collar. 'You've got a fine young woman on your hands here, Oscar. Beautiful *and* smart. I think I'm a little afraid of her.' Crest leaned back. 'She's the kind of girl that makes me glad to be queer — and I mean that in the nicest possible sense. There's just no way I'd be able to keep up with you, honey.'

'Well, thank you, Herbert,' she beamed. 'I aim to please.'

'Tell me, though. Why do you think your brother agreed to meet me today?'

Iris took a long time to respond, setting her knife and fork down neatly on her plate, in the half-past six position, as if to show off the good manners her parents had instilled in her. The restaurant was now empty and sunrays were beginning to whiten the windows. 'I think he wants to help you. I think he knows that if he can heal you — someone who'd never believe such a thing could be possible — then it might shake up the world a little bit, make people believe in things again. Believe in God, the soul, whatever. Or maybe he just wants the world to know how remarkable he is. He's convinced *me* of it . . . ' She breathed in a jolt of air. 'Why do you think he agreed to meet you, Herbert?'

Crest rubbed at his clean-shaven face. 'Because, deep down, he knows his delusions are spiralling out of control, and he's reaching out for my help. I've seen it time and time again.'

'Oh,' she said, sounding disenchanted by his answer. 'Well, I suppose you'll just have to ask Eden, won't you?'

'I will.'

She gave a fey little nod of her head. 'My brother's enormously intelligent, Herbert. You'll see that for yourself. He's not the kind of person who does things without thinking them through.'

Crest shrugged his eyebrows. '*Great minds are sure to madness near allied, and thin partitions do their bounds divide.*' He waited to see if Iris recognised the quote, but she didn't. 'John Dryden . . . The smarter they come, the more

252

sophisticated their delusions are. I knew a classics professor once who said he was Socrates reincarnate. He was pretty convincing, too. Had the knowledge and the intellect to back himself; knew all about the times, the history, the artefacts of the period. You just couldn't trip that guy up on anything.'

'Well, maybe he *was* Socrates. Who knows?'

'No, honey, he was just an ordinary man from Denver. He just loved history so much he tried to make it his reality. And *that*'s what we're really talking about here. No matter how much I love reading about Socrates and admire the man's ideas, I'm not going to go around pretending I'm him. Your brother's read too much Descartes and too much of this Johann Mattheson. Their ideas are great, but so outmoded. The world's moved on since then. And it sounds to me like your brother's trying to make them come alive again the best way he can.' Crest paused, seeing the change in Iris's body language — she'd folded her arms *at* him, one slow movement at a time. 'Look, who knows? I haven't met the guy yet. Maybe I'm wrong. But if you want my opinion, he's probably just another kid who's too intelligent for his own good. Way smarter than anyone else in his peer group. Probably even smarter than his parents. And because of that, he has trouble with intimacy. He thinks nobody else is on his level, nobody else is smart enough to understand him, so he doesn't let anyone get close to him. The only intimacy he gets is through books he reads, music he plays, written by people he considers to be intellectual equals

253

— your Matthesons and your Descartes — both of whom were child prodigies themselves, by the way, and that's no coincidence.' Crest padded his lips with his napkin. 'In case you're wondering where we all factor into this, I'm afraid we're just spokes in the wheel. Spokes in the wheel of one giant coping mechanism your brother's created for himself.'

There was a protracted silence. Oscar found himself wishing Jane could be there to smooth out the awkwardness of the moment with some bad pun or endearing quip. He knew that everything Crest had said about Eden was right — it had to be — but he wasn't going to admit this in front of Iris. Soon, the waitress came to clear the table and Crest insisted on charging the meal to his room. 'Listen, I'm feeling a little weary. I was thinking I'd take a nap before we go. You don't mind, do you, Oscar?'

'Not at all. I'll walk you.'

Out in the lobby, the old man kissed Iris goodbye — a short peck on each cheek which she accepted rather grudgingly — and she went off down the escalator, heading for her morning lecture with her X-rays under her arm. Oscar took Crest up in the lift and helped him along the too-bright corridor to his room. Crest swiped his card in the lock but the light wouldn't turn green. He tried it a few more times before his nurse pulled back the door and said: 'You're not doing it right, Herbert. Come inside.'

'I'll never get the hang of these things.' Crest headed into the room. 'Later, kid. Thanks for chaperoning.'

'Do you need any help?'

'Hang on,' the nurse said. She lowered Crest onto the bed, covered him over with a blanket the way Oscar had done a thousand times at Cedarbrook. 'I'm going out for a smoke,' she told the old man. 'I'll be back to give you your tablets when you wake up.'

She rode down in the lift with Oscar and they got to talking. She told him her name was Andrea and that she was originally from St Kitts, but moved to London with her family when she was thirteen. He told her that he was a nurse, too, and she said: 'Cool. Where did you do your training?'

'Oh, I'm just a care assistant.'

'*Just* a care assistant? Don't be doing yourself down now.'

'I mean I'm not qualified.'

'Well, why don't you take your qualification? It's not so hard.'

'I don't know,' he said. 'I suppose I've never really wanted to.'

'Prob'ly a reason for that.'

'I'm not sure it's what I want to do long term, that's all.'

Under the hotel carport, he waited while Andrea lit up a cigarette and drew on it thirstily. 'You think I wanted to be a nurse when I was your age? No way in heaven!' Her voice had that perfect Caribbean lilt. 'I wanted to be a drummer like Carlton Barrett. But I'm happy with how things turned out. I like my job. And when you have nice patients, it makes things easier. Like old Herbert up there — he's such a

255

kind old man. I feel so sorry for him.'

'He seems to be battling through.'

'At the moment, he's not too bad. But you know he's off the chemo now.'

'I thought that meant he was getting better.'

She shook her head. 'No. It means he's past the point of rescue.'

Andrea told him what she knew about Crest's illness. She said he had a glioblastoma multiforme tumour. 'That's a grade four. The worst kind. It means it grows these tentacles — *fingers* they call them — that are so tiny that the surgeons can't even see them. So although they can cut out the bulk of it, there's always tumour cells left behind.' She said he'd already had three surgeries and the doctors refused to do any more, because it would only worsen his quality of life. 'Compared to other tumour patients I've seen, he's a lucky man. They gave him no more than two years to live and almost three have gone by. He started writing the book about a year ago and I think it's really helped him. Sometimes he's too tired to write, but I sort of think it's keeping him alive, that project of his — having something to focus on, you know? He writes a lot at night, when he can't sleep. I try to keep his spirits up as much as I can. I tell him his hair's growing back since the chemo finished. He seems to like that.' She wet her fingertips and pinched out her cigarette; it fizzed like electricity. 'Anyway, I better go back and make sure he's sleeping. Promise me you'll look after him today, wherever it is you two are going.' She brushed the ash from her uniform.

'Don't worry,' Oscar said. 'I'll take good care of him.'

★ ★ ★

Mill Road cemetery was basking in a wide spray of sunlight when they arrived. 'I guess this is his idea of a joke,' Crest said, settling down on a wide wooden bench. 'Meeting a dying man in a cemetery. Don't know whether to laugh or cry.'

For a graveyard, everything seemed wild and alive: the holly bushes overgrown, the grass left to sprout in long tufts around headstones, the branches of trees entwined with creeping ivy. Elaborate tombstones were sunken into the soil, slanting out like bad teeth from the gums of the ground. Crest studied their surroundings with tired eyes. He was dressed for a Siberian winter — a parka, sheepskin gloves, and a brown fur Cossack hat — and still he complained of the cold. His skin was as pale as the late February sky, heavy with sweat, and it had that candlewax translucence again, like it had back in The Orchard. He was still gathering his breath after the short walk from the roadside, where he'd climbed from the taxi and taken the bend of Oscar's arm. Those fifty yards or so, following the tracks of mourners in the trampled grass, were enough to remind Oscar just how ill Herbert Crest was, and just how galling it must have been for him to lower himself to this kind of desperation.

'Well, punctuality doesn't seem to concern the kid,' Crest said, checking his watch. 'I guess that shouldn't surprise me.'

'Iris is late for everything too.'

'Runs in the family, huh?'

'Yeah. I think it's a boarding school thing. He'll be here, though.'

'I might freeze to death before he shows up. Then we'll both be screwed.'

They sat for a good while in the peaceful cemetery, waiting for Eden to arrive. Crest soon became restless. He pointed to the great marble tombstone in front of them — a white cross, raised up high on a granite plinth. 'Look at that. How's that for an epitaph, huh?' The top line of the inscription read: DAVID PALMER 1825–1862. CHERISHED FATHER, BROTHER, UNCLE. FOREVER IN PEACE. The bottom line read: MARY PALMER. WIFE OF THE ABOVE. 'Boy, what a kick in the guts. Her entire life reduced to four little words.' Crest rubbed his gloved hands together and blew on them. 'Just FYI, I'd like my headstone to say: 'Here lies Herbert Crest. Now fuck off and leave him alone.'' He crowed at his own joke, then stopped when he saw Oscar wasn't joining in. 'Lighten up, huh?'

Oscar couldn't help feeling it was discourteous to laugh in a graveyard. But he knew Crest's glibness was just his own kind of coping mechanism. Didn't dying men have the right to laugh in the face of what was coming to them, after all? The lighter death was made, the easier it was to bear.

Crest was still snickering when Eden appeared from behind the bushes, strolling towards them. He gave a genteel wave of his hand. The sun was behind him and it presented his thin shadow over the ground, shortening with every step he took in their direction. It seemed he'd made an extra effort with his clothes: aviator sunglasses, a yellow cotton polo shirt with a white jumper tied around his shoulders, and navy slacks. His hair was gelled back, parted at the side. All of this gave him the air of some old-time movie star, out for a stroll along the boulevard, though his body still had the ungainly profile of a folded-up parasol. He walked right up to the bench and stood in front of them, levering his sunglasses to rest in his hair. 'Hello again, Oscar. Isn't it a wonderful morning?'

'I suppose.'

'I hope you don't think this is bad taste. Didn't consider the irony of it 'til after we spoke.' He gestured to the jury of headstones that stood all around him. 'You aren't offended are you, Dr Crest?'

'It'd take more than a bad joke to offend me, kid.' With considerable effort, Crest got up to greet him. They shook hands tentatively.

'What should I call you?' Eden said.

'Anything you like.'

'I think I'll stick to Dr Crest.'

'Fine by me. Shall I call you Eden?'

'That's the only name I've got.'

'Alright then.'

Oscar watched the two of them. They were examining each other the way chess players do across the board, the way presidential candidates do from their podia — presenting their nervousness as amusement. Thin smirks drew

259

across both of their faces. There was quiet again, until Eden said: 'You look rather cold.'

'I'm alright. Just a little tired of waiting.'

Eden took a deep breath in through his nose and held it there. His nostrils closed over like the stops on a clarinet. Then he released the pent-up air from his mouth with a satisfied sound — *ppaahhhh*. 'It's always so quiet here. Really clears out those cobwebs.'

'You're too young for cobwebs,' Crest said. 'You want to see cobwebs, take a look in here.' He tapped his temple with a pointed finger. He was about to say something else, but suddenly he was stumbling on his feet. 'I'm sorry, excuse me, I'm feeling a little dizzy.' He sat back down on the bench.

'Are you okay, Herbert?' Oscar asked.

'Yeah, yeah, I'm alright. But I think we need to speed this up a little.'

'Good idea,' Eden said, and turned to Oscar. 'Would you mind giving us a moment alone? I'd like to examine him.'

'Examine him?'

'Yes.'

'You're not his doctor, Eden.'

'I'm well aware of that, thank you.'

'I don't think I should leave him,' Oscar said. 'I told his nurse I'd look after him.'

'He'll be fine with me. I'm here to help him, not harm him.'

Oscar waited for the old man to nod his approval.

Crest gave one slow, solemn blink. 'Go on. Do as he says.'

There was another row of benches on the other side of the cemetery, with a clear enough view for Oscar to keep his eye on things. 'I'll be over there if you need me.' He left them to face each other, feeling nervous about it, like a fist-fight might suddenly break out between them. By the time he got to the other benches and looked back across the lush grass of the graveyard, Crest had removed his hat and Eden was standing over him with two hands held against the old man's shoulders, staring down at the scar on the top of his skull. Eden stayed there, holding that position for several minutes, as if scrutinising every line and freckle on the old man's head. Then Crest seemed to fall into his arms. His body was a deadweight and Eden took the burden of it, carefully turning the old man around, lying him down flat against the bench. For the slightest moment, his head hung limp from the edge until Eden moved to cradle it in two hands. He crouched down on his haunches beside Crest and, with the dispassion of somebody testing the air in a football, began to knead his skull with the tips of his fingers.

Oscar didn't know whether to go over there or not — the old man didn't seem to be in any discomfort — but he watched Eden carefully. There was nothing sinister about what was happening. In fact, the whole process seemed almost brotherly, just one man tending the bedside of another. Eden's hands prodded and pressed around Crest's head. There was no sound but the wind in the trees, and the murmurs of couples as they went arm in arm

261

through the cemetery, stopping to read the epitaphs of sisters and mothers, husbands and fathers, wives of the above.

It must have gone on like this for ten, maybe fifteen minutes, until Eden rose from his haunches and turned Crest back into a sitting position, supporting his head the way you might hold a newborn's. Crest's body regained its stiffness; he flexed his elbows a few times and slowly rolled his head on his neck, a full rotation. He replaced his hat and sat there, saying nothing. Eden turned around. Bringing his fingers to his lips, he sounded a wolf-whistle that made the birds explode from the hedges in frightened packs.

Oscar took his time. He wasn't going to come running just because Eden demanded it. He got up and tied his shoelace on the bench, then the other one, even though it didn't need retying. Labouredly, he moved his feet through the long grass. The first thing he noticed when he got over there was that the old man's forehead was no longer sweating.

'Here's the situation,' Eden said. There was something very businesslike about him now — no more kidding around, no more cursory chat. 'Obviously, this man is very ill. You don't fool about with cancer. I'm going to need some time to think about this.'

'What's there to think about?' Oscar said.

'I — ' Eden paused. His self-confidence seemed to falter. That looseness in his shoulders, that movie-star brashness was starting to abandon him. 'I'd like some time to think about it, that's all.'

'Time isn't something I have much of, kid,' Crest said. 'You gonna help me or not?'

Eden straightened the tied-up sleeves of his jumper. 'Look, it's going to be very difficult. These aren't broken bones we're looking at here. You have a GPM tumour. It can't be fixed with a paean and a few towels like my sister's leg.'

'Are you saying it's beyond your capabilities?' Crest asked.

'No, no, I didn't say that.' Eden wagged his finger. 'I can do it, I just need a bit of time to think over the details.'

'How long?'

Eden removed his sunglasses from their perch in his wiry hair. Holding them by the hinges, he studied the lenses for smears, blew on them, wiped them with his jumper, and placed them back over his eyes. 'Two weeks,' he said. 'Let me get the Lent term over with.'

'I think we can manage that,' Crest said. 'Provided I can stick around that long.'

'And what then?' Oscar said.

'I'll let you know.'

'Now you're starting to talk like a *real* doctor,' Crest said.

'There's just one caveat,' Eden went on. 'Are you still taking your medication?'

'Of course.'

'I'll need you to stop taking it.'

'Right away?'

'No, not yet,' he said. 'But you have to be ready to stop when I tell you to.'

Crest raised his eyebrows at this. He thought about it for a few seconds, rubbing at his jaw,

263

leaving red fingermarks on his skin. 'Y'know what? That's fine. It makes me nauseous anyway. But you have to do something for me in return.'

Eden sniggered. 'Aren't I doing enough already?'

'I want you to promise me a sit-down when this is over.'

'A sit-down. You mean, you want me to lie back on a couch and tell you about my childhood.'

'No. I'd just like to talk to you some more. Get to know you.'

Eden shrugged. 'Okay. Fine. As long as I don't have to look at ink-blots or tell you about my dreams. I'm not shy when it comes to talking about myself. You can have as many sit-downs as you want.'

'Good.'

'In the meantime, go back to London and rest. I'll be in touch.'

Crest tried to stand up again but Eden waved him back down. 'Don't get up. I'll see myself out.' He smiled and shook the old man's hand cordially. 'You know where to find me, Oscar.' And with a casual flick of his finger, he pushed the sunglasses to the bridge of his nose, and walked away, along the same worn path from which he came. They watched his lean body strolling into the distance until it vanished behind the bushes.

'Well, that was a trip,' Crest said. 'He doesn't like *you* much, does he?'

'Not lately, no.'

'I wouldn't worry about it.' The old man got to

264

his feet with a groan. 'A guy like him has a hard time keeping friends. Reminds me of some of the guys I used to know back when I was at King's. Most of them ended up on the trading floor. He's got the same ugly confidence about him.' Crest sniffed. 'Shall we go?'

They walked back towards Mill Road, and though Crest made only gradual progress with each tired step, he no longer needed Oscar to help him stay upright. His skin seemed more opaque, and his breaths were stronger and more apparent in the air.

'Andrea's not going to be pleased about you stopping your medication,' Oscar said. 'You're not really going to, are you?'

'Way I see it, I've got to follow orders.'

'Why?'

'To keep things black and white, that's why. I don't want to give this guy a get-out-of-jail-free card for later. I don't want to give him the chance to say: *It didn't work because you carried on taking your medication when I told you not to.*' They reached the end of the graveyard where the grass turned to shingle and a dainty little church stood by the roadside, half-buried in weeds and overgrown trees. The quiet suburban neighbourhoods of Cambridge continued as normal, seeing and hearing no evil. 'Funny what he said about my tumour, though, huh?'

'He seems to know these things somehow. I don't know how he does it.'

Crest stopped. His exhalations swirled around his face. 'Thing is, I have a G-*B*-M — glioblas-toma multiforme. G-*P*-M? I don't even know what that is. That's not even *anything*.'

'So he was wrong for once. That's good. He's slipping.'

'Yeah, but that's not what bothers me about it. Don't take this the wrong way, but when I was talking with your girlfriend at breakfast, I think I might've said G-*P*-M — a slip of the tongue. My mouth was all dry with the bacon.'

'Oh. Are you sure?'

'I thought she'd correct me, her being a med student and all, but she didn't. That's why I remember it. Now her brother just made the exact same mistake. You think that's a coincidence?'

Oscar felt too shaken to answer.

'Yeah,' Crest said. 'I don't either.'

11

The Treatment of Our Mutual Friend

There was a time when Oscar would sigh at the very thought of Cedarbrook. He'd arrive at its black trellis gates in the winter to see the bare wisteria vines on the brickwork and the dour lights behind the early morning windows, and a heaviness would gather in his belly. He'd traipse towards the entrance, knowing the next five, eight, sometimes twelve hours would be nothing but a chore. The tang of iodine in the staff bathroom would make him cloudy-headed and he'd try to settle himself with a strong cup of tea before clocking on, and somehow it would never taste quite right — as if the milk was on the turn. But now he almost looked forward to work every day. He found himself enjoying the stroll along Queen's Road towards Cedarbrook, seeing the wide face of the building on the horizon like the genial smile of an old friend. He felt that Cedarbrook was the only thing about his life that was changeless — for all the headaches it gave him, and however exhausted he got from its routines, at least it could be trusted to remain that way forever. There was something to be said, after all, for predictability. There was comfort in seeing the same old fuzz-lipped women in the parlour every day, with the porridge stains on their dressing gowns and their balled-up tissues stuffed into their cardigan sleeves; and the bow-legged old chaps with their dogmatic way of reading broadsheets with magnifying glasses, column by column. He saw more of these people than his own family, and knew more about the day-to-day progress of their lives — sometimes he wondered if he even cared more about them. They were a cast of elderly relatives he was grateful to have adopted.

Most of all, Cedarbrook was a good place to hide. In the last week and a half, Oscar had taken on as many shifts as he could manage, because being at work gave him the perfect excuse to tell Iris when she called and asked why it had been so many days since they'd seen each other. 'Well, okay, but don't work yourself too hard,' she said, the first time she called. 'I know you need the money, but it seems like I haven't seen you in ages,' she said, the second time. 'I'm starting to think you're avoiding me,' she said, the third time.

On Saturday evening, he saw her number flashing on his mobile but chose to ignore it. He ignored her text messages too. He listened to the voicemail she'd left for him: 'Oscar, what's going on? You're not even answering the phone now? I miss you. I'm worried about you. I'm sort of afraid you've forgotten about me. You've met someone else? Is that it? Oh God, please ring me. Are you angry at me?'

'Angry' wasn't the right word. He felt betrayed by her, deflated and suspicious, and those feelings had grown into resentment. He wasn't sure he could trust her. When he saw her again, he knew he'd have to pay close attention to his words, worry about what he might let slip, in case she reported it back to Eden. And that made him think of all the times they'd lain together, held each other, walked through the Cambridge streets to each other's rooms, speaking with the kind of abandon that now seemed dangerous. He couldn't think of lying next to her, redolent from sex and second-hand smoke, with that same comfort he'd always felt with her before — the assurance that there was nothing in the world that he couldn't say to her. She had cheated on him — that was how he felt — not with her body, but with her spirit, her allegiance.

All of this must have shown on his face when he went to see Dr Paulsen that Friday. Though Oscar had been up to the old man's room many times in the last week or so, he'd managed to keep his disconsolation to himself somehow, held a cheeriness in his voice and a bounce in his step so nobody would notice the deflation of his heart. But that evening, Paulsen was lying flat on his bed in the dark, pillows and duvet strewn on the floor beside him. The curtains were drawn, and the only light in the room came from the Maglite torch that he was shining towards the ceiling — a ghost-white disc moving across the swirls in the Artex like a giant ophthalmoscope. The beam swung towards Oscar's face, and he squinted against the brightness of it. 'Turn that thing off, will you?' he said.

Paulsen kept on shining the torch into his eyes. He flashed his palm across the beam, laughing, and the light spat upon Oscar's face with a Morse code flicker.

'Cut it out, for God's sake!'

Startled, the old man clicked off the torch and the room went black for a moment. 'Alright, son,' he said, reaching for the bedside lamp, 'out with it. You've been tetchy all week. And I'm a man who knows what it means to be tetchy. Come on, let's hear it.'

'I don't want to talk about it.'

The lamp wouldn't go on at the push of Paulsen's fingers. 'I can't have my best nurse going about the place with a face like Armageddon. You need to put things into perspective,' he said. 'Think about Herbert, everything he's going through. If you think you've got it bad, son, you just remember what he's dealing with. Oh, for heaven's sake, help me with this thing, would you?'

Oscar kept quiet, fumbling with the switch until the lamp struggled on. He perched on the bed frame, unable to look the old man in the eye. There was a tightness in his chest. It had been almost a month since he'd gone to meet Herbert Crest in London and he still hadn't mentioned anything about it to Paulsen. It had been weighing on his conscience.

The old man's moods had been stable of late. He'd been less withdrawn, coming down for mealtimes more often, throwing fewer of his customary tantrums. Seeing Herbert Crest so close to death had been a strange kind of tonic for Paulsen, sobering and redemptive. Even the other nurses had remarked on it. But Oscar knew that if he uttered a single word about his meetings with Crest, all of this progress would come undone.

'What were you doing just then — with the torch?' he asked.

The old man smiled and flicked on the Maglite again, angling it towards the Artex. 'I was counting,' he said. 'It struck me yesterday that I've been staring up at this ceiling every night for years and I've never known how many grooves there are. A man can't go to his grave without closure on a matter like that. What if there's some sort of comprehension test at the gates of heaven, hmm? I'll be put in the cheap seats, and all because I didn't pay enough attention.'

Oscar could think about nothing but Herbert Crest as he left the old man's room. He'd made only one call to him since their meeting with Eden at the cemetery, just to check in, to make sure he was doing okay, and Andrea had answered the phone with her warm caramel voice: 'Hello. Crest residence.' She'd sounded so pleased to hear from him, saying, 'Oh, hey there, I was wondering if you'd call today.' Then she'd passed the phone to Crest, who'd wasted little time in getting to the point. 'I've already rewritten my introduction,' he'd said. 'I think you'll like it. Might just be the best thing I've ever written.'

They'd talked briefly about his state of health, glossing over it: 'Oh, you know, same old headaches, same old sputum. Any word from our friend?' Oscar had told him there'd been radio silence, and this had been Crest's cue to speculate on when — more like *if* — they would hear from Eden again. 'I'm sort of looking forward to seeing what he comes up with. I'm having visions of being stripped naked, lithe young virgins holding candles over my body, chanting mantras. Maybe that's just wishful thinking, huh?' Crest had said to call when there was any news. In the meantime, he was trying to keep his editor off his back, telling her what an exciting new course the book had taken, selling her the idea with 'some fancy talking', and doing preparatory research at the British Library. 'Turns out Andrea's a whiz with their Dewey system. She could find you a journal blindfolded.'

Before hanging up, Crest had lowered his voice, as if pulling Oscar to one side for a quiet word. He'd said: 'Listen, have you mentioned any of this to Bram? It's just, I'm not sure it's a good idea for him to know about it. If he hears I'm going to be in Cambridge for a while, he'll want to see me, and I really don't need that kind of distraction right now. I have to put everything I've got into this book, you understand?' Oscar had said he wouldn't tell Dr Paulsen anything. 'Good. I mean, don't get me wrong, I love that old man, but sometimes he can be suffocating.'

That Saturday night at Cedarbrook, Oscar came downstairs from the old man's room to find somebody waiting for him at reception. He saw a dark-haired stranger leaning on the counter, chatting with an agency nurse, and it took him a long moment to realise it was Iris.

272

She had dyed her hair coal-black and cut it into a bob, with a straight-edged fringe that rested upon her eyebrows; it made her look distinctly foreign, like some Balkan air hostess. It was only because of the merry whisper of her voice that he recognised her at all. 'I wasn't sure when I was sitting in the chair, but now I'm rather pleased with it,' she was saying.

'Yeah, it, like, really suits your face,' the nurse said. 'Makes your eyes, like, sparkle and stuff.'

'You think so?' Iris pushed at the back of her bob. It was then that she noticed Oscar approaching from the staircase, and she ran over to hug him. 'Hello, sweetheart,' she said, and stepped back dramatically to present her new hairdo. 'What do you think? You like it?'

'You look different.'

'In a good way, I hope.'

She hugged him again, kissed his cheek.

'It'll take some getting used to.'

He caught the synthetic fragrance of her hairspray — she didn't even smell the same any more. Her skin seemed chalkier when she kissed him, as if she was wearing more foundation than usual, and though he'd seen the clothes she was wearing many times before, there seemed to be something different about the way she was wearing them; a few more buttons undone, her skirt a little lower on her hips.

'Well, I had to get your attention *somehow*,' she said, looking hurt by his flippancy. 'You don't pick up your phone, you don't answer your messages.'

'I've been working a lot.'

273

'Every hour of the day?'

'More or less.'

'You're avoiding me, aren't you? Admit it — you've been avoiding me for weeks.'

The agency nurse was pretending to organise the files and papers on the desk. 'Let's talk about this outside,' he said, shepherding Iris out of the lobby by the taut cellist's muscles of her arm. They breezed through the porchway, into the clement March night, where everything felt so alive, full of scents. Instinctively, she moved to light a cigarette and he stopped her. 'You can't smoke here.'

'What?'

'If you want to smoke you have to go off the grounds.'

'Jesus, alright, fine.' She let her pack of cloves fall back into her handbag. This tiny disappointment seemed to upset her greatly. Tears began to show in her eyes. 'Oscar, are we drifting apart? It feels like we are. I mean, it feels like *you* are.'

'I don't know,' he told her. 'Maybe.'

Her eyes moved slowly to the ground. She pushed her shoe into the gaps between the flagstones, digging out the moss. 'I don't understand. Did I do something wrong?'

'Ask your brother.'

'What's *he* got to do with it? This is about you and me.'

'No, Iris, that's the point. It's never just about you and me.'

'But I thought we were together on this. Now that he's treating Crest, I thought — '

'Treating Crest? It's the other way round.'

274

'Yes, alright, however you want to see it.'

'That's how it *is*, Iris.' He was getting exasperated. 'This is exactly what I mean.'

'You don't have to shout at me,' she said, though he was sure he'd barely raised his voice. 'God, everything feels so different between us lately. You've changed so much.'

Now 'angry' *was* the right word. 'Oh, you've got to be joking.' He tried hard to contain the feelings that were building inside him. 'I know you tell him things, Iris.'

'He's my *brother*,' she said, emphasising the word as if he was not aware of their relation. 'Aren't I allowed to talk to my own brother about my boyfriend?'

'Not about private things. Not about stuff I told you in confidence.'

'I've never told him anything important.'

'There's no point lying about it. I *know* it. I've seen the proof.'

'Why are you being like this?'

'I'm not being like anything. I'm being real.' It was all coming out a little too quickly, in words that seemed unfair when he spoke them aloud, but he was too wounded by the sight of her to stop himself. 'I just wish I could have you without having *him*. You're not the same person when he's around you.'

She looked back at him with wide, wet eyes. Her mouth quivered with a pent-up sadness that fractured her voice when she spoke: 'Why are you being so cruel?'

'Because I'm hurt, that's why. You got me involved in all of this mess with Eden. I didn't even want to be a part of it. But you asked me to help you help him, so I did. Because I loved you — and I still love you — but this situation between us, it's just getting too much for me.' He took a breath, considering his next words. 'For you to go and tell him private things behind my back — I just don't know if I can forgive you for that.'

This seemed to get through to her. A kind of humiliation registered on her face, in the slackening of her brow, in the way she drew her eyes away from him in shame. All she said to defend herself was: 'Oscar, I — '

She began to cry. Tears rolled along her cheeks and streaked the foundation, revealing the truer skin beneath. He didn't move to comfort her at first, but the longer she stood there sobbing, the more she seemed like a frightened child who didn't understand what she was being scolded for. He took her by the shoulders, pulled her head towards his chest until he could feel the wetness of her tears through the cotton of his uniform. 'Look, I don't want to break up with you,' he told her. 'I just want you to be with me completely. I want what we have to be ours and nobody else's.'

'I'm so sorry, Oscar. I just don't know what's the matter with me lately. I feel so different. I just feel so *different* and I can't explain it. I've been thinking maybe I've got post-traumatic stress or something.'

'Maybe you do.'

'I've been having such awful dreams, you know — about the accident.'

'Why didn't you tell me that before?'

'I wanted to but — '

'But you told Eden instead.'

This set her off crying even harder. 'I'm sorry. You're right. I don't know why I always go to him. He never helps me.' She pulled her head from his shoulder, blinking up at his face. 'I even quit my chamber group. It seemed like the right thing at the time, but, oh, I don't know why I do anything any more. I can't seem to get my head straight.' He held her tightly, smoothing his hand along the line of her neck, where a wave of blonde hair once fell. 'I wish you would've called me, Oscar. I missed you so much. Just the sound of your voice. I've been so low this last couple of weeks.' She leaned into his chest, her arms around him. 'You're so important to me — I mean that. I probably don't say it enough. But you're the only man I've been with who's ever made me feel this way.'

'It's alright,' he said, kissing her. 'I'm here now. It's alright.'

'I love you,' she said, and that was all it took. In the quickness of one moment, as she wept in the glow of passing headlights, he realised he'd forgiven her. Something had released inside him and he could feel a warmth returning to his blood. This was the closest they'd been in months.

★   ★   ★

On Sunday morning, he woke early to make her breakfast. She was still sleeping with the

277

bedsheets twisted between her knees and a dusty bar of sunlight upon her back. He turned his computer on while he waited for the kettle to boil and found an email from Eden amid a bank of spam messages for hair tonics and hotel breaks. The subject line read: 'On the Treatment of Our Mutual Friend'.

Oscar

I'm ready to receive our mutual friend. Tell him to come out to my parents' house tomorrow evening. Let's say 8pm. He might want to bring an overnight bag, just in case. And he has to stop taking his tablets now — be sure to tell him that. Your own attendance isn't mandatory, but I should think you'll want to come along anyway. I'll explain more tomorrow.

Yours
Eden B

PS — Tell Iris, and I'll tell the flock.

Crest seemed surprised at this development when they spoke on the phone. 'Alright, but I'm going to have to bring Andrea along for the ride. She can stay in the car, go for a walk or something. I've got to say, I didn't think he'd follow through with this. It's been two weeks — we should give the guy some credit. He's a man of his word.' Crest coughed dryly and it took a moment for him to settle again. 'It's a little unusual — this flock thing.'

'Why?' Oscar said.

'Phoneys don't get their friends involved usually. It's more exposure than they can control. Widens the zone of scrutiny.' Crest coughed up the last of whatever was troubling his throat. 'My bet is he hasn't told those guys the whole story. They probably don't know what they're getting themselves into. We'll just have to see how things play out. Whatever happens, we have to let things take their own course. No getouts. You hear me?'

'I hear you.'

They decided it was best for them all to meet up at the Bellwether house. Oscar handed the phone to Iris so she could give the old man directions. When she hung up, her face was ridged with concern. 'Did he sound worse to you?' she said.

'About the same, I'd say.'

'Hope he's strong enough to make it through all this.'

'From what I've seen of that old man, he's got willpower coming out of his ears. He'll make it.'

They spent the afternoon in bed. It had been so long since they'd been able to do that, to relax in each other's company, idling away the hours. Oscar lay at the foot of the mattress, and studied the tiny scars on Iris's thigh. She had four short streaks upon her skin like chicken-pox marks, just above the knee — from a yard or so away, they were hardly visible, but up close they were clear, fleshy as bacon. When he traced over them with the back of his hand, she smiled and sighed. He moved to kiss them, but she pulled her leg away. 'I was thinking,' she said. 'I'm not sure if I want to live at Harvey Road next year. I think I'd like to live in halls.'

'Oh?'

'With it being my final year and everything, I think it would be better being closer to things. Don't you think so? I mean, we're not supposed to be off campus during term time anyway.'

He doubted whether her parents would allow it. Too often he'd seen her try to sell an idea to her father and fail. Like the prospect of doing a residency in a hospital overseas, or the possibility of going into dentistry instead of paediatrics, only for Theo to give his final, unanswerable verdict: 'No, darling, I don't think so.' Her mother would chime in with a few words of reinforcement — 'You heard your father; it's a bad idea' — and that would be the end of the matter. Iris would flop back in her chair, red-cheeked, huffing out her frustrations. This was surely how the conversation would go if she asked to move out of Harvey Road, but Oscar knew better than to point this out to her. It would only upset the balance that had been restored between them.

Later that day, he called Cedarbrook to rearrange his shifts for the week ahead, and Iris helped him pack some things into a holdall. They agreed that if Crest was going to stay over at the house, they should both stay over too. 'How's Eden going to get this past your parents?' he asked. 'All of us turning up unannounced tomorrow — they're bound to wonder.'

She folded up a round-collared shirt he never

wore and packed it into the bag. 'You should wear more green things,' she said. 'Green suits you.' She moved back into his wardrobe, skittling through his hangers. 'They're away. Barcelona. Some conference of Dad's. He invited me to go with him — can you believe that? Said it would be good for me to show myself amongst my peers. My peers! He thinks I'm a surgeon already. It's kind of sweet, when you think about it.' And she gave him a little peck on the lips, breezing past him on the way to the window, where she slid the pane upwards and leaned out, lighting a cigarette. This was more like her, Oscar thought — the girl he'd fallen in love with.

'Oh, did I tell you?' she said. 'I found the perfect cello. A friend of Jane's was selling it. It's not a Guadagnini or anything, but it has such a lovely tone. And, between you and me, I think I robbed the poor girl blind. It's worth triple what I paid for it.' She drew contentedly on her clove, blowing the smoke out into the pleasantness of the afternoon. 'I'll play it for you sometime.'

★　★　★

It was around eight o'clock, one quiet Monday evening in March, when Herbert Crest's black Mercedes came rolling along the tree-lined driveway towards the Bellwether house. Standing with Iris under the cold blue of the garden floodlights, Oscar watched it reach the end of the road and take a hesitant turn into the forecourt, make a slow circle around the fountain, and come to a stop behind Jane's mud-splattered

Land Rover. He could see Andrea's indignant face through the windscreen. She got out of the driver's side, slamming the door behind her, and helped Crest out of the back seat, walking beside him, step for step.

Oscar moved to greet them, and Andrea handed the old man over to him without a word, as if she was returning a rented tuxedo. 'Hi,' he said. 'You found the place okay.' She didn't reply, just gave him a hard stare and walked back to the car.

'Don't mind her,' Crest said. 'She thinks she owns me.' There was the sound of another slamming door, and Crest turned to look in its direction, shaking his head. Andrea was sitting back behind the wheel, arms folded. 'Oh, the kindness of women, huh? They just care too damn much about everybody. Even stubborn old assholes like me.' He smiled at Iris. 'You changed your hair. It suits you.'

She blushed. 'Thanks, Herbert. I'm not sure if I like it yet.'

'It'll grow on you,' he said, laughing at the cheap pun, and lifted his baseball cap, 'not like mine.' He eyed the vastness of the grounds, absorbing the white house, the pristine front garden, the fields and blossoms that surrounded them. 'Helluva place you've got here. Reminds me a little of home. Where's your brother?' he said. 'Not part of the welcoming committee?'

'We don't know,' Oscar said. 'Only just got here ourselves.' They'd come directly from Cedarbrook. He was still wearing his uniform, and his overnight bag was still in the boot of Iris's car.

'He's probably in the organ house,' Iris said. 'He's *always* in the organ house.'

'Right. The place from the videos. Intrigued to see it.' Crest looked up towards a light blinking off in an upstairs window. 'Maybe I could pop in to say hello to your parents while I'm here?'

'They're away,' she told him. 'On business.'

'Spain,' Oscar said, as if to endorse her honesty.

'Busy people, I imagine.'

'We hardly get to see them at this time of year. Always going off somewhere.' She gestured towards the back of the house. 'Shall we go through?'

It was pitch-dark in the atrium. Iris flicked the switch to turn on the chandelier and its crystals sparkled warmly. The house seemed empty, though it bristled with some invisible energy, like the excitement of guests hiding at a surprise party. All at once, there was a stir of voices from the floor above and, in a charge of activity, three sets of feet came vaulting down the staircase: Jane, Marcus and Yin, their faces pink with laughter.

'What were you doing up there?' Iris said.

Jane was giddy. 'Nothing. Just messing about.'

'We all got talking about your father's wine cellar,' said Yin. 'Spent the last hour trying to find the key. Do you know where he keeps it?'

'No,' Iris said. 'Ask Eden.'

'We did, but he's holding out on us.' Yin jumped the last stair. 'He says your dad's got a Screaming Eagle Cabernet in there. We don't believe him.'

283

'I wouldn't have the faintest idea,' Iris said.

Crest was still standing patiently in the atrium. 'Always been more of a cold beer man myself,' he said. 'Nobody pays more than ten bucks for a drink where I grew up.'

Yin pushed his hands into his trouser pockets. 'I guess it's all Sam Adams where you're from, huh?'

'And I guess you're one of those Napa Valley kids — wine on the inside,' Crest replied. 'We're both a long way from home.'

Yin smiled broadly. 'Yeah. We are.'

'So where's Eden?' Oscar asked.

Marcus piped up then. 'He's out in the O. H. We're not allowed in yet. He said to find a way of entertaining ourselves until you showed up, so we did. Nothing more entertaining than a good old root in people's drawers.' He was holding a cut-glass decanter in one hand and its shiny little stopper in the other. 'There are so many rooms in this house, it probably has its own micro-climate.'

Iris didn't seem discomfited by the idea of her friends scavenging in her parents' empty house. She just turned to Crest and said, by way of introducing him, 'I presume you all know who this is.'

'Sure,' Yin said, shaking Crest's hand. 'You're the guy we're here to help.'

Crest nodded politely.

'We're sorry to hear about your, you know — your condition,' Jane said. 'When Eden was trying to explain to me what music therapy was last night, I'm afraid it all went over my head. But I'll do my bit. I just hope we can help you with the pain.'

'I hope so too,' the old man said. He cornered his eyes at Oscar. 'You all seem very comfortable with the idea.'

Yin shrugged. 'Frankly, I don't see how a bit of music's gonna make you feel any better. But whatever — if you think it'll help, I don't see the harm.'

Marcus was the last to shake the old man's hand. 'Well, I think you've made a good decision coming here tonight. If there's even the slightest chance this can help you with the pain, it's got to be worth it. Eden knows what he's doing. Trust me. Nobody understands more about music than he does. If he says there's something to this music therapy stuff, there probably is.'

'Yeah, that's me alright,' Crest said. 'I'll take whatever's free.' He looked at Oscar, then at Iris, one eyebrow cocked. 'I know you probably think it's a crazy way for a man to get his medicine, but I'll try anything once.'

'I don't think it's so crazy. The five of us put Oscar under with hardly an effort — just a little madrigal Eden knocked up overnight,' Marcus said. 'Once he gets that organ firing, who knows what can happen? If he can put you to sleep for a while, at least that's a few minutes you're not in pain. Don't you think?'

Crest nodded, smiled. 'I do.' He turned to Oscar, winking. 'See, I told you they'd understand. Pain relief. That's all this is.'

Oscar realised what Crest was trying to say. It was clear that the others had not been told the full story about what they were involved in. They seemed to think they were only going to be helping the old man with his pain tonight — not working towards *healing* him. And as much as Oscar wanted to fill in the rest of the picture for them, he was aware of Crest's widened eyes, instructing him to stay quiet.

'Come on, I'll walk you to the O. H.,' Marcus said, placing his hand onto the old man's shoulder, and Crest allowed himself to be escorted through the dark house towards the kitchen. Oscar and the others followed behind. He listened as Marcus and Crest chatted amiably, walking towards an anaemic light that was filing in from the sitting room. 'Funny how things turn out, isn't it?' Marcus said. 'I read one of your books in school, and now here you are.'

'You did? Which one?'

'The one about the God Complex.'

'Ah, you're in a very small club there.'

The house was so vast it took several strides just to reach the middle of the hallway, where the hardwood branched off in three directions, and the solid doors of four other rooms hung closed. Oscar was starting to feel calmer now. Yin and Jane had a way of steadying his heart somehow, and the squeeze of Iris's hand was as grounding as it always was. He loved the way she hooked her fingers around his thumb.

'I hardly sold more than a thousand copies of that one when it first came out,' Crest went on, walking slowly beside Marcus. 'Now I'm obsolete my demographic is expanding. Typical luck. What brought you to reading it?'

'I took psychology A level. It was on the reading list — *suggested* reading, not compulsory.'

'Story of my life,' Crest said.

'Well, we had a very progressive teacher. John Fahey. Do you know him? I think he did his Ph.D. at Trinity, Dublin.'

'Can't say I've had the pleasure.'

Iris turned up the dimmer switches as they reached the end of the hall, and the sitting room revealed itself like a Polaroid image. Marcus continued, his hand upon the small of Crest's back, steering him. 'He's only been at Charterhouse for a few years, I think. I would've failed for sure if it weren't for Mr Fahey. Eden didn't like him very much, but he was definitely the best teacher I ever had. One of those people who really makes you *see things*, you know?'

Crest seemed to make a note of this in his head. He gave a short, curious hum. 'Why didn't Eden like him?' he asked.

Marcus took his hand away to fasten a loose button on his collar. 'Clash of personalities, I suppose.' They were nearing the kitchen now and Oscar thought he could smell something burning.

'Meaning?' Crest said.

'Meaning they were too similar. Mr Fahey was young and brainy. And so was Eden. Every lesson was like a — ' Marcus turned his head, briskly. 'What's that phrase you always use, Yin?'

'A pissing contest,' Yin said.

The kitchen was doused in a warm, wavering light coming in from the garden. The countertops were messy with apple juice cartons and an opened box of Jacob's crackers; the remains of a

287

blue cheese and a French loaf had been left to harden on the breadboard. Marcus opened the back door. He motioned his arm towards the winding path outside, its surface bright with the candle-flicker of mosquito lanterns flaming in the lawn borders. 'Here we are. The yellow brick road. Let me show you the way.'

They walked along the pathway as if it were some ceremonial march, and arrived at the great oak doors of the organ house, one of which was held ajar by a large white rockery stone. Oscar felt a spike of trepidation in his gut, remembering the times he had come here to visit Iris's bedside, wondering what they were now heading into. There was a strangely chemical smell in the air, like the burnt-out stench of a camping stove. He expected to hear music, but there was no sound except for the noise of their footsteps.

Herbert Crest went in first. He didn't seem to give it a second thought.

As the door swung back, a woozy orange colour radiated from the building, and Oscar could see a circle of twenty or thirty old-fashioned oil lamps with glass flame-covers, glowing in the middle of the room. There was no sign of Eden.

'Woah, check this place out,' Yin said.

'It's like the bordello of my dreams,' said Marcus, pressing further inside.

The organ console was adorned with tealights in jam jars. At the centre of the circle, between the lamps, was a worn green armchair. Everything else had been moved aside to make space: the four-poster bed was now shoved against the back wall, and the couches were turned on their sides, banked against each other near the entrance. 'Well,' Crest said, looking at Oscar and smiling, 'I might not have been so wrong about those lithe young virgins.' He seemed to think there was nothing disconcerting about what he was seeing, and casually wandered towards the organ to study its keyboard, its ornate stops and pedals, its pipework. The others followed. 'I bet these things aren't cheap.'

'It was here when my parents bought the place,' Iris said. 'The pipes are eighteenth century, so my brother says.'

'He's always tinkering with it, taking it apart,' Jane added. 'He fiddles more with that thing than he does with me.'

Marcus laughed. 'Have you ever tried getting the registration right on one of these things? They're much harder to please than women are. Can take years to get them humming properly. And you know Eden — he's a perfectionist.'

'Oh, I know Eden alright,' Jane said.

Crest ran his fingers over the ivory stops. 'My father had an old sailboat in the garage that he liked to fix up on weekends.' He turned to Iris. 'I guess this is your brother's version.'

Oscar thought about the Honda trail bike his father kept back home, leaned against the side of the house — a project he'd worked on so sporadically over the years that the flame-red paintwork had faded to a strawberry ice-cream pink, and the undercarriage had rusted away. He remembered that motorbike with a certain fondness. The only goal he and his father ever shared was to get it going again, even if they never got around to actually fixing it — even if it was sure to end up at the scrapyard with all the other father-son projects in the borough.

'What are you all standing around for?' came a voice from behind. 'We've got work to do.' Eden was looming by the entrance. He was wearing a white silk shirt with a patch of his bare chest showing through, tight black corduroy trousers, and no shoes.

'We're waiting for you,' Jane said. 'You haven't even told us what you need us to do.'

'First — ' Eden heaved the door closed and snapped down the metal latch. 'First, you can help Dr Crest into that chair.' He walked towards them determinedly.

Crest refused to be helped. He lowered his body into the armchair with a weary, pained moan. 'Alright if I keep my hat on?'

'No. Remove it, please,' Eden said.

The old man pocketed his baseball cap, smirking. He winked again, as if to say he had everything under control, but his apparent good humour was no consolation to Oscar. The nerves were still crackling inside him. He could tell by the arrangement of the room, the sheer consideration that had gone into the placement of everything, that Eden was taking this very seriously.

'The rest of you — ' Eden clapped his hands at them, getting their attention. Each little slap of his palms ricocheted in the rafters. 'I need you all to be quiet and do everything I ask of you,

290

okay? It's very important that you follow instructions. A man's health is at stake here.'

They all glanced at Crest, who was lounging in the armchair. He looked like he was taking pictures in his head, trying to capture every detail. Oscar couldn't help but wonder what he was thinking about. What did he make of Jane, and Marcus, and Yin, and the way they were waiting for instructions from Eden like hounds standing patiently at his heels? What did he think about Iris? She was beautiful in the dim candle-light, all free and easy in her summer dress, wool tights and topcoat, yet so removed from every-thing that was happening, absently lifting the tealights from the organ console and sniffing at them.

Most of all, he wondered what the old man was thinking about Eden, who was speaking now very plainly, eyebrows furrowed, organising every-one with a pushy composure. 'Iris, will you leave those candles alone and listen to what I'm telling you? Oscar, are you going to just stand there gawping at me, or do you actually want to be of some use?'

'Just let me know what to do,' he said.

'Hold that thought,' Eden replied, clapping his hands again. He walked over to the organ stool and flipped back the seat. It was a voluminous thing, and he pulled out a variety of objects from within it, setting them down on the floor: folders of sheet music bound in ribbon, a roll of gauzy fabric, a metronome in a walnut case, tuning forks of many sizes. 'Come now. Everyone, gather round me, please. You need to listen to me carefully.'

They stood there, studying the objects at his feet.

'We've all done this before — at least, a version of it,' Eden said, and began to hand out the ribbon-tied folders of notation. 'I don't want to hear anybody's scepticism or sarcastic comments tonight. If you don't want to help me, leave now.' He held a folder in front of Iris.

'But don't you *need* our help?' she said.

'It might not be possible to do this without you, I'll admit. But if you want to leave, we'll postpone it. I can always find someone else to take your place.' He looked at Oscar. '*His* role is expendable; but you lot, I need.'

'Well, I'm staying,' said Jane.

'Me too,' said Marcus.

'Me three,' said Yin.

Iris took the folder of music from her brother's hand. She looked down at Crest with sympathy. Then she folded her arms at Eden. 'So what exactly do you want me to do?'

'I brought your cello from home,' Eden said. 'Go and tune it. And stop being so sniffy with me. I don't have time for that tonight.' He pointed to a large white case at the far end of the room. She went to retrieve it, and Oscar watched as she took out the instrument and plucked at the strings. She stayed in a patch of darkness away from the others while she tuned it, sitting with her cheek close to the fingerboard, and he could hear the distant, muted pips of cello notes.

Eden pointed to Herbert Crest and looked right at Marcus. 'I want you to kneel at his eyeline, two yards away from his right ear. Got it?'

'Sure,' Marcus said. He flipped through the pages of the music before taking his place by the old man. 'Looks like a beautiful arrangement, by the way. Nice work.'

Crest stayed quiet.

'Jane, be a dear,' Eden said. 'Do the same as Marcus, only stand to the left.'

She nodded and went to stand by the old man. 'How exciting,' she said.

Eden placed two hands on Yin's shoulders. 'Yinny, my good friend,' he said, and paused. Then: 'I need that baritone of yours at the back. At his eye level, two yards away. But you must stay standing. No kneeling down for you, got it?'

'Sure. Fine. Whatever.'

Marcus feigned indignation — 'How come *he* doesn't have to get his knees dirty?' — but Eden dismissed this with a quick snap of his fingers: 'Quiet,' he said. 'Concentrate.'

Iris wandered back towards them, clutching a bow in one hand and the neck of her cello in the other. It was a wonderful rosewood colour with two little patches of faded varnish by the bridge — a prettier instrument than the one she'd owned before. 'Now what?' she said.

'One second.' Eden slid a short breakfast stool across the room — Oscar recognised it from the Bellwethers' kitchen — and it made an uncomfortable scraping sound upon the laminate as he positioned it directly in front of Crest. Eden gripped his sister by the tops of her arms and steered her towards it, practically pushing her down onto it. Her cello gave out a bouncy, discordant sound.

'Well, if I'm supposed to play from sight, I'll need a music stand,' she said, and Eden obliged by dragging one over. 'Happy?' he said, and she canted her head.

There was a perfect line now, from Yin, to Crest, to Iris, to that hulking organ. 'You lot are the y-axis,' Eden said, gesturing with a straight arm along the line. 'Understand?' Then he gestured towards Marcus and Jane the same way: 'And you two are the x-axis.'

Crest widened his eyes, rubbing at the top of his skull with his fingers. There was a moment of silence, which he broke with a polite little clearance of his throat. 'So, what?' he said. 'I just have to sit here?'

'Yes. You have to sit there and be as still as you can. But first — first — ' Eden picked up three tuning forks from the floor, wiping them against his sleeve. 'Here, grip it like this,' he said, placing one of the larger forks into Crest's right hand, manoeuvring the old man's fingers into a lobster claw around it. 'And the other hand — ' He put the second biggest into Crest's left hand. 'Open up,' he said, and like some family doctor investigating a child's sore throat, he took the old man's jaw and gently levered it apart. Then he placed the flat handle of the smallest tuning fork on the bottom row of Crest's teeth. 'Bite down on it — not too hard, just keep it steady.' Reluctantly, the old man complied. 'There, there, that's it.' Eden stepped away, studying him. 'Now — ' He went to retrieve the bundle of fabric, unravelling it quickly, until it became two separate strips. It was a light, diaphanous material, rather like muslin, and as he walked with it across the room, the air caught hold of it so easily, trailing it out through the slats of his fingers. He stood in front of Crest with the fabric then reached into the pocket of his trousers and drew out a small glass bottle, lifting the cork out with his teeth. He balled up the muslin and doused it with the contents of the bottle — a clear, thin liquid.

Oscar was so anxious he had to dry his palms on the back of his uniform. His legs felt hollow. Eden's momentum seemed unstoppable now. There was a kind of rapture about him.

'What is that, holy water?' Crest mumbled through the side of his mouth.

Eden just shook his head. He took one of the strips and set it in a straight line on the old man's skull, in the direction of Yin, Iris, and the organ — the y-axis. Then he placed the other one across it, along the x-axis, taking care that the cross-point met the centre of the old man's operation scar. Watery trails ran along Crest's face, dripped from his earlobes, hung in a wen at the tip of his nose. Oscar was amazed how much the old man was willing to tolerate — his face was creased up like he was about to sneeze, like he felt nauseous, and the others all looked on with wide, shifting eyes.

Eden clapped his hands loudly. 'Okay, now we're ready. Now we can begin.'

'Wait, what about me?' Oscar said. 'What do you need me to do?'

'Yes. Right. I almost forgot you were here.' Eden went back to his organ stool, hinging it open. He pulled out a new-looking video camera and, with a casual, aimless throw, he tossed it into the air for Oscar to catch. 'You've had some experience with these things, so I understand,' Eden said, his voice low and dry. 'Just keep it pointed at *him*, not at me, okay?' He jabbed a thumb in the direction of Crest. 'No fancy camerawork. We're not making *A Bout de Souffle* here. Just keep it simple.'

★　★　★

It began with *tick-tock tick-tock* — the toy-like gears of the metronome clicking out a steady rhythm. Eden rolled up the sleeves of his shirt, eyes closed, listening to its delicate percussion for several bars, and then sat himself at the organ and began to play a volley of notes, slow but intricate. Sounds layered on top of each other, the right hand marking out the path with a gentle, flowery melody, the left hand laying down great boulders of chords behind it. But although the music was languid, it was not exactly mellow. There was electricity underneath it, an energy that was gathering with every new movement of Eden's fingers.

Oscar kept the camera trained on Crest's face, struggling to keep his hands steady. He zoomed right up close and the frame shook wildly. The old man had a blank, relaxed expression, but he made for the strangest picture: there he was with a tuning fork gripped between his teeth and another in each hand, with a cross-hatch of wet muslin on his head. There was no more laughing or sneering, or any sign of the disparagement he'd shown earlier. In fact, Oscar thought he could see something in those wide-awake eyes: he thought he could see Crest *trying*. Trying not to jinx himself, trying to allow his rational brain to believe in the vague possibility that all this might actually come to something.

Iris, Yin, Marcus, and Jane followed every note of the music on their sheets, turning their pages swiftly. They were all caught up in the moment now, concentrating. Even Oscar felt connected. The organ had a rousing, cajoling effect on him. Everything felt momentous — the way he was holding the camera, the footage he was taking, the position of his feet on the floor, the angle of his body against the light — every last thing was important.

And then there came an enormous, jarring blast from the organ pipes. The pace of the music lurched forward. The volume rose. The timbre of the organ changed, from rasping to full-throated.

Oscar couldn't help but turn to look at what was going on behind him, keeping the camera trained on Crest. Eden was swaying, stamping his feet, clawing at the console. Gone was the lightness. Gone was the looseness in his shoulders. This was an energetic music, angry and contagious, something feverish and knife-sharp. It was music like gushing water, like frantic animals being herded on a hillside, like all of the conversations in the world being spoken at once, like an ocean prising itself apart, like two great armies converging on each other. With the pressure of Eden's feet, husky bass notes joined the teeming melody made by his fingers, putting flesh on its bones, thickening the sound. He picked out each low note with effortless pushes of his bare feet, not even glancing downwards, just heel-stepping like a seasoned ballroom dancer, adding brisk, jabbing chords, all the while continuing that smooth sailing of his fingers. Then he flicked on a switch, shifting his hands downward in the same easy motion, from the top rung of keys to the bottom rung, so that all at once the keys on every tier of the console were following the relentless movement of his fingers. The music grew heavier, darker. Keys were dropping and lifting themselves, as if invisible cats were running across them. Oscar had seen a working pianola once, in some backstreet pub in London, but this was something else — this was a machine that could make itself talk with five thundering voices.

He didn't think there was anywhere else for the sound to go. Surely the building wouldn't be able to contain it. Surely it would shatter the roof. But then Iris struck a high, trilling note on her cello, which cut through the dense breath of the organ. Her left hand slid along the neck, and she began to saw out quick, punchy chords with her bow — one two three four, one two three four — and they found their own place amid the rising clamour. Soon, Marcus, Jane, and Yin were singing.

They sang as if they were playing a game of catch, batting notes back and forth to each other over Crest's head. Short puffs of melody bounced off the chords of Iris's cello — *pah, pah, pum, pah, pah, pum* — and locked onto the unrelenting music of the organ. It went on like this for a good while, until they stopped to take deep breaths, eyeing each other. They flipped the pages of their notation. As the drone of Eden's organ began to fall away, they started to sing again with long, stretching notes in perfect harmony, as if to beckon the music down from the rafters. Yin's deep voice pierced the air, pouring out of his chest like one sad sigh; Jane's voice was the highest, the sweetest, the most fragile; and Marcus, the anchor between them, had a voice so sure and stable, never wavering with the beat of his arm as he kept them all in time. It was a smouldering lullaby. They sang no words, just sounds. The music was its own language.

Oscar remembered the camera in his hands. When he turned back to check that it was still pointed at Crest, he found that his grip had loosened and the lens was steering itself towards the floor. Quickly, he lifted it, zooming and focusing it again on the old man's face. He saw that Crest's eyelids were closed. There was nothing different about him other than that; he was still holding the tuning fork between his teeth and his neck seemed stiff and steady. The muslin was still wet upon his skull, glossing his forehead. His pale skin glistened in the sickly hue of the oil lamps.

The music stopped. There was not quite silence: it took a few moments for the organ's voice to leave the space around them. Though the pipes had no voice left in them, there was still the memory of their sound, and when it finally cleared, nobody spoke, nobody moved. Crest didn't open his eyes.

Oscar didn't know what else to do but keep on filming. The silence gathered. The mechanics of the camera kept on turning over. Then he felt a hand on his shoulder, and Eden leaned down to whisper: 'Turn it off.' And he did — he cut the power and, hoping that Crest might blink his eyes open and tell him not to, he handed the camera to Eden.

'I need you all to leave now,' Eden said softly. They all looked at each other, shrugging. Still, the old man's eyes stayed shut.

'So that's it?' Marcus said. 'Fun's over?'

'Fun's over,' Eden said. 'Go.' He threw something and Yin caught it. 'All yours. Take anything but the Pétrus. Now go.'

Marcus and Yin sprang up, letting their notation fall to the floor. They hurried off, and Jane skipped to catch up with them. 'You're not opening anything without me!' she called out.

The old man didn't twitch. He seemed to be passed out cold in the chair.

'I'm not leaving him like this,' Oscar said.

Eden stared at him. 'If you don't go, I can't do what needs to be done. You'll ruin everything and we'll have to start all over again tomorrow.'

'Come on, sweetheart,' came Iris's voice from behind him. She'd already placed her cello back into its case and was standing there waiting. 'It'll be okay.'

'But he's unconscious.'

'Of course he is,' Eden said, sounding almost affronted. 'What exactly did you expect?'

'If anything happens to him, Eden, I swear — '

'Oh, I'm not going to harm the man. He'll be wide awake again in a few minutes. Just go. Let me do what I need to do.'

Oscar felt Iris tugging at his sleeve, lightly at first, then more insistent. 'Come on. Herbert would want you to leave him,' she said. 'You know he would.'

She was right. *No getouts*.

He let himself be ushered away.

Out in the garden, the night sky was dusted with stars. The elms stood rigid as back bones and the countryside noises sounded mysterious, hard to identify. Iris leaned against the wall, lit a cigarette, blew out the smoke. The lights were still on in the main house and Oscar could see the silhouettes of the others moving against the sheer kitchen curtains. From the foot of the garden, it seemed almost unreal, like some theatre set: a trick house made of paper and paint, with nothing behind it but the brick walls of the stage. He felt cold, unsettled. 'What was that thing he just gave to Yin?'

Iris tapped a column of ash from her cigarette. 'Key to my father's wine cellar. They're probably tearing it apart as we speak. I should really go up there and make sure they don't cause too much damage.'

'You go. I'm staying here.'

She took a small step forward. 'He's really not going to hurt him, Oscar.'

'You don't know that for sure.'

301

'My brother's got his problems, but he wouldn't harm a fly.'

'Like he wouldn't put a nail through my hand, you mean? Like he wouldn't stab you with safety pins?'

'That's different.'

'Not much.'

'You're being dramatic,' she said. 'Herbert will be fine.'

Just then, Jane came out onto the patio, calling: 'Iggy! Iggy! You need to come up here! Yin just dropped something expensive!'

'Be right there!' Iris turned to Oscar, softening her expression. 'Why don't you come inside? There's no point waiting out here in the cold.'

He could hear no sound coming through the organ house doors. There was no music any more, no footsteps, not even a rumble of voices. Everything around him seemed placid and safe. Maybe he *was* just being dramatic. He went with Iris, back into the main house, where it was warmer, more comfortable. It was already getting on for ten o'clock; the time had passed in a blur.

Yin was in the kitchen, studying a mess of broken glass he'd swept into a dustpan. He carefully picked out the label with his thumb and forefinger, lifting it up close to his face to read it. 'Château Lafite,' he said. 'I'm so sorry, I was trying to pull out a cheaper bottle and this one just kinda gave way. I'll replace it, I promise.'

'Forget it, Yinny. He won't even know it's missing.'

'Not if I destroy the evidence.'

302

In the drawing room, Marcus was pouring a syrupy-looking wine from a dusty black bottle into three glasses. When he saw them coming, he began to fill two more. 'I was wondering when you'd be coming back.'

'It's all gone quiet out there,' Iris said.

Oscar could see the organ house through the French doors. He watched for signs of movement, but there were none. He took a seat close to the window, keeping the building in his line of sight.

'We were all just saying — ' Marcus handed Iris a glass. 'Wasn't that the strangest thing you've ever done in your life?'

'I've got to admit, there was something amazing happening in there,' Jane said. 'I mean, I could really *feel* something. It was like, I don't know, a pressure, right here.' She put her hand to her sternum.

'Yeah, totally,' said Yin from the doorway.

'We all felt it,' Iris said.

Oscar had felt it, too. The music had a weight, an energy he wasn't expecting. It had rattled through him. But until he knew for sure that Crest was okay, he wasn't going to admit it. 'How long did he have you all practising it?' he asked.

They looked at each other, confused.

'Practising?' Yin said. 'Man, we were just sight-reading in there. That's why the whole thing sounded so sketchy. Didn't you notice? My timing was way off. I had Marcus treading all over my harmonies. And we were all kinda presto with the counterpoint. A little practice and we

303

could have that thing nailed.'

'Didn't matter anyway,' Jane said. 'The piece had so much power to it.'

'I may have hit a few sharps that weren't sharps,' Marcus said.

Iris sat down beside Oscar on the settee, pulling her legs up underneath her. 'What about me? My fingering was appalling.'

'You all sounded fine to me,' Oscar said.

Jane took a seat on the other settee and discarded the cushions, one by one. 'Well, if we hadn't developed half an ear for each other after all these years, it'd be a sad indictment of our friendship.'

They stayed there in the drawing room for a long time, sipping their wine, until they fell into silence. Oscar wasn't in the mood for drinking; he didn't take a single mouthful. Iris rested her head on his lap, and he stroked her hair absently. All he could think about was what was happening in the organ house. He had a picture of Eden holding Crest's skull in his hands, squeezing it until the old man cried out in pain and the tumour fell out of his mouth like some hunk of meat that had been caught in his teeth.

'Don't you think it's unusual?' Jane said. Nobody responded, but she went on anyway. 'I mean, here we all are, most of us best friends who've known each other all our lives, and as soon as Eden's out of the room we hardly have anything to say to each other. Don't you think that's strange?'

They all seemed to ponder the question.

Jane continued: 'Don't get me wrong — it's

304

nice just to be in the flock — but I do wonder what it says about us that we get all tongue-tied when Eden's not around.'

Oscar felt Iris sighing against his lap. Then Marcus piped up: 'Actually, I think it's the opposite. We know each other so well there isn't anything left to say. Sometimes it's nice just sitting here with you all, thinking. It's only best friends who can be comfortable with silence, wouldn't you say?' Everyone sounded their agreement. 'And I include you in that too, Oscar. You're a part of the furniture like the rest of these degenerates.'

'Now why've you got to go and do that, Em?' Yin said, throwing a cushion at him. 'You've always got to ruin a nice thing with an insult.'

Marcus cackled. *'Ich bin wie ich bin.'*

Oscar had a warm sensation in his chest. He felt, perhaps for the first time since he'd known them, genuinely welcome in their company. They talked with greater ease after that. They spoke about the silly things that bothered them about the world: nose hair, tracksuits, airport tax, vegetarianism. Simple things. Bad films they'd seen, new books they'd read, tasteless jokes they'd overheard. Oscar started to relax. He didn't know how much time had passed, but there had been no movement outside the organ house, just the sullen flaming of lanterns in the garden.

Jane was telling them a limerick her father had written in a recent letter from Italy ('There once was a young man named Wyatt, who ate paperclips on the quiet; but his shits were belated, and badly collated, so he changed to an all-staple diet') and they were still giggling at the punchline when Crest appeared in the drawing room doorway. The laughter dropped away. Everyone stood up at once.

'Don't let me interrupt you,' Crest said.

Eden was behind him, clutching at the old man's forearm, steering him under the lintel the way Oscar often did with residents at Cedarbrook. It was the accepted method for guiding wanderers back to their rooms when they'd lost their sense of direction, sleep-walked, or just plain forgotten where they lived. Crest seemed confused. He walked with reluctant baby-steps.

'Everything okay?' Oscar asked.

The old man nodded. 'Let's just go, huh?'

'Alright.'

'I'll come with you,' Iris said.

'No, honey, that's okay.' Crest dismissed her with a wave of his hand. 'You wait here with your friends. Enjoy yourself.'

There was no fanfare, no round of goodbyes. Oscar took the old man straight out to his car, where he found Andrea sleeping in the passenger seat — he had forgotten all about her. She stirred when he knocked on the glass, checking her watch, opening the door. 'What the hell time do you call this? I been waiting in here for you all night, mister.' She helped Crest into the car without allowing him to answer. 'God Almighty, you look like death on a plate. I told you not to do this to yourself, didn't I? I told you. But oh no, you knew better. Well, now look at you, you silly stupid man.'

'I think she's mad at me. What do you think?'

Crest sounded groggy.

'She's right, though,' Oscar said. 'You don't look very good.'

'Well, I feel pretty great.'

'You do?'

'I'm all spaced out. Feels like I've had a long soak in the tub. Quite pleasant.'

'Oh.'

'Don't look so worried. I'm not saying I've been healed or anything. I'm not claiming any miracles. But my jaw's still tingling with that damn tuning fork. I definitely felt that.'

'What happened after we left?'

'We talked a little, that's all,' Crest said.

'About what?'

'Oh, come on now. I promised I wouldn't tell.'

'I thought we were in this together.'

'We are. It's like a doctor-patient thing. Bad ethics to break my word.'

Andrea tutted. 'Listen to you. You should be ashamed of yourselves.' She directed her words to the footwell as she fastened the old man's seat belt across his waist. 'I don't know what you got up to in there, but I was hearing all kinds of strange noises. I almost came running in to get you.'

'That's a sure way to get fired,' Crest said.

Andrea looked a little hurt. 'Well, it seemed like a lot of noise for a sick old man.'

'Is that all I am, a sick old man? A wife of the above.'

'A *what* now?'

Crest ignored her and beckoned Oscar closer. 'I'll have you know I learned a lot about myself in there tonight. There's something very exciting about that boy. He's a complex personality. Strange as hell, in my opinion, but there's nothing wrong with that. It's very exciting from a psychological standpoint to be around complex personalities. I'm a pretty complex guy myself.' He mumbled all of this with the lazy drawl of a town drunk and with the same glassy, desperate look in his eyes. Pulling Oscar down to his sight-line by the scruff of his sweater, he added, in a lowered voice: 'Listen, I'm going to be back here tomorrow. Same time. He wants me to do this every night for a week. A course of treatment, he said. I told him I'd stick around, stay in a hotel somewhere. What do you think?'

A few hours ago, Oscar would've thought the idea was ludicrous, but now he wasn't so sure. He'd definitely felt something in the organ house — a pressure, like Jane had said. He could still feel it now, the way you can still sense the gentle sway of a boat in your legs when you step back onto land. And even though the old man would probably never own up to it, Oscar thought he'd noticed a change in Crest as well. Maybe it was just his guard lowering. There was a new glimmer in his eyes, a deeper interest in his voice that he hadn't been expecting. 'If you think it's a good idea, then so do I,' he said.

'So I'll call you tomorrow?'

'Yeah.'

He shut the door. As Andrea turned on the engine and pulled the car away, he realised he'd forgotten to ask the old man about the music, whether he'd felt anything more than just the tingle of a tuning fork. Perhaps something as remarkable as hope.

★ ★ ★

When Oscar returned to the drawing room, Eden was leaning against the piano, pulling petals from the flower arrangement. The others were constellated on the furniture around him, and Marcus was talking about how wonderful he thought the music had been, how he hadn't enjoyed singing quite as much for a long time. Sliding Eden a glass of Pinot across the piano lid, Marcus said: 'I presume it was yours — your own composition, I mean.'

Eden nodded. He let another petal fall from his fingers. 'The entire arrangement came to me over the course of an evening. It was all rather hurried, but it's more or less perfect.'

Marcus said: 'The melody in the last movement, it reminded me of Mattheson, the opening of his first oratorio.'

'It was an homage,' Eden said.

'Oh, clearly it was an homage — very deliberate. A lovely touch, I thought.'

'Thank you, Em.'

'Please, stop it,' Iris said, burying her head under a cushion. 'Spare us the sycophancy.'

'Weren't you impressed, sis? I think you're the only one who wasn't moved by it. Even Oscar said he liked it.'

'Actually, I thought my cello line was rather basic,' she said.

'Yes, and deliberately so. Don't think I didn't

309

notice you trying to spice it up with extra glissando.' Eden pulled at the neckline of his shirt, as if it were bothering him.

'I'm just saying it wasn't very challenging.'

'My concern was for the architecture of the piece as a whole, not to entertain your ego.' There had always been a wilful exuberance about Eden, but that night Oscar watched it grow into something that was difficult to witness: sheer, unhinged reverence for his own ability. Eden paced around the room, gesticulating with his glass, telling stories about his great hero, Johann Mattheson, sharing the details of his grandiose theories, whether anyone was interested in these theories or not. ' . . . because music doesn't need any rules for its own sake,' he got to saying. 'It's only *us* that need them. I tried to override those rules tonight. I tried to write something without restrictions. Something to elevate the spirits, just like in the Baroque days. Mattheson said we impose rules and restrictions on music because of our own weaknesses and limitations. Because without rules, we wouldn't be able to comprehend music at all, we wouldn't even be able to discern a love song from, from — from a death knell. Music's a heavenly art so we have to find some way to harness it, to understand it, make it something earthly. You see what I'm saying? We can only understand music through our senses. *Nihil est in Intellectua, quod non fuit in sensu.*' He didn't seem to care whether anybody in the room was listening or not. He was talking *at* them, ranting as if he needed to get the whole thing off his chest, stopping only to refill his wine glass, or open another bottle.

It was late and no one had bothered to draw the curtains in the room, so even when Oscar had the temerity to turn his attention away, he could see Eden's wiry reflection bouncing back at him in the panes of the French windows. Soon, Iris fell asleep on his shoulder. The others gazed at the floor politely. But Eden was still bounding along: 'I hope you all noticed the scale. Quite deliberate. Mattheson said F sharp minor is the key that's most characterised by sadness. It's very different from any of the other minors. He said it's a scale that has loneliness and individuality — and *misanthropy*. Ha! Isn't that wonderful? F sharp minor is the misanthropic scale.'

'Well, it's hardly any wonder that we all liked it so much,' Jane said, trying to interject. 'We're all misanthropes here.' Her tone was pleading, as if she hoped she could make Eden aware of the rabid energy with which he'd been talking.

'Yes, yes, alright, Jane, but it's more significant than *that*. Why is everyone always trailing behind?' Eden looked at them all, bug-eyed. 'Dr Crest is the biggest misanthrope I know. If we weren't speaking the same language, I couldn't get through to him.'

'Maybe you should could call it 'Ode to Misanthropy',' said Marcus.

Eden shook his head, bothered by the interruption. 'It doesn't have a title. And even if it did, it's not an ode. I didn't write it to glorify his name. I wrote it to help him. It's a paean, that's what it is. A paean in the truest sense of the word. Read your *Iliad*.' He swallowed the dregs of his Pinot and shook the glass. 'Do we have any more of this?'

Oscar wanted to ask a question, but now that the whirlwind of Eden's chatter had finally begun to die down, he was reluctant to voice it. He had never read *The Iliad*, and only knew a few things about Greek mythology. There was a book about it in Dr Paulsen's room that he sometimes found himself thumbing through, drawn in by the weight of it. The paragraphs he'd read always troubled him; they seemed so epic and portentous — grave stories of punishments meted out by impatient immortals — and he could never read more than a few pages without shoving it back into the bookcase. Now he was too curious not to ask. 'What do you mean, read your *Iliad*?'

The question seemed to take Eden by surprise. His expression tightened. 'Don't tell me you've never read Homer?' He filled his glass from a fresh bottle. 'Paean — actually, Paion, with an A-I-O — was the physician of the gods. He heals Ares and Hades when they get injured. It's all there in Book Five. Don't they cover the classics in state school? You'll have to borrow my library card.'

'Join the queue,' Jane said.

★ ★ ★

There was plenty of space for the six of them that week. The Bellwethers had nine bedrooms;

most of them had not been used since Iris and Eden were children, though Mrs Bellwether had paid to have them redecorated only last summer. Each spare room bore the plain but expensive accoutrements of some interior designer's choosing: a flotilla of Japanese tube-pillows was organised at the foot of every bed; Indian tapestries hung from the walls; the furniture was all hand-made — blocky, characterless revisions of long-ago styles. While Oscar stayed with Iris in the rectory, Eden and the others had the run of the house, treating their rooms like their personal suites at The Bellwether Hilton. They would traipse downstairs into the kitchen, half-dressed, to load plates with buttery toast and grapefruit halves, to go noisily about the cooking of fried eggs, bacon, and tomatoes while Oscar and Iris silently played cards or swapped sections of the newspaper at the breakfast counter.

Oscar knew it would be difficult to spend a week in such close quarters, exposed to the realities of each other, to their everydayness. He found something unattractive about their lack of consideration for the Bellwethers' home, the way that Marcus and Yin cavorted around the house like unchaperoned children at a caravan park, the way Eden sat with his dirty shoes upon the furniture and how Jane's heels pressed little marks into the planks of the parquet floor. He tried to reason out their tactlessness as boarding school behaviour. Because they'd lived away most of their lives, they made the best of their days at home; they compensated for the discipline of the boarding house by loafing around in their own houses. Somehow, thinking about it this way made it easier to accept.

Oscar had already reorganised his shifts at Cedarbrook, giving himself the entire week off, and he tried to think of it as a holiday. In fact, the slackness of the days at the Bellwether house, the languid trawl of the clouds across the Grantchester sky, made him feel as if he *was* on holiday, staying over at some expensive private resort where everything was free, and there was no mobile phone reception, and even the sun rose brightly every day, giving the air an illusion of summer.

As he lay in bed with Iris that first Tuesday morning, she suggested they could use the coming days to be tourists — to visit the cathedral at Ely, to see a play or an exhibition in London, to drive to the Norfolk coast. They weren't unappealing ideas, but he told her he'd rather stay exactly where he was. He hoped that a week at the Bellwether house would give them a chance to spend some real time together, to finally settle in one place. He wanted to spend long hours in bed with her in the quiet of the rectory, with the batteries taken out of the clock and the curtains drawn. Maybe they could spread out on a blanket somewhere in the meadowlands across the river, in the high grass where nobody could see them, and let the time roll slowly by.

She didn't argue. 'I know, you're right, you're right,' she said, sliding a hand across his stomach. 'But it's not going to be easy. If we hide

314

in our room all day, the others will come calling sooner or later. Do you know how quickly Marcus and Jane get bored? It won't take long for them to dig up a croquet set or get the barbecue going. They'll be wanting to swim in the river, especially now it's getting a bit warmer.'

'Well, let's just make the most of it, that's all I'm saying.'

She got up, pulling on a T-shirt. 'Yin will eat everything in sight. He's got a killer whale's appetite. We might have a full fridge now, but leave that lot unsupervised for too long and we'll be boiling nettles by tomorrow, I guarantee it.' She went into the bathroom and turned on the shower. A while later, she came out, wrapped in a powder-blue dressing gown, drying her hair with a towel.

He made her sit down beside him on the bed. 'Promise me something.'

'What?'

'That no matter how things with Crest and your brother turn out, or how many times the others come banging on our door this week, we'll find a few hours to be alone every day.'

She stopped towelling the ends of her hair and looked at him, smiling. 'Easy,' she said, and kissed the tip of his nose. 'I promise.'

He reached through the folds of her gown and ran his fingers along the inside of her thigh. 'Don't get dressed yet.'

* * *

315

Herbert Crest had checked into the Crowne Plaza in the city and didn't arrive at the house until seven each evening. So they spent the afternoons the way young people are entitled to spend lazy spring days: drinking beer and sangria and endless cups of coffee, playing badminton on the back lawn until the grass wore down under their trainers, barbecuing steaks and peppers and burgers in the intermittent sunshine, dozing in patio chairs on the porch behind the rectory with their jumpers on, listening to Yin's mix tapes through a ghetto blaster. It almost felt like summer. The air was mild, and a drowsy daylight survived until five or six, and though dark clouds loomed above the rooftops sometimes, they only ever spat a gentle, lukewarm rain.

For Oscar, the afternoons were for sprawling with Iris on the riverbank, under the shade of the elms and willows, holding hands and peering up at the branches as they moved against the breeze. The afternoons were for finding a cool, dim room upstairs in the house, removing Iris's clothes and kissing her bare skin until the sound of some searching, beckoning voice came slicing through the hallway, and the slap of feet on the stairs made her turn away and scramble to pull on her skirt. The afternoons were for Jane and Iris to make daisy-chain jewellery, lying frontways with their legs kicking out from under their dresses, and for the boys to accept them when they were done, wearing them as proudly as diamonds until they wilted and broke apart. The afternoons were for group photographs, posed on the rectory porch, all smiles and bunny-ears and arms around each other's shoulders; as well as quickly taken snapshots for which nobody was prepared, shut-eyed and funny-faced. The afternoons were for sitting in silence around the big wide patio table, reading books they found in the house; other times they were for contagious laughter, the sharing of jokes, silly ideas, idle thoughts; to speculate, to ruminate, to reminisce. Most of all, the afternoons were for the simple enjoyment of being together.

The longer he stayed in the tranquillity of the Bellwether house, the more Oscar understood the need the wealthy had for distance, for acreage. There was something to be said for being so removed from civilisation — the rest of the world became an afterthought. There was nobody here but the Bellwethers and the flock. Nothing could disturb them. They'd all turned off their mobiles, tired of struggling for reception, but a call would come through on the landline every now and then from Barcelona. Oscar would hear Iris talking to her parents, assuring them that nothing had gone up in flames. 'Did you want to speak to Eden?' she'd ask, each time. 'Well, alright, I'll tell him you rang.'

Most days, Eden wouldn't get out of bed until past eleven, and after spending an hour with everyone at lunch, he would go off into the organ house alone; 'to think,' he said, or sometimes, 'to get my head in the right place'. They would hear him tuning the organ and testing the registration for the better part of the afternoon, while they got on with the task of enjoying themselves. Usually, he would emerge around two or three o'clock, and insist that everyone join him in taking a ride along the Cam in the family punt. He'd pack a picnic basket in the kitchen, fill it with cheese and fruit and a few bottles of wine, and carry it down to the riverbank. Oscar would help him drag the punt out of the bulrushes and they'd load the provisions together. He found he liked Eden at these moments; there was something friendly about the way he'd take the ghetto blaster and ask, 'What do you think will do the trick today, Oscar? I've got Schubert, Mahler; I've got Brahms and Liszt. You choose.'

All of Eden's pretensions seemed to abandon him the instant he got on that boat and took the pole. 'All aboard, all aboard,' he would call to them in a sea captain's voice, and they'd climb in one by one, with Eden helping them down, steadying the boat against the bank. He was a graceful punter and would glide them along the river with effortless pushes of the wooden pole. In fact, his skill for punting was the only thing he didn't brag about. 'Oh, it's not difficult,' he told them once, 'it's *a priori*.' After a while, he'd give in to Marcus's constant pleas for a turn at the pole, and they'd switch places. The ride would become turbulent as Marcus staggered around on the till, wetting their heads with drips of silty water each time he made a manoeuvre. Eden would lie back then, with his feet upon the treads and his head against the lip of the boat. He'd run his hands through the tall grass on the bank as they limped along the river, or conduct the

318

up-and-down music bleating from the ghetto blaster with two pointed fingers, eyes closed.

It was only during their first punt ride together on Tuesday afternoon that they talked about Herbert Crest. For the rest of the week, they used their excursions on the boat to get merrily drunk and tell stories about their school days. It was Yin who brought up the subject. Eden was standing high up on the till, punting like a master, his stringy silhouette bearing down over them. They were drifting along soundlessly when Yin said: 'So how come we gotta do this seven nights in a row? Seems a little excessive.'

Eden lifted the pole out of the water, holding it across his body like a tightrope walker. 'I've explained that already, Yinny. You should've listened.'

'I listened. Just didn't really understand it.'

'We're relieving his pain,' Jane said.

Yin squeezed the bulb of his nose. 'Sure, okay, it's just — he seems like a pretty nice old man to me, and I don't know, I feel like maybe we're taking things a little far. I don't see how this is gonna help him.'

'We're taking it as far as the situation requires,' Eden said.

'I just think we might be subjecting this poor old guy to a bunch of stress he doesn't need. I don't want his heart to pack up or something. You see what I'm saying?' Yin's cheeks were flushed a shade of red. He kept pulling on his nose as if it was itchy. 'It was different when we were just goofing around with Oscar — he's young and healthy — but I don't see what good

319

can come from hypnotising this guy. It's fun and all, but I feel bad about it.'

Everyone kept their eyes on the water. Eden just carried on punting them along. The pole made gentle splashes as it broke the surface. Finally, he said: 'Don't you trust me after all these years, Yinny?'

'Sure, but — '

'He wouldn't do anything dangerous,' Marcus said.

Eden nodded. 'I know what I'm doing.'

'Yeah, look, I know you explained it already,' Yin went on, 'but I'm just not comfortable with it. I feel like we're taking advantage of the guy, that's all.'

'Herbert knows what he's getting himself into, don't worry,' Oscar said, feeling moved to speak up on Crest's behalf. But he was glad that someone had found the courage to question Eden. It was the first real murmur of defiance he'd heard amongst the flock.

'He's got a brain tumour,' Yin said. 'How much can he really be in control of his mind right now?'

Marcus dismissed this idea. 'We're relieving his pain. It's good for him. It can only be helping him, not making him worse. Hypnosis never hurt anyone. We're doing him a favour, the way I see it.'

Oscar might have told them everything at that moment, but he kept his mouth shut, for Crest's sake, and remembered the feeling that had kept him awake last night: that vague inkling of doubt that had stayed with him after Eden's paean.

Yin shook his head. 'We've pulled a few stunts

in our time, Edie, but this seems pretty crazy.'

'I don't see it that way. I see it as progress.'

Oscar couldn't help peering at the wide stance of Eden's deck shoes on the till. They didn't have a single drip of water on them.

Yin folded his arms and stared out beyond the high bank, where the distant steeple of a church was needling the orange-purple sky. Everything went very quiet. Eden turned the boat around. As they headed back towards the house, he said: 'You know, Yinny, I don't see what you're so bothered about. In your country, people do this all the time.'

Yin's back was turned and his arms were still folded across his chest; he didn't seem to be in much of a mood for talking. They drifted a few yards downriver, then Yin said: 'What the hell does *that* mean?'

'I'm talking about the good old U-S-of-A,' Eden said, cheerily. 'That great country of yours. I love it over there. Do you know I've been to nearly every State?'

'Yeah, you've only told me about a million times. So what?'

'Well, have I told you what happened the first time I went there?'

Yin shrugged. 'Maybe. I can't remember.'

'You're not going to tell the Disneyworld story, are you?' Iris asked.

'No, no, that's old news.' Eden punted on. 'I was going to tell them about the time we went to that church in Florida.'

'I don't remember any church,' Iris said.

'You were only five.'

'Oh.'

'Anyway — ' Eden pushed the shirtsleeves up on his forearms. He looked blankly at the clouds. 'It was my mother's idea to go there. She must have been getting one of her migraines after walking around Epcot all week, all that muggy weather they have over there. So she took us into this Pentecostal church that someone had told her about. It was near Tampa, one of those giant barn-like places. You know the kind I mean?'

Yin nodded.

'Well, there were already hundreds of people in there when we arrived. It was sweltering hot inside, too — Florida in the summer, no air conditioning. Horrible. The shirt was sticking to my back. Anyway, there was a big banner above the altar — actually, it was more like a Broadway stage than an altar — but that's beside the point. This banner was enormous, and I can remember it clear as anything. It said: 'Salvation and Revival Week with Pastor John Hoolihan. Come for Your Deliverance!' I remember feeling so excited. It was like being at a concert. Everyone was chattering, waiting for the pastor to come out. And after a few minutes, a choir came running in through the doors, and an organist started to play up above us. The music was only basic, but the sound was incredible, and the congregation went mad for it. People were flailing their hands about, speaking in tongues. Total gibberish. And then — boom! — pyrotechnics are going off and golden ticker-tape's shooting out everywhere. Next thing, this preacher runs up onto the stage. He's got this terrible spray-on tan, and white teeth — I mean, ridiculously white. Straight away, he starts proclaiming the wonders of the Lord Jesus Christ, shouting and screaming and praising his name, and the people are chanting back: *Amen, Amen to that!* Meanwhile, the organ's still playing, and the choir's still singing hallelujahs.'

'I really don't remember *any* of this,' Iris said. 'Where was I?'

'Oh, you were there too. Somewhere. Maybe you stayed in the car, I don't know.' Eden ducked to avoid an overhang of hedgerows, steering them around it. 'Anyway, after a few minutes, the preacher calls up a little boy from the crowd and pushes a microphone into his face. And the boy — he's not much older than me, maybe seven or eight — starts saying how he's had a sore throat for months, asking if Jesus can make it go away. So the preacher just laughs and goes, *Of course he can, son. You were born with the love of Jesus in your heart!* Of course Jesus will cleanse him of his sins and take away that sore throat. No problem. So he puts his hand on the boy's head and pushes it backwards and the choir's still singing hallelujah, hallelujah. The boy's just completely bewildered by the whole thing. He's got this anguished look on his face. But suddenly his legs start to go.'

Eden paused, letting the boat drift along on its own. He crouched down to put his hand on Yin's scalp like Pastor John, calling out in a faulty Southern accent: '*Praise Jesus, son! For he has redeemed you for your sins and healed you of your ailments! Praise Jesus our Lord in Heaven!*'

323

He stood up, stomping around on the till for a while, flailing his mad preacher's hands before settling down. Yin was smiling now, but Eden wasn't. There was a steely concentration in his eyes. He took up the pole again and propelled them downstream. 'Next thing, the kid falls back into Pastor John's arms and starts clutching his throat, like all the pain has been suddenly lifted out of him. *Hallelujah! Hallelujah!* Oh, I'm telling you, it was an amazing thing to behold. It went on for hours. The preacher kept dragging people out of the crowd. People were wheeling their relatives up the ramp and Pastor John was blessing them. He had them eating out of his hand. Everyone was in this state of delirium, just complete and total ecstasy. People were fainting in the aisles . . . And I remember seeing my mother standing there, waving her hands in the air like some little kid at a pantomime, just dying to be chosen. She was actually shouting *Over here! Over here!* I'd never seen her quite so animated before.' Eden stopped to take a rest. Holding the pole across his chest like a rifle, he stared down at his wavering image in the spreading wake. They coasted towards the bank at the foot of the Bellwethers' garden. Everyone was waiting for him to finish, but Eden didn't say anything further, and the punt gradually lost its momentum.

Oscar leaned forward. 'Did she get chosen?' he asked.

Eden seemed to be expecting the question. He smirked and tore his eyes away from the water. 'That's not the point of the story.'

'Of course it is,' Iris said. 'If Mum got up there, I want to know about it.'

'I was *trying* to explain something, that's all.'

'That there are crazy old people in Florida?' Yin said. 'Big revelation.'

'Did she get up there or not?' Iris asked.

Eden stayed quiet.

'Fine,' she said. 'I'll ask her myself.'

When they reached the bank, Eden jammed the boat against it with the pole. He took Jane's hand and helped her onto dry land, then reached out for Iris's. She let herself be lifted, but skipped over the side by herself. 'All I'm trying to explain,' Eden said, staring after her, 'is that there are plenty of people in the world who believe a preacher can rid them of their pain.'

'So what?' Yin said, climbing out.

Eden threw him the tether and huffed out a heavy sigh. 'So if Pastor John Hoolihan can do it with nothing but a spray-on tan and a smile, what makes you think *I* can't? I'm better equipped than he is. I understand things that he couldn't even come close to understanding.'

Oscar jumped onto the bank, linking arms with Iris. The fresh air had roughened her skin.

'That's different,' Yin said, hitching the rope to a stump. 'Nobody can argue with Jesus.' And he went off through the tall grass, laughing, before Eden had a chance to respond.

★　★　★

Every night at seven, Andrea would drop Crest off at the house, leaving the engine running while she helped him to the front door. She'd ring the bell and leave the old man standing there by the great glass entrance, and wouldn't return until around ten thirty, the milky daub of her headlights brightening the flowerbeds. Oscar would go to greet Crest in the atrium and he'd take him to the drawing room and pour him a glass of water. The old man would sit there gulping it down every time, like it was the first drink he'd had in months. Then he'd hand the glass back and ask for another. He'd drink the second more slowly and, if the others were around, he'd take the opportunity to ask them a few questions: How did they all know Eden? What were their best memories of Eden? How did they all learn to play so well — did Eden teach them? What could they tell him about Eden's parents? After a while, they seemed to get tired of these questions. They started to avoid being in the house when Crest arrived each night, and would wave at him from the far end of the garden, or from the top of the stairs.

Oscar couldn't tell what Crest thought about Marcus, Yin, and Jane — or if it really mattered in the scheme of things — but Crest *did* seem to care about the impression he was making on them: 'I bet they see me as a sad, strange old man, huh, coming here every night to get my head wet? They must think I'm desperate as hell.'

'I think they just feel sorry for the pain you're in,' Iris told him.

'Well, haven't they heard? Sympathy's a waste of time.'

When he was done with his third glass of water, Crest would go out to the organ house and rap his knuckles against the oak. Eden would let him inside and they'd spend an hour together, just the two of them, with the doors locked. Crest liked to call these moments 'our little sit-downs'. As much as Oscar tried to see in through the windows, as much as he leaned his ear against the gap in the doors and tried to hear what they were discussing, all he could make out were a few dull mumbles and two fuzzy shapes. He couldn't even tell which of them did most of the talking — from outside, their voices had the same rhythm, the same dry timbre — and Crest would never tell him anything afterwards. He said it would be wrong to betray Eden's confidence, and if it was all going to end up in the book anyway, what was the problem?

On the phone each morning, he'd be just as elusive, speaking to Oscar in vague phrases he knew would placate him: 'Oh, it's like drawing blood from a stone in there sometimes, but I'm satisfied with how things are going'; 'We still have a long road ahead of us'; 'I know I don't have much time to play with here, Oscar, but I've never rushed anything in my life and I'm not about to start.'

The longer it went on, the less they all seemed to think about what they were involved in. What took place in the organ house each night became perfunctory, an ordinary social event as mundane as a band rehearsal or a visit to the cinema. Around eight o'clock they would file into the organ house, barely a word passing between

327

them. They'd take up their usual positions and go through the precise routine of it all over again. There was something quite pacific about the ceremony of it.

Iris would go straight to her cello to tune it. Marcus and Jane would kneel, opening their folders of notation. Yin would stand with his arms folded, staring down at Crest with a kind of pity. Oscar would change the tape in the camera, clean the lens with his jumper. Crest would dust off the tuning forks and ready himself without a smirk, without a shrug, accepting each wet strand of muslin like a Catholic taking his communion wafer. As soon as Eden struck the first organ note, they fell into gear — the music took over them; the thrill of playing, of being involved in something, no matter how crazy, held a certain power over them. They knew their parts well and performed them with a kind of involuntary focus. And although they knew better than to glance towards Eden for a nod of approval when they sang their counterpoint harmonies in perfect sync, Oscar would catch some of them doing it now and then.

Only Iris wavered from the routine: she couldn't help but embellish moments of her cello line, adding new runs, new flourishes. For the most part, she would stick to the pattern of things, but there were chords that she bowed differently, notes she held a fraction longer every night. Oscar knew that she wasn't doing this to steal the limelight from her brother; it was just how she played. If she couldn't add her own individuality to a piece of music, she grew bored.

Eden must have noticed it. But he seemed to tolerate her ornamentations; he'd furrow his brow or give a little shake of his head, but wouldn't admit to his frustration.

Then, late on Thursday, after Crest had gone home and the others were winding down in the drawing room, Oscar looked through the French doors and saw the two of them arguing outside the rectory. He didn't like the way Eden was clutching so tightly at her elbow, how Iris was struggling to prise herself from his grip. Her face was flushed and the sleeve of her cardigan was snagged between her brother's fingers. Oscar could hear their raised voices as he hurried out through the back door. 'Come and look,' Eden was shouting. 'Come and look at it on the page, if you don't believe me. Don't argue.'

'No. I'm going inside. Get *off* me!'

Oscar was ready to put himself between them. But when Eden heard him calling out, 'Iris, are you okay?' and saw him running down the path, he let go of his sister's elbow with an easy motion, like he was releasing a kite string.

'Are you okay?' Oscar said again, facing her.

She wouldn't look at him. She smoothed out the twists in her cardigan. 'I'm fine. Everything's fine.' There was an unusual flatness to her voice.

'Was he hurting you?'

'No. We were just talking.'

'Sounded like shouting.'

'Okay fine, we were arguing. We're allowed to argue *sometimes*.'

'What were you arguing about?'

'Nothing. Just — ' She began to rub her arm

329

where Eden had been holding her. 'Just leave it, okay? I'm getting cold out here.' And she went striding off, brushing his hand away as he tried to stop her.

'Iris, wait.'

She kept going until the security light came on at the back of the house, and went into the kitchen.

Oscar turned to find Eden leaning against the wan bricks of the rectory. The light blinked off again, darkening the space between them. 'She's been ornamenting her cello parts all week,' Eden said. 'It was getting so bad it seemed almost like sabotage. But it's okay, we've talked it through now. You can climb off that high horse you just rode in on.'

Oscar realised he was breathing heavily. Steam was rising from his mouth. 'You were hurting her.'

'Oh, please. I was barely even touching her. Why don't you just go back inside and enjoy the fruits of my hospitality? There's a good chap.' Eden pushed himself away from the wall abruptly, and shuffled off, into the safety of the organ house. Oscar heard the cold slide of the bolt across the door. He looked back towards the kitchen. Iris was standing at the sink with both taps running. When he headed up to meet her, she moved into the drawing room to sit with the others, and for the rest of the evening, she avoided the subject.

In bed that night, she was quiet, distracted. She turned off the bedside lamp and rolled away from him. He could tell by the way her fingers kept tapping on the mattress that she was thinking about what had happened. But she refused to talk any more about it and he fell asleep an arm's length from her.

She woke him a few hours later, kissing his neck. Her mood seemed brighter. 'I was thinking,' she said, and began to walk her fingers down his body, from his chest to his stomach. 'We aren't using the hours of two a.m. to four a.m. very effectively.' She moved lower. Her hand felt dry and hot around him. 'I think there are better things to do than sleep, don't you?' And she ducked her head beneath the covers.

The next night, there were no hints of elaboration in her cello line. She played robotically, her back straight and her shoulders tight, and that was how it stayed for the rest of the week. The music seemed better because of it — more unified — but something else had been lost.

Through all of this, Herbert Crest showed few signs of improvement. He was still ashen-faced and walked away from the organ house each night with a heavy gait, crooked and unstable. He tired very easily and complained of the cold. His dizzy spells were just as frequent. He still got headaches. Sometimes, he would lose words or slur them: he'd mean to ask for a coaster for his glass but would struggle to remember what to call it; he'd mean to say 'wonderful' but it would come out as 'wandffer', and when these things happened, his eyes would glaze over with fear. Other times, he seemed perfectly tuned in. Though it was clearly an effort, he'd play old

331

songs on the piano now and again, just a few bars to amuse himself. 'I play worse than a horse,' he'd say. Often, he'd wander through the house looking at family photographs in silver frames — 'Your mother's a good-looking woman, huh? Strong genes' — and each night, he'd wait in the drawing room for Andrea, reading the paper, quoting news stories that took his interest: a maths prize founded by the King of Norway, a new strain of flu that was taking over China. He still had the vocabulary of a debate team captain, and would point out grammatical errors in most of the articles ('An apostrophe in 'yours' — how do they get away with it?'). At the very least, his condition didn't seem to be deteriorating; he was holding steady. The hair was even beginning to grow back on his head in thin, babyish tufts of blond and his eyebrows were fuller, darker. But every time Oscar asked if he was feeling better, he'd shake his head wryly and say: 'No dice.'

On Sunday night, as Eden's organ melody was in full flow and the voices of the flock were falling away, Oscar watched the old man through the camera lens. There was something new about his expression, something not quite at ease. His breathing seemed quicker than usual and he was struggling to stay upright. The music went on — lilting and slowly coming to rest — but Crest only grew more agitated. The tuning fork began to wobble between his teeth. His whole head began to shake. And then his neck, his chest, his arms, his legs were shuddering. The tuning forks fell to the ground — an awkward music, like three bells clanging off-key — and then the old man began to rock in the chair, his entire body convulsing. He rocked so hard that its legs toppled over, and the chair hit the floor by Iris's feet. She stood up instantly, casting aside her cello. Oscar dropped the camera. Yin, Marcus and Jane stopped singing. They gasped, frozen with panic, as Crest lay there, juddering on the planks like a grounded fish before them. 'It's his heart,' Yin said. 'Oh, Jesus fuck, it's his heart.' Crest was writhing so much that his feet came close to kicking over the oil lanterns before Iris pushed them a safe distance away. The room darkened, closed in on them. Time became heavy. And through it all, Eden carried on playing.

Oscar knew what he had to do. He could see the fear on the faces of the others, but he tried to keep himself calm. He got down on his haunches, turning Crest onto his side. 'Give me your coat,' he said to Marcus, and when Marcus didn't move, he shouted it louder until he jolted into action, ripping off his coat as if it were on fire. Still the organ kept on playing. Eden hadn't even turned around to see what all the noise was about.

Rolling up the coat and putting it under Crest's head, Oscar tried his best to settle him. 'Steady, Herbert, steady,' he said. He waited for his convulsions to slow, and, soon enough, the old man's body was at rest again. 'He'll be okay now.' He almost had to shout it over the sound of the organ. 'It was a seizure, that's all. He's had plenty of them before.' Crest lay there, exhausted.

'Thank God for you, Oscar,' Jane said. 'I was really panicking.'

'Yeah,' Marcus said. 'Well done.'

'Good job, man,' Yin said, squeezing his shoulder.

Finally, the organ stopped; the last note choked in the rafters. Eden turned around on the stool. He didn't seem shocked to see Crest on the floor. 'What are you all doing?' he said.

Nobody answered.

Oscar looked at Yin. 'Can you help me carry him?'

'Sure.'

'We'll put him in the rectory.'

'On the bed?'

'Yeah.'

'Be careful,' Iris said.

Eden stood over them. 'What the hell is going on?'

'Oh, Edie, it was awful. He had a seizure,' said Jane. 'But he's okay now. Oscar was amazing — so calm.' She turned to look into Eden's briny green eyes. 'Didn't you hear?'

'No. I was — ' He trailed off. 'I suppose I was somewhere else.'

Yin took the old man's weight. Crest was limp as a puppet in his arms, feet dangling, heels clapping. At the exit, he stopped to allow Oscar to unlock the doors. He looked hard at Eden, his big chest heaving. 'I warned you, man,' Yin said. 'I knew we were taking this too far.'

Eden wetted the corner of his mouth with his tongue and said nothing.

In the rectory, Yin laid Crest down on the

mattress and stood at the foot of the bed, hands on his knees, catching his breath. He wanted to stay and help — 'Maybe I can just wait with him, make sure he's okay?' — but Oscar told him it would be better not to crowd him, so he went outside to join the others, looking in through the window.

Oscar drew up a chair by the old man's bedside. He mopped his brow with a flannel, checked his pulse. Crest slept soundly on his side, breathing against the pillow. For a while, the only sound was the singing of the crickets in the garden, but soon, the others began to congregate outside. They started to bicker. Their lean shadows stole in through the window and performed a weary pageant on the wall behind Crest's head. He went over to shut the curtains and put some gentle music on the stereo to drown their voices out, but he could still hear the tenor of their argument.

'It's not *his* fault, Iggy. Why do you always have to blame him for everything?'

'She's right. We're all in this together.'

'I can't believe you guys. How long have I been saying this was a bad idea, huh? All fucking week, I've been saying it.'

'Yeah, yeah, change the record, will you?'

'*Ssshhhh.* Keep your voices down.'

'He can't hear.'

'Of course he can hear.'

'Let's go inside then.'

'I want to stick around, make sure he's okay.'

'Oscar will find us if he needs us.'

'I wouldn't be so sure about that.'

'What's *that* supposed to mean?'

'Nothing. I'm just saying — he looked upset.'

'You mean angry?'

'No. Just upset.'

'He'll get over it.'

'*Sshhh*. You're being loud.'

'Alright. Fine. Let's go in.'

Oscar heard the clamour of their footsteps as they all headed for the house.

He stared down at the old man, placed his hand against his forehead. It was clammy and cold and smooth as glass. 'This is what happens when you stop taking your medication,' he said.

By the time Andrea came to pick him up, Crest was awake and back on his feet, though he moved with tiny, uncertain steps and seemed reluctant to talk, or just too tired. He mumbled his gratitude to Oscar for taking care of him, straightening out his collar, pulling on his baseball cap in front of the dressing table mirror and reshaping the peak. He was still groggy and could hardly muster the energy to walk up to the house, so Oscar took him around the side way, through the big iron gate that swung back, pleasingly heavy, ducking under the trellis arches, veined with ivy. When he saw Andrea ahead of them, parked up like always in the same little spot behind Jane's Land Rover, Crest stopped walking. He held a knotty finger to his lips and said: 'Let's keep this little incident between us, okay?' The words came out of his throat with a kind of resignation, like they would be the last words he ever got to speak.

12

Her Ideal Life

Cedarbrook was typically quiet when Oscar arrived on Monday morning, an hour early for his shift. The lobby was empty as always, and the lights had yet to be switched on at the nurses' station. A cleaner's cart stood at the foot of the stairs and a short, broad-shouldered Filipina woman he'd never seen before was dousing the seat of the stairlift with disinfectant spray. The place was still half-asleep: thirty-four beds were still thick with dreams. In the dim light of the staff room, he made himself a coffee, browsed the front and back pages of the paper so he'd have something to discuss with Deeraj and the other nurses later. Then he went to find Jean in her office, to hand in the time sheets she'd been asking him for since the start of the month. She had her own little room marked MATRON, between the kitchen and the parlour, and he knew she'd be there sitting at her desk with her portable TV on as always, watching a repeat of some American sitcom with the volume down low and laughing her dockyard laugh.

It was when he got to the parlour that he saw Dr Paulsen. He was sitting dull-eyed in a wingback near the window. A plate of scrambled eggs was set on the tray-table in front of him and he was peering down at it vacantly, turning his plastic spoon around in his right hand. The features of his face were drawn to the left as if they were caught on a fishhook. There was an atlas of foodstains on the front of his pyjama top. He looked like he'd been sitting there for hours.

'You're down early, aren't you?' Oscar called out, but the old man didn't move a muscle. 'Dr Paulsen?'

Slow as the winching of a crane, Paulsen moved his right eye to look up at him. His body stayed rigid, apart from the spoon he kept turning around in his dry fingers — flick, flick, flick.

'Dr Paulsen, are you alright?'

Flick, flick, flick.

The eggs were cold to the touch. When Oscar went to move the plate, the old man didn't try to stop him, and after it was taken away, he just gazed down at the space where it used to be, probing the corner of his mouth with his tongue. 'I'm going to get you some more, okay?' Oscar said. 'I'm going to get you some more.' A numb feeling was starting to gather in his feet. He felt something clutching at his heart, trying to drown it, like the way his cousin Terry used to duck his head under the water at the swimming pool to time how long he could hold his breath.

Flick, flick, flick.

'Just wait there. I'll be back.'

Jean was sitting at her desk just like he knew she would be. The clock in the corner of her TV screen read 7:06. 'Hello, lovey,' she said. 'Can't pay you any extra for being early, you know.'

His voice was steady, even. 'Is everything okay

with Dr Paulsen? I just saw him in the parlour.'

'Right. *Him*. He's in a bad way, I'm afraid. Been leaving you messages all week. Haven't you been home?'

'No. I've been — I went on holiday.'

'Anywhere nice?'

He looked back at her blankly.

She gestured at the empty chair in front of her and he sat down. 'Well, sorry, it's not good news.' With her eyes on the television, she talked him through the whole thing very matter-of-factly. Late on Wednesday night, she said, Dr Paulsen had had another stroke. 'It was a big 'un, too. Not a TIA, a proper ischaemic.' She smiled at the TV. Canned laughter filled the room. She clicked it off and turned to look at him, putting on a serious face, assuming a proper tone. 'Doctor reckons he had a full-on thrombosis in his brain. That's why his left side's a bit, you know, tensed up. He should be alright in a few months, but who knows? Hard to know anything for sure when it comes to strokes.' She tilted her head, reached out her hand. 'Aw, lovey, I know you two are close. I *did* leave messages for you. But there's nothing you could've done about it, even if you'd been here.'

When he went back into the parlour, Paulsen was still in the wingback, peering down at the empty tray-table, and still absently twirling the plastic spoon in his right hand.

He crouched down beside his chair. 'Dr Paulsen, it's Oscar. I know you remember me. I know you understand.' The old man didn't move anything but the thumb and finger of his right hand around the spoon. His left side was tight, unbending. 'I'm going to take you upstairs and get you dressed, okay? We can't have you down here all day looking like you've just crawled out of bed. That wouldn't do now, would it? A man has to have standards.' He went to take the spoon from Paulsen's hand, but the old man wouldn't let go — his fingers viced around it and Oscar couldn't wrest it from his grip. The old man grunted, and flung out his right arm. It nearly struck Oscar on the side of the head. 'Mine. Mine,' he slurred.

'Alright, okay, you keep hold of it.'

Oscar didn't know what to do. Upstairs, he struggled to get the sleeve of a clean jumper over the old man's arm. The jumper hung half on, half off his shoulder — a saddening Argyle sling.

For the rest of the day, Oscar felt lost. The corridors of Cedarbrook seemed endless. He could barely bring himself to visit Paulsen all afternoon. It was too difficult to watch him sitting there, staring into space with those big snuffed-out eyes and a lengthening trickle of drool in the corner of his mouth; his jaw was like a glovebox with a broken hinge. But despite how low the sight of Paulsen made him feel — and despite how much the guilt weighed on his shoulders — he forced himself to go up to his room every hour to make sure he was okay. The old man had nobody else.

Later that night, Oscar put his head around the door one last time before the end of his shift. Paulsen was lying flat on his bed with an arm across his ribs, the spoon at rest between his fingers. There was a sombre darkness in the room; the curtains were drawn. He thought the old man was finally sleeping, so he went to lay a blanket over him, but as soon as the fabric touched Paulsen's skin, his right eye opened.

'Didn't mean to disturb you. Go back to sleep.'

Paulsen made a movement with his arm, lifting the spoon up and releasing it. 'Okay, Herbert,' he said, shutting his eyelid slowly. 'Okay, Herb.'

★   ★   ★

Oscar was surprised by the strength of Crest's voice on the answer machine. He skipped past four messages from Jean and was about to delete the fifth when suddenly he heard a bright and cheery intonation fizzing in the speakers: 'Oscar, hey — just Herbert. Letting you know I'm doing fine. Call back if you want to. Bye for now!'

He expected Andrea to pick up when he rang back, but Crest answered the phone himself with a merry, 'Hey there, kiddo, good of you to call,' and waded right into telling him about how much he'd written that day. He talked with the enthusiasm of a schoolboy, one sentence spilling into the next, barely stopping for breath: 'I'm a little giddy here. Things are really going great with the book right now. Six thousand words today and counting, can you believe that? The old brain feels like it's firing again, not just *ticking over.*' Then he said: 'Hey, tell you what: I'd like to send you what I have so far. Just the intro, maybe; I don't know. I wouldn't usually share anything before it's ready, but, oh boy, it's been a really great day. I'm on such a high.' Finally, Crest exhaled — more of a sigh than an outward breath — and that's when he said, 'Sorry to talk so much. What's happening with you, kid?'

Oscar explained what had happened to Dr Paulsen and Crest took a long moment to respond. All the *joie de vivre* seemed to leave his voice through the sudden puncture in his heart. 'I — I really — God, I really don't know what to say to that. Boy, oh boy. Poor Bram, huh?' Oscar invited him to Cedarbrook, but Crest seemed reluctant to pay a visit. 'I hate those places,' he said, 'they give me the jitters. Besides, I'm not sure I have the time right now, with the book and everything. We'll see, huh?'

Oscar went on trying to convince him, though he sensed it was a lost cause. 'It would mean so much to him if you came. I just feel so bad about it all. If I'd just been there . . . '

'Oscar. Stop. Believe me, thinking about What Ifs will drive you crazy.' Crest went quiet then, deliberating on things. He made short little clucking sounds with his tongue. 'Look, maybe I can make it out to see him sometime this week. I guess I owe Bram that much. Leave it with me.'

★　★　★

At the Great Gate of Trinity College, Iris stood waiting. The soft light of the porters' lodge pooled on the flagstones at her feet. She had on a

342

royal-blue evening dress with a white satin shawl and the luminous wire of her headphones hung in a V against her bare neck. Seeing Oscar, she removed the tiny buds from her ears, coiled the wire up quickly, and put the old Walkman into her glitzy little handbag. She took his hand and kissed him squarely on the mouth. 'Where's your suit?' she said, gesturing at his jeans and leather jacket; his worn-in trainers. 'It's a Formal. It's meant to be, you know, *formal.*' Behind her, the impeccable lawns of Trinity were dusted with a fine, forgotten rain.

For a moment, all he could do was look at her. She had taken him by surprise with the dress and the tiny diamond earrings. The way she'd drawn her fringe across her forehead in a side-parting made her look older, less studious. 'What's the matter, sweetheart? What is it?'

He told her about Dr Paulsen and she comforted him with whispers of sympathy, pressing her nose upon his temple. 'Oh, I'm so sorry, Oscar. I feel silly now, dressed like this. We'll go another time. There'd be nothing worse than a formal right now, all that tightness and etiquette.' She took his hand again, kissed his cheek. 'Come on, let's go to mine. I need to change out of these clothes.'

'What about the others?'

'They won't mind.' She glanced across the empty court towards the college buildings, where silhouettes of men in dinner jackets stood chatting with vague outlines of girls in evening gowns. 'Probably won't even know we're missing.'

Part of him still wanted to go inside. The formal dinner had been his idea, after all. Last week, Jane had mentioned that the BA Society at her college held formals over the holidays and he'd been so enthusiastic about attending that Jane had gone to the trouble of arranging tickets for everybody: 'It'd be a nice, low-key introduction to the formal scene,' she'd said, 'and then, if you want, we can take you to a bigger do when term starts.' Even Eden had agreed to go. 'It'll be worth it just to see Oscar in a white collar,' was how he'd put it.

Thinking about their week at the Bellwether house was the only thing that took Oscar's mind off Dr Paulsen. He missed them, the comfort of being among the flock. He remembered how Yin and Marcus would come out to sit with him and Iris on the rectory porch each night after Crest went home, chewing cigar-tips, swirling brandy, picking the wax from the citronella candles. They would hardly talk, just watch the motion of the clouds across the moon, timing the pulses of the stars above them. Yin had a way of making Oscar feel at ease by saying nothing at all, just by leaning back on his chair-legs, venting cigar smoke from his nostrils. Sometimes, they would play Pontoon or Hearts, and Marcus would go ballistic every time he lost a hand: '*Fuck* you, Iggy, and your *fucking* jack of diamonds! How many of those *fucking* jacks of diamonds can you get in one game!' Jane would hear the commotion and come down from the house in her pyjamas, leaving Eden in bed. She'd refuse to be dealt in to whatever game they were

344

playing, but she'd talk to them while they eyed their cards, bringing smiles to their faces with her commentary.

There was a strange solace in being a part of the flock. Oscar liked the way they considered even the most pedestrian of subjects from an intellectual angle: 'What's surprising about badminton,' Marcus would revel in telling them, 'is that it goes back centuries. Started in ancient Greece, worked its way through India, to Britain, via the army. The rules haven't changed since the eighteen hundreds.'

Oscar couldn't help but enjoy the sheer unpredictability of their discussions, how Jane would start out by asking Iris a simple question: 'Are your parents going to build out any further towards the road?' and Iris would answer: 'God, I hope not. It's already like *Last Year at Marienbad* around here.' Then Marcus would give his forthright opinion: 'Ugh! I hate that pretentious piece of nonsense — hate it. I get a headache every time I see it. Alain Resnais stinks. He's got a decent aesthetic eye but that doesn't give him licence to be incoherent,' and he would segue into a diatribe on the sadness he felt about the obsolescence of celluloid film and the soulless digitalisation of photography; this would lead into Yin pondering the extinction of the audio cassette, how he couldn't imagine a world where a guy couldn't give his girlfriend a mix-tape on her birthday, and Oscar would chime in then with a few opinions of his own. When Eden wasn't there, they could all talk like this — ruminate on matters, get their points of

345

view across without being interrupted.

And yet part of him missed the simple quiet of those punt-rides with Eden, too, the brightness of the spring sun on their faces, the sight of birds winging across the river. He liked the way Eden would hum along so tunefully to the Boston Pops on the ghetto blaster. When he thought about the week in Grantchester — leaving out the madness of what took place each night in the organ house — he was sure it had been the best week of his life.

It was too late to go to the formal now. He was underdressed and unprepared. 'Come on,' Iris said, wrapping her shawl around his neck, pulling him close. 'I know what you need.' She kissed him hard on the mouth.

They walked to Harvey Road. There were few cars on the streets but there were plenty of people out for a stroll in the gathering dark — couples about their age, holding hands; packs of polo-shirted men heading for the centre of town, drenched in cologne. At the end of Regent Street, she said: 'I was reading your poem today. I really think it's a lovely thing. You should write more.'

'Maybe,' he said.

'I mean it. You have talent.' She looked towards the changing traffic lights in the distance. '*A concession to a coming afternoon*. That's so perfect. I cry every time I read it.'

'You're just trying to make me feel better.'

'I mean every word. You could do so much more, Oscar. God knows you can't be a care assistant your whole life.'

346

He stopped.

She looked at him and he couldn't tell if her expression was apologetic or incredulous. 'There's nothing *wrong* with being a care assistant, it's just — oh, come on, you know what I mean. I'm saying you could be more than that. If you wanted to be.'

'There's no way I could be a poet. That's a pipe dream.'

'I'm not saying you should be a poet. I'm saying you should write more poetry, that's all. You should do whatever makes you happy.'

'Things don't work that way in the real world. Trust me.'

She seemed hurt by this, creasing up her mouth. He felt her fingers reaching for his hand. Then her head fell against his shoulder, sighing. 'I'm just trying to support you. I know you think about this stuff, too. You keep it all inside, but I know you think about it. And I know you don't want to be at Cedarbrook forever.'

'Maybe I do. There's nothing wrong with that.'

'No, look, of course not. It doesn't matter to me *what* you are — I don't care if you're a bloody sea fisherman — but it matters to me that you're fulfilled, and I'm not sure you are.'

He didn't want to get into an argument. How simple it was for her to say these things to him, to drop slogans like *Do whatever makes you happy* into the conversation, as if happiness and fulfilment were easy things to acquire. To Iris, the world was a clear-cut place where anything could be achieved with a little perseverance, or the right connections. Failure didn't scare her, because she had the crashmat of her inheritance to fall back on. She had the comfort of knowing the house she lived in was her own, bought and paid for by parents who spent more money on cognac than most people could retire on.

Sometimes, it seemed that Iris had gone through life so weightlessly that she couldn't imagine the kinds of struggles other people had. It wasn't that she couldn't identify the most wretched poverty when she saw it — the distended bellies of Lesothoan families plagued by famine, Romanian orphans crammed eleven to a cot — and he knew that when these things flashed up on the news, she felt the sorrow profoundly and was moved to help. But she often seemed unaware of the regular, financial stresses of ordinary people: the constant hustle for that little bit of extra money to fix a broken boiler, to buy another school jumper, to pay the orthodontist's fees. If he asked her the price of petrol, she probably wouldn't know it, but she could tell him everything about the distillation of petroleum and the importance of renewable energy. There were times when he couldn't help but resent her for what she had, for the nineteen years of good schooling, skiing holidays, fine dining; for being told every day that she could have whatever made her happy. But he'd come to realise how wrong it was to resent her for these things. Because they were the same things he wanted for himself, the same things he would like to afford his own children one day. To begrudge Iris her ideal life was just plain jealousy, the kind of bitterness that had ruined his father. He had to bite down on his tongue sometimes to remind himself of that.

'I'm fine,' he told her. 'It's just been a bad day and I don't want to talk about it, okay?'

'Okay, okay.'

They were quiet for the rest of the walk. When they got to the house, she went upstairs and ran a bath. She asked him if he wanted to get in with her, but he said he was too tired. 'Oh,' she said, glassy-eyed, 'well, if you change your mind . . . ' He waited for her in the bedroom, reading her revision notes and the scrawled comments in the margins of the textbooks on her pillow. He looked at the display of St Mary's School rosettes that were pinned up on her notice board: First Prize (Latin), First Prize (French), First Prize (Music). There was a photo of her parents in a gold enamelled frame on her bedside table. He would always turn it away when he opened the drawer to get a condom, and he'd always find it set up again in the morning: the faces of her ambitions.

She came in from the bathroom with a white towel wrapped around her, and the skin of her shoulders mottled, beaded with water. For a moment, she sat at her dresser, brushing her hair, and he watched her, trying to imagine her fifty years from now, wondering if he would still feel the same exhilaration at the sight of her. And he realised how easy it was to picture her that way, still tidying her hair with the same little gestures of her brush, half-naked in the shade of some future bedroom.

'Will you play for me?' he asked.

She kept on brushing her hair. 'Now? I'm not even dressed.'

'It doesn't matter. I just want to hear you.'

And so she went to get her cello from the corner. She took off her towel and sat at the foot of the bed with her back towards him. She played something he'd never heard before — a plaintive, drawling tune with notes so low they rattled the perfume bottles on her dresser. He watched the slow flight of her shoulder blades as she bowed. It was all he needed to make that dry ache inside him disappear.

13

Ibidem

Herbert Crest emerged from Dr Paulsen's room like a man defeated. It was a muggy Thursday afternoon in late March and the underarms of his cotton shirt were dark with sweat, his upper lip glistening. The peak of his baseball cap had been a perfect horseshoe shape when he'd knocked on the old man's door, but now it was creased along the middle, forming a gable above the solemn features of his face. 'Well,' he said, 'I tried.'

Oscar had been waiting outside the door for a while, hoping that the sight of Herbert Crest might jog the old man's memory. There had been some improvement in Paulsen's physical state (he'd regained some of the strength in his left side) but the wires of his brain were still tangled up. All week, the old man had been staring back at Oscar with a misty panic, a terrifying blankness, calling him 'Herb' and 'Hebb' and 'Herbie'. One morning, down by the parlour window after breakfast, Paulsen had pushed a pair of used ticket stubs into his hand. LARKIN'S BALLOON TOURS: REDEEMABLE FOR ONE RIDE ONLY. It had near enough broken his heart.

'I think I made things worse,' Crest said, standing in the corridor, trying to hide the

351

sadness in his voice by laughing meekly. 'He didn't really recognise me, I don't think. I tried to get him talking but he just sat there. Didn't say much.'

'What *did* he say?'

'Yes, no, mm-hm, okay — not much more. Oh, and 'What time is it?' He asked me what time it was. I couldn't even tell him *that*.' Crest raised his left arm to show his bare wrist.

'He didn't use your name?'

'Nope.'

'Sometimes he mumbles. Maybe you missed it.'

'Oh, I'm sure I would've heard it.'

Oscar didn't know what else to do. 'He must've been happy you came, at least.'

'Hard to tell,' Crest said. 'He was pleased to see the carpet, I know *that*. Barely even looked at me . . . Listen, this is kinda difficult for me to take right now. I could use a little air. Take a walk with me?'

They went out into the back garden, where the tended lawns were freshly striped and flowers bloomed in hanging baskets and window boxes. Residents sat out on the patio in wheelchairs, noses white with sun cream. Crest walked along the path with confident strides. There was definitely a new range of motion in those stout legs of his. Though his chest was heaving slightly when they reached the far end of the garden and sat down on the stone wall beside the fishpond, Crest didn't take too long to steady himself. He removed his cap to let the sunshine fall upon his face. 'Y'know, of all the nursing homes I've seen, this is definitely the nicest. I never thought Bram would end up in a place like this, but I'm glad it *is* a place like this. Does that make sense?'

'I think so.'

'Look at this garden. It's impeccable.'

Oscar was so used to the Cedarbrook grounds he hardly noticed them any more. Looking now in the fervid spring sunshine, he could see what Crest was talking about. Everywhere was its own shade of purple: there were azaleas in the lawn borders, and clutches of hyacinths in the rockery, and that perfect covering of wisteria on the walls of the building like a fine velvet jacket.

'I'm sorry about — you know,' Crest said. 'I had to get out. It's not easy, seeing him like that.'

Oscar realised he hadn't even thought about how Crest would feel. It would be tough for anyone who knew the old man to watch him silently dribbling in his chair, absent from the world, but Crest was the person who'd known him in the best years of his life, when he was Abraham Paulsen, a young academic with things to say and places to go.

'I'll bet you think you know that old man better than anyone, huh?' Crest said. The question caught Oscar a little off guard. He opened his mouth to speak, not really knowing what was going to come out, but Crest went on: 'I mean, you probably think you've got him all figured out — am I right? That's how I used to feel too. But you can be sure there's plenty he hasn't told you. Like I'll bet you don't know about his ex-wife.'

'No,' Oscar admitted. The shock, the intrigue

was clear in his voice, and he felt ashamed of himself for sounding like some gossiping neighbour. 'God, I had no idea.'

'Oh, yeah, she's out there somewhere. Doubt she'd ever come to visit. They're a long time divorced. But she's still out there alright.'

'He never even mentioned her.'

'That's Bram. You've got to pry things out of him. Let's face it, most of the time he's pretty hard to like. That temper of his. Boy!' Crest went about straightening out the peak of his baseball cap, pressing at it with his thumbs. 'I'm amazed that *anyone* still gives a damn about that guy, truth be told. He's pushed a lot of people away in his time, myself included.'

A melancholy came over Crest's face. 'All I could think about on my way over here was the first time I saw him, up there teaching my freshman Lit class. I'm talking way back now, long before you were born . . . ' Crest gave a little smile of recognition, puffing air from his nostrils. 'I hated that class — *everybody* hated that class. He was always in such a bad mood. Tyrannosaurus Paulsen, we called him. One guy, Teddy Pugh — I remember this clear as day — he was reading out a passage from a Donne poem in a seminar one time and I guess he must've misread a line. The thing about Teddy was, he kind of stumbled over his words when he got nervous. I think he said, 'as *sun-burned* souls from graves will creep' instead of '*sin-burdened* souls', and Bram, well, he just went crazy, started pacing around like he'd been personally insulted. He made Teddy write the whole poem on the board and recite it to him at the start of every class. That was Bram for you. Tyrannosaurus Paulsen. Ha.'

Crest shook his head wistfully, eyeing the upstairs windows of the building, as if trying to see through the walls, into the old man's room. 'I guess that's what I must've liked so much about him back then — he seemed a little dangerous — but I guess it's also what held me back in the beginning. I was a grad student by the time we got together. Maybe if I hadn't made my move on him, things would've worked out differently; maybe the two of us wouldn't be all alone. Two lonely old men with only our nurses who really give a shit.'

'That's not true, Herbert. I know he doesn't think that way. He told me you were the love of his life.'

'Really? He told you that, huh.'

'Yeah. I've never seen him happier than when you came to The Orchard.'

Crest mused on this, the shape of the garden reflecting in his eyes. 'That's good to know. Maybe the time we spent together was worth something after all.' Then, in a spasm of his shoulders, he turned to Oscar and said: 'I'm sorry, I've been talking way too much. That's how I seem to be lately. Got more energy than I know what to do with.'

Oscar was almost afraid to ask Crest how he was feeling. It was only because he saw something in his expression — an openness, a willingness to be questioned — that he even voiced it. It came out more tentatively than he'd intended:

'So you've been feeling better, you know, since — since last week?' He couldn't bring himself to use the phrase he'd originally thought of: 'since your treatment'.

'I don't know if *better* is the right word for it, but I definitely feel *different*. More productive lately, that's for sure. It's all placebic, of course. Nothing to get worked up about.'

'What about the seizures?'

'Haven't had one since last week.'

'That'll be the medication.'

Crest shook his head. 'No, that's what's strange — I've stayed off the pills. I mean, I still get the headaches, but they don't seem to last as long, and they aren't — I don't know — they don't seem so intense. All I can tell you is, at the rate I've been going these past few days, my book'll be done in no time.'

'That's great, Herbert.'

'Yeah, well, don't get too excited. I'm meeting my consultant next week. We'll find out the real picture then.' Crest edged forward on the stone wall and idly fingered the scar on his skull; then, with a quick, easy motion, he tugged the cap down onto his head. The peak was now straight as an airstrip. 'Look, I can't believe I'm even suggesting this, but did you think about maybe asking Eden if — ' He stopped himself, laughing. 'No, forget it, forget I said anything. Seriously. Wow. That was almost a moment of true dumbness. Let's go back inside.'

'I know what you were going to ask,' Oscar said.

'You do, huh?' Crest shook his head at the ground.

'The thought's crossed my mind. Every time I look at Dr Paulsen now, I think about it. I hate seeing him this way.'

'But you can't bring yourself to do it.'

'No.'

'Good. Don't. Once you surrender to hope, it's a long road back to reason.' There was a certain tone of self-loathing in the way Crest said it. He got up. 'Walk me back to the car? I should try to beat the traffic.'

★　★　★

Iris said that revising medicine was like digging a well: you had to get your head down and keep on working through it, and trust that every spade-load of dirt you were lifting out was actually bringing you one step nearer to striking water. This was the philosophy she'd been sticking to all evening. The Easter term was still a few weeks away, but she'd been studying since they came back from dinner — by Oscar's count, that was three straight hours — and she'd only just allowed herself a bathroom break.

It was dark out. A gallery of her textbooks lay open on his bed: pages of dense, blocky paragraphs; precise anatomical drawings of the brain and diagrams of cranial nerves; minuscule footnotes in italics, referencing other books containing even more paragraphs, diagrams, footnotes and references ('Ibid., pp. 291, 482, 886'). Each book was thick with a luminous rainbow of page-markers onto which Iris had scrawled letters and numbers. Each colour corresponded to a topic, and each letter and number corresponded to something else. She'd tried to explain the nuances of her system to him over dinner and he'd nodded his head, pretending to follow everything she was telling him. ('So when I need to remember, let's say, that the trachea is level with the *sixth* cervical vertebra, to the upper border of the *fifth* thoracic vertebra, where it divides into the two bronchi, I just think Pink B-8, Yellow K-4. It's simple . . . ') But it had been very hard to hear her voice above the Algerian music bleating through the restaurant speakers and the sound of the sizzling grill. Now all he wanted to do was gather up those textbooks and throw them out of the window.

She left the bathroom wearing one of his old T-shirts, the lace of her underwear showing and the light glistening upon her bare legs. She lay frontways on the bed, feet upon the pillows, and took to reading again, chewing on the cap of her highlighter pen.

'How much more have you got to read?' he asked.

'I've already read these chapters, sweetheart, I *told* you. I'm annotating now.'

'Oh.'

'Five more chapters, then I'm done.' She lay her pen down on the page and looked at him. 'Why don't you put some music on or something? It'll help me concentrate.'

'Okay.' He needed to concentrate, too — on something other than the smooth pale skin of her calves, and the slow enticing way she was

358

bending her heels towards her thighs. She was raking her fingers through her hair now, pulling it over to one side of her face, and he could see the polite little nape of her back above the waistband of her underwear.

He chose a CD at random, hit play on the stereo, and went over to sit beside her on the bed. His hand reached out for her shoulder, and she tilted her face against it, until he could feel the gentle pressure of her cheek. There was a jangle of acoustic guitars now, and Tim Buckley's voice was breaking over them; he was singing about searching for dolphins in the sea.

She wriggled forwards. 'I can't,' she said, 'I have to read this.' But he moved his hands to the small of her back, running one fingertip along her skin, under the cover of her T-shirt, from the base of her neck to the bottom of her spine. She quivered, ticklish. 'Don't,' she said, giggling. He bent to kiss the backs of her legs — that gentle flesh where the skin was silken, scented with sweat — and she hummed along with the music and gave out quiet little moans. 'You're going to make me fail. Do you really want that hanging over you?' He just kept on kissing, stroking her legs. And then, in one motion, her whole body spun around, and he was staring down at the cute recess of her belly button. 'Alright, *stop,*' she said, and took off her glasses. 'If we're going to do this, we're going to do it properly.'

She pulled him forwards and kissed him, and soon she'd manoeuvred herself into the groove of his body, twining her legs around his. He lay on top of her, feeling her breath on his neck, her fingers against the buttons of his shirt. She stole the shirt from his shoulders, her palms cold against his stomach, and looked up at him alert, ready, clutching for his belt buckle. He lifted off her T-shirt and kissed her; she became a fragile body in his hands, light as paper. The music in the room seemed distant and formless now, like some argument playing out many storeys above them. His breath fogged upon her shoulder. As he pushed himself inside her, the textbooks dug into his knees. She gasped. Her legs wrapped him up and turned him around, so he was on his back, gazing up at her. Cars passed by outside the window, brightening the room with slow, pale flashes; her shadow swiped across the ceiling, angular and gaunt. She rocked herself upon him, eyes closed lightly. Then, like some old piece of furniture giving way under too much weight, she collapsed. There was a sudden jolt from her body, and a low judder of the mattress beneath them, and the strangest sound like a tiny object dropped from a great height. He knew something was wrong, badly wrong. She fell down onto him, winded and screaming. Her agony rang in his ear. Before he even knew it, she'd rolled away from him, onto her side. She was clutching at her thigh and beating the pillow with the base of her fist, shouting: 'My leg! My leg! My leg!' He could see the blood on his sheets and a husk of bone protruding from the skin above her kneecap, and for a moment, all he could do was stare down at her, tense and frightened. Then he heard her small voice pleading for his help.

14

Elephants

The fringes of Theo Bellwether's loafers edged under the curtain. He was continuing a conversation that had likely started somewhere in the car park: 'And I've already told them they have to get rid of that hideous gazebo before we do anything, so it'll be months before we can exchange on it. That's what's so annoying about the whole situation — is it this one? Nurse? Is she in *here*? Right, okay, thank you.' He peeled back the curtain and poked his head through the gap, peeking in at his daughter and Oscar with the dubious expression of a man who'd spent too long sizing up the menu boards of Barcelona restaurants for the last two weeks. 'Oh my goodness, look at her,' Theo said, seeing Iris in the bed, 'they've got her in a bigger brace than before.'

He and Mrs Bellwether pushed into the room — a small, plain space as confining as a shower cubicle. Eden trundled in after them, closing the curtain. He stood slackly beside his mother, sheepish and distant, hands in his pockets.

Nobody gave Oscar so much as a glance. They didn't thank him for being there with Iris, for riding with her in the ambulance, for waiting under the acid-bright striplights of the A&E while she was taken into X-ray and, later, the

361

operating theatre. They didn't even bring flowers.

Theo went right over to kiss Iris on the cheek, clocking the surgeon's name scribbled on the whiteboard behind her. 'Oh, good Jesus, not *Barnfield*. Not that old hack. The man needs five Glenlivets inside him before he can even scrub in. Anyone but Barnfield.' He stared down at Oscar, folding his arms. 'I told you to call me with the name of the surgeon. I could've organised somebody much better.'

Iris was still drowsy from the operation. Her face was damp and her hair was wild and matted. 'Dad, relax — you were on the plane,' she said. 'And anyway, I feel fine. It went fine.'

'You should've waited until we touched down,' Mrs Bellwether said. 'Your father specifically asked Oscar to ring when — '

'I told him not to,' Iris said.

Mr Barnfield had seemed more than capable to Oscar. He was about the same age as Theo and had a broad, owlish face with a suntan that faded at the cheekbones. Crouching down at Iris's bedside, he'd spoken with a composure that made everything seem better, casually uncapping a biro and handing it over for Iris to scrawl her name on the consent form. After three hours of surgery, Barnfield had come out to tell Oscar it had gone smoothly. He'd removed the original nail in her leg because it was 'structurally unsound' and replaced it with a new one. There was another fracture, too, just below the hip, and he'd had to place a pin inside the hollow of the bone to fix it. He'd used a lot of

362

words that Oscar didn't understand: 'Unfortunately, the interposition materials that her first surgeon packed around the bone to tease out some physeal growth ended up migrating, and I'm afraid they left the femur rather prone to pathological fracture. I've never been a fan of these new intramedullary techniques for intra-articular breaks; they can damage as many as they help, in my opinion. I'm afraid the days of wait-and-see and the good old plaster cast are long gone.' It was all about rest and recuperation from this point, Barnfield had said, and keeping the brace on until he told her to remove it.

'Well, it's all damage limitation now.' Theo leaned against the bedside table, exasperated, then reached out a hand to tuck a loose strand of hair behind his daughter's ear. 'I want you out of this place right away. The post-op here is diabolical. I don't know what I was thinking keeping you in here the first time.'

'I tried to tell you that,' Eden said. His voice was lazy, smug.

Theo ignored him. 'Where's that bloody Akingbade anyway? The whole job was a cut-and-shut from the start. I should've stopped it, but oh no, he wanted to do it his way, practically bullied me into it. Well — I'm going to see what my solicitor thinks about that.'

'Dad, calm down, I'm fine. Really,' Iris said. 'There's no need to start talking about lawyers. And anyway, I like Mr Barnfield.'

But Theo wouldn't be placated. 'He should *never* have let you come home so early. I told him at the time — didn't I, Ruth? Didn't I say to

363

him it was much too early?'

Mrs Bellwether gave a slow nod. She seemed satisfied to affirm that Theo had been right about everything all along, as if it made her righteous, too, by reflection.

Eden stayed silent. He fidgeted with the clasp of his earring, trying not to catch his sister's eye.

'Don't you worry, honey,' Theo said, going back for the same strand of Iris's hair. 'We're moving you tonight. I've already called Madigan Hall and they've got a bed waiting.'

'No, Dad, you don't need to do that. I'm fine. It's fine here.'

'And I'll be putting in a call into Subramanyam at UCH tomorrow. He's the best orthopaedics man in the country and I'm sure he'd be glad to do me a favour. Lift up now, come on.' He waited for Iris to raise her head, then pulled out her pillow and fluffed it, placing it back underneath her and giving it two firm pats. 'From now on, they're not offering you so much as a paracetamol in this place without my say-so. Just wish I could've made it back sooner. We tried to change our flight, but — '

'*Dad*,' Iris finally snapped. 'Will you just for God's sake sit down, you're giving me a headache.'

There was a sudden quiet in the ward, as if all the other patients had muted their television sets.

'We've already wasted too much time,' Theo said. He turned, searching the rail of her bed. 'Where's your chart? Who's taken it?'

There was resignation — capitulation — in the

364

downbeat way that Iris responded: 'The nurse has got it.' She looked down at Oscar and pulled her lips into a tired smile.

'Which nurse? The blondey one or the redhead?'

'I don't know.'

'The blonde,' Oscar said. 'Her name's Yvonne.'

Theo rolled his eyes. 'I don't care if her name's John Addenbrooke — she's got no right removing the chart from my daughter's bed.' With that, he tugged back the curtain to let himself out.

'Wait,' Eden said, 'I'm going with you.' He practically reached out to grab onto his father's coat-tails. A wen of sweat slid from his hairline, past his temple to his cheekbone. The colour had drawn completely from his face. 'Please. I promise I'll let you do the talking.'

Theo stopped. 'Come on then. But I don't want you chipping in. Let me handle it.' The two of them headed off along the ward.

Mrs Bellwether stayed. There was a moment's quiet. She eyed the curtain, letting it settle. Then she stepped forwards, pulled a tissue from the box on the cabinet, and wiped down the chair beside Oscar. 'Your father's a bit wound up,' she said. 'It was a long conference, and a bumpy flight and — and well, now *this*. It's a lot to take.' She leaned in close to Iris, but didn't try to take her hand. 'Tell me again how this happened. You just *fell off* the bed?'

★　★　★

365

When the rain struck the windows of Iris's room at Madigan Hall, it hardly made a sound. There was an eerie numbness to the building and its grounds — about an acre of landscaped gardens that included a private man-made lake called Madigan Pond. For all the postcard views of the Cambridgeshire countryside that it boasted, for all the Axminster carpets, organic meals, and satellite television, Oscar felt it lacked the strangely comforting bustle of Addenbrooke's, and Iris agreed.

Not once did Eden visit his sister at Madigan Hall. He didn't telephone through to her room or write a simple card to wish her well. Sometimes, Jane would show up in the evening, bearing his apologies: 'It's his week at the chapel — they're preparing for the Easter festival. He sends his love. Said he might be in tomorrow.' She would give Iris a peck on each cheek, Paris style, and nothing more would be said of it. Next day, she'd bring a textbook that Iris had asked her brother to check out of the library, saying, 'Sorry, he's just so busy at the moment. I'm sure he'll be in tomorrow. Would you like me to bring you anything else?' For the most part, Jane would drone on about how pretty the hospital was, saying how pleased they all were that Iris had decided not to let 'this little setback' stop her from taking her exams. 'It's so wonderful that you're keeping on top of things. You must be in terrible pain. Eden's been so upset about it all, he really has. I'm sure he'll be here soon to tell you that himself.' But it was very clear that Eden would not be coming to Madigan Hall, and Oscar knew perfectly well why.

He tried to avoid talking about it during his visits. The longer Eden stayed away, the less Iris enquired about him. She seemed happy to go along without mentioning his name or bringing up the fact that only a few weeks ago she'd been telling Oscar how remarkable her brother was, how absolutely certain she was that he had healed her. They didn't talk about the conclusions that could be drawn from her being in hospital again, with her leg broken in the same place and with the doctors telling her the bone wasn't suitably repaired the first time. She was looking at a long hard road to recovery with plenty of bed-rest, and possibly traction, and most definitely a sustained course of physical therapy. Oscar knew that she had no choice but to acknowledge the truth now. Her leg was not healed. Eden could no more heal her bones than he could heal Crest of his brain tumour. Of course he couldn't. *Of course not.* The whole idea was preposterous. But did she really need to say any of this aloud? Wasn't the shame already written on her face? Oscar didn't want to force the conversation out of her, so the subject became a snuffling great elephant in the room that they ignored every time they were together.

She had been in Madigan Hall for over a week by the time this silent truce finally broke down. Oscar went to see her after work, arriving in the heart of visiting hours, when the corridors were backed up with bored children playing hide and seek, and infused with the scents of Get Well presents. She was fast asleep in her room — a deep, snoring slumber. He sat by the window and waited, reading through an issue of the *Spectator* that Theo must have brought in earlier that day. He was halfway through a feature on sustainable fishing by the time she woke up. 'Hey, you,' she said, sleepily. 'What are you doing over there?'

'Learning about rainbow trout. It's sort of interesting.' He put the magazine down. 'How are you feeling?'

'Alright. A little better, I suppose.' She yawned. 'Would you do something for me?'

'Of course.'

'There's a pack of cloves in the drawer there, hidden away at the back. You see them?'

He found the pack, tucked underneath her socks and bras. 'Got them.'

'I want you to go outside and smoke one.'

'Why?'

'Because I can't move out of this bloody bed, that's why, and I'm just dying for the taste of one. Every time I wake up I've got this awful craving.' She smiled. 'So I want you to go out and smoke, then come back in here reeking of cigarette fumes. And then I want you to kiss me. You're the only one I can ask.'

He went and sat on a bench at Madigan Pond and smoked one and a half cloves, which was as much as his lungs could bear. He blew the smoke into his clothes, tried to waft it into the pores of his skin. The moon was a sliver in the sky and it reflected back in the rippling surface of the water, bent out of shape. He felt nervous. They hadn't kissed since she'd been hoisted into the ambulance and now he was reluctant to touch her again. He felt partly responsible for what had happened, and wasn't sure if she blamed him for it. If he hadn't coaxed her away from her textbooks, she wouldn't have broken her leg, and — oh, there was no point in worrying about that now. He put another clove in his mouth but didn't light it, put off by the taste.

When he went back inside, the smell of the cigarettes had faded a little on his clothes. Iris didn't seem to notice. 'How many did you smoke?'

'Two.'

'Two!' she said. 'You're so lucky. Quickly, come on — kiss me before it wears off.' Once their lips met and her tongue found his, all of his nervous feelings eked away. She clutched his neck, his shoulder, breathing in his scent. 'Oh, thank you, darling,' she said. 'Thank you. I needed that.' She lay back in silence, peering up at the magnolia ceiling, and stayed like that for quite a while, until he thought she was falling back to sleep. But then she began to cry. Tears strolled along her face and made little ink-blots on her pillowcase. She looked at him with wet, heavy eyes. 'I should have listened to you,' she said, reaching out to take his jaw in her soft hands, kissing his mouth. The brackish taste of tears was on her lips. 'I just — I wanted to believe in him so much. He's my brother. I wanted to believe in him. Was that so wrong?'

He didn't know what to tell her.

'I was so sure he'd healed me. I mean, I — '

'It's okay,' he said. 'You don't have to say it.'

'I thought I could trust him.'

'I know you did, Iris. I know you did.' He held her sobbing face upon his shoulder, smoothing her hair, until she moved away, drying her cheeks on her hospital sheets.

'Being bedridden is good for something, though,' she said. 'It gives you a lot of time to think. Staring up at the same ceiling for hours, it puts you into a state of meditation, makes you remember things.'

'Like what?'

She gave a sad exhalation through her nose. 'I was thinking about what Herbert asked me the first time we met, about trying to remember how this whole mess might've started. A trigger moment — I think that's what he called it.'

'Yeah, I remember.'

'Well, I've thought of something.'

For a second, she kept her eyes away from him, pondering the memory again. Then she slowly rolled her head towards him, making a straight line out of her mouth. There was uncertainty in her voice as she told him what she remembered — her words came out on tiptoe. But there was also a kind of confidence in her tone, as if she was sure that, amid all the misrepresentations and the sketchy details, there was a kernel of truth that justified the telling.

'I'm not sure exactly when it was, but I think I must've been about seven or eight, because I didn't have my glasses yet, and my eyes only started to get bad when I was nine. It must have been the summer, because *all* my memories are of the summer, but it was kind of a cloudy day — I mean, not rainy but gloomy.' She stopped, realising the picture she was painting was a little abstract. 'Sorry, the weather probably isn't that important.' She stroked the back of his hand with her thumb. 'Let me start again.'

It had happened in the summer holidays, a regular, grey afternoon. She'd been in her father's office, playing around with one of his old stethoscopes. 'I was listening to things with it. Not just my own heartbeat and stuff. I mean the walls, the wardrobe, *everything*. When you're little, the world seems so fascinating.' And soon, she'd begun to hear a sound almost like wedding bells. It was Eden, practising his piano in the drawing room. 'I tried to ignore it, but after a while it really started to annoy me, because I couldn't concentrate on anything else. So I went in to tell him to shut up for a minute. There was a smell in the air, I remember, like a cake was baking, and my mother was pottering in the kitchen, loading the dishwasher or something. And I had the stethoscope around my neck like my dad used to wear it.'

When she'd got to the drawing room, she'd found Eden at the piano. 'He was playing something slow, something gentle, and his eyes were shut. He didn't see me come in. I seem to remember the French doors being wide open, and this cold draught against my feet. The curtains were all flapping against the windows. The whole room just felt weird.' She'd got halfway towards Eden and stopped. 'There was something on the piano lid. I didn't know what

371

at first, just a mound of something, black, kind of greasy, and it was only when I got right up to it that I knew what it was. It was this bird, a blackbird, just lying there on the piano lid, not moving. And I felt like I should scream, but I didn't. The noise wouldn't quite come out.'

Then she'd remembered the stethoscope around her neck. It had seemed like a chance to use it properly, on something real. She'd placed the chestpiece against the breast of the bird and listened. 'Ugh, the smell of it, the feel of it — all oily and cool. I had to hold my head away from it, trying to hear its little heartbeat. But I couldn't hear anything. Maybe the piano was too loud, or maybe I just wasn't using the stethoscope right, I don't know, but the thing seemed dead enough to me.'

Eden had stopped playing then, eyeing his sister across the piano lid. He'd told her not to touch the bird. 'I asked him how the thing had got inside and he said he'd just found it on the front doorstep. It had flown into the glass. He goes, *Tell on me if you want to. I don't care.* He was very calm about it all, considering. Didn't seem bothered that my mother was only in the next room. And he walked over and scooped the thing up in his hands. Its little head flopped down over his fingers. I said, *Okay, I won't tell*, and he looked almost disappointed about it. He carried the bird over to the French doors — they were still open, and the cherry trees were all shaking about outside. I said he probably shouldn't be holding it like that. It could have all kinds of diseases. But he didn't seem to hear me. He stood there for a while, with that creepy-looking blackbird in his hands, just staring at the garden. Then my mother began to call us.'

At this point, Iris paused. She shook her head, remembering. 'We were all supposed to be going off somewhere — a church event or something. She was shouting out to us, *Kids! Come on! I want you ready in ten minutes!* And she came through into the room, drying her hands on a tea-towel. Oh my God, the look on her face when she saw what Eden was doing. She was going, *Put that filthy creature down right this second!* And she started running over to him, but she must've caught her knee on a table or something, I don't know, and the next minute she was all bent up, rubbing her kneecap. And the next thing — ' She trailed off, widening her eyes at Oscar. 'Why are you're looking at me like that? I swear to God, I'm not making this up. Honest, I'm not. You've got to believe me — '

'I believe you,' he told her. 'Just tell me what happened.'

'You're going to think I'm imagining it.'

'What happened, Iris?'

She took a breath. 'The bird started moving again. It was making this little sound like *flupp-flupp, flupp-flupp*. Started twitching, squirming around in his hands, screeching — this horrible screeching — and he was struggling just to keep hold of it. His arms were juddering around, and then — *woosh!* — he just let the thing go, gave it a little throw upwards. And it flew. It went right out through the French doors, easy as that. I watched it go straight into the trees like nothing

373

had even happened to it.'

'What did your mum do?'

'Nothing. That's just it.' Iris tried to shift herself closer to him, but the pain of moving caused her to wince. 'I think she was just glad the bird was out of the house. She wasn't even that angry with him. She told him to wash his hands with Fairy Liquid right away and not touch any of the furniture.'

'She didn't punish him or anything?'

'Nope. She told me to get changed, and we all went off to the church thing with her, and nothing more was said about it. I bet if you asked her about it now, she wouldn't even remember.'

Oscar let go of her hand, leaning away. 'You just thought of all this today?'

'Not exactly. I've sort of been sitting on it for a while. I know, I know — don't start. I wanted to tell Herbert about it when he asked me at the hotel, but — oh, I'm so stupid. I felt so differently about things then. I thought everything would be okay.'

'Well, you have to tell him now,' he said.

'You don't think it's too late?'

'No. He needs to hear it.'

'Then I'll tell him.' She tapped the telephone on the Pay-TV that hung over her bed on a mechanical arm. 'Get him to call me. I won't be holding back any more.' She folded back the bedsheet, making a crease around her waist. 'You know I don't think he healed it, right? The blackbird, I mean.'

'Good. I don't either.'

'It was probably stunned or something. Just happened to wake up at exactly the right time.'

'That would make sense.'

'But I don't think my brother sees it that way. I think somehow he got the idea in his mind that he could do anything if he just willed it. God, if my mother had just said *something* to him . . .' She levered herself upright, slowly, holding her hand against her breastbone. 'You know, when I was little, I used to get this feeling all the time, right here, a kind of burn. I'd feel sick with it sometimes. The doctor said I was just swallowing my food too fast. It went away over time. But with everything that's been going on with Eden lately, it's started again. And I think I finally understand what it is.'

'What?'

'It's my heart trying to overrule my brain. It's my heart saying *forget what's reasonable and listen to me*. That's how Eden always manages to get to me. He knows which voice I listen to most. Well, it can shout as loud as it wants from now on — I'm not going to let it win.' She went quiet again and Oscar held her hand, soothing her. After a while, she pushed her tongue out as if there were a bad taste on it, and tried to douse it with water, but this didn't sate her. She asked him to get her some juice.

He went down and bought her a few things from the gift shop: cartons of Ribena, a romance novel called *Sorrento Lust* he knew she'd find amusing, a pack of playing cards in case she got bored of studying and watching TV. All the time he was in there, he couldn't get the image of

Eden and the bird from his mind. He didn't quite know if he believed the story or not. The only thing he knew for sure was that he'd never seen Iris like this before — so weary with regret, so unhappy with the world.

When he got back to her room, Marcus and Yin were there, setting up the ghetto blaster on the windowsill, and she was going through a stack of CDs they'd brought along. 'We thought we'd rescue you from the hell of hospital radio,' Yin was saying. 'I was gonna make a mix tape, but I ran out of time. Oh hey, Oscar, how's it going?'

'Hi.'

'We're having a party in here. Grab a seat.'

They spent the rest of visiting hours listening to Yo-Yo Ma playing Bach, while Marcus told them all about the intricacies of his exam timetable, and about some girl on the Trinity College hockey team whom Yin had kissed at the formal last week.

'So what's the deal with the leg?' Yin said, changing the subject. 'When are they letting you out of here?'

'I'm not sure. A few weeks maybe.'

'Yikes. That sucks. I thought you were a fast healer.'

'Yeah,' Iris said, 'so did I.'

'And they're gonna let you take your exams if you're not recovered?'

'Might have to do them in a room by myself, but yeah, my father's arranged it.'

'Damn,' Yin said, adding his usual guffaw. 'There's no escaping old Theo, is there?'

'Never mind that,' Iris said. 'Tell me about this girl.' Yin's face and neck blotched red. 'Do I know her?'

'Nope.'

'That's why he likes her,' Marcus said. 'She's an outsider, like Oscar.'

'There's a lot to be said for outsiders.'

'Sure.' Yin nodded. 'If she fits in half as well as Oscar, I'll be happy.'

Oscar had to admit he felt a certain pride welling in his chest, and he was going to say something about feeling honoured or even touched, but Marcus gave him a friendly slap between the shoulder blades before he could: 'Oscar Lowe. We do hereby induct thee into the circle. Please accept this Ribena as a memento.' Marcus reached for the carton on Iris's table and pushed it into his hand. 'Do you have a few words for the assembled media?'

'Save it for the press conference,' Yin said.

It brought a smile back to Iris's face. When they left her bedside that evening, she seemed brighter, warning Yin not to get that poor young lady of his in trouble, and telling Marcus to shine his shoes next time he came to visit.

Oscar kissed her goodbye and she held onto his fingers. 'Thank you,' she said.

'What for?'

'For being so good to me.'

'Any time.'

'Get a room, you two,' said Marcus from the doorway.

'This *is* her room, idiot,' Yin said.

They gave Oscar a lift back home. With the

calm lights of Madigan Hall growing distant in the wing mirror, he began to realise just how exhausted he was. His neck felt tense, his mind was leaden. He listened to Yin and Marcus bickering about the best route to take to Cambridge, and shut his eyes, resting his head upon the shuddering window. He thought about his parents arguing: his father flailing the map around, his mother saying, *Slow down, slow down*. It was getting on for five months now since he'd spoken to them.

He had the strangest, most conflicted feelings going home that night. It was hard to reconcile where he was now with where he'd come from. Was it really so wrong that he preferred the leather upholstery of Yin's BMW to the scratchy seats in his father's van? Did it matter that he liked the peaceful aria that was on the stereo more than the David Bowie song he'd heard on the cab ride over? And what if he *didn't* want to be a care assistant his whole life — did that really make him so high and mighty?

He would call his parents when he got home — that's what he would do. He would ask his father how everything was going with the business: was he picking up enough work lately? How was his back these days? Was the van still holding out? And, yes, he would tell his mother about Iris, and say he was in love with her. It was not such a daunting thing any more, to let them know he'd found someone.

'Oscar, hey, Oscar — you hear me back there?' Yin was calling now from the driver's seat.

He hadn't been listening to their conversation;

it had been nothing but a dull burr in the background. 'Huh?'

'I was just saying, don't you think there's something wrong about putting him through it again?'

'I'm not sure what you're talking about.'

'Herbert Crest,' Marcus said. 'We thought you knew about it.'

'He's coming back,' Yin said, making a turn. 'Who told you that?'

'Eden did. Just this morning.' Yin sniffed. 'Sorry, man, I really thought you knew. I gotta say, I don't feel so great about it. I told him I'd think it over, but the way I'm feeling, he'll have to find someone else. Are you gonna go?'

There was no reason for Yin to lie to him. It had been a few days since he'd heard from Crest, after all, and he didn't want to start refuting things that might have been true. So he said, 'I didn't think Herbert had spoken to anyone about it. When did you see Eden, anyway?'

'We had a study date today,' Marcus said. 'At the UL.'

'Did he mention when he might be visiting his sister?'

Yin and Marcus looked at each other.

'No,' Marcus said. 'He's been in a bad mood lately.'

Yin puffed out a raft of air. If he could have held his hands up in surrender, he probably would have, but he kept them both planted on the steering wheel, turning right. 'I did talk to him about it, but hey, I can't force the guy. He hates hospitals. They creep him out or

379

something. I think it's like a phobia.'

'Nosocomephobia,' Marcus said. 'It's a real condition. My grandmother had it.'

'Well, whatever,' Yin went on, 'you know the old guy better than we do, Oscar. I'm not sure I want to get involved with it. Not after last time.'

'You're just being a sissy,' Marcus said.

'It's about *graduating*, dickhead. I don't have the time to spend another week out at that house.'

'Admit it. You're scared,' Marcus said.

'Hey, the guy had a seizure last time. I'm not putting myself through that again, and I don't think he should put himself through it either. You know what I'm saying, don't you, Oscar?'

'Yeah,' he said, 'completely.' He could feel his heart quickening. All he wanted was to get home and dial Crest's number.

Yin turned his eyes to Marcus. 'See. I told you he'd be on my side.'

'Well, I think it's unfair to Crest if we don't go back,' Marcus said. 'It's obviously helping his pain.'

Oscar kept quiet. When they reached the traffic lights on East Road, just fifty or so yards from his flat, he told Yin to stop and let him out. 'No problem, man. Are you sure I can't drop you at the door?'

'Here's fine. Thanks for the lift.'

It was only a short walk to his building, and he took deep breaths to settle his stomach. The air was warm and fragrant with freshly trimmed hedges, the pavements dry and cool. He crossed the road without having to check for oncoming traffic. Everywhere was so still that, when he reached the walk-up to his flat and saw a movement of shadows under the porchlight, it startled him. Somebody was waiting by the doorway, leaning a bony shoulder against the bricks. And with every step he took towards the flat, it became clearer and clearer who it was: the rangy build of him, the way the flaps of his cardigan hung down like badly measured curtains, the pearly glimmer of his eyes. He was holding a carrier bag, bulky and sagging with the weight of its contents. 'Hello, Oscar. I was just about to give up on you.'

He was not exactly surprised to see Eden standing there — he had such a knack for the unexpected that it felt somehow inevitable — but the shock of Eden's voice was enough to make him check his stride a little. He brushed past him, into the narrow porch, and put his key in the lock. 'What are you doing here?'

'Oh, I thought I'd come and see how you're getting on. It's been ages since I saw you.' Eden must have realised how implausible this sounded; his expression caved in. 'Just trying to be cordial,' he said, grinning. 'I have something I need to talk to you about. Can we go inside?'

Reluctantly, Oscar opened the door and turned on the landing light. The heel-worn carpet of the stairway felt soft under his feet as he scaled the two flights to his flat, Eden following behind him, fingers squeaking on the balustrade. He felt uneasy walking ahead, sensing Eden's presence behind his back like ominous weather.

The lights were still on in the flat; he must have forgotten to switch them off.

'Have a seat,' Oscar said. He gestured to the armchair, but Eden went right over and perched on the edge of the bed, placing his carrier bag on the rumpled duvet beside him. Saying nothing, he removed his cardigan, balled it up and clutched it between his knees, then spent a long moment studying the flat: his eyes flitted from wall to wall, floor to ceiling, object to object. 'Don't you know it's polite to ask your guests if they'd like a drink?' he said finally.

Oscar hung up his jacket. 'I don't have much to offer you.'

'Water is fine.'

He rinsed a glass and filled it from the tap. Eden took it, taking a small sip, and set the glass down on the floor beside his dirty canvas shoes. 'This isn't about my sister. Not directly, anyway. I'm sure you think I've been avoiding her.'

'You shouldn't presume to know what I think, Eden.'

'Right. But you *do* think it — you both do — I can tell by the way you're looking at me right now. All righteousness and consternation.'

'Well, I think it's fair to say your absence hasn't gone unnoticed. And not just by me.'

'Has she been upset?'

'I wouldn't say that.'

'Well then — ' Eden pinched at the creases of his trousers. 'I don't see what the problem is. She'll see plenty of me once she gets out of that place. Have I ever told you about my condition?'

'Your condition?'

'Nosocomephobia. Fear of hospitals.'

'I thought you meant your other condition.'

'And what condition would *that* be?'

'I'm not sure yet. I'm waiting for a professional opinion.'

'You know, you needn't behave this way towards me, Oscar. I'm not your enemy. We both want the same thing.' Eden began to straighten out the wrinkled plastic of the carrier bag attentively; Oscar could only see the loosest outline of whatever was inside. 'It's true, I haven't been to see Iris, and I do feel a certain pressure about that. But, it's not for the reason you think.'

'There you go again. Presuming to know what I think.'

Eden smiled. 'You want to hear me say it?' He picked up his water and took two small sips. 'You want me to say I haven't been to see her because now she's back in hospital it proves that I'm — that I'm some kind of fraud. At the worst, a kind of failure.'

'Well? Aren't you?' It came out exactly as Oscar intended: dry, nonchalant.

Eden didn't blink. 'No.'

'Right. It must be a coincidence.'

'Look, I can't explain it, I'll admit that. But if you want my honest opinion on the matter — '

'You really think you're still entitled to an opinion?'

'Well, I'm still her brother. That counts for something.'

'I wouldn't be so sure.'

Eden gave a tiny noise from his throat, like a valve being released on a tyre. 'I haven't been to visit her because I want her to get better, that's all. And I'm very aware that seeing me right now wouldn't be the best thing for her rehabilitation. And anyway, where do you get off lecturing me on this? We're talking about my sister here. I've known her a lot longer than you have.'

'*Oh*. You're keeping away for *her* sake.'

'Yes. Exactly. It's for her own good.'

'And here I was thinking you were ashamed to face her.'

Eden stayed quiet for a second, gazing at his shoes. He lifted his head gradually. 'Why should I be ashamed? It's not my fault the surgeon was inept. If he'd done his job properly, she'd be fine by now. And if I'd got to her first then all of this would be — '

'You're really something, aren't you, Eden?'

'Yes. Actually, I am.'

'You still think you healed her. I mean, you *really* think it.'

'I don't just think it. I know it.'

There was nothing Oscar could do but shake his head and stare back with disbelief and pity, and hope somewhere in Eden's mind all of this might register. 'I've never met anyone so arrogant or deluded in my whole life. I'd like you to know that. For the record.'

'Noted.' Eden smirked. 'But given the calibre of people you associated with before you met my sister, I'm hardly surprised.' He stood up, dredged the water from his glass, and set it down on the bedside table, noticing the picture tacked to the wall above the alarm clock: a snapshot of Iris posing outside the rectory in a T-shirt and denim shorts and big Sophia Loren sunglasses.

Jane had taken it weeks ago and given it to him; he'd put it up there on the wall so he could wake up to it every morning. 'Anyway,' Eden said. 'I didn't come here to get into a debate with you about this.'

'Then why did you come?'

'Because you owe me a favour.'

'I don't think so.'

'Yes, you do, Oscar — you owe me big time. If it weren't for me, you'd never have met my sister in the first place.' Eden went back to the bed and picked up the carrier bag. He turned with a kind of pirouette; the bag spun with him. He held it out by the handles. 'I need you to keep hold of these for me. That's the favour.'

When Oscar opened the bag, he saw a collection of black rectangular cartridges in clear plastic jewel cases. He recognised them. They were the miniDV cassettes he'd used to film Crest's sessions in the organ house. There were fourteen in total, each of them labelled with Eden's slanting cursive:

Dr Herbert Crest, Revival, Session 1, March 2003 (Some Footage Obscured)
Dr Herbert Crest, Revival, Session 2, March 2003 (Complete Footage)
Dr Herbert Crest, Revival, Session 3, March 2003 (Complete Footage)
Dr Herbert Crest, Revival, Session 4, March 2003 (Complete Footage)
Dr Herbert Crest, Revival, Session 5, March 2003 (Complete Footage)
Dr Herbert Crest, Revival, Session 6, March

'What am I supposed to do with these?'

'Put them somewhere safe. A deposit box at the bank would be best, but they're expensive. Perhaps you have a safe at that nursing home of yours? I'm trusting you to think of somewhere suitable.' Eden crouched to retrieve his cardigan from the floor. He dusted it down and put it on. 'Don't worry. Jane and Marcus have copies too. Didn't give any to Yin because, well — that's another matter. We've had a little falling-out. But it's not like I'm trusting you to look after the master copies or anything.'

'So why *are* you giving them to me?'

'Just a way of fireproofing. Spread the valuables out. That's what they used to tell us in fire safety at prep . . . Anyway, there are two sets in there. One's for you, the other's for Dr Crest. I need you to send them off to him tomorrow, first thing.'

'Send them yourself.'

'I would, but he doesn't give out his address so willingly. I find him very peculiar on the telephone. He's rather suspicious. The man is really quite difficult to understand.'

'I'm sure the feeling's mutual.'

Eden didn't look amused. 'Be that as it may, he said you'd take care of it.'

'I'll send them tomorrow.'

'Good. He's very eager to watch them. Don't keep him waiting.'

'Is that all?'

'No.' Eden pursed his lips and waited, pushing back his cardigan sleeves. He pointed to the bookshelf where Oscar's telephone sat with its cord in an unsightly tangle, and where the tiny red bulb of his answer machine was blinking. 'You should really check your messages more often. What if it's good news?' He placed two hands on Oscar's shoulders, gripping his collarbones, peering down into his face. Then, with a click of the door latch, he was gone, and the flat felt suddenly empty. The only movement was the persistent red flash of the machine against the wall.

The message went like this: 'Call me, kid. Call me as soon as you pick this up. It's Herbert. Just — just call me back, okay? There's been a development.'

★　★　★

The next morning, Oscar stood in Jean's office at Cedarbrook, waiting for a fax to come through. He had the telephone clutched to his ear, and Crest was talking away on the end of the line. They'd spent the last twenty minutes back-and-forthing about technical matters; about which buttons to press and which numbers to dial, and it was all starting to get chaotic. He wasn't due to start his shift until eight, but Jean had already passed by the corridor a few times to remind him that she wanted her office back sooner rather than later.

'Hey, I think it's sending.' Crest's voice rose with delight. The fax began to bleat out electronic cat-fight noises, and the blank paper fed through the machine and came out printed in greyscale: four near-identical square images, each of which housed a black-grey oval with a white daub at its centre.

Oscar had never seen a brain scan before. It seemed to him like four little weather charts promising torrential rain. 'What am I supposed to be looking for?'

'The grey stuff, that's my brain tissue,' Crest replied. 'The white stuff in the middle — that's the cancer. What you're looking at are my last four MRI scans. The picture on the bottom right was taken a few days ago.'

Oscar squinted to focus on the images. In the oldest scan there was a large white glob in the centre of the brain, about the size and shape of a hazelnut. The newest scan seemed to be darker overall, but how much could he really see from a fax machine printout anyway? It was hard to tell black from dark grey, and light grey from white.

There was a rustle on the phone as Crest transferred the receiver to his other hand. 'Take a look at the two pictures on the bottom row. They were taken a month apart: the newest and the second newest. You following me?'

'Yeah.'

'See any difference between them?'

Oscar studied the two scans closely, the way he would study the wordsearch in the back of the paper at breaktime. In each of them, there was a cluster of tiny white spots at the centre of the brain, covering about the same area. 'Not really.'

'The white splotches — they're the fingers of the tumour. That's the cancer left behind after surgery. They look about the same size to you?'

'Yeah.'

Crest paused. 'Well, there you have it, kid. The tumour's stopped growing. Millimetre for millimetre, it's not getting any bigger.'

'Jesus, Herbert. I don't know what to say.'

'Just don't say congratulations — *please*. That's what the consultant said. Dumbest thing I ever heard come out of her mouth.'

'I thought you'd be thrilled.'

'Hey, don't get me wrong, I'm happy about it. But congratulations are a little premature. This is just a plateau, that's all, not a remission.'

There was something different about Crest this morning. He was playing the whole thing down, as if a good night's sleep had given him a sober new perspective on the matter. Last night, when Oscar had called him back, swing music had been pounding in the old man's apartment — a huffing, exuberant brass section that distorted in the earpiece, with Nat King Cole singing along brightly. 'Hang on, Oscar, hang on, I gotta turn this down,' Crest had said, almost shouting over the music. A gentle fizz had settled on the line. He'd underplayed it, but there'd definitely been a kind of elation in the old man's voice as he'd told Oscar the news, talking him through the details of his last appointment with the neurosurgeon, describing the tests, the bloodwork that had been taken, the scans that he'd been put through. He'd enthused about the look on the surgeon's face when she announced the news — 'gleeful and bemused' was how Crest had described it. And he'd insisted on faxing over the scans so that Oscar could see them. But this morning, Crest seemed more pragmatic about the situation.

'So do you actually *feel* any better?' Oscar asked. He folded up the scan and put it in his pocket.

'Well, that's hard to say. On the one hand, it still takes me an hour to get myself dressed in the morning, and on the other, I have fewer headaches, fewer seizures, fewer dizzy spells. I've got more energy, but could I run to the post office and back? Hardly. I used to do a lot of running, you know. Five miles a day.' Crest allowed a moment to pass, and Oscar could hear the London traffic rolling by his apartment. 'Look, kid, I meant to bring this up last night but it got kinda late and I didn't want to get into it, and I guess I was a little reluctant to tell you about it. I arranged to see the boy again.'

Oscar had been waiting for him to mention it. 'Yeah, I heard,' he said.

'You did?'

'These things tend to filter down.'

'I didn't mean to go behind your back. We've all been doing enough of that lately. That's just how it worked out.'

'It's okay.'

Crest sighed. 'First off, I wanted to get a look at the tapes again, that was all. But once I had him on the phone — I don't know — I guess he was talking in a way I hadn't heard him talk before. He seemed depressed about something.

390

So I asked him what was up, and he said he was feeling down because his sister was in hospital. I said, Oh, I'm sorry to hear that, what happened? And he said she'd broken her leg again. That's when I realised: the kid was reaching out to me.'

The gardeners were firing up the lawnmower outside now, and Oscar was aware of Jean walking by the office.

Crest went on: 'He didn't have to talk to me about it — usually he wouldn't — but he did, and I knew it was a breakthrough. Then he asked me how I was doing and, well, I guess there was no reason to lie to him. But once he heard my news about the tumour, it was like he went right back to his old self. That's classic NPD behaviour. He wasn't upset about Iris being injured — he was upset for himself, because of how it made him look — and as soon as he heard my news, well, a light just switched on again. Started telling me how I had to come back for more treatments right away. I told him I'd think about it. He got pretty insistent, and I thought: this could be a chance to really help the kid, you know? I could really sit down with him and help him understand himself a little better. He said three weeks, come over in three weeks, and I agreed, with one condition: I get to meet his parents. He told me it could be arranged. That was the last I heard.'

'It's a relief to hear it from your side,' Oscar said. 'The way Eden told it, it was like you came begging for his help.'

'I wouldn't expect anything different. But you can tell your girlfriend I'm gonna see that he gets some help, okay? I'm gonna talk to some top-level psychiatrist friends of mine and see if they'll take his case.'

'That's all she ever wanted.' The day Iris had first asked for his help was a distant memory to Oscar now. Somehow they seemed further than ever from achieving what they'd set out to do. 'She told me something yesterday. She's been thinking about what you asked her, about a trigger moment.'

'Oh yeah?' Crest said. 'She remember something?'

He told the old man Iris's story about the summer day at the Bellwether house with Eden and the dead blackbird. Crest didn't interrupt, and he made Oscar wait for his response. He gave no suggestion that the memory was significant. All he said was: 'Thanks for the info. You tell your girl to get well.'

15

A Light Went Off in the Organ House

Under the heading VOLUNTARY in the Festal Evensong programme were the words 'Toccata in B Minor (Gigout), arrangement for chamber organ (E. Bellwether).' There was no applause when Eden took his place at the modest-looking instrument at the far end of the chapel — the awkward etiquette of the occasion demanded it. He stretched his fingers, straightened out his back, and carefully set his hands upon the keys. The music came fast out of the pipes like greyhounds breaking the traps — a hard-sounding, impatient melody. Powerful chords blasted through the chapel, and layer upon layer of frenzied notes clambered for the ceiling. Half the congregation took the organ voluntary as their cue to leave, gathering their coats and heading for the exits, but the people who stayed behind kept their eyes trained on Eden. As his fingers sprawled across the keys, the music began to thicken. It flooded the cavernous building like a mist.

Oscar searched the last of the crowd, looking for the Bellwethers. It had been a long, dreary service, and Iris had given him the impression that her parents would be there. 'If I can't go myself, I at least want to experience it vicariously,' she'd told him. 'God knows I can't rely on my father to describe it. You're the only person who understands why I love that choir so much.' In fact, the choir was the only thing that had made the service bearable, until the moment Eden took to the organ.

Oscar tried to focus on the music and forget about who was making it. He tried to detach himself from everything and enjoy the sound. But he couldn't. The more the music came surging towards him, the sadder he felt — because as surely as he could picture Eden as an organist at a magnificent cathedral like St Paul's or Notre-Dame, he could also picture him as a patient in some white-walled psychiatric wing, playing silent toccatas on the windowsill.

After a while, Eden held down the final chord like he was damming some great power below his fingertips. He released the pressure with a flourish and the chapel fell silent. What was left of the congregation rose to its feet, applauding. Eden hardly smiled. He stepped away from the organ, gave the slightest of bows towards the pews, and walked along the aisle, into a private room near the choir stalls. The ovation subsided, and Oscar filed out with everybody else.

Rain was slanting steadily across the Front Court. People were sheltering in the vestibule, waiting for it to ease, but Oscar headed straight out into the downpour. His umbrella was cheap and water ran down onto his shoes. He was relieved that the others weren't around to ask what he thought of the performance. If Jane had been there to tug at his sleeve and say, 'Scale of one to ten: how good was Edie tonight?' he would've had to admit what he'd left the chapel feeling — that, despite it all, Eden Bellwether was a genius.

He made it as far as King's Parade before he noticed Mrs Bellwether on the roadside. All around her, the rain was tinged blue by the old-fashioned streetlamps. There was no way to get by without her seeing him, so he made a point of calling out to her. She turned around, curious. 'Oh, hello there. Theo's just bringing the car. Can we give you a lift?'

'No, it's alright. I don't live too far from here.'

'Okay. Well, do keep dry.' She turned away, seeing a spray of headlights in the distance, but when she realised they didn't belong to Theo, she looked back at him, lifting her eyebrows. There was an awkward moment of quiet.

'I didn't see you in there,' Oscar said. 'Did you enjoy the service?'

'No. I'm afraid I didn't.'

'Oh?'

'Much too secular for my taste. It felt like a concert in there, not worship. When I go to church, I expect people to be reverent. But there was so much chattering I could hardly hear the lessons.'

'Well, I'm not really qualified to judge any of that.'

'No,' she said. 'No.' And she turned away again, staring down at the slick cobbles. 'Eden was wonderful, of course. He plays so well.'

'You didn't want to stay and talk to him?'

'He's always so busy after a service. No point in waiting. And, oh, perhaps I'm just being a stick-in-the-mud, but a chapel is *really* no place for a standing ovation. I can't understand how the vergers allow that kind of rowdiness. My old uncle Charles would've been appalled.'

Oscar didn't know what to say. 'Sorry you didn't have a good time.'

'I'm sure I'll get over it.'

They stood there quietly as two giggling women sharing a golf umbrella emerged from the Gatehouse, heading for Market Square. Then Mrs Bellwether looked his way again and said: 'Do you mind if I ask you something, Oscar?'

'Not at all.'

She waited, drawing in the corner of her mouth. 'Would you say that my son is liked by people? I don't mean popular exactly, just, you know, *liked*.'

He wasn't sure how to respond.

'Oh, look,' she went on briskly, 'I know he has friends — but Jane, Marcus, Yin, they were raised in the same sort of environment. Prep school, boarding school, Cambridge. You know what I mean. Sometimes I wonder how the average person sees him. I wonder how he's going to cope in the outside world. I look at other boys his age — boys like you — and I can't see him ever fitting in.'

'Everyone's trying to fit in somewhere, Mrs Bellwether. Me included.'

'Yes, well, I'm sure that's the case. But sometimes I worry that it's all been handed to him much too easily.' She didn't seem interested in his answer to her question any more. The tension was easing from her voice. 'The only trouble he's ever had was being born, and heaven knows he was a difficult birth. But all we've done since then is try to keep him comfortable. No stresses or struggles. We've sheltered him, indulged him. I don't think he's learned to cope with disappointment.'

She paused, switching her umbrella into her other hand. 'Oh, I'm getting myself into bother here. I shouldn't be saying any of this. You don't want to hear it, I know. It's just that everyone in my family went to boarding school, then Oxbridge, and there's an assumption that it didn't do any of us any harm. That we're all somehow *better off*. But I wonder about that. I look at my son in there and I think, have I raised someone exceptional or someone abnormal?'

She let her words hang in the air. It occurred to Oscar that this was the first time he'd ever thought that Iris and her mother were similar. There was something about the way she looked as she waited under the streetlight: she had the same shallow slope to her face as Iris, the same straight hairline that bent when she frowned. But hers was a beauty that had aged into something ordinary. 'You know,' he started to say, and she squared her eyes at him eagerly, 'I'm not sure it's possible to be exceptional without being a bit abnormal too. Goes with the territory.'

'Yes, I'm sure you're right. I really don't know why I brought it up.' Right then, Theo's Alfa Romeo rolled up to the kerb. The passenger door swung open. She collapsed her umbrella, calling: 'Goodness, Theo, what kept you? My shoes are ruined.'

Iris was discharged from Madigan Hall on Easter Monday. She phoned Oscar from her parents' house that afternoon, sounding less than enthusiastic about the prospect of spending the whole of the exam term in the company of her father. 'You have to come over for dinner tonight,' she said. 'Dad's roasting a lamb — he's driving me spare. It's supposed to be family only, but that means Eden will be coming and I don't think I can face him on my own right now. Please tell me you can make it.' He took the call in the front garden at Cedarbrook. Inside, the residents were tucking into their own lunch, and the smell of lamb and mint sauce had pervaded the corridors all morning, making him nauseous. But he told her he'd be there.

It was Theo who answered the door. Everything he had on was white — his trousers, his shirt, his shoes — apart from a red cooking apron, which was so shiny that it seemed to strobe when he moved. 'Ah, Oscar, good,' he said, 'do you like your lamb pink or brown? Say brown and you'll break my heart.' He took Oscar's umbrella before he had a chance to reply, dumping it into a large ceramic pot by the door. 'Go on through, why don't you? I've got to run upstairs quickly and change.' He gestured to the blots of oil on his shirtsleeves. 'Chef's prerogative.'

Oscar found Iris reclining on the sofa in the drawing room, her leg braced in the foam and metal contraption she hated so much, elevated on a velvet cushion. She had on a pair of jogging bottoms with one leg snipped off above the knee, and a hooded varsity sweater. Eden wasn't in the room, but Jane and Mrs Bellwether were there, and he could see that a light was on in the organ house outside — a simple glow behind the misted-up glass of the French windows. 'Hey, there you are — *finally*,' Iris said. 'I was starting to worry.'

'Sorry. Held up at work.'

Mrs Bellwether opened her palm out towards the furniture. 'Sit yourself down, Oscar. Can I get you something to drink?'

'No thank you, Mrs Bellwether.'

'Please. Call me Ruth.' She smiled at him.

Jane waved hello. 'Eden's out in the O. H., in case you're wondering.'

'Doing what?'

'Tinkering,' she said. 'Like always.'

He bent to kiss Iris on the cheek and took a seat beside her. Ruth picked up the conversation they'd been having when he came into the room — something about a certain style of property that you only ever saw in a certain region of France called the Auvergne, where she was taking a trip with Theo next week; they were going out there to look at some holiday houses.

Soon, Theo came bounding through the drawing room in a clean shirt, retying the cord of his apron. 'Alright, I hope you're all hungry.' He went into the kitchen and they heard him opening and closing the oven. After a moment, he popped his head back around the door. 'Another few minutes for the potatoes,' he said. 'How about some sherry to get things going?' He brought out six little glasses on a silver tray and handed them out, one by one. 'Where's Eden? Will somebody bring him in, please? I want to make a toast.'

'I'll go,' Jane said.

It was noticeably quieter in the room without Jane. Even when she wasn't talking, she had a way of making noise, and now there was an unbearable hush amongst them. Theo sat down on the arm of the couch next to his wife. 'So, Oscar, how's that patient of yours doing? Dr Poulter, wasn't it? Dr Pointer?'

'Paulsen,' he said.

'That's right. How's the old fellow doing?'

'Not good, actually.'

'Oh, I'm sorry to hear that.'

'He had a stroke a few weeks ago. A bad one.'

Theo shook his head in consternation with the world. 'I suppose it comes to us all in the end,' he said, as if this platitude really got to the heart of the matter.

'How old is he?' Ruth asked.

'Eighty-six.'

'Hm,' she said. 'My father had his first stroke at fifty-seven. Terrible thing.'

There was a noise from the kitchen as Jane and Eden came in through the back door, arriving into the room with damp hair and shoulders dotted with rain.

'Oh, good, we're all here,' Theo said. He dinged the sherry glass with his fingernail and stood up. 'This is what you might call a multifarious toast, so I'll try to keep to the bullet points, but I make no guarantees of brevity. You all know how much

400

I like to make a speech.'

'We do,' Eden said. 'So get on with it.'

'First, I'd like to drink to Iris.' He raised his glass by its spindly neck. 'To her steady and *lasting* recovery.'

'Hear, hear,' Oscar said.

Eden shuffled his feet in the doorway.

'Second of all, to Eden, who put on a heck of a show yesterday. It brought to mind that old Wordsworth poem — does anyone recall it? — *Where light and shade repose, where music dwells* and so on and so on . . . It's been a trying year so far, and, yes, we seem to have had a few setbacks lately, but I'd like to think we can have a successful exam term now to make up for it.' Theo sipped at his sherry, and everyone presumed the toast was over, setting their glasses down. 'Wait, wait, I'm not finished. Let's not forget it's Easter Monday. We must give our thanks to God, who gave His only begotten son to die on the cross for our sins. May we live by the example of Our Lord Jesus Christ on this day and always, in his name and memory. Amen.'

'Amen,' Ruth said, sipping. 'That was lovely, darling.'

'Amen,' the rest of them murmured.

Oscar just pursed his lips and nodded. Even if he didn't believe in the prayer, he had to respect the sentiment of it. Then Theo clapped his hands — one loud buckshot. 'Okay, everyone, if you'll please make your way to the table.'

Oscar helped Iris onto her crutches. She struggled towards the dining room, one movement of her arms and one swing of her heel at a time. She took her place at the end of the table that was usually reserved for her mother, and Oscar sat adjacent, a buffer between her and Eden. The tablecloth shifted as she lifted herself slowly down onto her chair, and he had to reach out and stop it being drawn away from underneath the tableware like some disastrous magic trick.

Iris didn't say a word to her brother at dinner. After dessert, Theo pinged his glass, and everyone groaned at the prospect of another toast. 'Alright, enough. I have an announcement to make. Actually, it's not just *my* announcement — your mother's involved in this, too.' He reached for his wife's hand across the table.

'Please don't say you're pregnant,' Eden said. 'I don't think I could bear it.'

His father cleared his throat, undeterred. 'Your mother and I will be going to the Auvergne next week, as you know, to look at some properties.'

Eden said: 'You told us already. So what?'

'Well, there's a particularly good-looking *gîte* out there that's frankly a steal at the price, and really it has so much potential — more acreage than we have here — and if we can do some work on it in the next few years, it will really turn out to be quite an investment. It'll be a lovely place to live and something to pass down to the pair of you in the future when you're raising children of your own.' He stopped, drinking his wine.

'I don't understand,' Iris said. 'It sounds like you're thinking of staying there permanently.'

Theo raised his eyebrows and took a deep

breath, ready to continue, but his wife leapt in: 'What your father's trying to say is — what we've decided is — after giving it some serious thought, and considering all the factors — '

'Look, it's simple,' Theo said. 'If this place we've got our hearts set on measures up, we're going to buy it and move out there.'

There was a palpable tension in the room now. Iris sat there with her mouth ajar, and her brother's face was screwed up with shock.

'But — but what about your work?' Eden said.

'Well, that's the good thing about consultancy. It's a moveable feast.'

'What about *your* work, Mother?'

'Oh, I can always keep in touch by email.'

'You can't just *emigrate*. Not just like that. You don't even speak French.' Eden's anger was rising. The skin of his neck was dappled red.

'Of course we can emigrate. That's the joy of the EU. And anyway,' Theo said, 'if everything goes well, I'll probably retire. I'll have plenty of time to learn the language.'

'Well, I think it sounds wonderful,' Jane said, stroking Eden's forearm. 'My parents have never been happier since they left for Italy.'

'Yes, but — but — ' Eden pulled his arm away and stood up. His chair scraped on the marble and his napkin clung to the front of his trousers with static. 'What will *we* do? I'll be starting my Master's in the autumn and Iris still has a year of the Tripos left. And the house — what will you do with the house?'

'We'll sell it,' Theo said flatly. 'That's what we've decided.'

'Oh, you've got to be joking.'

'It's not exactly going to happen overnight, Eden. I can't imagine we'll be moving for at least six months, maybe even a year.'

Eden balled up his napkin and threw it at the table so hard it knocked over his wine glass. Burgundy oozed across the white linen and Ruth leaned over to dab it dry. She said: 'Will you calm down please, Eden. You're behaving like a child.'

That's when Iris finally decided to speak up. She gazed at her brother. 'You should just be glad for them.'

'Don't tell me you're happy about this,' Eden said.

'I'm not thrilled about the idea, but I'll get used to it.'

Ruth was still padding the stain on the tablecloth, pouring salt onto the fabric. 'Your father's worked hard for you all his life,' she said. 'He deserves his retirement. You're not children any more, and both of you are just going to have to live with our decision.' She didn't lift her gaze from the table. The stain was now a sickly brown colour.

Her words only seemed to make Eden more indignant. His glossy eyes swelled. 'And what about the organ house? Have you even thought about that? Or are you just going to go away on your little jaunt and leave me to deal with having no organ to practise on next year?'

'We'll sort something out for you,' Theo said. 'You'll manage.'

'I don't want to manage. I love that organ. I

want things to stay just as they are. Why can't you just move out there *and* keep the house? What if — ?' His face brightened. 'What if Iris and I stay here next year? Together. What about that? We'll make sure the place doesn't go to ruin.'

Iris folded her arms. 'No chance. I'm moving back into halls next year.'

'Don't talk stupid.'

'I am. I'm moving out of Harvey Road.' She looked at Oscar for support, taking his hand. 'I've already put my name into the lottery.'

Eden glared at Theo. 'Did you know about this?'

'Yes. In light of our own plans, we're okay with it.'

'Oh, I see, so you're *all* abandoning me. I suppose you've all been plotting this for ages behind my back. What about you, Janey? Did you know about this?'

'No, of course not.'

'Don't be silly,' Theo said. 'Sit down. Nobody's been plotting anything. You're being paranoid. Things change. People move on.'

But Eden didn't sit down. He stared right at Oscar. 'I bet *he* knew.'

Oscar stayed quiet. There was no point making things any more tense than they needed to be. Eden was chewing on his bottom lip so hard it looked like it might come apart under his teeth. His lungs heaved in his chest, up and down, like two great accordions trapped behind his ribcage. He had the same dazed look about him that he'd had at the hospital, weeks ago, and Oscar could tell that whatever thoughts were running through

405

Eden's head now, he wouldn't let them settle.

'Eden, come on, sit down,' Theo said.

But Eden wouldn't listen to his father. He shoved hard at the table. It slid and lifted up slightly on its legs, but somehow none of the glasses toppled over; they teetered and came to rest again without a drop being spilled. Turning fast, Eden kicked his chair out of the way, his force so strong that it hit the floor with a crack. He rushed out to the kitchen, slamming every door behind him, and soon they could hear the stutter of his feet on the path outside. A pale light came on in the garden, illuminating the rainspots on the windowpanes and making the dining room seem smaller, barer.

'Excuse me, I'm sorry,' Theo said, and made to go after him, but Ruth stopped him: 'Let him cool off,' she said.

Nobody said anything for a while. Theo leaned his elbows on the table and knuckled his beard. Iris ran her fingers through the crown of her hair. Oscar rolled the last bead of liquid around in his wine glass. No matter how many of them he went to, he thought, he'd never get used to these Bellwether family dinners.

It was Jane who found a way to break the gloom: 'So will you keep horses at this *gîte* of yours?' she asked. 'Because if you keep horses I'll come out to visit you all the time.'

Theo smiled, then began to laugh, and the heaviness in the room seemed to lift. 'Jane,' he said, the colour rushing back in his cheeks again, 'we'll keep a stable full of them just for you, I promise.'

Still, when they all went back out into the drawing room, Theo seemed to be in a downcast mood. He poured cognac for everyone, apologising to Oscar for Eden's behaviour — 'I just don't know what gets into that boy sometimes, I really don't' — and sat there, warming his expensive brandy, taking no part in their discussion about the French way of life and what Ruth called 'the liberal stance' the country had taken over the invasion of Iraq, though Oscar supposed he had plenty to say on the issue. As the conversation drifted into silence, Theo said tiredly: 'Okay, everyone. I think we should call it a night.'

'Yes, I'm exhausted,' said Jane. 'Back to the library tomorrow.'

They all gave each other polite hugs and handshakes. Ruth told Oscar there was no sense in ordering a taxi — he could stay in one of the guest rooms upstairs — and Jane volunteered to give him a lift back to Cambridge in the morning. Everyone went off to their rooms.

A bed had been set up for Iris in the sitting room. 'Can't handle stairs or flagstones at the moment,' she said to Oscar. 'I need more practice on the crutches.' They lay together, kissing and holding each other, until her leg got too uncomfortable. He sat on the floor with his neck against the mattress and her fingers combing softly through his hair. She was wide awake and talkative, and seemed pragmatic about the idea of her parents moving away. 'It was bound to happen sooner or later. Dad's always talked about buying somewhere in Nice or Cannes, so I'm a little surprised they're looking around in the Auvergne, but it doesn't matter much to me. So long as they're happy. And besides, they spend most of their time away from this house, anyway. I suppose it makes sense to sell it. Can you believe the way Eden was acting?' She checked herself. 'Wait, what am I saying? Of course you can.'

They talked about the prospect of Crest coming back to the house again. Oscar told her he'd been wondering why Eden had put the old man off for three weeks, but tonight, after the drama at dinner, he'd realised why — because Eden was waiting for his parents to leave town. 'It's almost like an admission that he's doing something he shouldn't be,' he said. 'If your dad found out what was going on here next week, he'd go ballistic.'

'Oh, I wouldn't be so sure about that.' Iris's fingers stopped moving, settling on his head. 'You saw him tonight — he's too soft on him. Put it this way: what would *your* dad have done if you'd kicked up a big scene like that at the dinner table?'

Oscar knew exactly what his father would've done, but he didn't want to tell her about it. 'We never really ate at the dinner table much.'

'What about if you slammed a door?'

He wanted to change the subject. It was in his mind now: that horrible banging of the back door latch, loud as a gunshot; a gust sweeping right through the house as his father arrived home. Then the urgent thump of his father's feet on the stairs: 'Oscar! What've I told you about leaving the back door open. You're gonna take that fucking door off its fucking hinges. Where are you?' This wasn't something he ever wanted Iris to hear. 'I never slammed any doors,' he said.

'Well, you know what I mean. Eden's just allowed to make a big scene then go away somewhere without anybody telling him off. Everybody in this house just hides and pretends there's nothing the matter. Maybe I'm expecting too much of people, I don't know.' She sighed, pushing her head deeper into her pillow. 'I just wish this whole thing was over. I'm so tired of my brother, the way he talks to me like he's so superior, when *he's* the one who's crazy. I just wish somebody would take him off in a white van.'

'I know you don't mean that,' he said.

'You're right, I probably don't, it's just — I'm so exhausted with it all. I'm not sure how much longer I can go on living like this. I feel like he's swallowing up my whole life. And Herbert was supposed to help him, but he only seems to be encouraging him.'

'That's not how it is.'

'Well, it just seems like he's getting what he needs for his book and then that's it — he's going to leave us all in the lurch.'

'It's not like that. I told you, he's going to speak to some people he knows, get Eden some proper help.'

'Why do you trust him so much anyway?'

'Who? Crest?'

'Yeah.'

'I just do. I've got to know him quite well lately. He's a good man.'

'Well, I hope he's going to come through for me.'

'For us.'

'Yeah.' She smiled and pulled his hair lightly. 'For *us*.'

That night, the air in the guest room was stuffy and Oscar couldn't sleep. Rain was still coming down behind the drawn curtains, rapping on the glass with every gust of wind, and all he could think about was Herbert Crest and the question Iris had asked: why *did* he trust the old man so much? That faded dust-jacket photo from *The Girl With the God Complex* was stuck in his mind — the image of a young, broad-nosed man with a head of dark hair and features not so different from his own. He'd trusted Herbert Crest the moment he'd seen him. He had no doubt that Herbert Crest was a good man, somebody to aspire to — somebody his father would've called a butterfly catcher because his brain was too active, too ambitious to settle for doing the same work day in, day out, when it could be exploring the deeper facets of the world.

The wind blew another shiver of rain against the house. Oscar opened the window and the fresh air began to pacify him. Soon, he drifted into a restless dream in which he was swimming in a quiet brown lake where old women were washing cotton nappies and a pack of horses had come to ford. He woke abruptly, feeling tense and thirsty, and went across the hallway into the bathroom to get some water. But when he turned on the light, his eye caught the bleary

410

reflection of something in the mirror, and his heart shook. There on the floor tiles, shivering against the bath panel, was Eden. His hair and clothes were sodden, and he'd removed his shoes and socks; they were drying in the bidet. His fingers were stained black with something: mud, or ink, or oil.

Oscar was breathless with shock. 'Jesus,' he said, trying to steady himself, 'how long have you been in here?'

Eden didn't answer. He leaned his head against the lip of the tub.

Oscar took a towel from the rack and handed it over. Eden didn't say thank you, didn't even unfurl it from its neat little quarter-fold, just began dabbing his face. The extractor fan whirled above them for a moment, then Eden said: 'When all of this is over, you know what I'm going to do?' He was slurring his words, either too drunk or too worn out to speak.

'When all *what* is over?' Oscar said, staring down at him.

Eden wiped a bead of water from his nose. 'I'm going to build myself the most incredible organ you've ever seen. That's what I'm going to do. Better than the one I have here, better than the one at King's. Look — ' He got to his feet gingerly, clutching the sink. He opened his left hand and revealed a tiny scroll of paper, rolled up as tight as a cigarette. He unravelled it, spreading it over the counter, holding it flat.

Oscar was expecting a refined sort of drawing, as precise as something an architect had drafted. But it was a fairly awkward sketch in spotted,

411

smudged ink — not exactly child-like, but not remotely skilled. The lines of the organ pipes were loose, wobbly, and the keys and stops of the organ console looked more like the fixtures of a gingerbread house.

Eden stood beside him now, dripping. 'I based it on the St Michael's organ, but the registration will be different. It'll have German pipes, but I'll probably get them zinc-lined over here. And I'll have a Claribel Flute stop as velvety as the Harrison at King's. It doesn't need to be big, it just needs to be pure. And if I get the specs right, it'll rattle your bones when you hear it. I'll be able to do anything with it. Whatever I want.'

Oscar was still half-asleep, but he couldn't help noticing the change in Eden's eyes: they weren't so pearly any more; the pupils were dilated. 'What are you doing in here, Eden? You're soaking.'

'Raining out there,' he replied. And he went over to sit down on the floor again, on the same little patch of wet tiles. 'I came here looking for something.'

'What?'

'I don't remember.' He smiled dreamily. 'But I found my sister's tablets.' He laid himself down flat. 'If you take two at once, you get a nice giddy feeling.'

Oscar took a glass from the cabinet and filled it with water. 'Drink this,' he said.

Eden pushed it away. 'I don't need a nursemaid.'

'Drink it or you're going to get sick.'

'What do *you* care?'

412

'I don't.'

Eden took the glass, but didn't even sip at it. 'He'll have to make an appointment like the rest of us.'

'Who will?'

'Dr Crest. If he wants to meet my parents.'

'Okay.'

'Why is it so hot in here?'

'It isn't.'

'Then I must be getting a fever, because it feels like I'm on fire.' Eden gulped down the water in one long mouthful. He exhaled and dropped the glass. It broke against the tiles in a few clean pieces. 'Oops.'

'You better go to bed, Eden. Sleep it off.'

'Don't tell me how to behave.'

'You're going to wake everyone.'

'Tssh. They don't care what I do. Nobody bats an eyelid.' He lifted himself to his feet again, clutching onto the washbasin. 'But that's okay. I'm going to build my own organ. And then I can do anything, and everyone will listen.' He staggered towards the door. 'Get out my way,' he said, pushing at Oscar's chest weakly. 'Everyone's always in my way.' And out he went along the dark hall, down the stairs, through the atrium.

Oscar hurried to the window in the guest room. The rain was still driving across the garden. He saw Eden come out through the kitchen door below, stumbling over the patio, along the path. He stayed there at the window, watching, until the light went off in the organ house and the night began to settle.

16

Waiting

Dr Paulsen didn't miss a single movement of the weather all week. He studied every last twitch of the sky through his window, as if he was trying to lure the sun out by sheer will. When Oscar came into his room each day, the old man was rooted to the same spot as the morning before, eyes pointed up towards the clouds, and the only thing that seemed to change was the shade of the sky beyond his shoulders. Tuesday: heavy rain. Wednesday: brighter. Thursday: grey again. Friday: greyer. On Saturday, the sun was finally beaming through the glass and the room was heady with the smell of damp wisteria, but Dr Paulsen still kept staring, and by Monday morning, Oscar realised it wasn't the sunshine that the old man was interested in — he was waiting for God to finally show his face and take him away.

Oscar had tried to prepare for another long week in Grantchester the same way as last time — by not preparing at all, by booking the whole week off to enjoy his afternoons at the Bellwether house with Iris and his friends. But when he'd gone to Jean's office to ask for the time off last weekend, she'd refused him outright. So he spent the better part of Monday at Cedarbrook, performing his usual duties and counting down the minutes until five o'clock, when he was due to meet Herbert Crest at the Crowne Plaza. It had been arranged for Andrea to drive them to the Bellwether house and drive them back later that night.

After making a final sweep of the rooms, swapping pillow-cases and fitting calipers and emptying one last colostomy bag, Oscar went to the staff room and changed out of his uniform. He dabbed his neck and face with aftershave and wet his hair and combed it. He brushed his teeth, packed his stuff back into his locker, and went up to check on Dr Paulsen.

The old man was reading a book on his bed. It was written in a foreign alphabet — Russian or Greek or maybe Farsi. For the first time all week, Dr Paulsen noticed he was there, and it took Oscar slightly aback.

'What are you reading?' the old man asked.

'Funny,' he replied, 'I was about to ask you the same question.'

'What are you reading?' Paulsen repeated.

'Just making sure you're okay.'

'I'm okay.' He moved his eyes back to the book. 'What are you reading?'

Oscar put a blanket over the old man's feet. He felt elated to be having a conversation with him again, even if it was strained and looping. 'I haven't been reading much lately, Dr Paulsen, I'm sorry to say.'

'It's good to read.'

'Yeah. Yeah, it is.'

'Rain today,' Paulsen said. 'Take my umbrella.'

There wasn't a drop of rain outside — not that

he could see or hear from the old man's window — but Oscar took the umbrella from the coat-stand anyway. It was an expensive leather-handled thing, with a Paisley awning. 'Thanks,' he called out from the doorway, but the old man was no longer aware of their conversation. He was turning pages over, wetting the tip of his finger.

Oscar walked into the centre of town, swinging Paulsen's umbrella, along Queen's Road, past the playing fields of St John's College where a few rangy students were tossing a frisbee around. He took the short cut over Clare Bridge, winding through the back of King's, around the tall imposing chapel where a line of tourists were already queuing with their Nikon cameras and their pop-out guidebooks. He felt the weight of the building against his back as he made his way through the Front Court, like he was dragging it behind him on a rope, but once he made it past St Catharine's and onto Pembroke Street, the heaviness began to ease away. The Crowne Plaza was not far ahead. Three silver Audis were parked under the carport, and nine or ten businessmen were standing in a huddle as the porters unloaded their luggage onto trolleys. They were checking in at the front desk when he got off the escalator and arrived into the lobby.

He was five minutes early and there was no sign of Crest or Andrea yet, so he took a seat near the window and waited. The businessmen piled into the lifts and went off to their rooms, and the next thing he knew, they were coming back down again in their pinstripe suits and heading for the bar. It was quarter to six. He began to watch the lifts, keeping his eyes alert to the movements of the lights as they ascended and descended, studying the people who stepped out: old women in flowery two-piece outfits; a father and son in football shirts. With every slide of the doors, he held his breath, expecting Crest or Andrea to come out waving to him, apologising, but it was always just a porter bringing back an empty trolley, or a cleaner with a cartful of dirty linen.

The phone rang steadily at the front desk; as soon as one call was answered, another came through. Oscar picked out a few pamphlets from a display stand and read all about the must-see local attractions and organised tours. Sometime after six o'clock, the phone rang again at the front desk — another booking, he thought, another room service order — but soon he heard a voice behind him saying, 'Excuse me. Excuse me, sir.' He turned around and saw the brassy-haired receptionist bending towards him with her hands on her thighs like she was addressing a stray dog. 'Excuse me, sir, is your name Oscar?'

'Yes.'

'There's a call for you at reception.'

'Oh.'

'It's a woman. I think her name was Denny? Miss Denny?'

'Okay. Thank you.'

He'd never heard the name before, but something inside him knew exactly who was calling. He got up and followed the girl to the

417

front desk, and before he picked up the receiver that was waiting on the counter, he took a deep breath in through his nose and out through his mouth. 'Hello?'

'Oscar, is that you?' A soothing Caribbean voice came flowing through the earpiece, and he didn't need to hear anything more. 'Oh, I couldn't remember your last name, but I knew you'd be there. I knew you'd still be waiting.'

'What is it, Andrea?'

She took a long moment to respond. Across the gleaming floor of the lobby, the businessmen were in the bar, drinking pints and guzzling peanuts. Their laughter felt excessive, bruising. He plugged his ear with his finger.

'It's Herbert,' Andrea said, and he knew right away what she was going to tell him. 'He's gone,' she said. 'The Good Lord took him in his sleep. We never even made it out of the apartment.'

There was nothing he could say, nothing he could do but exhale.

'I guess you better tell whoever needs to know,' Andrea went on.

'Yeah.'

'I'm glad I reached you.'

'Yeah. God, I'm just so — '

'I know, me too,' she said. 'There'll be a funeral soon. If you give me your number, I'll keep you posted, okay?'

'Thanks.'

'Try not to feel bad. It was going to happen sometime.'

'I know, but with his last scan and everything, I — '

'He was hopeful,' she said. 'We all were.'

'He told me he'd been feeling so much better lately.'

'Well, it makes no difference now. But look, I'm really glad I reached you. He would've wanted you to be one of the first to know.' She hung up and Oscar stood there for a while, holding the bleating receiver as the hotel walls closed around him like a clamshell, and then the girl at the front desk said: 'Sir, are you alright?' He gave the phone back to her without a word, and headed off down the escalator.

The dusk was gathering outside. He staggered out of the hotel, feeling punchdrunk and hazy. His feet seemed to take him where he needed to go all by themselves, towing him through town, until he found the floodlights of Cedarbrook shining warmly before him. He went through the gates, up to the entrance. The parlour door was open and all the floorlamps were on but there was nobody inside; a John Wayne movie was playing quietly on the television. The young auxiliary at the nurses' station smiled at him, and he tried to smile back but could hardly move the muscles in his cheeks. He passed right by her, trudging up the stairs and along the quiet corridor.

Dr Paulsen's door was ajar. The old man was back in his usual chair again, gawping at the blank pane of his window. Oscar went in, crouched at his side, and held his hand. The skin felt dry and brittle. 'Dr Paulsen,' he said, 'I need to tell you something. It's important that you listen to me, okay?' The old man moved his face

419

towards him first, then his eyes followed. 'Herbert Crest is dead. He died today. I thought you should know. I'm so sorry.' But Paulsen didn't say a word. He simply rolled his head away and began to make a tutting noise — tt-tt-tt-tt-tt-tt — as if his tongue was trying to hack through the prison of his teeth.

★ ★ ★

As he waited on the front step with the doorbell echoing, Oscar felt a coldness against the back of his neck. He looked down towards the Bellwethers' driveway, where grey dust was settling in the aftermath of cab wheels, shining like moonrock. There was no easy way of telling them, he realised. There were no *right* words to say. It was past eleven, and here he was, standing outside the door the way policemen stand to deliver bad news to unsuspecting families, wringing his hands and shifting his weight around on his feet. He was tired — tired of Cambridge and its changeless scenery, tired of Cedarbrook and Dr Paulsen, tired of his small dim flat and his answering machine, tired of cab rides to Grantchester, tired of Eden and Marcus and Yin and Jane, tired of his parents. He hoped that it would be Iris who answered the door, because she was the only person he wasn't tired of, and he knew that he'd start to feel better the moment he saw her.

But it was Yin who came peering through the glass. He was holding a bottle of cider, and struggled to unlatch the door. 'Hey. I was expecting Marcus. You didn't see him pass by or anything, did you?'

'No. Why?'

'Doesn't matter. Listen, buddy, I'm — ' Yin was slurring. 'I'm really fucking sorry about your friend.' And before he could ask him how he knew about it, Yin placed a hand on his shoulder and said: 'We got your message, man. It was pretty garbled, but we got it.'

Oscar didn't think it had recorded properly; the signal had been so intermittent. His calls kept going straight through to Iris's voicemail, and he'd hung up the first few times because he didn't want to leave the bad news waiting in her mailbox like some letter that began *Dear Miss Bellwether, It is with profound regret that I must inform you* . . . But after an hour of trying to get through, he'd finally left a message after the beep. As he'd said, 'You better let your brother know,' he'd thought of Eden's apple-sheen eyes growing wide and wet, of slamming doors and falling chairs and that light going on and off in the organ house. The connection cut out before he could say he was coming over.

'I don't know why everyone's so surprised,' Yin said. 'I mean, the guy was pretty sick, right? You kinda had to see it coming.'

'Doesn't make it any easier to accept.'

'Yeah, but still — a brain tumour. Nobody comes out the other side of that.'

He could tell Yin was drunk because he was talking too much, swigging his cider with big, slack movements of his arms. A sober Yin would've known when to shut up and keep his opinions to himself, but the drink always brought out the conversationalist in him. 'Where is everybody?' Oscar asked.

Yin shrugged and sniffed. 'There's only the three of us here. Eden took off and Marcus went after him. That was — shit — ' He looked at his watch. 'That was a couple hours ago. You sure you didn't pass by Marcus on your way over?'

'No. What do you mean, he took off?'

'He *took off*, man. Drove away. I don't know how else to say it.' Yin pointed towards the light at the end of the hallway. 'Rest of us have been sitting around, wondering what to do. I figured, hey, we got free time on our hands, right? Might as well get wasted.' He took another swig of cider.

They were in the drawing room with the lights dimmed and the television flickering in the walnut cabinet. Jane was watching some wildlife documentary showing animals in slow motion. She'd been crying; her eyes were puffy and she was blowing her nose into a damp, frayed tissue. Iris was fidgeting with her leg-brace, scratching the underside of her thigh with a chopstick. It was not the most graceful vision of her that Oscar had witnessed, but it brought him some comfort. 'Oh, sweetheart,' she said, holding out her arms.

'You've really got to do something about your phone reception out here.'

She held him for a while, whispering how sorry she was. 'I know how fond of him you were,' she said, her warm breath upon his ear. 'I really liked him too. We should never have got him involved in all this.'

'It was what he wanted.'

'I know, but I can't help feeling guilty.'

'He went peacefully. I suppose that's something.'

He looked at Jane. She was hunched forwards with her hands in her lap, clenching her tissue, and the television screen was reflecting in her pupils, two little squares of blue. He lowered his voice to ask Iris what had happened with Eden.

'I tried to let him down gently,' she said. 'We all went out to the O. H. and knocked for him. By then he was all wound up about Herbert's no-show.' She said that Eden had demanded to listen to the message himself. 'I gave him my phone and he stood there and listened to it a few times but didn't say much.' Eden had gone back into the organ house, and the next thing she knew he was locking the door behind him. Jane had tried for an hour to coax him back out, talking to him through the door, but he wouldn't respond. 'I thought, okay, he's just doing what he usually does, hiding himself away when reality bites,' Iris went on, 'so I told everyone to leave him alone. We went back into the house.' Some time later, they'd heard the sound of wheels spinning in the gravel outside, and they'd looked through the window to see Jane's Land Rover missing from the driveway, and two rear lights speeding through the trees. 'He must have been going about a hundred and twenty,' Iris said, then nodded at Jane: 'She's been like that ever since. Hardly said a word.'

Yin took a seat on the sofa next to Jane and

put his arm around her. On the TV, two large green creatures were slinking across a patch of grass. 'Are they Komodo dragons?' Yin asked her.

She shrugged. Then, ever so softly, she said: 'They're trying to mate.'

'They seem angry.'

'That's just how they do it.' She pulled Yin's arm tighter around her like a blanket. They all watched the screen for a while, as the Komodo dragons engaged each other, writhing violently in the dirt. And somehow, just this — just watching the television quietly in the middle of the night, four of them together — took away that awful tiredness that had come over Oscar in the Crowne Plaza.

But Jane still seemed dejected. By the time the credits of the wildlife programme were rolling, she was staring out towards the dim hallway expectantly, as if Eden might come bounding in from the atrium to apologise to everybody. The longer she waited for movement out there, the more defeated she looked. She began raking the hair away from her face, and, finally, her eyebrows furrowed and tears started to skim along her freckly cheeks. 'I've got a bad feeling,' she said, rubbing at her forehead. 'After everything that's happened lately . . . I've just got a horrible feeling.' There was a sudden scrape of footsteps in the garden, and she sprang to her feet. The world behind the drawn curtains brightened.

Marcus came in through the back entrance, lingering in the kitchen doorway. He set his car keys down on the cabinet.

'Well?' Jane asked. 'Did you find him? Where is he?'

Marcus shook his head. He began rolling up his sleeves like he was preparing to deliver a baby. 'I lost him at a level-crossing,' he said. 'He shot right through before the barrier came down. Tried to get him to pull over, was flashing my lights at him, honking the horn, but — *argh*. Will somebody pour me a drink? I don't understand *any* of this. My heart's going like a rabbit.'

Jane collapsed onto the couch. 'We have to go to Harvey Road.'

'Already checked there,' Marcus said. 'I drove past the house and the lights were all off. Didn't see your car either.'

'We have to go anyway.'

'Why?'

Jane didn't answer. She had a faraway expression, biting down on her lip. The string of pearls around her neck was rising and falling with her short, worried breaths.

'What is it, Jane?' Oscar said. 'What aren't you telling us?'

17

New Wrongs

The sun had not yet risen when they arrived at Harvey Road. Oscar parked the Alfa Romeo and waited with his hands still sweating on the steering wheel, watching as Marcus reversed his car into a space further along the street.

'I'm going to need some help,' Iris said from the back seat, her leg stretched out on the leather upholstery. He took her weight as she hauled herself out of the car, and helped her up the steps. They stood at the front of the house, breathing hard. 'I'm afraid,' she said, taking her crutches from his hand. 'Are you?'

'Yeah.'

The others came traipsing along the pavement, shoes clapping the concrete. Jane bounded up the steps and took out her keys. She unlocked the front door and went inside. 'Before you see the mess in there,' she said, turning at the threshold, 'I want to say it again — '

'You already explained,' Iris said. 'Let us in.'

'Okay, but just remember that I found it like this, like you're all finding it now. There wasn't anything I could do.'

They walked in through the porch, single file, and Jane flicked on the light.

Oscar couldn't see anything different about the hallway. It was as plain and narrow as it had always been, with the same old pile of shoes near the door and barely a scuff on the hardwood or a fingermark on the dado rail. But he thought he could smell something strange in the air, like clothes left to fester in the washing machine.

Jane led them towards the living room. They all seemed to hold their breath as she pushed back the door.

'What the hell — ?' Yin said.

The antique clavichord was a mess of pieces on the floor. Its ivory keys were smashed and spread across the floorboards like punched-out teeth; hunks of varnished teak lay splintered and held together with frayed piano wires. When Jane described the damage to them back at the Bellwether house, she'd made it seem almost cosmetic — fixable, at least. But Oscar could hardly believe the wreckage that was before him now. The instrument was a junkpile of parts, as if Eden had razed it with a bulldozer.

Yin walked over to survey the ruins, crouching to pick up an ivory and tossing it back onto the pile. 'Guys,' he said. 'This is seriously fucked up.'

Iris was just standing there with her soft little mouth hanging open. 'Jane, I can't believe you didn't say anything about this.'

'I wanted to tell you. Honest, I did. I was just so upset when I saw what he'd done to it and — ' Jane stopped. She rested her head against the doorframe. 'I thought maybe it was just one of those things, like he'd needed to let off some steam.'

Marcus went over and began prodding the clutter with his toes. 'This is more than letting off steam,' he said. 'I've never seen him do anything as violent as this.'

'It's like he went at it with a sledgehammer,' Yin said. 'You didn't see what happened?'

'No, I told you. This is how I found it.'

'But . . . it doesn't make any sense. He paid a fortune for this thing.'

'I know.'

'Was he even upset about it?'

'Not remotely,' Jane said. 'He wouldn't even let me clean it up. He said he wanted to keep the mess there forever, as a reminder.'

'A reminder of what?'

Jane shrugged. 'I asked the same thing.' She looked glumly at Iris then, as if apologising. 'I should've said something to your parents the other night — I nearly did. But everybody seemed like they had enough to worry about. And Eden said — ' She trailed off. 'Never mind.'

Iris stood upright. 'Eden said *what*, Jane? Did he threaten you?'

Jane could hardly bring herself to glance in her direction. 'No — well, not exactly. It wasn't really a threat.' She turned her head, examining the rug. 'He said he'd break up with me if I told anyone, that's all. I don't know if he was serious or not, but it seemed like it at the time, and I didn't want to test him. It was weeks ago, before they moved you to the other hospital. He was so mad.'

Yin stood up, dusting off his hands. 'We need to find him. I've been saying it all year: he's been acting weird. We better find him before he does any more damage.'

'We should probably take a look around before we go,' Oscar said.

'He's not here,' Marcus replied. 'He wouldn't come back here. Why race off at a hundred miles an hour just to go back where you started?'

'We should check anyway,' Yin said. 'He's probably not thinking straight. I'll start looking upstairs. Who's coming with me?'

Oscar volunteered. He followed Yin up the narrow staircase, hearing Marcus's heavy steps over his shoulder. An acid began to bite at his stomach. His palms were sweating again. Jane and Iris peered up from the hallway, whispering to each other.

He checked the bathroom. It was empty and undisturbed but for a tiny spider-web crack in the shaving mirror and a shallow pool of dirty water in the bathtub. He came out to find Yin up on the landing, feeling along the wall for the switch. A mild yellow light stammered on. Marcus went straight to Eden's room, taking bold, purposeful strides, as if to say *What's everyone so afraid of?* The handle turned in his fingers but the door wouldn't move. 'Huh,' he said, arms dropping to his sides. 'It's locked.'

'It can't be,' Yin said. 'Let me try.' When it didn't open at the first attempt, he threw his weight at the bare wood — three short punches of his shoulder — but the lock held firm. 'Edie! You in there? Eden!'

Nobody answered.

Yin pointed across the landing. 'Try Iggy's.'

Oscar went to Iris's room and twisted the handle. As he pushed back the door, there was a sudden flutter of birds' wings, loud as applause. He stopped in the threshold, unable to move. A flock of mangy-looking blackbirds flew up from around the feet of the bed, scrambling against the ceiling, rebounding against the walls, shedding their feathers with every frantic burst of their wings. There were at least ten of them, maybe more, and they'd left their mark all over the room: everything was spattered with gobbets of silvery-white bird shit. A single bedside lamp was on, casting a frenzy of shadows against the curtains. The dank, fungal smell of caged animals was everywhere.

'Shut it, man,' Yin called. 'Shut it.'

Oscar pulled the door closed. A wordless shock came over him. He was shaken, repulsed, and when he looked at Marcus and Yin, he saw the full whites of their eyeballs; they were both holding their hands to their mouths as if they might throw up.

Yin was the first to move. He leaned over the balustrade, shouting down: 'Iggy! Jane! You better come up here!'

They had already heard the commotion. Iris was crutch-stepping up the stairs as fast as she could, with Jane holding on to her back, saying: 'What? What is it?'

'Take a look,' Yin said.

'It's not pretty in there,' Oscar warned them. 'I don't think you should go in.'

'Let me through,' Iris said, stepping forwards. 'I need to see.'

When Jane opened the door, the noise of the panicked birds came at them with a jolt, and

430

there was that smell again — that awful, mouldering stench. Iris gasped and staggered backwards, and Oscar had to catch her by the shoulders to stop her falling. Jane gave out a shriek and slammed the door. She stayed there with her fingers on the handle, recovering her breath. 'I swear I didn't know about this, Iggy,' she said. 'I swear on my life I didn't.'

Oscar held onto Iris tightly, kissing the side of her head. 'Don't worry, we'll clean it up. If we open the windows, they should fly right out.' She didn't seem able to talk. Her crutches creaked in her grip.

'We can't get into Eden's room,' Marcus said. 'Where's the key?'

'I don't know,' Jane said. 'He keeps it with him.'

'You don't have a copy?'

Jane shook her head.

'Maybe we should bust it open,' Yin said. 'He could be in there.'

'Are you sure it's locked? Sometimes it sticks.'

Yin stood back. 'Go ahead.'

Jane went over and jimmied the handle. After a moment of struggle, the door released, and she stepped inside tentatively, clicking on the light.

'Be careful,' Iris said.

Oscar had never seen the fullness of Eden's room before. A few times, he'd peeked in as he went sleepily to the shower, but he'd only ever glimpsed things — a sliver of a bedpost, the corner of a duvet. It wasn't so different from how he'd pictured it. The floor was a landfill of assembled junk: faded hardbacks, notepads,

431

newspapers and sheet music were stacked in towers around the bed, like some great city of books rising up from the carpet; shirts hung from the windows on wire hangers and dried-out socks were draped over the radiator. Eden was nowhere to be seen. 'Looks like it always does,' Jane said, coming out. 'A total mess.'

'Told you he wasn't here,' Marcus said.

With this, Iris turned on her crutches and headed for the stairs. 'I need a cigarette.'

'We'll take care of things up here, don't worry,' Yin said. 'Why don't you girls go sweep up what's left of the clavi?'

'Okay,' Jane said, her voice faltering, 'okay, yeah. Let's go, Iggy.'

Iris lingered on the top step, looking back at Oscar. She held her hand to her breastbone the way she'd done back at Madigan Hall, her eyes teary and reddening. He knew she wasn't thinking of the blackbirds in her room any more, but of the blackbird squirming from her brother's hands when she was eight years old. He gave a solemn nod and she carried on down the stairs with Jane's help.

'Alright,' Yin said. 'Let's do it.'

The birds were still frantic inside the bedroom. Squawking and screeching, they flapped and scurried away, landing on top of the shelves and the wardrobe, beyond reach. 'Calm down, little things!' Marcus called out, stooping to open the curtains. 'We're here to help you!'

Oscar opened the windows as wide as he could. An urgent breeze came sweeping into the room, but the birds didn't seem to sense the world outside. They didn't go racing towards the windows, just cawed and jumped and side-stepped, clacking their claws on the wood, pecking everything with their bright yellow beaks.

'What now?' Yin said.

'It'll be light soon. They'll go for the windows then.'

The three of them went out to the landing. Oscar sat down with his back against the door.

'Shit,' Yin said, his short laugh hollowed by the cove of the ceiling, 'you sounded so confident about them flying right out. I thought you did this kind of thing all the time.' He guffawed nervously. 'We're gonna have to call pest control.'

'Don't laugh,' Marcus said. 'Don't either of you laugh.' He stood clicking his knuckles. He had a stern, concentrated look about him. 'Edie's gone too far this time. I'm not sure he's thinking straight.' Marcus directed his words to the floor. 'We all know the pranks he used to pull back at school, but this — I've never seen him do anything like this. I just don't understand what's got into him. I mean, that clavichord was one of his favourite things in the world. It cost him a fortune just to ship it over. I don't understand why he'd trash it unless something was seriously wrong. And I don't see why he'd speed off like he did tonight, either, just because some old man who he hardly even knew is dead. It doesn't add up.'

'That's because you've only got half a story,' Oscar said. 'It makes sense when you know the rest of it.'

'What are you talking about?' Yin said.

'Yeah,' Marcus said, 'what do you mean, *half a story*?'

Oscar looked at them, blinking. There was something about their faces — about the tightness of Yin's eyes and the slackness of Marcus's mouth — that made him feel the need to tell them. They needed to understand who Eden really was. They had seen the blackbirds of the present, but they didn't know about the blackbirds of the past. And, yes, they might deny the truth once they heard it, but they were his friends — he was sure they were his friends — and they deserved to know.

He told them everything: from Iris's childhood stories, to her broken legs, to NPD and Crest's book, right up to Andrea's phone call. He didn't try to spare their feelings or dance around the issue, and he did his best to answer their questions and to calm them when they got angry. It took a long time to get through it all. And by the time he was done, it was light outside and the cawing of the blackbirds had weakened in the room behind his back.

★   ★   ★

There were small death notices for Herbert Crest in the *Guardian*, the *Independent*, and the *Daily Telegraph*. Each paper ran a tiny paragraph about him, devoting fewer column inches to the achievements of a man's entire life than to news of a skimpy dress some actress had worn to some London film premiere. But when Oscar went to the homepage of *The New York*

Times that afternoon, he found a link to a full obituary.

Herbert M. Crest, Psychologist and Writer, Dies Aged 69

by Peter McLury

Herbert M. Crest, a psychologist and writer best known for the intimate portraits he drew of his patients in award-winning volumes of case studies, died on April 28 at his home in London, England.

Dr. Crest had been fighting cancer since a brain tumor was diagnosed three years ago, and had been receiving treatment from specialists at University College Hospital. He died in his sleep in the early hours of the afternoon, reported his nurse, Ms. Andrea Denny. News of his death received little coverage in the British media, though it was widely discussed in professional circles.

Dr. Crest was the author of a diverse range of accessible works on psychology, which sought to investigate the foundations of disorders such as Schizophrenia, Narcissistic Personality Disorder, and Borderline Personality Disorder. In 1974, he received a gold medal from the American Psychological Foundation for his book *The Girl With the God Complex*, which developed the ideas of Ernest Jones in detailing the delusions of a young girl convicted of drowning her five-year-old brother. Though the book sold modestly, its publication made Dr. Crest one of the foremost authorities in the study of Narcissistic Personality Disorder, precipitating further works on the subject, including *Selfhood in the Modern World* (1984).

Herbert Montague Crest was born July 7, 1934, in Harwichport, Mass., to Arthur Crest, a British expatriate and teacher of mathematics, and Katherine, a homemaker. He moved to Boston when he was 11 after his father took a position at MIT. After leaving for England at the age of 18, he graduated from King's College, Cambridge, in 1961 with first class honors in Philosophy and Psychology, and remained in England to complete his doctorate. During his time at Cambridge, he was convicted of stealing a houseboat owned by an esteemed literature professor at his college; a civil suit was settled out of court before his return to the United States in 1971 when he took a position at the University of Connecticut.

A proud gay man working in an era of widespread homophobia, Dr. Crest never married and had no children. His younger sister, Tabitha, died aged 14, after falling from her school building in 1950. He is survived by a cousin, Nancy, of Vancouver, WA., and her two children.

Described by *New York Times* book critic Marek Stoor as 'writings of humane eloquence,' Dr. Crest's thought-provoking case studies, articles, and essays found a wide lay readership in the United States. At the time of his death, he was working on a new book detailing his battle with cancer, entitled *Delusions of Hope*, in which he was investigating the authenticity of alternative therapies. His editor, Diane Rossi at publisher Spector & Tillman, commented: 'Herbert had an amazing mind, and right to the very end he was making changes to the book, which we all knew would be wonderful. We're devastated by the news of his death.' The book was scheduled for release in fall 2003, but it is now unclear if publication will be delayed.

When Oscar arrived at Golders Green Crematorium, pushing Dr Paulsen down the aisle in his wheelchair, the service was already underway. Turgid organ music was playing — one strained, macabre note after the other — and he couldn't help but think of Herbert Crest looking down and smiling at the desperate irony of it. The room was only a quarter full. Andrea was sitting on a pew in the front row, and she turned to see him wheeling the old man along the carpet. He parked Dr Paulsen at the front of the chapel, where scarlet drapes hung and a bouquet of white lilies stood in a tall black vase. Crest's coffin was laid out on the brick altar, polished to an impossible shine, waiting to be disappeared.

Andrea gave the eulogy. She'd been crying and the chapel lights caught the tracks of her tears as she moved her lips. 'Herbert didn't want a religious service,' she finished by saying, 'so

437

instead of a Bible passage, I thought I'd leave you with a few of his own words. In his book *Unpopular Mechanics* he wrote: 'My father used to say it's better to mean something to no one than mean nothing to someone. That's a maxim I've always tried to live by.' I think that gives you a good idea of the man Herbert was.' With that, she stepped down from the pulpit and took her seat. A Nat King Cole song began to play on the speaker system, and the coffin was lowered into a pit of hidden flames.

Outside the crematorium, Oscar introduced Dr Paulsen to Andrea. She stooped to shake the old man's hand, though he didn't seem to notice her or understand what he was doing outside. 'So you're the one, are you?' she said, winking. 'You're the old fool who broke his heart. Don't worry, he forgave you, I know he did.' Paulsen peered blankly across the road. Andrea stood up.

'Herbert would've been touched by your speech,' Oscar told her.

She smiled wanly, and lit up a cigarette. 'So where are your friends, hm? The kids from the big house.'

'They didn't think it was right to come. Most of them hardly knew him. *I* hardly knew him.'

'Nah, you knew him alright. He liked you a lot.'

'I wish I could've got to know him better.'

'Yeah. But you saw the best of him. I think you reminded him a little of how he used to be.'

The way she said it — so breathy, so earnest — made him uncomfortable for lying to her about where the others were. 'The kids from the

438

big house' — that was how he used to think about them, too, but now he saw them only as his friends, people he had to cover for when called upon. They'd all had good excuses for not coming: Iris couldn't make it all the way to London with her leg as bad as it was; Marcus and Yin both had exams on Friday and couldn't afford to give up the study time; and Jane was so worried about Eden that she couldn't handle the solemnity of a funeral service. But they were all just excuses, not reasons.

'Sorry there's no wake — he didn't want one,' Andrea said. She told him she was shipping Crest's ashes to America by Fed-Ex. 'His cousin's going to scatter them in the family plot, next to where they buried his sister. It's how he wanted it.'

'That's nice,' Oscar said, and the words seemed stupid the moment they came out of his mouth.

They said their goodbyes and he started to wheel Dr Paulsen back towards the car park, but Andrea grabbed his arm. 'Hey, hold on,' she said, then gestured at the old man with her head, lowering her voice. 'He ever talk about what happened? — between him and Herbert, I mean?'

Oscar looked down at Paulsen, at his veiny hands drooping over the armrests. 'I heard it was something about a boat. That's all I know.'

'Yeah,' Andrea said, grinning at the sky. 'I never found out either.'

★ ★ ★

439

There hadn't been so much as a whisper from Eden in twelve days — not even a simple text message to say he was okay — and on 10th May, when her parents called again from the Auvergne to check up on her, Iris finally decided to tell them he was missing.

Lying beside her on the bed in the too-big guestroom, Oscar listened as she explained to them why this wasn't just one of her brother's usual jaunts to Prague or Heidelberg or Florence, the kind of impromptu trip they were all used to him taking. For a long while, she struggled to get across the gravity of the situation, arguing first with her mother, then with her father, about the importance of cutting their trip short. 'No, no — it's different this time,' she kept saying. 'I wouldn't have bothered you with it if I thought — no, okay, but listen — ' It was only when she reminded them that Eden's first exam was on the 26th and that she didn't think he was likely to come back for it that the conversation took a sudden, serious turn. Her father's voice grew thicker in the earpiece, and Oscar could hear his every sputtering word.

'Alright, good, so you'll come home?' she said. 'Okay. Monday then. Good.' It was finally decided. She hung up, flushed and exhausted.

It was late on Tuesday evening when Oscar noticed the sound of a car engine outside his flat. He peered down from the window to see Theo Bellwether emerging from the driver's side of his Alfa Romeo. There was something about the shape of his body in the dusk; he liked to wear a

440

camelhair overcoat at night, even on warm summer evenings, and its padded shoulders made him look thin and tapered, just like his son. The buzzer went off, and the voice on the intercom was thin and ghostly. 'Hello? Can you hear me? It's Theo Bellwether. Can we talk?'

Oscar let him inside. 'I'm sorry, it's a bit messy in here. I've been at work all day and haven't had time to — '

'Relax, Oscar. I'm not your landlady. I couldn't care less about a few unwashed dishes.' Theo removed his coat. He was not an especially tall man, close up, but he held himself in an upright way: two arms held behind his back, shoulder blades pulled tightly together, as if by strings hidden underneath his clothes. 'You mind?' He motioned towards the couch, and sat down before Oscar could answer. With a weary twist of his fingers, he loosened his tie, crossing his legs. 'Don't bother putting the kettle on, I've had three cups of tea already — you're my last stop of the evening.'

'I had a feeling you'd be coming to see me.' Oscar wasn't sure what to expect from Theo now that he was here. He felt underprepared. It didn't seem as if Theo was especially upset: he seemed neither angry nor melancholy, only composed, like a man who knew the cards he'd been dealt and exactly how he was going to play them.

'Funny. The others told me the same thing.' Theo recrossed his legs. 'Suppose I'll give the same speech I gave to them.' Standing over him now, Oscar could see Theo's white hair was

441

thinning, and the skin beneath it was dry and spotted. 'Look, sit down, would you?' Theo said. 'I don't like talking at different eye-levels.'

Oscar sat on the edge of his bed, leaning forwards. 'I suppose Iris told you everything, or you wouldn't be here.'

Theo peered at the floor and twisted his beard. Then he gave a little dry cough. 'She showed me the videos.'

'You're not as upset as I thought you'd be.'

'Well — ' Theo looked at him blankly. 'The way you've all been keeping me in the dark about this, quite frankly I'm furious about the whole bloody fiasco, but my being furious isn't going to solve anything, is it? So that will have to wait for another time. Right now I'd appreciate it if you'd just sit still and listen to me and not interrupt me until I'm finished. I have a lot to say to you.' He gave another cough. 'It's important that you know I'm not coming here as a sort of defence counsel, but as a father — that's first and foremost. I saw the videos, and I'll be honest, they frightened the life out of me. To see my own son behaving that way, well, you don't need me to tell you how I feel about that. The thing is, though, I've *always* been frightened by Eden. Not by his behaviour — that's only just become a cause for concern — I mean frightened by how much he knows. He's always been such an intelligent boy, far more talented than I was at his age. I could master a lancet, but I couldn't pluck a decent note on the violin if the fate of the nations rested on it, and I certainly didn't have as many friends as he seems to have, not close friends, people who genuinely liked my company, you know?' Theo blinked at last. 'But we're alike in so many other ways. All of his brashness and exuberance — he gets that from me. All that arrogant self-assurance and stubbornness he has, how he likes to make you think he's so complex and interesting, like everybody's either too stupid or too insignificant to understand him — that's exactly what I was like at his age. I've made a lot of enemies that way.' Pausing, Theo glanced towards the ceiling, at the wiry strands of cobwebs stretching from the cornices to the lampshade, as if he wanted to reach out and sweep them all away. 'So you see, I understand Eden more than he thinks. And yes, okay, I go easy on him sometimes, I admit it; maybe I let him get away with too much, but it's only because I understand that side of him. My father couldn't empathise with that side of me, and I always promised myself I'd be lenient with my own kids. Once you have children of your own, your whole perspective on life changes. You try to right the wrongs your own parents made but you only end up doing new wrongs, making new problems. That's just how life is . . . But the important thing I want you to grasp here — and I hope the others grasp this now too — is how long it took for me to understand myself. Do you follow? It took me a very long time to get any kind of self-awareness. Just seemed to click itself on one day like a light switch. Really, it took meeting Ruth and having children of my own for me to lose that arrogance, that sense of self-importance. I'm sure they'd diagnose me

443

with all kinds of things these days, disorders and whatnot. Do you see what I'm getting at here? I don't want you to think I'm being arrogant when I say this to you now, but I know my son better than anyone, Oscar. More than some two-bit psychologist who spent — what? — a few hours with him. No, please, don't interrupt me, okay? You'll have your turn to speak. I'm telling you something now, so, please just listen . . . I know exactly how my boy's mind works because it works the same way mine used to work. Just like I told Iris yesterday, and just like I just told Marcus and Jane and Yin tonight: I'm not worried about Eden. Not in the long-term, because I know that one day he's going to reach that level of self-awareness I've been telling you about. The only thing that concerns me is the here and now, do you understand? I am his father, and it's my responsibility to look after his best interests. Until Eden reaches that point where he truly understands himself, I have to protect him from himself. Are you listening to what I'm telling you?'

Oscar stayed quiet.

'It's okay,' Theo said, 'you can talk now.'

Oscar took a steadying breath. 'I don't really know what you're trying to tell me. But if you're saying that Eden's perfectly fine — that he doesn't need help — well, I'm sorry, but I just can't agree with that.'

'No, I didn't expect you to.'

'Dr Crest wasn't just a two-bit psychologist. He was an expert in his field. He practically defined the whole subject.'

'And he said my son had a narcissistic personality?'

'Yeah. He was sure of it.'

'Oh, come on.' Theo gave a dismissive laugh. 'We're human beings — we're *all* narcissists. We're all selfish. Just because somebody is extraordinary, or ambitious, or self-motivated, that doesn't mean they have a disorder. It's just human nature. Survival of the fittest.'

'How can you say that?'

'Because it's true. I've read the diagnostic criteria for NPD, and yes, there are a few things you might level at Eden — need for admiration, a certain lack of empathy, okay, okay — but I just don't recognise my son in most of them, I'm sorry.'

'Mr Bellwether, I — '

'Oh, call me Theo, will you?'

Oscar sighed. 'I can't believe you're saying that — you're a doctor.'

'I'm a surgeon,' Theo said, 'but that's beside the point. What I'm saying is, I know my son, and he'll be fine. He's just going through a bad phase right now, and the last thing he needs is for some idiot shrink to go advertising his troubles to the world — worse, to go tarnishing my son's reputation, and my own for that matter, with some glib diagnosis.'

'Theo, with the greatest respect, I think you're lying to yourself.'

'Please don't psychoanalyse me, Oscar.'

'I'm not. I'm just saying maybe you can't accept Eden's ill because you think it'll reflect badly on you somehow. And it doesn't.'

445

'Oh, so now *I'm* a narcissist. I *see*.' Theo let out a whipcrack of a laugh. 'I know my son, and I don't believe he's ill. Misguided? Yes, perhaps. A bit too big for his boots sometimes? Clearly. But he doesn't need any kind of intervention from the psychiatric profession, I want us to be very clear on that. He just needs some stern words and a little tolerance.'

There was resoluteness in Theo's eyes now, and Oscar knew that it wasn't coming from a place of reason, but from somewhere deeper, more emotional. It was the kind of look his own father had never shown in public, or anywhere for that matter: sheer blind love for his son. 'If you could just see him, Theo,' he said. 'If you could see the way he's been behaving — '

'I've seen the videos. I've been through all of this with Iris, I'm not going through it with you, too. I haven't come here to argue with you.'

'Did she tell you about Harvey Road?'

'Yes.'

'We had to sweep up the clavichord into cardboard boxes.'

'I know.'

'It took us all night to clean up Iris's room. The birds might've gone but you can still smell them.'

'Yes. Look, I know all that.'

'It doesn't bother you?'

Theo took a long breath in and a long breath out. 'I don't have time to get upset.'

'You wouldn't be saying that if you'd seen the state of the place. If you'd seen the look on Iris's face when she opened the door.'

446

'Don't start telling me what I would and wouldn't think. I won't be lectured to. Eden's clearly been acting very oddly, and he's handled things badly. Nobody's arguing with that. But my concern isn't for the state of Harvey Road right now. It's for my son's future. He's going to achieve big things in his life, we all know that, and he doesn't need any setbacks. That's why I'm here: to protect him from himself. And I think you know what I'm referring to.' Theo leaned forwards, making a steeple with his fingers. 'I need the tapes he gave you, Oscar.'

'I don't have them.'

'Come on now. Marcus and Jane already gave me their copies. They were only too happy to help me. Why are you being so obtuse?'

'I don't have them.'

'Oscar, I'm asking you nicely. Don't make things difficult. It's very important that you give me those tapes.'

'They're not here. I put them somewhere safe, like he told me to.'

'Then we'll drive there, wherever it is.'

'Now?'

'Yes, now.'

'That might be difficult.'

'Just put your coat on and let's go.'

They drove silently along Queen's Road, heading for Cedarbrook. The sky was dark and starless and streetlights flashed across the windscreen in a steady ticker-roll of blue. Operatic music played quietly on the stereo. Back in the flat, Oscar had felt certain about the idea, but now, as Theo steered the car through the gates and pulled up

447

in the driveway, he didn't feel so sure. And as he walked inside, flashing his ID badge at the duty nurse, his stomach felt loose and he was trembling a little. He went upstairs and strode by the snoring patients in their closed-off rooms. Slowly turning the handle on Dr Paulsen's door, he went inside and saw the old man sleeping on his back with his mouth half-open. He retrieved a carrier bag from the back of Paulsen's wardrobe and found the tapes still inside, plus the original videos he'd shown Crest all those months ago in London.

Treading gently, he left Dr Paulsen sleeping, went back downstairs, waving at the duty nurse, and got back into Theo's car. The engine was still running. He handed the carrier bag over.

'Good,' Theo said, eyeing the contents of the bag under the dashboard light as if there were used banknotes inside. 'Thanks for making this easy. I might get some sleep tonight, after all.' Theo put them on the back seat and reversed out of the gates.

It was only then that Oscar felt sure he'd done the right thing. He thought of the copies he'd posted to Herbert Crest, seeing a Jiffy envelope somewhere in his apartment, amid a pile of unopened condolence cards and health insurance policies. He knew he wasn't betraying anyone.

18

The Ordering of Material Affairs

Oscar couldn't remember time ever passing as slowly as it did that fortnight in May. In the lead-up to their exams, Marcus, Yin, and Jane were just like all the other Cambridge students, sandbagging themselves inside their colleges to study, stopping only for sleep and food, coming out into the fresh air only to make it to the University Library before it closed. At night, the city felt empty and eerily quiet, but there was a strange kind of energy inside the boundaries of the colleges whenever he passed by, like secret meetings were taking place behind closed doors, operations being plotted by candlelight. He saw little of his friends in those two weeks, though he thought about them often as he worked his shifts at Cedarbrook, wondering how they were getting on and hoping they were thinking about him, too. His days at work were even more drawn out than usual: he would try not to count the hours, because measuring out his shifts only made the time pass more slowly. Tasks he thought would kill several minutes, like helping Mr Foy into his varicose vein stockings or segmenting grapefruits for the residents at breakfast, hardly seemed to take any time at all. He couldn't even talk to Dr Paulsen any more. And when he got home, there was nothing to do but sit around, watch TV, listen to the radio. He was too bored to clean the flat, too heavy-hearted to read a book, and this only made things worse, adding guilt to loneliness. For those two excruciating weeks, he felt alone again.

It seemed like forever since he'd last seen Iris. She spent her days studying at her parents' house and, apart from an awkward telephone call every night (in which she was not quite herself, always making him feel like he'd phoned at the least convenient moment) they hardly spoke at all. Her leg was growing stronger and she was getting regular physio now, but she was still on her crutches and couldn't drive herself to Cambridge even if she wanted to. 'I can't be putting myself in a cab just to give you something to do,' was how she put it, 'it's going to be hard enough making it out there to sit my exams. With all the painkillers I'm taking, God knows what kind of gibberish I'll end up writing. I need to use this time properly.'

With Eden still missing, she seemed more focused on her studies, and more determined than ever to prove herself to her parents. She talked about them a lot in their nightly conversations. 'I think this is the longest stretch they've spent at home all year. My mother keeps bringing me cups of Darjeeling and telling me to eat, and Dad seems to be on the phone a lot, so if you can't get through to me, that's why.'

She said that her father had been talking to his credit card company to check if and where Eden had been spending his money. The account was in her father's name, so they'd given him the

450

information he asked for, but it wasn't showing any activity. 'He's making a lot of calls to France, too. He thinks I can't hear him down there in the study, using his French phrasebook from the seventies; it's embarrassing. They're about to exchange on that *gîte* of theirs by the sounds of it, so obviously nothing's going to get in the way of the big retirement plans — massive shock. And yesterday, they were arguing about Eden. I don't think I've ever heard them argue like that before.'

She said that her mother wanted to involve the police, that she was starting to think Eden wasn't going to come back at all. 'I suppose technically he *is* a missing person by now, so she has a point. But Dad wouldn't have it. He's convinced he's coming back. He said, *Can you imagine how that would look? Police cars in the driveway? No thank you* . . . Still, my mother seems worried. It's true what she says — a month is a long time, and he'd normally have been in touch by now. But I'm trying not to get caught in the middle of it. I'm trying to get my head down and study. I feel bad for saying this, but — ' She trailed off. 'I feel awful for saying it, but I'm sort of glad my brother isn't around at the moment. It's taken the pressure off a little bit.'

Every day was another cross on the calendar.

On the morning of 23rd May, Iris had her first exam, and Oscar went to meet her later that afternoon at Jesus Green. He came straight from Cedarbook and was still in his uniform, and the sight of her there on the grass before him, the way her face brightened as he approached her,

451

only made him more aware of how much he'd missed her. Her hair was longer, nearly back to blonde. She was happy and relaxed, lying on a plaid blanket that she'd spread across the grass, and it seemed as if the sun had come out just for her. 'Ask me,' she said, 'ask me how it went.'

He lay down next to her, kissed her mouth softly. The ground was damp and spongy beneath the blanket. 'How did it go?'

'Wonderfully. If the next five go as well as that, I'll be delirious.'

'That's great.'

'We need to celebrate,' she said.

'Okay. Let's do something tonight. Dinner?'

'No, I can't, I have to go back and study. Another test in the morning.'

'Well, whenever you want then.'

It was the oddest feeling: when Eden wasn't around, they were so much freer. They could make plans that didn't revolve around him; they could do things on a whim, without any regard for what a certain somebody might say about it. So then why did everything feel so uncomfortable? Why didn't life seem the same without him? Somehow Eden's absence had given him a greater presence. He was an unspoken word that underscored every conversation. A face that flickered behind every shopfront. A punter's shadow gliding away along the Cam. And though Iris did her best to cover up the moments where she'd zone out as they were talking, though she busied herself with revision so Oscar wouldn't think she'd fallen apart completely, he knew that she missed her brother. How could she not?

'I was thinking we could go to the May Ball at St John's,' she said. 'I think it's a Japanese theme this year. It'll give us a chance to dress up. Exams will be over by then — we can get Jane and Marcus and Yin to come, really let our hair down. It'll be fun.' Her words came out in monotone. She looked across the green, towards a group of shirtless men playing volleyball over a badminton net. 'And besides, I've only ever been to the ball at King's, which isn't the same thing. I could never find anyone to take me. Eden always said the fancier parties were a big waste of effort.'

Oscar noticed the past tense. 'Maybe he was right,' he said.

'Yes, but for once in my life, I'd like to find that out for myself.'

She lay on her back, brushing the hair out of her eyes. 'My mother says you were talking to her after the Easter service. I don't know what it was that you said to her, but you made some kind of impression. In a good way, I mean.'

'I did?'

She nodded. 'We had one of those difficult, silent dinners last night — the type you just want to crawl under the table and hide from. My dad wasn't saying much, and everyone was messing with their food, not eating, and I suppose I must've looked depressed or something, because my mother put her fork down and said — I can't do her voice — *So, darling, when are you next seeing Oscar?* Took me completely by surprise. She never asks me about you, not really. And I said, well, I don't know, soon I hope, it's hard

453

with my leg and everything, and she starts gathering the dishes up. Then — this is the best part — she says to me: *Well, I think you should make more of an effort. He's good for you, that boy.* So there you go. Seal of approval. How do you do it, Oscar?' She smiled at him. 'How do you make people like you without even trying?'

'Oh, there are plenty of people who don't like me,' he said.

'That's not true. Name one.'

'Your brother for starters.'

'No, you're wrong about that. He liked you.'

There it was again, Oscar thought: the past tense. 'How do you know?'

'I just know.'

'Well, I suppose it doesn't matter. You're the only Bellwether I want to love me.'

She raised his hand to her mouth and kissed it, holding her lips there, warm and dry. He felt two long exhalations upon his skin before she released it. 'I do love you,' she said. 'You're the only good thing to come out of all this mess.'

They lay there for a while in each other's arms, watching the grey clouds trawling the sky. It was good to be close to her again, to have her breathing quietly beside him, her chest rising and falling, her fingers gripping his. But he knew her mind was a long way away. She was glaring at clouds, never blinking, and he could tell by her soft, persistent sighs that she was thinking about Eden. The whites of her eyes seemed to dance with her every thought, nervously twitching. 'I was going through some old study notes the other day,' she said, stretching to retrieve her bag, rooting through it. After a moment, she pulled out a spiral-bound notepad, leafed through the pages, and presented it to him. 'Look what I found.'

Oscar struggled to read her messy handwriting. He remembered the night when she had copied out the passage from Herbert's book: *Sometimes, NPD sufferers are trapped in an endless cycle of trying to prove their abilities; they may set themselves impossible challenges to solve or overcome, only to battle with the feelings of failure and ineptitude that these self-imposed challenges create.* The last part of the quote, she had underlined several times: *If this rage is held inside, directed inward, it can lead to self-harm and suicidal ideation.*

She looked at Oscar now, squinting into the sun. 'I can't stand waiting any more,' she said. 'I need to be doing something.'

'But your dad said — '

'Forget about my dad. He's being so bloody obtuse. Everyone can see Eden's not coming back by Monday. We need to start looking for him.'

'Where?'

'I don't know. But I can't do it on my own, not in this condition.' Her voice had a defeated tone, as if she were tired of its sound. 'Oscar, he's going to lose everything — his scholarship, his place at the college — it's all going to be wasted. We can't just sit here letting it happen. He's got to know we're trying to find him.'

'Then let's start.'

She turned her head sharply. 'You mean it?'

'Just tell me where to look.'

There was a familiar cold pressure upon Oscar's neck when he got to the landing. He had switched on every light on his way upstairs, but it only made the furthest reaches of the house seem darker, and even though Iris had given him the keys, he couldn't shake the feeling that he had broken in. There wasn't much furniture amongst the clutter of Eden's room: a double bed and a small chest of drawers, a dressing table and an antique wardrobe with a streaky mirrored door. He decided to start with the drawers. There were plenty of clothes left inside: vests and thermals, white sports socks, silk boxer shorts, ties and cummerbunds. He slid the bottom drawers out, emptying them onto the bed. There was nothing of interest, only musty corduroy, denim, polyester. But then, as he was putting the last drawer back in place, he noticed something — a strip of black electrical tape on the bare insides of the unit. He ran his fingers over it, feeling a bump, and peeled the tape away. A small key fell into his hand. It was brassy and tarnished and didn't seem to fit any lock he could find, so he put it into his pocket, and slid the rest of the drawers back in.

There were so many books and papers on the floor that he could hardly see the carpet. He had to skim-read his way through them: pamphlets and pamphlets of sheet music; anthologies of classical notation; single foolscap pages with Eden's scrawls and doodles; brand-new books with shiny dustcovers that looked as if they'd

456

hardly been opened; frayed hardbacks with torn jackets or no jackets at all; whole chapters ripped from unknown paperbacks, held together by hard yellowy glue; old newspaper after old newspaper; worn-out copies of the *Spectator*, the *New Statesman*, the *New Yorker*, the *Sunday Times Magazine*, the *British Medical Journal*; outdated university prospectuses; journals in which essays had been mapped out, and musical compositions sketched, and self-portraits drawn in blunt pencil. Inside every book, inside every newspaper and magazine, there were corners folded over to mark pertinent pages. Sometimes a single word was underscored in biro, sometimes a sentence or a whole paragraph. Though there seemed to be no particular system to the way that all of the books and papers had been assembled, Oscar knew they'd been arranged exactly how Eden wanted them. Where the rest of the world saw chaos, Eden saw logic and order. His room was an atlas of his mind.

It took Oscar an hour just to get halfway through the stacks. He felt like he was in the archives of some abandoned library. He leafed through essay collections on art history, architecture, economics, philosophy; language textbooks on Anglo Saxon, Norse, Medieval German, Latin, Ancient Greek; journal articles on engineering, materials science, geology; simple instruction booklets on pyrotechnic displays, set design, landscape gardening. There were many different books on Descartes, and by Descartes — from early French editions to modern translations — and fat, daunting texts with their titles embossed in gold letters: *Mesmerism and Other Forsaken Arts. The Awakening of Memory. Animal Magnetism: The Genesis of Hypnosis.*

He wasn't even sure what he was looking for. By the left foot of the bed, there was a pile of books that seemed to share a single theme: music. His eyes studied their spines, starting with *Observations on the Correspondence between Poetry and Music*, reaching thicker books like *Sacred Music: An Anthology of Essential Writings, 1801–1918*, and *The Organ: Its Evolution, Principles of Construction and Use*, and theoretical volumes on the works and lives of great composers, from Francesco Landini to Guillaume Dufay; from Henry Purcell to Benjamin Britten; from Tchaikovsky to Bartók. He had to take a breath when he stumbled upon a copy of *Der Vollkomenne Capellmeister* by Johann Mattheson. It was a well-thumbed German paperback, and Eden's jottings in the margins were mostly in German too — apart from one section in the text, numbered 59, by which he'd written in ballpoint: '59. *Hope is caused by an elevation of the spirits. Despair, on the other hand, is a casting down of the same. These subjects can be well represented by sound . . .* '

Oscar wasn't sure if this was a translation or just an idle note, but the handwriting was different: inkier, less hurried. He picked up the next work in the pile. *Johann Mattheson: Spectator in Music* by Beekman C. Cannon. He flicked through it, not really sure what he was

458

expecting to find. The pages stopped turning at 107, where there was a highlighted paragraph of text:

The year before his death he presented all his books and manuscripts, totaling one hundred and twenty-eight volumes and *Convolute*, to the Hamburger Stadtbibliothek. Thus were spent the last few years of his life, and on April 17, 1764, in his eighty-third year the valiant old gentleman, '*der wohlgebohrne Herr Legationsrath*,' died. He was buried according to his wishes in the St Michaelis Kirche five days later. His epitaph, recently discovered in the church, bears the inscription:

> *Ruhe Kammer*
> *für Herr*
> *Johann Mattheson*
> *weyland*
> *Grosfürstlicher*
> *Holsteinischer*
> *Legations Raht*
> *und dessen*
> *Ehe Genossin*
> *Zu ewigen Tagen*

On April 25, a special service was held in the church in his honor, as a leading citizen of Hamburg. For two-and-a-half hours, the bells of all the chief churches were tolled.

He flicked back a page and found this:

In June, 1753, Mattheson made his second will, which left a sum necessary for the construction of a proper organ in this church (should he die before it was finished). According to his records, Mattheson's chief concern in the last ten years of his life were the ordering of his material affairs and the progress of the St Michaelis organ.

St Michaelis sounded familiar.

St Michael's?

He remembered Eden mentioning something about a St Michael's organ back at his parents' house. It was a lead, or the closest he'd come to one. He read more highlighted passages from the book, and the more he read, the stronger the feeling built in the reaches of his gut — not exactly a certainty, but an optimism — and the louder the voice grew in his mind that kept on saying *Hamburg*. It wasn't so far beyond reason that Eden would go there: somewhere his hero had been laid to rest, where he could speak a different language, be somebody else for a while. It was perfectly possible that he'd gone to visit Mattheson's grave, to commune with his headstone, to see the famous organ Mattheson had paid for, to feel those centuries-old keys under his fingers. Maybe all of this had been in Eden's mind when he'd gone speeding off in Jane's Land Rover. Maybe he hadn't been thinking he was running away, but heading for home.

The wardrobe was the only place left to look. Oscar tried to open the door but it was locked, and for a moment, he almost gave up on it, until he remembered the key that was still in his pocket. It was a perfect fit in the tiny, intricate lock, and it turned with an easy click. There were no clothes inside, just a column of identical black storage boxes — eleven of them, maybe twelve. He slid out the top box and found it was filled with handwritten notation, bound with green ribbon. There must have been fifty different scores in there, and though none of them was titled, each page bore Eden's name and his angular signature. The marks on the staves were wild, drawn freehand, and they swept from left to right in exaggerated waves, dense and complicated. There was more of the same in the next couple of boxes — more sheet music, more of Eden's own compositions — and the one after that held labelled photocopies of works by Beethoven and Mozart and Handel that had been cut out and pasted together, reassembled into an awkward medley of paper. In the next box, there were photographs of musical notation, and folders of slides that showed nothing but ancient-looking sheet music when he held them up to the light. The music in these pictures seemed more balanced, written in a steady, almost clinical hand, as if each crotchet had been drawn with a ruler. Right at the bottom of this box, he found two very old editions of *Der Vollkommene Capellmeister*, their covers pre-served with clear polythene wrappers, and there was a large plastic wallet that contained letters

461

and envelopes, the paper jaundiced and brittle, bearing German words in faded black ink, and signatures too intricate to make out.

Oscar felt his heart clenching as he opened the next box. He could hardly breathe. Inside, there were ten first editions, wrapped in tissue paper.

Engines of Grief
Distant Relations
The Predatory Instinct
Selfhood in the Modern World
The Fraudulent Mind
Solitude and the Self-Image
The Psychic Policemen and Other Case Studies
Towards Yesterday: The Meaning of Memory
Unpopular Mechanics
The Girl With the God Complex

Every book that Herbert Crest had ever published was right there before him. Their pages were stiff and clean. There were no marks or comments in the margins. Some of them still had the shop receipts tucked inside the back flap: at 4:36 p.m. on 04/28/96, Eden had paid $35.00 for *The Girl With the God Complex*, at Powell's bookstore in Portland, Oregon.

Oscar opened another box. He found lever-arch folders with photocopies and printouts of every article Herbert Crest had ever authored; there were copies of every article that had ever been written *about* him, each one in its own plastic sleeve. Only the old man's obituaries seemed to be missing. As he leafed through them, Oscar saw images of Herbert Crest he'd never seen before, watched him ageing before his eyes like stop-motion footage of a plant growing from seed to flower. His hands paused on a small, single-column article. The headline caught him by surprise:

Cambridge Daily News, 5 NOVEMBER 1966

PROFESSOR SUES STUDENT OVER HOUSEBOAT THEFT

by Leda Cotter

KING'S COLLEGE RESEARCHER, Dr Herbert Crest, 32, appeared before magistrates this morning charged with causing damage to a houseboat owned by eminent literature professor, <u>Dr Abraham Paulsen</u>, of Clare Street, Cambridge.

The defendant stole the houseboat, which had been moored on a stretch of river near the Victoria Bridge, and sailed it as far as Ely, where it was left abandoned for several weeks and damaged by local vandals. Dr Crest was arrested in June on suspicion of theft, and later convicted and sentenced to 72 hours community service by the Magistrate, Mr Franklin Hulme.

Now Dr Paulsen has brought a civil proceeding against the defendant — a postdoctoral researcher in the Psychological Laboratory, Cambridge — to reclaim repair costs amounting to £300.

At Cambridge Magistrates' Court this morning, the defendant stated that the boat

463

was bought for him as a birthday gift by the 51-year-old King's College professor; the two men had been close friends but had fallen out over Dr Crest's career plans. Therefore, ownership of the houseboat is still being disputed.

'This is a nuisance case,' said solicitor James McAnthony of Bronwen Boyle Solictors. 'My client was wrongly convicted of theft in the first place, but he has served the sentence handed down to him. He cannot now be held accountable for the senseless actions of hoodlums, and should be remunerated for the undue stress this action has caused.'

Dr Paulsen's counsel refused to make comment. The case continues.

The name Abraham Paulsen had been underlined in red. Oscar stared down at the page, his mind turning like a carousel. The text began to blur at the edges, spreading and connecting in the blank spaces. He turned through more of the articles, scanning each line for the old man's name, and when it came, he almost missed it.

At the back of the folder there was a small square of newsprint. It seemed like nothing — a picture from the local paper, a group photo. But when he looked closer, he recognised the building in the background, the shape of the wisteria growing thickly on the walls. And he recognised the face of a young Jean squinting back at him, posing in a clean white uniform.

Beside her, two men in business suits were holding up a certificate in a frame. On the far right, there was a thin-faced old man in tweed with spectacles hanging from a cord around his neck and a cane in one hand. Oscar didn't have to read the caption to know who it was:

Staff and residents of Cedarbrook Nursing Home on Queen's Road celebrate the People's Award for Dignity in Care in the NHS Health and Social Care Awards 1993. Pictured (L — R): Jean Hogan (matron); Darren Glover and Tony Spears (owners); Abraham Paulsen (resident).

19

The Visits

The police came for him at Cedarbrook. It was a dreary Tuesday afternoon in May, and he was in the parlour, doling out teacups and digestive biscuits, when he saw the squad car parking in the drive. There were no sirens, no flashing lights, but the younger residents — always hawk-eyed around that time of day — noticed the flare of luminous paintwork, and gathered at the window to watch the two uniformed policemen striding up the ramp towards the front door. The bell rang and Jean went to find out what they wanted. There was a brief, murmured exchange, and she came back into the parlour to say: 'Can you come with me for a minute, Oscar?'

The policemen asked for somewhere private to talk, so Jean showed them into the staff room and closed the door behind her. Oscar leaned on the counter while one of constables — the shorter of the two, but the stockier — took out a notebook and a biro. He said his name was PC Towne; the other man's name was PC Walsh.

'Don't worry, sir. You're not in any trouble. We'd just like to question you in regard to a friend of yours, a Mr Eden Bellwether. Can you confirm that you know him?'

'Yeah. I know him.'

'You're friends?'

'Sort of.'

'Sort of?' said PC Walsh. 'What's that mean?'

'We hang round together, but whether we're really friends, I don't know. I'm going out with his sister.'

'Yes, we've already been informed about that.' PC Towne licked the nib of his biro, and left it poised on the paper. 'Mr Bellwether's parents reported him missing last night. Seems he's been gone for a few weeks, though.' Towne turned to his partner. 'When was it, end of April?'

Walsh nodded, keeping his eyes on Oscar. 'We're making initial inquiries, that's all. Just a few questions. Won't take long.'

It took less than fifteen minutes.

Their questions were basic: 'How long have you known him?' 'When was the last time you saw him?' 'Was that the last time you heard from him?' 'Any idea where he might be now?' Oscar gave brief, courteous answers and PC Towne wrote them down with little movements of his pen, while PC Walsh just stood there, arms folded. He didn't mention his theory about Hamburg; it sounded stupid in his head, and he was sure it would sound twice as stupid out loud. There were many things he didn't mention, in fact, because he knew they'd be too difficult to explain to a couple of small-minded constables who were clearly just going through the motions, and besides, where would he even begin?

'Okay, thank you, sir,' Towne said. 'That'll do for now. If you hear anything, call the station. We'll find you if there's anything else we need.'

★　★　★

They only had a couple of hours together that evening, and they wasted the first part of it arguing over where they should have dinner. Iris insisted it had to be somewhere central, because she couldn't walk far, and her father was coming to pick her up from the gates of Downing at seven thirty. It had been nearly three months since they'd last eaten alone in a restaurant. They had a nice table on the veranda at Galleria, overlooking the river, but all through dinner Iris sat with a glum face, picking at her food. She drank two glasses of Chardonnay and made three awkward trips to the ladies' room with her crutches, leaving him sitting there every time, looking down over the water. They talked a lot about her last exam — the big Pathology test that she'd been dreading all year. The confidence and bluster of a few days ago was gone now; despair had set in. Oscar was sure that she was exaggerating when she told him her mind had blanked halfway through the multiple choice section, that she'd forgotten the most basic information, simple facts that even a nine-year-old could learn, and he listened, not really taking any of it in, just watching her lips moving. He knew that it was good for her to talk like this, to get it out of her system. He tried to comfort her by telling her it was perfectly understandable if she failed her exams, given the duress she'd been under lately, with all the night calls from the police, all the questions she'd had to answer, all the anxiety that surrounded her brother, but she

468

didn't seem to hear him. He told her that, in the grand scheme of things, her exams weren't really that important anyway. She looked at him, annoyed. '*What?*' He knew it was the worst thing he could have said, and when he tried to take it back, she got impatient. Her voice turned into a whine. '*Not important?* How can you say that? I mean, it's only my whole bloody life, my whole future on the line. Do you know how much pressure that is? Sometimes I feel like we're a million miles apart.'

'I'm just trying to support you.' He knew that she wasn't really upset with him — she was upset with her brother, her parents, her whole situation — and if she needed somebody to vent all of this resentment towards, he was happy to be that person for a while. She shook her head and finished off her wine. 'It's bad enough having to study every hour of the day without having to brace myself every time the bloody phone rings, in case it's my brother, or the police, or, I don't know, the bloody coast guard. You should've seen the looks on those policemen's faces when I was telling them about everything with Herbert. They were just smirking the whole time I was talking. And I said to them: *Look — you asked! If you don't believe what I'm telling you, that's your problem.*' She exhaled — one long protracted huff from the deepest reaches of her lungs. 'God Almighty, I'm so bloody sick of this. Why can't things ever just be simple? Why can't I just have a normal life with a normal family?'

'That's what everybody wants,' he told her. 'There's no such thing.'

'I don't believe that. Somewhere in the world, somebody has to be living a normal, happy life. Maybe those monks in Tibet are happy. They look peaceful whenever I see them on TV. Maybe I'll become one of those.'

'Did you ever ask your mum about that church in Florida?' he said.

She shook her head. 'I can't seem to find the right moment to bring it up. She's too tightly wound.'

'Maybe ask your dad.'

'Yeah. Maybe.' She checked her watch.

'Better get the bill,' he said. 'We're going to be late.'

'Okay. But I'm serious — I'm going to Tibet and you can't stop me.' It was the first time she'd smiled all evening. She gathered up her crutches and he caught the eye of the waiter.

They got to Downing College around six fifteen. Yin and Jane were already waiting for them on the cool green lawn by the Fellows' garden. It had been a long, miserable afternoon, and although the sun was out, it seemed weak, phlegmatic, and there was a listless kind of breeze in the air that hardly stirred the roses in the flower beds. Jane was sitting shoeless and cross-legged with her hands in the bow of her dress. She saw them coming and waved. Yin was lying on his side, pulling grass out in clumps. As they arrived beside him, he peered up at Iris and said: 'If that face is anything to go by, your exams are sucking as much as ours.'

'Urgh, don't get me started.' She ditched her crutches and lowered herself carefully to the

470

ground. Oscar sat down next to her.

Yin smiled at him. 'Times like these you should be thankful you're not a student.'

'I suppose.'

'I mean it, man. Look at this.' Yin lifted his hands. Nearly all of his fingertips were covered with plasters. 'Paper cuts.' He guffawed. 'It's the new textbooks that get you. The older ones are made of sturdier stuff, but the new ones? Edges like razors. I swear, I've lost a pint of blood.'

Iris straightened out her leg. 'Where's Marcus, anyway? Aren't we technically trespassing without him here?'

'He went to get the beers,' Jane said. 'Exams are nearly over now for him, lucky sod.'

'You're kidding.'

'Only one to go,' said Yin.

'I've still got four.'

'Yikes. That'll teach you to do medicine.'

'Yeah, and I hear it doesn't get any easier,' Jane said.

Iris threw a clod of grass at them and it broke apart in the air. 'You lot were supposed to be cheering me up.'

Yin lay back, grinning. His shirtsleeves were rolled up tight around his biceps. 'So I guess you all had the visit from the Keystone Kops by now, huh?'

'They came for me at work,' Oscar said. 'I've never seen so many old people so excited.' He tried to make a joke out of it, not wanting to bring Iris down; she was only just starting to brighten up again.

Yin said: 'They were waiting for me outside

my room after my exam. Just what I needed.'

'Came for me this morning,' Jane said. 'I was still in my pyjamas.'

'Oh, I bet they liked that!' Iris said. It was good to hear her laughing.

'Yeah, that taller guy — what was it? — Walsh?' Yin said. 'He was giving me the fish-eye. Marcus said he called him *sunbeam*. I don't think he liked that so much.'

'Actually, I thought the small one was quite nice,' Jane said. 'He had a kind face. And he drank Earl Grey with a slice of lemon, which I thought was funny, you know, for a policeman.'

Oscar hadn't seen Jane and Yin since the night they'd all cleaned up the mess at Harvey Road. Jane had been so quiet and ashen-faced back then, and she'd thrown herself into the task of washing the bedsheets and scrubbing the carpets to keep her mind off things, the way his mother used to do. Twice that night, he'd found her crying in the kitchen with the lights off and the tumble-dryer whirring. But now she seemed a little happier, or maybe she was just resigned to things. For the last two weeks, she'd been applying herself to exam revision the same way she'd applied herself to cleaning up that house — with a determination to continue until someone told her to stop.

There was a gentle sound now in the distance. It was like the noise of people throwing glass into the bottle bank, an erratic clinking. Oscar looked across the courtyard, across the patterned lawns. A man was running towards them, as fast as his legs would take him. He was holding two stripy carrier bags that swung with each frantic stride he took across the shingle path, hitting his knees and thighs. The nearer he got, the louder the sound became. *Clink-clink, clink-clink.*

'Hey, that's Marcus,' Yin said. He sat upright. 'What's the big hurry?'

'He's fizzing up the beer,' Jane said.

Marcus was sprinting as hard as he could, stones spewing under his feet. He was only a few yards away now. His face was almost purple; his shirt was soaked with sweat. 'Germany!' he shouted. The word rebounded between the college buildings. 'Germany!'

Yin stood up. 'What the hell?'

Marcus came tearing into the Fellows' garden. He dropped the carrier bags and stooped, panting, his hands on his knees. He couldn't find enough breath to speak. Then he reached into his pocket and pulled out his mobile phone, jabbing at the keys. 'Look,' he said, 'he's in Germany. Look!' and he thrust the phone at Oscar. The screen displayed a text message:

> M. Your country is beautiful in the springtime. How go the exams? E

* * *

Theo rolled down the window as far as it would go. 'Speak up,' he said. 'I couldn't quite hear that last part.'

Oscar raised his voice over the traffic that was inching along the road outside the college gates. He picked another dried-up cherry blossom from the roof of the car, and looked down at Theo in the driver's seat. He'd already been talking for so long that his throat was beginning to itch. The others were standing around him like security guards, listening. 'I said he was telling me about this organ he was going to build — when all of this is over, that's how he put it. I didn't know what he meant. He showed me this drawing he'd done. And that's when he mentioned St Michael's — something about getting the pipes from Germany, how he was going to do something special to them, I can't quite remember what.'

'Why didn't you say anything about this before?' Theo said.

'It was only a hunch then. I didn't know if it was right. But now that he's sent this text to Marcus — and after everything I found in his books — it seems more definite. Mattheson was buried in Hamburg. His organ is in Hamburg. It makes sense that Eden would go there, don't you think?'

For a long moment, Theo said nothing. He sat there, fidgeting with the key-ring dangling from the ignition. He jogged his knee up and down, combed his beard with his fingernails. Then he looked through the window at Jane. 'You agree with this?'

Jane nodded emphatically. 'He used to talk about Hamburg all the time. It does make sense that he'd be there. And I really don't have much faith in those policemen we saw.'

Theo lifted his chin at Yin and Marcus. 'How about you two?'

474

'Worth a try,' said Yin. 'We don't have much else to go on.'

Marcus shrugged. 'It's not a lot, I know, but it's something. He speaks the language. If he's *somewhere* in Germany, why not Hamburg?'

'Hmm.' Theo twisted round to look at Iris. She was sitting in the back of the car with her leg across the seats. 'I suppose I don't have to ask if you're on board?'

She pushed herself upright. 'It feels right to me, Dad. We need to do something.'

'Okay. I think I get the picture.' Theo took a breath in through his nose and gulped it down. He started the engine. 'Thank you, everybody. I'll handle it from here.' There was such a confidence and finality to the way he said it — the consummate surgeon taking over from his interns.

'If you're going out there, I want to come with you,' Jane said, gripping the window as it rode up, stopping it dead.

'I haven't decided what I'm going to do yet.'

'Please, Theo.'

He tightened his lips. 'I'll think about it. In the meantime: study. All of you. Don't let your hard work go to waste.'

Jane stepped back from the car and Theo reversed and drove towards the gates. As they waited to turn onto Regent Street, Iris blew kisses from the rear window. Oscar waved back. The car moved off, and the reflection of the dimming sky came sweeping over the glass to vanish her.

20

Caterwaul

The summer was just getting started. Oscar stood in the dusty heat of his flat with a desk-fan blowing out lukewarm air, checking his dinner jacket in the mirror, redoing his bow tie. His shoes were shined and his hair newly cut, and he was wearing the expensive aftershave the shop-girl had persuaded him to buy yesterday with her clever saleswoman's compliments. A bouquet of carnations was sitting in water on the nightstand; the card was already written. He couldn't tell if he was sweating because of the mugginess of his room, or because he was nervous about the evening ahead. When he'd told one of the agency nurses at work that he was going to the ball at St John's College, she'd been much more impressed than he expected. She said she'd never known anyone lucky enough to get a ticket. 'I've heard they fill up all the punts with champagne bottles, and they put purple lilies in the water, and they have all the top DJs playing, and anyway — make sure you take plenty of photos. It's gonna be like a fairytale.'

Around seven, there was a beep of a car horn outside. He looked down from his window to see a silver Mercedes by the pavement, engine running, and Yin standing there in a jet-black dinner suit, beckoning him with big semaphore

476

movements of his arms. He grabbed the flowers and went down to meet them.

Jane was in the back seat in a pink gown and long white evening gloves. A necklace with a single, clear diamond hung at her neck, and her hair was curled and waved, somehow darker. She was wearing more make-up than usual, concealing most of the freckles on her face, and it gave her a duller, flatter look — prettier maybe, but much less remarkable. 'You look great, Jane,' he said, seeing that she felt awkward in her formalwear. She smiled back at him, dim-eyed, distracted. There was something subdued about the way she spoke: 'What are they, carnations?'

'Yeah.'

'She'll love them.'

'You think so?'

'Definitely. Roses are so unoriginal. I always preferred tulips . . . Mind if I — ?' She motioned to the flowers. When he handed them over, she pressed her nose upon the petals daintily and took in their scent. She went very quiet then, as if remembering every flower she'd ever smelled in her lifetime, all the bouquets that had been delivered to her doorstep on special occasions.

Yin leaned over from the passenger side. 'The black tie thing suits you, man. You look like a diplomat.'

'Thanks. I'm not used to these starched collars.'

'Ah, you won't notice it after a while.'

'Can we go now?' Marcus said. He flicked on a right signal, eyeing the wing mirror for a gap in traffic. 'I'm sweating like a boar and the roads are getting busy already.' There were no objections. Marcus slid his window down to throw his chewing gum to the tarmac, and off they went along East Road.

It was cold with the air conditioning on, and there was a sullen atmosphere in the car once they started driving. As they left the city, heading for Grantchester, Oscar saw other groups in formalwear just like them, walking in the opposite direction — happy young faces, brighter for knowing that another long year was behind them, for better or worse, and that the summer had finally arrived. But the end-of-term spirit seemed to have bypassed his friends entirely. Nobody talked for a long time, and the silence was uncomfortable. Jane quietly gazed at her shoes; Marcus concentrated on the road; Yin fidgeted with the lightswitch on the vanity mirror until Marcus told him to cut it out. The sun flared in the windscreen.

'This doesn't feel right,' Jane spoke up at last. 'I should be over there with Theo, not going to a stupid party. I should be doing something.'

'I know what you mean,' Marcus said. 'This whole thing just feels — '

'Hollow,' said Yin.

'Yeah. That's it exactly.'

'Nothing's the same without Eden,' Jane said. She leaned forward to tap Marcus on the shoulder. 'Have you got your mobile switched on? Just in case.'

'Yeah, yeah, relax.'

There'd been drips of positive news from Theo since he'd left for Hamburg at the end of May.

The information was passed on by Ruth, then Iris, and by the time it reached Oscar, all traces of pessimism had been filtered out of it. He'd heard that Theo had begun a city-wide search, starting with St Michael's church, where a chorister had recognised Eden's face from the photograph he'd shown her — she said she might have seen him at an afternoon service. Next, a waitress in a café on the Reeperbahn had recognised the boy in the photograph, too, and said he might have been to eat there a couple of times. Then a taxi driver said he'd dropped someone who looked like Eden at the opera — he remembered, because the fare was only eight euros, and the boy had given him a twenty and walked away. That was the last anyone had heard. There'd been no more text messages, no more sightings, and Theo was getting tired of the hunt, but he wasn't giving up until he'd exhausted all the options. He was still confident that he would find his son amid the hustle and dirt of Hamburg, and everybody else was, too.

Iris seemed a lot more upbeat about the situation, knowing that somebody was out there looking for her brother, and now the exams were over she'd started to ease off on the cigarettes. She was easier to talk to on the phone. Her laughter had returned.

Oscar had gone with her to a violin recital at West Road last week, and she'd spent the night at his flat afterwards; for the first time in months, they'd slept together and woken up in the same bed. On Wednesday evening, they'd had dinner with her mother in the vast, echoing dining room

479

at the Bellwether house, and they'd stayed up late watching movies while Iris talked over every scene, telling him how much she was looking forward to the year ahead. She was excited about spending the summer in Grantchester and doing nothing but reading and swimming and playing cello in the garden, and she was thinking of taking a trip with him somewhere once her leg was better (maybe Paris — 'clichéd but romantic,' she said; or maybe Reykjavik, because she'd always wanted to splash around in the geysers). She couldn't wait to move into halls in September and be a regular student for a while.

The first thing she was looking forward to was the ball at St John's. 'Oh, I can't wait to just let my hair down, and *breathe* for a while,' she'd whispered into his ear. 'I know I should be thinking of my brother and everything, and I feel guilty for being excited about a silly party, but I just feel like I need something to celebrate that's *mine*. Does that make sense? I miss Eden, I *do*, but I want to have at least one memory of Cambridge that's all mine.'

She'd already imagined how the night was going to go. 'I was thinking you could pick me up, all handsome in your dinner suit, and we'll have Marcus park somewhere close, so I don't have to stumble around too much, looking like an invalid. As soon as we get inside, I thought we'd have champagne — three or four glasses before the dancing starts, at least, though I'm thinking the music will already be playing when we arrive — that old-fashioned Cole Porter-type music, probably; trumpets and clarinets and oboes and a proper jazz singer. Then you can ask me to dance and of course I'll accept, and you can waltz me around the ballroom as long as you want, all night if you want to. We should probably sit down for a bit then, I suppose. Rest my leg. Mingle. Be sociable. And then afterwards, leg permitting, we've got to walk barefoot on the college lawn. I've always wanted to do that.' Her voice had sounded so breezy; her face had been alight. 'I bought this incredible white dress — you're not allowed to see it yet, but it fits me like a dream — and my mother's helping me decorate my crutches with this fabric she got in India. I'm aiming for convalescent chic.'

Now, Oscar could just make out the verge of the Bellwethers' driveway in the distance: that familiar regiment of pine trees that led up to the house, nestled beyond the main stretch of road. How he'd come to love this place, and how well he'd come to know the journey. He almost knew it better than the route to his parents' estate. He seemed to walk these roads in his sleep.

Jane was still wordless beside him. She was twisting at her bracelet and keeping her eyes on the accelerating world outside the window. The sun was hanging in the sky, grapefruit red, and the distant fields were spotted with grazing livestock. It was strange to see her so quiet, so removed. Usually, when she couldn't find a way into a conversation, she'd start one of her own. But her lips were tightly closed and she didn't seem the least bit interested in talking. Her mind was in another country.

Marcus and Yin discussed their summer plans: 'Are you going back to the States?' 'Probably. Haven't seen my folks all year. They're renting a place in Santa Barbara over August.' 'Jealous.' 'Come if you want.' 'I'd love to but — ' Oscar had already tuned out by the time they turned into the Bellwethers' driveway. He was thinking of Iris, wondering what she was going to look like in her dress, imagining the bare slope of her shoulders. He would kiss her the moment he saw her.

The tyres shuddered on the gravel, and suddenly the house appeared before them, a great surfacing block of white that grew bigger and wider as they approached. In the sunlight, it seemed almost waxen, the glass atrium glinting like a telescope lens. Birds darted from the trees in the garden; they seemed to head straight for the atrium, mistaking the perfect glass for air, only to pull up at the last second, using the updraft to steer themselves away. All it would take was one small miscalculation, he thought, just one rotation of their wings too many and they would stun themselves and fall to the ground.

Marcus parked by the garage and switched off the engine. He leaned into the back seat. 'It doesn't take four of us to knock for her,' he said, looking at Oscar.

'Don't be such a misery,' Jane said. 'We'll *all* go.'

'But it's so lovely and cool in here . . . '

Jane clicked open her door. 'Shut up. You're coming.'

Yin had one foot out of the car already, and when Marcus saw they were all leaving him, he quickly unlatched his seat belt and got out. They stood around the car, adjusting again to the heat. A humid air pushed at them from all sides. Oscar checked his reflection in the tinted window, dabbing his face with his handkerchief. The flower-stems dripped on his shoelaces. They trudged towards the house, labouring up the front steps.

Before he rang the doorbell, Oscar got their attention. 'Listen, everyone, I know you're not in the mood for a celebration right now, but can we at least pretend to have fun tonight, for Iris's sake? She's been looking forward to it.'

Yin pushed his hands into his pockets and nodded. 'Okay.'

'I can manage that,' said Marcus.

Jane put on a silly, ventriloquist's grin. 'Shiny happy people,' she said through her teeth.

He rang the bell and waited. When there was no reply, he rang again. They all shuffled their feet, shrugging at each other. 'Ring it again,' Yin said. 'They're probably upstairs.'

'This house is just too massive,' Jane said, 'it's no wonder they can't hear anything.'

Oscar pushed the bell a few more times.

They waited.

No answer.

Yin stepped forward and pushed the button — five urgent trills. 'This is ridiculous. It's too hot for this.' Still, nobody came to the door.

Oscar put his face to the glass, blanking out the sunshine with his hands, and peered into the

483

empty atrium. The ceiling fan was spinning slowly on the landing. 'You see anybody in there?' Marcus asked.

'No.'

But right then Oscar saw something that brought a tight feeling to his chest, as if a fist was closing around his heart. There, at the back of the room, a white dress was hanging from the highest baluster, wrapped in dry cleaner's plastic. With every rotation of the ceiling fan, the tails of the plastic quivered and shone, and the longer he looked at it, the more the fabric of the dress seemed so intensely white — it stood out in the bareness of the atrium like a flag of surrender. He pulled his eyes away.

Jane noticed the worry in his face. 'What?' she said. 'What's the matter?'

'Her dress is there.'

'Are you sure?'

'Typical. She's not even dressed yet!' Marcus said.

Jane pushed past him to look through the window. 'He's right. She hasn't even taken it out of the wrapper. We *did* say seven thirty, didn't we?'

'Yeah.'

Yin sniffed. 'So what now?'

'I'll call her,' Oscar said. He got out his mobile and dialled Iris's number. No signal; it went straight to voicemail. He called the landline. They could hear it ringing out in the atrium, could see the green light pulsing on the telephone table, but nobody answered. 'I guess we should try the back way,' Yin said.

They went down the steps, heading for the side gate. The others walked with casual, trundling strides, but there was an urgency now in Oscar's step — something wasn't right. He could feel it.

The side gate was locked. Marcus tried to reach through the iron rails to unlatch it, but he couldn't quite stretch far enough.

'Alright, stand back,' Yin said. 'Let me get a decent run at it.' He gave himself a good run-up and hurled himself towards the gate; he leaped out with his front foot and landed it halfway, pushing himself upwards, clutching at the brickwork. He hauled himself over the wall and dropped down on the other side. His suit was streaked with dirt and he spent a moment patting himself clean before he unbolted the gate.

They made their way through the garden, winding along the landscaped path, under the hang of weeping willows and past rockeries of hibiscus and roses and lavender. The decking at the back of the rectory was dark with the shadows of elms and cherry trees, but the lawns seemed impossibly green, and the sprinklers were giving out a fine and gentle spray. As they neared the back of the main house, Oscar noticed a curtain billowing. One of the French doors was wide open. Yin saw it too: 'Hey, I guess we're in luck.' Oscar led the way up to the patio, around the swing-seat and the folded-up sunlounger, to the open door. He knocked on the glass, calling out for Iris and Ruth as he went inside, hoping to hear their soft, friendly voices

485

coming back at him.

The drawing room was empty. On the marble floor, there was a long, meandering streak — he saw it right away — a wavy black line, like a child's crayon doodle, or a scuff mark left by chair casters. It was a solid, thin trail that weaved across the room, from the far end of the hallway to right where he was standing.

'I don't get this,' Jane said. 'Where is everybody?'

Yin crouched to inspect the black mark. He rubbed at part of the streak with his fingers. On his haunches, he followed the trail back to the lip of the French doors, back outside, everyone walking behind him. The trail continued across the patio, stopping at the steps, where the path turned into gravel — the stones were disturbed there, bunched together in little heaps — and it carried on as far as the rectory. Yin stood up. 'I guess they've been moving the furniture around.'

Jane turned to Oscar. 'This is so weird. Where is she?'

'We should check upstairs,' Yin said.

Marcus huffed. He swung his car keys around on his finger. 'Well, I'm going back to the car before I sweat right through this jacket. If she comes out the front, I'll toot the horn.' And off he went, back the way they'd come. But before he could even get down the patio step, a jarring noise rang through the garden. Marcus stopped the instant he heard it, turning back to them. 'What was that?'

'I don't know,' Yin said.

The noise came again. It was like the sound of

486

a shipyard, of metal striking metal — short atonal notes resounding through the air. The four of them stood waiting, listening, as the noises got louder, more frequent. 'Where's it coming from?' Jane said.

The sound came again. *Kuh-langg. Kuh-langg.*

Oscar knew exactly where it was coming from. He had a perfect line of sight now from the patio. Across the sun-bright lawns, the door of the organ house was hanging ajar. He heard the noise again — *kuh-langg, kuh-langg* — and started to run towards the building. He ran with his arms flailing, and the carnations shed their petals behind him, until his fingers loosened around the bouquet and it fell to the ground. He heard Yin trampling over it as he came bounding after him. *Kuh-lanng. Kuh-lanng.* The metallic noises kept on coming and he could feel that fist around his heart getting tighter. *Kuh-langg.* He was breathless and panicked by the time he reached the organ house. He struggled to push back the door.

Another black drag-mark ran like a train track along the aisle. It ended at the rubber heel of Iris's leg-brace. She was crumpled on the floor in a nightdress, her body as limp as bundled laundry. The frame around her leg had snapped, bent up like a hairpin. One side of her face was lying square against the hard floor and her skin was silvery pale. Her eyes were closed. She wasn't moving. She didn't seem to be breathing.

There were no more noises.

A few yards from his sister's body, Eden was

sitting on the battered keys of the organ console, barefoot and shirtless. He was breathing hard. Sweat was teeming from his face. His hand was curled loosely around a pickaxe. Behind him, the metal pipes of the organ were punctured and twisted, hammered flat and mangled.

Oscar felt his whole body seizing. He could hardly move his fingers, let alone his feet. But then he heard Yin's voice behind him — 'Fuck, man, what the hell have you done?' — and he saw Eden raising his head, slowly, slowly, so that the sheen of his eyes was like a cat's glare.

'I made a mistake,' Eden said, 'I made a mistake.'

The words seemed to unlock Oscar's body. He couldn't have run any faster down that aisle to reach her. He couldn't have made it to her side any quicker than he did. He dropped to his knees, searching her neck for a pulse, but he couldn't feel one. 'Call an ambulance!' he called out. 'Somebody! Hurry!' Marcus backed out of the organ house, heel after heel, so startled and frightened that he nearly tripped over himself. He rushed off to find the telephone.

Oscar stared down at Iris. He felt for her pulse again, but there wasn't even the weakest beat. Her skin was dry and cold. He listened for her exhalations. None came. Her lips were pinched and blue. He tried to resuscitate her, desperately pushing his mouth against hers, but she didn't stir, she didn't gasp, and there was no pressure coming back upon him. He broke down, then. He wasn't ashamed to cry, to scream out in pain, to fall apart. The tears came rolling down his face onto her mouth and he wiped them away, kissing her cheek. He held her head against his chest and smelled the shampoo in her hair. And he did all this with Eden sitting there on the organ console, watching him, making no sound.

'Is she — ?' Yin couldn't even get the words out. His fists were balled at his sides. 'Is she dead?'

Oscar could only just bring himself to nod.

Yin turned away. 'Oh fuck . . . Oh my fucking God . . . '

Jane was still standing by the doorway. She had to lower herself into a chair, two hands cupped over her mouth, as if she were praying. Her eyes were wet and round. 'Did you do this?' she said.

Eden let her voice fall away. 'I made a mistake,' he said. 'I couldn't bring her back.'

She stepped along the aisle towards him. 'What did you do?'

'I couldn't revive her.'

'What did you do, Eden?'

'I — I just — it all happened so fast.'

'Where's Ruth?'

Eden stared at the floor.

'Where is she? Where's your mother?'

He didn't respond. As Jane moved closer, his fingers tightened around the pickaxe handle.

Yin was heading towards Eden now, too, his fists still balled up at his sides. Eden stood up, clutching the pickaxe across his chest, spinning it as if it were a tennis racket and this were all just a backyard game. 'Don't come any closer!' he said. Yin and Jane slowed, holding their hands in the air. 'I mean it, stay back!'

Eden began to swing the pickaxe. He was standing high up now on the organ console, towering over them. They stopped in their tracks. 'Edie,' Jane pleaded, 'you're not going to hurt me. You love me. Come on, put that thing down and let's try to sort this out, together, you and me.' But Eden just swung the pickaxe again and again, in wide, slow arcs, until they stepped backwards. He jumped down from the ruined keys of the organ and his feet slapped against the floor. Swinging the axe, he made Jane and Yin retreat further, turning them around, backing them against the wall to give him a clear path along the aisle. 'Don't move,' he said. 'Don't make me hit you!' With the momentum of one last swing, he started to run for the door.

Oscar was only a few yards away, still holding Iris's limp body in his arms, and he wasn't close enough to reach out and stop Eden escaping. But the axe was heavy, and Eden had to let go of it halfway along the aisle — *kuh-langg* — and when he got to the door, he found Marcus standing in his way. If Marcus expected that sheer resolve would bring Eden to a halt, he was wrong. Eden kept on going. Like a rugby forward, he dipped his shoulder and barged straight into Marcus's ribs, throwing his weight right into him, and Marcus fell back against the door, hitting his head against the wood. After a moment, he sat up, clutching his skull, bewildered. Eden slipped out into the bright evening.

Oscar was sprinting after him now, and Yin

490

was coming up behind, shouting: 'Stop him, Oscar, stop him!'

'Left,' Marcus said, pointing, 'he went left.'

Eden was running for the river. Oscar went after him, spearing through the warm air, running so hard his muscles pounded and his lungs burned. As Eden dived into the water, he was only ten or twenty yards behind him. Flinging off his jacket, he got to the riverbank and dived in, too. He didn't care that Eden was a better swimmer. He didn't care that the water was deep and briny and green with algae and that it flooded his ears as he broke the surface. All he cared about was catching up with Eden. He could see his shining back a few yards downstream.

Eden battled to haul himself onto the high bank — the marram grass was tall there, and he clawed at it, trying to find something to grip so he could escape to the meadow on the other side — and while he struggled, Oscar got closer and closer. With every passing second, Eden grew larger in his sights. He was nothing but a target to him now. He would bring him down like an animal.

Eden heaved his body onto the bank, mauling the bulrushes. He'd only just made it out of the water when Oscar reached out and grabbed his ankle, pulling him back. With his other hand, Oscar gripped the marram grass to keep his head above the waterline. Eden kicked and jostled, but he didn't have the strength or the will to shake himself free, and he slipped and fell to his knees, sliding back into the river with a great splash.

Oscar watched the water settling. For a few moments, the river was strangely peaceful. The swallows gossiped in the reeds. Then there was a rush of pressure beside his waist, and Eden popped up, gasping, his hair drenched and slick as seal hide. Before he could even blink the river from his eyes, Oscar threw his arm around Eden's neck and tightened it. He held him in the crook of his elbow and squeezed. Eden began to choke. He squeezed harder. Eden's face turned beet red and his arms flailed and clawed. But Oscar didn't release him. He pushed Eden's head below the water, until it bubbled with his desperate breaths, until he could see his eyes bulging white and swollen. He wasn't going to let him go until he drowned. He was sure of it. Thoughts entered his mind — sirens, policemen, hospitals — but they weren't enough to stop him. In that moment, he thought revenge was all he had left. Drowning Eden right there in the placid green water was the only way he could help Iris now, the only way he could stay close to her.

As Eden writhed under his arm, he tried to picture her face. He wanted to see it the way it had looked on the day they met — bright and hopeful, looking back at him with that guarded curiosity she had for everything — but he could only see it now the way it was: still and pale on the organ house floor. He could only see blue lips, and dead eyes, and tight white skin. And the cruellest memories came visiting him before the sweetest ones: he remembered the things he'd said wrong, the times he'd annoyed her, the moments he'd let her down, occasions she'd shaken her head at him or sighed. He heard her voice saying, 'You should do whatever makes you happy,' and he knew, looking down at Eden's harried, popping eyeballs, that happiness was a long, long way from here and he would never get to reach it.

He tightened the clench of his elbow around Eden's throat and pushed him down lower, waiting for him to give up. Clinging to the riverbank, he steeled himself. Eden went on thrashing beneath him, his flailing arms getting slower, losing their energy. He was going to kill him. He was resigned to it. He understood now that he was capable of it, the way Eden was capable of it, the way his cousin Terry was capable of it, the way his father was probably capable of it, too. He remembered how his cousin would hold his head below the water when they were kids at the local pool — just like he was holding Eden's head now — to train him to hold his breath, Terry would say, to teach him how to survive. He could almost hear his father's voice now from the poolside, husky and thrilled, goading him the way the voices of The Fates had once spurred on Jennifer Doe. And that's when he found himself thinking of the helpless little boy she had killed. Her own brother. Pink and wheezing. Desperate and confused.

He stopped.

He loosened his hold.

Eden gulped in a stream of air and the colour came flooding back into his face. But Oscar didn't let go of him. He swam cross-river, with Eden passed out under his arm, to where the others were standing solemnly at the foot of

493

the Bellwethers' garden, ready to bring them both in. They'd been watching the whole thing. They must have been shouting, but he hadn't heard them.

Yin reached down to heave Eden onto the bank first. He laid him flat on his back in the reeds and Jane crouched down to tend to him. 'He's alive,' she said, feeling his heart.

They all helped to pull Oscar out of the water. He sat on the bank, getting his breath back, saying nothing. Eden lay unconscious in the bulrushes and canary grass; there were bruises on his chest and scratches on his shoulders.

Oscar felt a warm hand on his neck. 'You alright, man?' Yin was standing over him, tears in his eyes. 'You okay?' And from somewhere, he found the strength to nod.

His drenched clothes were heavy and tight, and he peeled off his shirt and twisted the river out of it, then just let it fall onto the grass. He sat silently, the world hazy and foreign. They let him settle there for a while. The sun shimmered in the water and the crickets called out for each other. A steady breeze had gathered, shaking the willows. It was cooler now, and everything seemed almost like it used to be — like one of the nice spring evenings they'd spent together back in March, when they'd piled out of the punt and walked wearily to the house for dinner before Herbert Crest came. But it wasn't one of those evenings, and no matter how hard he tried to convince himself that everything was going to be alright from here, he could only manage to feel a raft of nothing. He was beyond sadness, beyond rage, beyond despair. There was only blankness and vagueness and torpor.

'Come on, let's get you inside and get you dry,' Jane said softly, touching his shoulder. 'They can stay out here with *him* until the ambulance arrives. The police are on their way.' Oscar got up. His legs were shaking, buckling.

Jane took him to the back of the rectory, not up to the main house. He sat in one of the deck chairs while she went inside to fetch a towel, and he studied the garden in a kind of stupor. It was the exact same garden he'd stared at many times before. They were the same trees, the same flowers; it was the same grass, the same soil, the same decking under his feet. But it was not the same sky above him. The clouds were different; they were sharper, angrier. And the grey bricks of the organ house were different now too, because he could no longer look at them. He felt sick to be so close to that building. The breeze was gathering strength and every time it swept across the garden he could hear it blowing through the broken organ pipes — a weak and tuneless drone that sounded on and off, on and off, with the steadiest of rhythms, like some machine that had found a way to breathe.

He couldn't bear it any longer. He tried to stand but his legs wouldn't hold his weight, and he slumped back down into his chair. Jane came out onto the deck, holding a blue dressing gown. 'I couldn't find a towel,' she said, 'but this will do. Here.' She wrapped it around his shoulders and he felt the warmth rising through his body. She rubbed the tops of his arms the way his mother used to do when she'd take him out of the bath.

They sat quietly together for a while. When he turned to look at her, he saw that she'd started to cry. She was padding her eyes with the sides of her fingers. 'I can't believe this is happening,' she said. 'I can't believe he could do something like this. He just isn't the kind of person who — ' She stopped, knowing he didn't want to hear it, and dipped her eyes to the deck. 'Ruth is dead, too. Marcus found her.'

'Where?'

'In her bedroom.' Jane broke down again, sniffing back tears.

He stood up. 'Show me.'

'No, please, let's just wait here.' She reached out for him. 'I don't want to go in there. I don't want to see it.'

'You have to see it, Jane,' he told her.

'Why?' she asked. Her voice was like a child's.

'Because if you don't believe he could do something like this now, you'll never believe it.'

And so they walked into the Bellwether house for the last time, through the sitting room and the hallway and the atrium, up the stairs into the master bedroom, following the trail of rubber from Iris's leg-brace, with river water running off his trousers and his shoes.

The master bedroom was dim and warm. On the four-poster bed, Ruth lay on her back with her eyes closed and her mouth partly ajar. Oscar didn't need to touch her cheek to know that she was dead. There was a pillow on the floor beside her, and the linen slip was wrinkled and streaked.

496

She'd been suffocated in her sleep.

Jane backed up against the doorframe, biting on her thumbnail, trembling.

A wave of nausea built up in Oscar's stomach then, and he had to hold it in until he could make it down the stairs and out of the front door. He threw up on the steps, and the sight of Marcus's car, still parked in the driveway, made his body weaken again. He thought of the little speech he'd given to the others. He thought about a party happening far away, people dancing to old-fashioned music, punts filled with champagne bottles, purple flowers, eveningwear, carnations, new aftershave. He wiped his mouth on the sleeve of the dressing gown and sat down. There was a bulk of something in one of the pockets and he lifted it out: a half-empty packet of clove cigarettes. In the other pocket: a book of matches.

'Are you okay?' Jane said, coming up behind him.

He just sat staring across the forecourt. The fountain was glinting in the dying sun. The pine trees stretched out before him in a perfect line. He opened the pack of cloves, put one in his mouth, struck a match and lit it. That sweet, cloying smoke unfurled around him. He felt it like a warm coal inside his lungs. Jane lowered her thin body down to the step beside him. She held his arm and leaned her head upon his shoulder. And they waited there together at the front of the Bellwether house, listening for the caterwaul of sirens.

DAYS TO COME

Truth is the torch that gleams through the fog without dispelling it.

— *Claude Adrien Helvétius*

21

Testimony

Oscar waited on the courthouse balcony, looking through the streaked glass at the reporters and news crews huddling on the street below. There were some faces he remembered from the funeral: the fat-mouthed men who'd swarmed around the cortège and pushed their lenses against the windows, trying to capture his misery on film, who'd pawed so rabidly at the sides of the car that they dislodged and flattened one of the wreaths; and the orange-skinned women who'd pushed microphones up to his chin and asked him vile, insulting questions like 'Is it true she was pregnant?' and 'Can you confirm she was sleeping with her brother?' Now they were gathered like wolves in the grey afternoon light, prowling outside the courthouse. Cameramen and photographers were perched on high ladders with dark equipment, and press reporters were jostling for position behind a metal barrier, clutching onto dictaphones. As the lawyers ushered Theo through the doors to face them, there was a surging din of voices. The reporters called out their questions — one great shrieking disharmony — and the *tick tick tick* of flashbulbs brightened the street like fireworks.

Theo's barrister was calm and upright. With a simple gesture of his arms, he managed to quiet the crowd. 'I have a statement to make on behalf of Mr Bellwether,' he said, 'and then — listen to me, please, because I'm only going to say this once — we will not be taking any questions.' Another shimmer of flashbulbs. A headache of light. Theo averted his eyes.

Lowering his glasses, the barrister read from a piece of paper: 'I am satisfied that the judge, the Honourable Mr Justice Phillips, has seen fit to hand my son the maximum sentence of life imprisonment, despite the jury's finding of diminished responsibility. From this point forward, I would appreciate it if you would all stop calling me in the middle of the night and refrain from parking your news vans across my driveway. Thank you.' Voices clamoured as the barrister turned away. The cameras went on flashing and rolling. Policemen held the press corps behind the barrier while Theo was escorted across the street to a waiting car.

Oscar looked on from the balcony, watching the wolves disperse. They packed up their equipment, smoked their cigarettes, laughed and joked, leaving their sandwich wrappers and drinks cans on the pavement. The traffic was flowing by the courthouse steadily, taking people somewhere he could not imagine, a place he wanted so badly to be. If he thought he had known tiredness before, he was wrong. The waning he felt now in his bones was the most unbearable kind of exhaustion, a persistent lag that rose with him each morning and spread throughout the day. He went down the dim stairway, hoping to see nobody on the way home.

It was only when he was away from the courthouse and the jousting of the lawyers that he could remember Iris for the person she was, not just a victim or a name in a file. The more everyone talked about the facts of the case, the less she was alive.

For the last few days, he'd sat in the courtroom, willing it to be over. He'd watched an artist making pastel sketches of Eden entering his plea on the first morning, and seen the drawings appear later on the news: badly proportioned, strangely coloured, like something from an old cartoon. He'd listened to Theo's lawyers outline their case, describing the events with cold, considered voices: how the defendant suffocated his sister, then his mother, as they lay sleeping in their beds in the early hours of the morning of 7th June; how the defendant then proceeded to drag his sister through the house later that afternoon, into a detached building outside, whereupon, according to the defendant's own statement, he tried to revive her. 'The defendant believed he could resuscitate the victim by playing organ music, Your Honour,' the prosecuting barrister had said, and Oscar had watched the reaction of the judge and the jury, their clenched, disbelieving faces.

When it came time for the defence to present their case, Oscar had listened with rising desperation. 'We do not wish to refute the facts put forth by the prosecution regarding the events of the seventh of June,' the defence counsel said, 'but we wish to argue diminished responsibility in this matter, Your Honour, and press for a

503

ruling of voluntary manslaughter.' Oscar knew that he was going to be called to testify to Eden's state of mind. Theo's lawyers had prepared him for it. But as he answered their questions in the crowded court, he couldn't shake the feeling that his honesty was somehow a betrayal, that he was hurting Iris with every word. He tried so hard not to look at Eden in the dock, knowing the sight of his face in the daylight would send his blood raging. Instead, he kept his eyes on the prosecution table, where Theo sat, slouched with grief, his bald head blotched with eczema, looking thin, and lost, and beaten.

When the defence counsel played the videos, Oscar saw the jurors fidgeting and ruffling their brows at the screen. He answered questions about Iris's leg, how it had come to be broken the second time, and the sniggers from the gallery turned his stomach. *Mr Lowe? Mr Lowe, can you please answer the question?* His mind kept leaving the room as the defence counsel grilled him about Eden's 'behaviour' and 'character' and 'lifestyle'. They asked if he'd ever suggested to Herbert Crest that Eden suffered from a condition known as Narcissistic Personality Disorder, and he answered truthfully. But stepping down from the witness box, he felt a sinking in his gut. What use was the truth to anyone now?

On the third day, the defence had called a leading neurosurgeon to show the jury the scale of Eden's delusions and, later, the prosecution had been allowed to cross-examine her. It was unsettling to hear Theo's lawyers lending

504

credibility to Eden's claims of healing, but Oscar had been told what they were trying to do: it was important to show that Eden had been in full control of his faculties so that the jury would not reduce his crime to voluntary manslaughter.

'Correct me if I'm wrong here, Dr Reiner,' the prosecuting barrister had said, 'but aren't the uses of hypnosis and music therapy considered to be perfectly acceptable forms of treatment for brain injuries, as well as cancer?'

'Yes, that's right, they are, but — '

'In fact, as a neurosurgeon, you provide information to your patients about both hypnotherapy and music therapy, don't you?'

The expert didn't take kindly to being interrupted. She was a thin-lipped woman with her hair pulled tightly in a bun, and every time the barrister interjected she gave an angry little cough and looked at the judge. 'Yes, I do. But only as part of a full, post-operative treatment plan. I like to give my patients a range of options. I admit, some patients find those kinds of treatments helpful, but I would not consider them to be anything but placebic.'

'I'm sure those patients would disagree with you.'

'They might. But they aren't here.'

The barrister waited. 'Music has also been proven to benefit sufferers of Parkinson's disease — hasn't it? — helping to calm their symptoms? It's also achieved some positive results with stroke victims and Alzheimer's patients. Is that correct?'

'Yes. That's true. It can have certain temporary

effects — *temporary*.'

'But the defence counsel would have us believe that the defendant was acting with diminished capacity in regard to the treatment of Dr Crest and his sister, the victim. Your testimony infers that the defendant was perfectly aware of his intentions. He was providing hypnosis and musical therapy, was he not? Perfectly normal forms of post-operative care — not delusions at all.'

The woman paused and cleared her throat. 'That might be true,' she said, 'but hypnosis, music therapy, quite frankly they're just complimentary treatments. We call them Mind-Body Interventions. They're no more scientific than dance therapy, or herb therapy, or, well, I was going to say prayer.'

The barrister shook his head. 'Dr Reiner, forgive me, I was under the impression that numerous clinical trials have proven the efficacy of music therapy. Are you telling me I'm mistaken?'

'There've been clinical trials on music therapy, yes, but they haven't proven anything except the obvious. Certain types of music can reduce a person's heart rate or blood pressure — that's natural. Music helps anxiety. Less stress equals better health. I don't think we needed a clinical trial to tell us that.' She scoffed, smirking at the jury. 'It certainly couldn't heal a Grade Four brain tumour. And anyone who says so is severely deluded.'

'Objection, Your Honour. Conjecture.'

'Sustained. The jury will ignore Dr Reiner's last comment.'

As the barrister continued to question her, Eden sat grinning in his seat. He seemed thrilled to be the centre of attention, knowing his ideas were being openly discussed, even endorsed. He kept toying with the furls of his fringe, and spreading his fingers on the tabletop, as if he was dreaming up some new musical arrangement, picturing the desk as an organ and the court as a cathedral.

The jury returned a verdict of voluntary manslaughter the following afternoon. Oscar thought he would feel relief at the judge's decision to hand down a life sentence, but all he felt was a vague satisfaction in seeing Eden led away by the bailiffs towards a darkened hallway, an expression upon his face like a climber staring up a mountainside.

Afterwards, Oscar didn't know where to go. He stayed in the courtroom until everyone else had gone, feeling hollowed-out, redundant, wondering if there was enough strength in his legs to carry him home.

On his way out, he saw Theo conferring with his lawyers and a uniformed policeman by the balcony. He went over, and Theo looked at him wearily. 'They want me to face the rabble out there, Oscar. Make some kind of statement. What do you think?'

He sat down on the bench. Outside the window, the sky held clouds as dense as battleships. 'If you feed them,' he said, 'they'll keep coming back.'

Theo rubbed at his scalp. 'Yes. I expect you're right.'

Now, in the quiet foyer downstairs, Oscar could see Marcus and Jane at the end of the corridor, standing under the tinted hood of a payphone. They were ordering a taxi: 'We don't exactly know yet,' Marcus was saying. 'Can't we just tell the driver when he gets here?'

'Tell them to pull up outside,' Jane said. 'There might still be reporters in the car park.' She looked drawn, her eyes rimmed with darkness. She lifted her fingers slowly when she saw Oscar, leaning her head back against the wall. 'Are you coming with us?'

'Where are you going?' he asked.

'Somewhere quiet,' she said. 'You should eat something, too.'

'I'm fine.'

'Come with us,' she said. 'We miss you, Oscar.'

He gave a narrow smile. 'Another time maybe.'

Yin came down the stairs behind him then, carrying a coffee from the vending machine. 'Oscar, hey,' he said, almost whispering.

'Hey.'

For a moment, Yin just stood there, blowing across his plastic cup with fey little breaths. The harsh scent of coffee made Oscar feel queasy. 'You see his face when they took him away?' Yin said. 'He seemed kinda — I don't know — terrified.'

'Good.'

'Yeah. Still, though — '

'Still what, Yin?' He stared back coldly.

'Nothing. Forget I opened my mouth, okay? It was stupid.' Yin took a few strides along the corridor, then halted, twisting around. 'Look, we're going to eat lunch or something, try to get back to a little normality or whatever.' Further up the hall, Marcus had hung up the payphone and was coming towards them. 'What do you say?'

'I think I'm just going to go home,' Oscar said.

'You sure?'

'I'm exhausted.'

'Alright, man. Catch up soon, huh?'

When he got back to his flat, Oscar found it was a clutter of unlaundered clothes and unwashed plates. There was no relief in being home at all. Everything reminded him of Iris: the CDs she used to browse and moan about, the books that she'd pull down occasionally from the shelf and skim through, the saucer on the bedside table still holding her clove ashes, the picture of her still tacked up on his wall. He couldn't bear to disturb any of it. It was still too soon. He didn't turn on the TV because he didn't want to see the news headlines; he didn't turn on the radio because strange voices would be passing the subject back and forth, and he would only have to hear the name again, over and over — Iris Bellwether, Iris Bellwether — like the whole world was out to haunt him with it.

He wanted to talk to her, that's all. To hear her voice. He wanted to spend his next shift at Cedarbrook knowing that even though he couldn't see her, she was out there somewhere, in the quiet hustle of the city — rehearsing for a chamber group recital, say, or studying at the University Library. He wanted to take her existence for granted, the way the ocean beats against the shore without anyone having to monitor it. All he had now was a dirty flat and a week of double shifts and thirty-four residents to tend to. He needed sleep, so he lay down on the bed, but he could only think of her. She was an apparition who lived inside his skull. Her face flashed before him whenever he blinked, as if she were drawn on his eyelids. She wouldn't let him sleep. She never let him sleep.

By midnight, he was still awake. His mobile was vibrating on the nightstand, and he was so tired he thought it was a dream. It kept on buzzing until he answered. 'Yeah? Hello?'

There was a moment of quiet. He could hear what he thought was motorway traffic on the end of the line. 'Oscar, it's me — did I wake you?' Theo's voice was solemn and husky.

'I don't really sleep these days. How are you, Theo?'

'I don't sleep either. I wrote myself a script for Zimovane, but I can't bring myself to take any. Want me to prescribe you some?'

'No.'

'Probably not a good idea,' Theo said. 'I'm just calling to let you know I'm going away for a few weeks.'

'Okay.'

'In case you need me. That's why I'm telling you. I'm going to stay with some friends in Devon. Need to get out of the circus for a while.'

'Right.'

There was a long quiet. He could hear Theo's steady breaths, then a rising, desperate noise like a sob.

'Are you okay, Theo?'

'No. Not really. I'm lower than I've ever been in my life, but thank you for asking. You're a kind boy — Ruth always said that about you. I know she never said it to you directly, but . . . ' Theo cleared his throat. 'I was just thinking about them, that's all. The circus. Iris used to like the circus — did you know that? Ruth and I would take her in the summer holidays. There was one every year on Midsummer Common. She liked the elephants.'

'She never told me that.'

'Oh, yes. It was a big thing for her. When she was a little girl and she got in a strop, she'd say she was running away to Paris to join Cirque du Soleil, until we told her there weren't any elephants in Cirque du Soleil, only acrobats, and that Cirque du Soleil were from Canada.'

Oscar found himself smiling. 'Really?'

'Funny girl. She begged us to take her to see them when we visited Montreal — Cirque du Soleil, I mean. I've never seen anybody so thrilled. But somewhere along the way, I suppose she lost her passion for it.'

It was nice to think about Iris as a little girl, in a time when everything still lay ahead of her. 'Do you remember taking her to Florida?' Oscar asked. 'She mentioned a church you all went to.'

'We had a holiday in the Keys, years ago. I don't recall the church. Why?'

'Just something she talked about, that's all.'

'Uh-huh.' Theo paused. Traffic thudded by. 'Listen, there's something else I've got to tell you. I thought you should hear it from me first.

It's about the book, Herbert Crest's book. I've been speaking with my lawyers about it.'

'Lawyers? Why?'

'I'm filing an injunction to stop publication.'

Oscar didn't quite know what to say. It hardly seemed important any more.

Theo seemed to mistake his silence for consternation. 'You understand why, don't you? I mean, it's not because I want to protect Eden or anything like that — we're far beyond that now.'

'Then why?' he heard himself saying.

'Because I don't want people lining their pockets out of this. I don't mean Crest, I mean the publisher. Nobody has the right to make a profit out of tragedy. Nobody.' There was a crackle on the end of the line. 'But it's not just that. You've seen how the bloody media have been salivating over it already. I can't leave my house without being harangued by some idiot with a camera. I've become a celebrity, for heaven's sake. I'm a celebrity because my wife and daughter were murdered in their beds. There's something wrong with the world, Oscar. Do people not realise how unseemly that is?'

There was nothing he could tell Theo now. The man just needed somebody to listen, to agree with him. 'It sickens me. All of it.'

'You want to know what the worst part is? Eden is a bigger celebrity than anybody. I'm hearing his name every day on the news. I can't escape him. He's on the front pages of the tabloids *and* the broadsheets — I thought they knew better, but I suppose the only way they can sell papers is by pandering to the lowest common denominator. That's what's wrong with this bloody country, Oscar. I need to get out. He's getting everything he wanted out of this. They're making him a bloody star.' Theo stopped, settling himself, calming down. 'So do you see why I can't allow the book to come out? It's only going to add more fuel to the fire. And I can't allow that. I can't bear it. I'm sorry, I know that Dr Crest was your friend but — '

'Theo, stop,' he said. 'You can stop. It's okay. I understand.'

'You do?'

'I don't want that, either. I told you, it sickens me. The whole thing sickens me. It just — ' He broke off.

'What, Oscar?'

'Nothing.'

'It just *what*?'

'It just wasn't supposed to end up this way, that's all. She only ever wanted to help him.'

Theo stayed quiet. 'I can't tell you how many regrets I have,' he said. 'I just want the time back. I just want to be able to talk to them again.'

'Me too.'

'I want to be able to see them standing in my kitchen in their dressing gowns and their hair all muzzed-up and sleep in their eyes.' Theo let his words fade. 'Thank you for understanding about the book. If anything good has come out of this, it's — well — you know what I mean.'

'Thanks for calling, Theo.'

'Yes. Goodbye, Oscar.'

He hung up the phone, and lay back on the

513

pillow, studying the bare white ceiling. The streetlights on the pavement below gave his curtains a tireless glow, like the windows of an all-night supermarket. It was too bright to sleep. He got up to get himself a drink of water and stood in the kitchen gulping it down. On his way back to bed, he thought about turning on the radio. There would be no news now, only classic ballads and sports chatter, but even that seemed too much to handle, too much like moving on. Instead, he pressed play on the stereo. He didn't even know what disc was inside. He got back into bed and closed his eyes. The CD changer went through its motions. After a moment, he could hear a lone chorister singing a high, sweet note. Soon, that one fragile voice turned into several. A slow, delicate melody poured from the speakers and surrounded him. The music thickened around his body. He felt it like a warm fog gathering in the room, like ether lulling him to sleep. And just for an instant — a second, maybe half that — he couldn't see Iris at all.

DELUSIONS OF HOPE

HERBERT M. CREST

Introduction

'In old age, the consolation of hope is reserved for the tenderness of parents, who commence a new life in their children; the faith of enthusiasts who sing Hallelujahs above the clouds, and the vanity of authors who presume the immortality of their name and writings.'

EDWARD GIBBON

I couldn't save my sister Tabitha from falling off the rooftop of our high school fifty-four years ago, but I saw the whole thing happen. She had gone up to the roof alone — not because she was the kind of rebellious kid who skipped class to smoke hand-rolled cigarettes (like her older brother) but because she was the kind of smart, keen student who liked to raise bacteria in Petri dishes to get extra credit from her science teacher. She would go up there every recess to observe how variables like direct sunlight or extreme shade affected their growth. I am not quite sure how she came to fall. The school building had a pretty high parapet

515

and I don't think she stumbled. She may have climbed up there for some reason, maybe to find a particularly shady nook for one of her Petri dishes — I don't know. But I do remember the sight of her falling as if it were yesterday.

At recess, I liked to sit with my friends on the bleachers and act tough as other kids went by. That's what I was doing as my sister fell. I was talking tough, leering at some freshman boy and calling him names, and I guess I looked up for a tiny moment and saw it: a dark shape dropping towards the ground. Then I heard the horrible, haunting smack of her body against the cement parking lot. And I remember my friend Thomas laughing and saying, 'Holy hell. Somebody just bought it.'

It is difficult for me to describe the grief I felt when I realized that dark shape was Tabitha. Although I've managed to box my grief away over the years, like some old photo album containing too many painful memories, the feeling of loss has never really left me. It is triggered whenever I hear her name spoken (which is not often), and whenever I think about high school (which is often), or whenever I see a Petri dish (which is more often than you might think).

I wrote about the sensations that come with bereavement a great deal in my book *Engines of Grief* and I don't wish to retread old ground or dwell on the issue for too long here. This is not another book about grief, after all, it is a book about hope. But there is one last memory about Tabitha I would like to share here, if only to demonstrate how those two seemingly divergent states of being — grief and hope — are forever linked in my mind.

Roughly a year after my sister died, I attended a meeting of a local spiritualist church near Boston. Rather, I should say, my parents attended a meeting, and they took my begrudging sixteen-year-old self along with them. I was rattled by the despair of losing my sister, of course, but despondency seemed to affect my parents a different way. It possessed their minds, consumed their every conversation. My mother went from being a happy-go-lucky housewife who always had a smile for everybody and a pie cooking in the oven in case the neighbors dropped by, to being a cheerless, downtrodden person who didn't like to venture outdoors and saw doom lurking around every corner. My father's way of coping was to apply himself to the task of investigating the circumstances of my sister's death. Because he was a scientific man, a math teacher whose favorite phrase was 'in mathematics there are no accidents,' he wasn't satisfied by the police report that ruled Tabitha's death as accidental. He set out to explain the circumstances of my sister's death like some private detective. For a while, he harassed one of Tabitha's schoolfriends, Liz, to such a degree that her parents threatened to obtain a restraining order. My father became so obsessed with finding out what happened that he seemed to forget himself.

During this desperate process, I think he began to realize that everything in life is not understandable according to the laws of mathematics. Somewhere along the way, I don't exactly know where or when, he found himself drawn to other things in his pursuit of answers. He started to look beyond what he'd always believed in — beyond the pure reason of science.

We were not a church-going family. I was not baptized and neither was Tabitha. It was much too late for my father to 'find God' in any conventional sense. He'd railed against organized religion his whole life. Instead, he found comfort in what people refer to as 'the supernatural,' but which he preferred to call 'the metaphysical.' He began — as many grieving people do — to believe in things like ghosts, angels, the spirit world. By the time I was seventeen, he had as many books in his study on spiritualism and mediumship as he had on calculus, geometry, or algebra. He began to attend meetings at a spiritualist church near Boston — the Waltham Church of Spiritism.

When we moved to Waltham in the spring of 1953, my mother and I thought we were moving to be closer to my father's work, but later we realized we'd moved because he wanted to be nearer to the spiritualist church. He'd been attending three meetings a week there for several months before he finally convinced my mother to join him. She left for the Waltham Church one summer night, indifferent about the prospect, but when she came back she was giddy about what she'd encountered there.

The resident medium, she said, had claimed to be receiving the voice of a spirit whose name had the initials TC. Of course, she had taken this to mean Tabitha Crest and raised her hand. The medium had said he was sorry, he had lost the signal from the spirit world, and the voice of TC had gone — perhaps if she came back next week, he could try again? She reported all of this to me in the kitchen over cocoa, while my father stood by the counter, nodding.

The following week, we all went off to Waltham Church together. Despite my father's great conviction that I would find it all very enlightening, and despite his advice that I should retain an open mind about metaphysical things, I was wholly skeptical about what I would find there. When a forty-year-old man with a bad shirt, a crew cut, and horn-rimmed glasses took to the pulpit and began to ask everyone how they were doing, I felt no better about it. When he just stood there, finger in one ear, breathing loudly through his nose like some folk singer pitching a harmony, I almost laughed. When he raised his hand to stifle the mumbling congregation, and said in a dry Bostonian voice, 'Please, everybody, stay quiet now. I must be able to commune with the spirits coming forward to me tonight,' the needle on my cynic-o-meter began to peak. 'Yes, spirit,' he said, 'I do recognize you, spirit. Ladies and gentlemen, this is a spirit who's been with us before. Somebody with the initials — what's that now? BC?' The congregation stayed quiet. 'TC?' My parents fidgeted. 'TC, yes, that's it now,' the medium said, 'TC.' No gender had been assigned to these initials, but this did not matter to my parents, both of whom held their arms aloft. 'Here!' my father said. 'That's my daughter!' The medium fluttered his eyes open and said: 'Yes, sir. She is with me now.'

You have to forgive me: I am an old man and I can't recall the rest of that evening with complete accuracy, but there are certain things I know for sure. First of all, the medium, whose name was Kendall Johnson, never addressed the spirit as Tabitha (he might well have convinced me of his psychic powers had he plucked such an unusual name out of thin air, instead of a set of initials). He also talked about a diary my sister kept in her bottom drawer, as if this were absolute proof that he could only be talking to Tabitha Crest, surely the only girl in the history of the world who'd ever kept a diary. 'You must read it,' he told my parents, 'she wants you to read it. It'll answer a lot of your questions.'

But my lasting memory of that night is of the congregation itself. The church was crammed. Fifty, sixty, maybe a hundred people. And it occurred to me then, as it occurs to me now, that everybody in the room was grieving for someone. Whether it was a sister, a brother, a mother, a father; whether it was a daughter or a son or an aunt or an uncle; they were all mourning the passing of somebody they loved and had come to Waltham Church for one reason: the slightest hope that they might be able to talk to that person again.

My rage began to grow when I figured this out. I wanted to stand up and shout, 'You're all such frauds! You're all such phoneys!' but I didn't. Here was a place that preyed upon the most anguished and helpless people. It purported to give hope when there was none to give — and, worse, it charged a price for admission. It was immoral, I thought, abhorrent, and I told my parents so on the car ride home. I said I would never go back there as long as I lived. 'How can you say that, Herb? You heard the man,' my father replied. 'The thing about the diary?' When I told him it was only coincidence, suggestion, sleight of hand, my father scoffed. 'Fine,' he said. 'You can stay home next time, and I'll go talk to your sister.'

But a few months later, my mother stopped going to the Waltham Church with him. She claimed she was too busy for it.

Around the time I was graduating high school, my father started going to another spiritualist church in Watertown, and then another in Dorchester, and then another in Roxbury, and soon he stopped attending spiritualist churches altogether. He took to working longer hours and returning home later, spending nights alone in his study with the lights off and a bottle of Johnnie Walker for company. He became melancholy. Some weekends, he wouldn't get out of his pajamas or even take a shower — and for a man who'd always prided himself on his appearance, this was a significant backward step. One night, I came into his study and he was passed out drunk. On the desk in front of him sat my sister's diary. He'd pried open the tiny lock. Every page was blank, apart from one, which bore a faded scribble, as if Tabitha had used it to test a pen.

My father died three years later, when I was living as an undergraduate in his native England. It was only after he died that I realized how much my angry response to the spiritualist church had affected him. I had trodden roughshod over something he had placed his faith in. I had destroyed the one thing he had left of Tabitha: the hope of her continued, peaceful existence in some other, better place. And I understood that the reason I hadn't stood up in the church that night and shouted 'You're all such phoneys!' was because I knew that I would be taking away the last thread of hope for an entire congregation.

At the time of writing my book *Engines of Grief*, I co-chaired a symposium at the University of Denver with a psychiatrist colleague of mine, Dr. Evan Meade, in which he touched upon an idea that struck a chord with me. He posited that in times of great anguish and bereavement, the most valuable thing a person can possess is a single thread of hope, even if that hope is entirely baseless. He referred to it in terms of religion, in regard to what is often termed 'blind faith.' I recall the conversation sliding past me (as most conversations now do), and the symposium was over all too quickly, but that kernel of an idea stayed in my mind for a long time after.

Then, ten years later, I was diagnosed with a malignant brain tumor. A grade four glioblastoma multiforme tumor — the worst kind. I won't get too much into the complexities and modalities of this now, because I will be discussing them at length in later chapters, but I will say this: on the day my doctor told me the bad news, I thought a great deal about my sister, about my parents, and about the ideas my colleague Dr. Meade had discussed at our symposium. In fact, I began to think a lot about hope, about what it meant — specifically, what it meant to *me* — and the more I thought about it, the larger the issue became, until it felt like something I had to write about.

One of the most important things I have come to understand through the course of my experiences with the myriad healers, mediums, and wannabe prophets you will read about in the chapters that follow is how my father — such a mathematically minded man — could abandon his convictions and place his faith beyond the laws of science. It had always bothered me that, even when the claims of the mediums at the Waltham Church were so obviously bogus, he seemed utterly convinced by them. I think I had always resented him for being so easily duped. But I understand now, after the personal battles I have been through lately, that when my father talked this way, behaved this way, he was not really my father at all. Like a drug addict, he was under the influence of something much stronger than he could rationally control. His mind had been seized by a delusion.

It is the same delusion my own mind has been prey to in the years since my diagnosis. It is the same everyday delusion that makes a crippled man shout Hallelujah and fall from his wheelchair when a preacher touches his head. It is the same delusion that sends a fireman into a burning building when there is no chance of survival; that makes a rocket scientist drop to her knees and pray to a God she's never believed in when her son is kidnapped; that makes a farmer keep on planting the seeds in the arid soil when the rain doesn't come and the crops don't grow;

that encourages a father of five to place his last fifty bucks on a rank outsider at the dog track; that makes a barren woman spend her life savings on an IVF treatment with a five per cent ratio of success; that makes a respected psychologist with a brain tumor and a profound skepticism for the metaphysical world attend five sessions a week with a faith healer called Padre at some backwater dive in Bigfork, Montana; that makes a simple man called Kendall Johnson believe he is endowed with the ability to commune with the dead.

It is the delusion we all know as hope. And what this book will investigate is whether this simple delusion is as benign as we believe it to be, or if it is something considerably more harmful.

'Keep reading,' Dr Paulsen said, blinking his eyes open. 'I wasn't asleep, I promise — just concentrating on the words.' But Oscar knew that the old man's attention span was limited, despite the progress he'd made in the past twelve months. At least he could hold a conversation now without forgetting the name of the person he was talking to; at least he no longer looked back at everyone with blankness.

Oscar folded the dust-flap between the pages and closed the book. 'We'll pick it up again tomorrow. It's almost three. You're due a sleep.'

Paulsen sighed loudly but he didn't argue. 'What time will you be coming tomorrow?'

'Same time as always.'

'Eleven?'

'One,' he said, helping Paulsen onto the bed. 'It's always one. You know I can't get out of class 'til then. You remember that, don't you?'

'Yes, yes, I remember that.' Paulsen turned on his side. 'I'm old, I'm not an idiot.'

As Oscar went to close the curtains, he saw the gardeners working in the Cedarbrook grounds — three men were clipping back the wisteria vines and dumping the off-cuts into a trailer. A pleasant, grassy smell rose up towards him. He could hear the quaint snips of pruning shears. When he turned back to say goodbye, he found the old man was fast asleep.

That morning, Oscar had woken early to get to the bookshop in town before class. He'd seen it there on the New Arrivals table, with its gleaming white cover and its simple black lettering: DELUSIONS OF HOPE BY HERBERT M. CREST. It had felt as weighty and important as he'd imagined it would be, and the pages still bore that fresh-off-the-press scent. On the inside of the dust jacket, there was a new picture of Crest, grinning under the peak of a Red Sox cap. It had been a thrill to take the book to the counter and hand over his money, and to hear the cashier say, 'Oh, right, I heard about this,' as she rang it through the till. 'Wasn't this supposed to be out, like, ages ago?'

He'd taken the book to Jesus Green, thinking he should read it in the same spot he'd first read *The Girl With the God Complex*. After a few lines of the introduction, he'd felt like he was having a private conversation with Herbert Crest again, as if the old man had simply picked up the phone to say hello. It was a fine book, maybe even his best. It had all the Herbert Crest hallmarks: the earnest prose, appealing to the informed as well as to the layman; the softly spoken address to the reader; the loving way he reported his personal memories to support his psychological arguments.

But Oscar knew the book had not been published the way Crest had intended, and it gave him an uneasy feeling as he turned the pages. There was no mention of the Bellwethers — Theo's injunction had seen to that. It was an older version of the manuscript, the draft that Crest had finished and submitted to his editor just a few days before Oscar had introduced himself.

He'd followed the progress of the civil suit in the papers. It had been announced in full-page articles in the summer. By the time the court ruled in February, the public's interest had waned, and the story was reduced to single paragraphs in the outer columns, under dispassionate headlines like: *Killer's Father Wins Book Injunction*. All of Crest's notes and manuscripts, barring the original, had been permanently sealed by the judge. Spector & Tillman had released a statement to say they were disappointed with the ruling, and that the original version of the book would now be released; it was a version they were pleased with, despite 'fundamental differences' from the final draft. ('It's still a terrific book,' Diane Rossi had told *Publishers Weekly* back in March, 'so everyone should run out and buy it. But, at heart, it's not the same book. The final draft is edgier; it reaches more surprising conclusions than the original version, that's all I'm allowed to say. Even the title is different. And, no, I can't tell you what it is. That's court ordered.') When the book was finally released, a year off schedule, the buzz surrounding it had died down. The public's imagination had been seized by somebody else's misery, some other disaster.

Reading in the dreary light of Jesus Green, Oscar had found himself wondering — as he'd often wondered — about Crest's final version. He'd thought about the sit-downs in the organ house, all those conversations with Eden he would never get to hear. Part of him was glad of the injunction, because knowing these things would only have left him feeling numb and helpless all over again. He couldn't bear to face Eden again on those pages, to hear the tenor of his thoughts, his justifications, his dangerous, high-minded ideas. What good were answers now? What good were Crest's observations and judgements? He didn't need another opportunity to pick apart the details, to look for the places he could have done something to prevent what happened. He was already living with the burden of those missed chances. Only Theo, his lawyers, and a few senior editors at Spector & Tillman knew what Herbert Crest had really thought. And, for now, if not for ever, Oscar was comfortable with that.

He'd gone to college that morning, feeling fairly bright. It was still difficult to be back in a classroom where the other students were three or four years younger than he was, but he tried to see it as an advantage. He'd already read most of the books on the reading list for his English Lit class and been awarded an A+ for his last assignment, an original poem. Because he was only there to learn, he wasn't distracted like the boys in his history lessons were when some girl bent over to pick up a pencil. He was taking psychology, too — he was compelled by it. He liked learning about Stanley Milgram and the release of free radicals in the brain. When his A levels were over, he wasn't going to be taking a gap year in Australia or New Zealand. He'd already wasted too much time. But he was thinking of taking a short holiday — to Paris maybe, or Reykjavik.

It was past three o'clock now, and Dr Paulsen was snoring. Outside, the afternoon was honeybright and the roads were slick with rain. He left the old man with *Delusions of Hope* on his bedside table, ready to be picked up again tomorrow, and made his way through the corridors and stairways of Cedarbrook. All the same old faces were in the parlour — Mrs Brady, Mrs Lytham, Mrs Kernaghan, Mrs Green — and a couple of new auxiliaries were chatting with Deeraj at the nurses' station. He could hear Jean's voice bounding from her office. Sometimes, he missed working here. He missed the residents and their gratitude for a good deed, the way the place smelled, how it creaked under his shoes. He still came by twice a week to visit Dr Paulsen, and he still borrowed books from his shelf, one at a time. There was comfort here — the safest, most reliable kind — and he didn't want to let it go completely. He'd been working at a hotel in town for a while now. It was lighter work, better paid, and easier to fit around college, but it wasn't the same as Cedarbrook.

When he got to the front garden, he stopped. Across the old city, the ground was slowly drying out and the air was thick with petrichor. He could almost taste it, like a sweetness on his tongue, and he stood there for a long while, just breathing it in. He lived for moments like this now: for a fleeting scent of the damp earth, for the whiff of a clove cigarette. They were the only things that ever brought her back to life.

He didn't take the shortcut because he knew the North Gate would still be closed. The pavements were busy with students and tourists and girls with clipboards hustling him to hire punts or take the sightseeing bus. He passed along St John's Street, stepping out of the way of cyclists, breaking through the crowd. Ahead of him, the grey spires of the King's College Chapel stood against the sky like gun barrels. There was a queue of people near the Gatehouse. The college would not be open to visitors for a couple more hours, but Oscar kept on walking towards the entrance. When the porter saw him coming, he gave a tender smile, and moved aside to let him through.

In the Front Court, the grass was so plush and green it seemed almost embroidered. The cobblestones felt blunt and familiar beneath his feet. He walked past the chapel, past the ashen gables of the Gibbs' building, down the gentle slope of the back lawn to the riverbank. He could see his friends ahead of him now, gathered by the tiny patch of ground where they'd planted the bulbs last autumn. Yin was standing tall and wide, his thumbs hanging from his belt-loops. Marcus was right beside him, a full backpack on his shoulders. Jane was kneeling by the flower-bed, raking the soil with her fingers. He called out to them and they turned, waving. He was glad to see their faces again.

'Look,' Jane said, 'they made it.' She pointed to the mound of fibrous soil before her. The first blue petals of *Iris milifolia* had begun to bloom and seemed so fragile in the bright afternoon. 'I can't believe they're flowering already.'

Once a week since last November, Oscar had come to check on them. They were difficult plants to grow — requiring just the right amount of moisture and sunlight, and he'd had to cover the roots with coconut husks to protect them from the wind and cold — but he didn't care how much attention they needed. It was better to go to the peaceful grounds of King's each week and tend to one small corner of earth, thinking of her, than to talk to a gravestone.

He stood with his friends beside the flowerbed, and while they filled him in on the things that had happened since they'd last seen each other, the river flowed by with the quietest of movements. He'd almost forgotten the sound of their voices, and he listened to them talk with a warm feeling growing inside him. Marcus was halfway through his Master's and was doing an internship at the Royal Opera House in the summer; he was clearly excited about moving to London, though he tried his best to play it down. Yin was leaving next month to join a start-up company in San Francisco: 'Silicon Valley,' he said, 'right back where I started.' And Jane — 'Well, I still have another term to get through,' she said, 'and then I'm thinking of retiring.' There was consolation in knowing that the gears of their lives were still turning, despite everything.

They seemed pleased that Oscar was back in school. 'Look around you, man,' Yin said. 'You belong here more than any of us. I know King's is probably the last place you'd want to go, but you should think about it. The place could use more people like you.'

They stayed there talking beside the irises for over an hour, until the sky turned glum and the rain began to fall again. He felt better in their company and didn't want to say goodbye. 'We'll go for dinner or something,' Jane said. 'We'll call you.' But he knew he wouldn't see them again for weeks, because their lives were just too different now, their schedules too complicated to manage. Jane hugged him farewell at the North Gate, and he shook Yin and Marcus by the hand. Then he watched the three of them go trundling along the old brick lane, slow and spirited, silent but together.

He stared up at the needling spires of the chapel. At five o'clock, the tower bells would sound, and the porters would open the college to the public. People would soon come streaming in to wait outside the vestibule for evensong. And he knew that once those big oak doors were open and the voluntary began, he'd have to be far away from here. The sound of the organ was impossible for him to be around; his heart would capsize with the slightest note. So he turned his back on the Front Court and went striding through town, hoping he might see something in the darkening sky that hadn't been there yesterday.

Author's Note

A number of texts informed the writing of *The Bellwether Revivals*, but there are a few works that I am particularly indebted to:

Herbert Crest's newspaper article on hypnotism is a fictitious reworking of Andi Rierden's 'A Hypnotist Taps the Mind's Power in North Haven' (*New York Times*, 12 December 1993). I have embellished upon the facts at the heart of Rierden's piece to suit the requirements of the novel; in doing so, I have stayed close to the style and structure of her original article to retain a sense of authenticity.

Aspects of Elsa Ronningstam's book *Identifying and Understanding the Narcissistic Personality* (Oxford University Press, 2005) helped me to define the limits of Eden's 'condition'. Richard Kivy's *Music Alone* (Cornell, 1990) and *The Corded Shell* (Princeton, 1980) are key to my understanding of music aesthetics, though I'm sure Eden would take issue with some of his assertions about Mattheson. I relied on Hans Lenneberg's translation of *Der Vollkomenne Capellmeister*, as published in *The Journal of Music Theory* (1958), when beginning to construct Eden's musical philosophy.

Finally, Beekman C. Cannon's comprehensive book *Johann Mattheson: Spectator in Music* was enormously valuable to my research, and I am grateful to Yale University Press for giving permission to reprint excerpts from it.

Acknowledgements

I would like to thank everyone who supported me in the writing of this book, and those who helped bring it to the attention of readers. My agent, Judith Murray at Greene & Heaton, offered sage editorial comments and believed in the novel from the beginning; Grainne Fox and Suzanne Brandreth found it loving homes in the USA and Canada. I am very grateful to my editors — Francesca Main, for her perceptive readings and invaluable notes, Josh Kendall and Lara Hinchberger, for their additional insights and suggestions — Maxine Hitchcock, Jessica Leeke, and the hard-working teams at my publishers, Simon & Schuster, Viking Penguin, and McClelland & Stewart.

I owe a big debt of thanks to Adam Robinson for taking me to see the college choirs and making Cambridge feel like home, and to Birkbeck College for keeping the roof over my head while I wrote the book. Thanks for the help, advice, and encouragement of Ailsa Cox, Michael Marshall Smith, Robert Paul Weston, Meryn Cadell, Steven Galloway, Keith Maillard, Derek Dunfield, Amanda Lamarche, Carla Gillis, Cathleen With, Susan Olding, Catharine Chen, Cliff Flax, Alice Kuipers, Patrick Neate, Hellie Ogden, Luke Brown, Mark Wainwright, Bobby Kewley, Laura Brodie, Phil Kielty, and Anne

Seddon. Thanks also to Kit Holland and Tim
Marwood for shedding light on unfamiliar
aspects of student life, and Shaban Javed for
kindness and numerous free meals.

Thank you to my girlfriend, Stephanie, for her
love, belief, and stabilising presence (Opi did us
proud). Thanks to my family for their great
encouragement along the way: Alex and Nick
— my brothers and kindred spirits — Ali, Dad,
my grandparents, Uncle Harry and other absent
friends.

Most of all, thank you to my mother, Lynn, who
has read every draft and incarnation of this
novel, and without whose love, resilience, faith,
support, and wisdom I could never have written
a word.

We do hope that you have enjoyed reading this large print book.

Did you know that all of our titles are available for purchase?

We publish a wide range of high quality large print books including:
Romances, Mysteries, Classics
General Fiction
Non Fiction and Westerns

Special interest titles available in large print are:
The Little Oxford Dictionary
Music Book
Song Book
Hymn Book
Service Book

Also available from us courtesy of Oxford University Press:
Young Readers' Dictionary
(large print edition)
Young Readers' Thesaurus
(large print edition)

For further information or a free brochure, please contact us at:
Ulverscroft Large Print Books Ltd.,
The Green, Bradgate Road, Anstey,
Leicester, LE7 7FU, England.
Tel: (00 44) 0116 236 4325
Fax: (00 44) 0116 234 0205

THE UNCOUPLING

Meg Wolitzer

A strange, formidable wind blows into Stellar Plains, New Jersey, where Dory and Robby Lang teach at Eleanor Roosevelt High School. Dory is suddenly and inexplicably repelled by her husband's touch, whilst back at school, life imitates art. The new drama teacher's end-of-term play is Arisotophanes' *Lysistrata*, in which women withhold sexual privileges from their menfolk in order to end the Peloponnesian War. And all across town, there's a quiet battle between the sexes: relationships end abruptly and marital issues erupt. Women continue to be claimed by the spell — from Bev Cutler, the overweight guidance counsellor to Leanne Bannerjee, the sexy school psychologist — even the Langs' teenage daughter, Willa, is affected — until everything comes to a climax on the first night of *Lysistrata* . . .

THE MIDWIFE OF VENICE

Roberta Rich

Hannah Levi is famed throughout Venice for her skills as a midwife, but as a Jew, the law forbids her from attending a Christian woman. However, when the Conte di Padovani appears at her door in the dead of night to demand her services, Hannah's compassion is sorely tested. And with a handsome reward for her services, she could ransom back her imprisoned husband. But if she fails in her endeavours to save mother and child, will she be able to save herself, let alone her husband?

HEART OF THE MATTER

Emily Giffin

Tessa seems to have the perfect life. Married to a world-renowned pediatric surgeon, she has chosen stay-at-home motherhood over her career. But Tessa is beginning to question her decision, concerned that it is affecting her marriage . . . Valerie, a single mother and attorney, has given up on romance. Things never turn out the way she plans, so she believes it is best not to risk more disappointment. Although both women live in the same Boston suburb, the two have relatively little in common aside from a fierce love for their children. But one night, a tragic accident causes their lives to converge in ways no one could have imagined . . .